CUDDY - PLUS ONE

Jeremiah Healy

CUDDY - PLUS ONE

Crippen & Landru Publishers
Norfolk, Virginia
2003

Cover and dust jacket painting by Carol Heyer

Cover and dust jacket design by Deborah Miller

Crippen & Landru logo by Eric D. Greene

ISBN: 1-885941-94-3 (limited edition)
ISBN: 1-885941-95-1 (trade edition)

FIRST EDITION

Crippen & Landru Publishers
P. O. Box 9315
Norfolk, VA 23505
USA

E-mail: info@crippenlandru.com
Web: www.crippenlandru.com

To Doug and Sandi Greene
for helping to drive these scattered sheep
into a warm and lovely herd

CONTENTS

INTRODUCTION

In this space for the first collection, *The Concise Cuddy*, I expressed my gratitude to Doug Greene for asking me to submit roughly the first half of the John Francis Cuddy short stories to Crippen & Landru. I'd like to do the same for this new anthology, roughly the next half (if you'll pardon the metaphysical liberty). If you're happening upon Cuddy for the first time, he's a Vietnam veteran who survived the Tet Offensive in Saigon only to return home to Boston and lose his young wife, Beth, to cancer. There have been thirteen Cuddy novels, from *Blunt Darts* in 1984 to *Spiral* in 2000. In the novels, Cuddy evolves from a grieving widower to a man developing a fulfilling life outside his profession of private investigation. However, in the shorter pieces, I've kept him in the original mode, partly because of space limitations on "back-story," but also partly because the chronological "freeze-frame" lets me return to the character as originally created, kind of like an actor reprising a favorite old role. And, as in the first collection, the stories are printed in the sequence in which they were written, not published, so that any improvement or decline in my abilities can be more easily noted.

I'd like to comment on only a few of the entries in this second anthology. "Rest Stop" is drawn from my attending a prizefight with a fellow attorney who used to represent Marvin Hagler, the great middleweight champion from Brockton, Massachusetts. It was nominated for a Shamus Award as Best Private Eye Short Story of its year, as were "Turning the Witness," "What's in a Name?," and "Hodegetria." I'm proud to add that both "Eyes That Never Meet" and "A Book of Kells" were selected for Houghton Mifflin's *Best American Mystery Stories*.

A brief observation on "Decoys," the "plus one" in the title of this anthology. It is the first short story featuring Mairead O'Clare, a female attorney just past the bar who, disenchanted with large law-firm practice in Boston, throws in with an older male attorney representing mostly criminal defendants. The first novel in the series, *Uncommon Justice*, appeared in April, 2001, but we decided to go with the pseudonym of "Terry Devane" to distinguish it, as a legal thriller, from the private eye books with which my own name is most associated. I hope you enjoy reading this "change of character" as much as I've enjoyed writing her.

Finally, in May 2001, I had the honor of presenting the Mystery Writers of America "Ellery Queen Award" to Doug at the Edgar Banquet in recognition of his immense contributions to the field of mystery publishing. My dedication of this volume to him and his wife, Sandi, co-founders of Crippen & Landru, is just a small footnote to all that the Greenes have done for the rest of us.

Jeremiah Healy
Boston, Massachusetts
October 8, 2001

REST STOP

ONE

STARING through the glass windows of the vending machine, I tried to decide what to buy with my last four quarters. I was torn between a single slice of soggy poundcake and a cellophane package of oatmeal cookies that looked two days older than dirt.

I took a sip of the hot chocolate I'd gotten from another machine, mainly for the caffeine. It already had been a long December drive from New York City, and I was only halfway back to Boston. The president of a small company in my office building had hired me for a simple courier trip, the woman liking the cachet of having a private investigator run something too important to fax. It was an easy way to make my daily rate, but I was already so sleepy coming through Connecticut at nine P.M. that I didn't want to risk nodding off at the wheel of my old Prelude.

So I'd pulled into the rest stop.

There was an eclectic collection of vehicles in the angled parking slots near the flagstone path to the hokey cabin. One was a seventy-eight Chevy with a busted taillight and some people in it drinking coffee from a thermos. Another was a Mitsubishi pickup truck sporting a sullen hound dog tied to a toolbox but no tailgate and only a wired-on bumper. At the other end of the scale we had two entries. The nearer was a Cadillac El Dorado coupe, the spare nestled in an extension of the trunk. At the back of the lot, a Toyota sports car hunkered down, looking as though it had been melded in a wind tunnel.

Sensing kinship, I parked my Prelude between the Chevy and the pickup.

Inside the little lobby of the cabin, a guy in work boots and dirt-caked blue jeans passed me as I moved toward the hot drinks machine. Just in front of the restrooms was a cut-out counter, a black man maybe sixty years old sitting in a high chair behind it, his nose buried in a copy of *RING* magazine.

My hand was hovering over the button for the cookies when a voice from behind the counter said, "I'd go for the pound cake, myself."

I looked over at him. He'd lowered the magazine, and I could see that the nose was crooked, a couple of swipe lines of scar tissue through the eyebrows.

11

His hair had thinned like water eroding a midstream island, but he kept it short enough that you wouldn't notice but for an overhead fluorescent.

He said, "Those cookies, they a bit past their prime."

"Thanks." I hit the cake button and retrieved my prize from the bottom bin of the machine. As I moved over to the counter, an elderly woman met her husband outside the Men's Room and they walked by me.

I extended my hand to the man in the high chair. "John Cuddy."

"Elvin Tyson."

We shook. Closing on his hand was like gripping a bag of wood chips.

I nodded to the magazine. "Any relation to Mike?"

"I used to wish."

I took a little more hot chocolate. "What was your weight class?"

"Light heavy. Had the legs but not the punch. Got to have the punch for light heavy. You never boxed."

"No."

"Always tell from the hands, you know."

A yuppie couple came past, barely glancing at us. They were dressed like L.L. Bean mannequins and split for the restrooms.

Tyson said, "You from Boston, right?"

"Good ear."

"This job, you get so's you can hear it. Only been there once myself, but give me three Bostons over one New York, I got to listen to them try to repeat directions I give them. You ever see Marvin Hagler when he was fighting?"

"Just TV."

"Oh, man, you missed something then. Marvin, he the reason I went up to Boston that time. Hynes Auditorium, musta been fifteen years ago, before he got famous and all. He was fighting Willy the Worm Monroe. Remember him?"

"Uh-unh."

"Willie, he from Philly. I was setting up in the balcony with these brothers from down there, and they telling me how the Worm put Marvin away like a year before, only one to do it ever. Only I knowed that Marvin, he had the flu bug when he fought Willy that first time, so I figured the Worm had a date with the robin, you know?"

I laughed, and so did Tyson. The L.L. Bean pair left their restrooms at exactly the same moment and walked out, hand in hand and no doubt still on schedule.

"But first five rounds, Willy, he *owned* Marvin. I mean the Worm come in at like six-one and still made his weight, maybe one-fifty-five, you know he got a reach like a cherry-picker. But Marvin, he a solid boy, chest and arms like a man your size, and he kept bearing in and burying these body punches. Also,

Marvin, he a lefty, and that always keep you off-balance some."

A couple in their late twenties came through, stylishly turned out in ski parkas. The man led a boy maybe three years old in a matching parka. The man and the woman exchanged brief comments in Spanish before he went with the boy into the Men's and she used the other door.

Tyson said, "Then the fifth and sixth, Marvin, he started gaining ground. You could see Willy wasn't breathing just right no more, all the punishment he took to the mid-section, but the Worm still kept Marvin off a bit."

"With his reach."

"That's right."

A trio came in, all fairly short and dark, not saying anything to each other. The two men were dressed in jeans and Army field jackets, the woman in jeans and a cloth coat. One of the men had a scraggly goatee and sized me up as they went by. The other man and the woman looked a little nervous as they divided at the doors.

"The seventh and eighth, now, Marvin, he really come on. Pounding and boring, driving Willy around the ring. The Worm, he rallied some in the ninth and tenth, but Marvin still won those, which give them five rounds apiece on anybody's card."

The short woman came out of the rest room and moved quickly back toward the cabin door. Then the two short men came out, the clean-shaven one seeming shaky, the goatee not looking at me but walking fast enough to pass his friend. There was only one problem.

The clean-shaven guy was carrying the little boy in the ski parka, hefting him in both arms like a heavy bag of groceries. The boy seemed to be asleep, but I didn't see either of the two people I'd assumed were his parents.

Tyson said, "Then come the eleventh—"

I started toward the Men's Room. "Elvin, see which car they get into!"

"What?"

"See which car the guy with the kid gets into."

"But I ain't finished my story yet."

I was already through the washroom door, thinking my Smith & Wesson Chief's Special was locked in my trunk because I'm not licensed outside Massachusetts. The place was quiet and lean, but not spotless. There was a pool of red expanding from under one of the stalls.

I got to it and pulled open the door. Even if he spoke English, he couldn't have heard me. The knife was still sticking out from under his breastplate, the eyes out of sync, like each was intent on a different point of the compass.

I came out, Tyson not behind his counter. Barging into the Women's Room, I saw the dead man's companion on the floor at the sink. The contents of her handbag were scattered over the tiles, but no blood joined them. The pulse was steady at her neck, a strong whiff of something like chloroform coming off her face.

I ran back through the lobby and out the cabin door.

Tyson was standing at the end of the flagstone path, hugging himself and stamping his feet against the cold. When he heard me running, he turned and said, "What do you want to know their car for?"

I got my keys out as I hit the Prelude. "Which one was it?"

"Old Chevy. The man without the boy got in this Mercedes."

I turned the key in the ignition. "Colors?"

"Couldn't say on the Chevy. Mercedes was yellow."

"Plates?"

"Plates?"

"License plate on the Chevy?"

"Don't know. What the hell—"

"Call the state police. Have them check the next five exits north. Then check on the woman in the bathroom and call an ambulance."

"What the—"

But I was already hitting forty on the ramp back to the Interstate.

TWO

It took me two miles to get them in sight. I figured rightly that they'd stick to fifty-five, while the Prelude's speedometer was flirting with eighty. I eased off when I picked up the Chevy's broken taillight. It was like following a firefly.

They went only two exits, then turned off. I lost the Mercedes at the traffic signal for a crossroad, but I stayed with the Chevy easily enough for six or seven wandering miles. Our route got increasingly urban until we were going through the center of an old mill town, wooden three-deckers perched on a hillside over the main drag.

The Chevy wound up a steep street, and I dropped back a little. When I topped the crest and rounded a curve, I saw the broken light just disappearing into a narrow driveway between two rows of houses. I pulled past, slowly. The clean-shaven man was getting out of the driver's side, the woman now carrying the baby toward a house.

I edged into a parking space and killed the engine. I thought I'd wait to be sure they were staying, then find a phone.

After a minute, the Prelude's windshield and rear windows fogged up, probably from my breathing and body heat. When it got to the side window as well, I rolled it down rather than start the engine for the defroster.

I had just put my arm on the sill when a muzzle nudged my left ear. A voice veneered with a Spanish accent said, "Thought you smelled like cop."

THREE

"Private in-ves-ti-ga-tor, eh?"

The one with the goatee took a swig from the jug of wine and passed my identification holder to the clean-shaven one, who didn't look any less nervous. We were on the first floor of the three-decker. Goatee was sprawled in a gut-sprung easy chair under a badly framed seascape, the Saturday Night Special he'd poked in my ear lazing in his lap. Nervous was squatting next to the chair. I was sitting on the floor Indian-style in front of them, my hands tied tightly behind me, my feet tied a foot apart with the same stout rope. When Goatee wasn't talking, I could hear the woman in another room, speaking quietly to the child in Spanish.

Nervous mouthed the words on my ID while Goatee said, "I spot your tail when we come off the Interstate. You suck when it come to following people."

"I wasn't following you. I was following them."

Nervous looked at Goatee. "Cristo, the man is a detective, he will—"

With some crispness, Goatee backhanded him across the cheek. "José, how many ..." Then Goatee laughed and in Spanish said something soothing to Nervous. Goatee gargled some more wine before turning his head to me. "You *habla español*, Mr. P.I.?"

"No."

"Well, maybe you lying to me, but I take your word for it. I hit my cousin here because he say my name in front of you, but then I use his name, so I apologize for it. We all under the pressure, no?"

"This is your first kidnapping."

"You could say that, yeah."

"But not your first killing."

Something moved inside José, who gave Cristo back my ID, then rubbed his stomach a little with his other hand.

Cristo just smiled, drained more of the jug. "Let me guess. You see the knife we leave in the rich boy, you figure we real bad dudes, eh?"

"It was probably smarter to leave the knife than carry it away, but it was pretty stupid to kill the man when you had chloroform to start with."

"You got a good nose, Mr. P.I. I got a good nose, too." Cristo pointed to it. "I see you at the rest stop, I say to myself, 'Cristo, this one is cop. Maybe not now, but sometime.' "

"You saw me on the way in."

Cristo looked a little puzzled. "So?"

"So you thought I was a cop, that's all the more reason you don't kill the man in the bathroom."

At that point, the woman walked into the room. She was just this side of pretty, with a white blouse and jeans, a tiny gold crucifix on a delicate chain around her neck. Cristo muttered something to her in Spanish with a questioning lilt at the end of it. José spoke up petulantly, but she answered Cristo.

The goatee swung back in my direction. "My cousin is a little angry with me, I call his wife a bad name. Luna, this is Mr. P.I."

The woman looked at me, maybe trying to picture my last name in letters. I said, "How's the boy?"

Luna didn't hesitate. "He's fine."

"Did he see your relatives here stab his father to death?"

José flinched, Cristo not noticing through his wine laughed as he set down the jug and picked up the gun. The cylinder looked like it held six rounds and would explode before you got past three, but I didn't expect to still be counting that far.

Cristo waggled the business end of the barrel at me. "Mr. P.I., you trying to start my people here against me?"

"Why'd you have to kill him, Cristo?"

The muzzle wavered as he shrugged and went back for the wine with his free hand. "Man recognize me."

"From where?"

Cristo considered that, then shrugged again and took a few more swallows. "I working in this nursing home, bunch of old farts with more money than time to spend it. One old one in particular, he got lots of money. Rooms, whole houses of money. He has his son and the son's wife from the rest stop come visit him, bring the old one's grandson. They rich, too, but they come because they want to get richer. They play up to the old one, they bring him stuff he don't need and can't use. They bring the kid to scream around the room, make a mess and noise the old one would yell at he not so sick he can't move. Then they start to run low on small talk, they tell the old one about this rest stop they use, every time on the way home from visiting him. They go on and on about what it look like and what they can get the little monster there and I hear them one day and I say to myself, 'Hey, that's the rest stop around where my cousin José and his Luna live.' So I wait till the rich boy go out for a smoke, out on the patio, and it's cold but I go out there anyway, I try to be a human being, and I say to him, 'Hey, that rest stop. That's by where my cousin José live.' And this rich boy, he look at me like I am something the pooper-scooper clean up, and he crush his smoke under his shoe and go back in without he even answer me."

"And that's where you got the idea to take his child."

"Not so much his child as the old one's grandson, eh?"

"For ransom."

"For maybe one of the grandfather's houses of money."

"And to kill his son."

Some more wine, eyes to the ceiling. "He recognize me, man. No choice."

José was watching Cristo, Luna was watching me.

I said, "You were going to kill the man from word one, Cristo. The plan was to take the child in the Men's Room. Mirrors everywhere. The man's going to see you."

Now José started watching me, Luna on Cristo.

"The man's going to see you and remember you after he wakes up from the chloroform. You can't let him remember about that and your cousin José who lives near the rest stop."

Cristo picked up the gun, both the others watching him. "Time to shut up, man."

I played my last cards. "And you're going to have to kill me now because I know and the child because he might remember you, too."

I don't know where José and Luna were looking after that, because Cristo came out of the chair in a half-dive and cracked me across the face with the butt end of his popgun. I didn't think the handle grips broke, but I wasn't as sure about my jaw.

FOUR

I ran my tongue around the inside of my mouth and under the gag. One molar was still a plateau, but the one next to it had become a jagged peak.

Lying on my side on the cold floor of a back bedroom, I was a foot away and twice that down from the little boy, sleeping peacefully on an old iron twin bed. Luna had tucked him carefully under a blanket, but his breath came out in little streams of gray, sweet as an after-dinner mint.

I rocked around on my rear end until I could roll over, my ankles and feet all pins and needles from the tighter bonds. There was a low, wide window that seemed to face onto the driveway, because I could just see the top of the Chevy.

I figured they'd keep me alive as long as they could, since it would make my body less smelly and therefore more convenient to carry and dump somewhere. I was looking around from radiator to closet door for a sharp enough edge to work on my ropes when the room door opened.

Luna put her index finger to her lips and closed the door silently behind her.

She first walked to the bed, stepping over me to check on the child. Then she stepped back over me, kneeling next to my head and leaning down close to my ear.

"If I cut the ropes, you will take the boy and not hurt my husband?"

I nodded.

She produced a knife from her back pocket and had the hand ropes loose in ten seconds, the feet taking a little less. I got the gag out, but when I tried to stand, my legs were shaky from lack of circulation. Luna gathered up the boy, who rubbed his eyes and fussed a little, but quietly. I got to the window and tried to ease it up. No go. I checked for the lock, but there was none. I tried again, got a squeak within half an inch, and stopped.

The boy seemed to rise to the squeak and cried out.

Luna hissed at me and tried to shush him.

I heard something from the front of the house and just heaved up on the window, which shuddered and screeched. The boy began to howl, and I turned back to Luna.

She said, "Quick! Out the window and I will hand him to you."

I got out the window, but given the trussing and the darkness, I twisted an ankle hitting the ground. It took me time to get back up and turn toward Luna.

The light that precedes a swung-open door silhouetted her from behind. She said, "Catch him!"

Luna dropped the wailing child from three feet above me. I caught him like a punted football and reached up a hand to steady her.

From inside the room came a yell from Cristo and the sound of hands clapping twice. An exit wound bloomed on the center of Luna's chest, just below the crucifix. Her mouth formed an "O," a choir member holding her note. Then she sagged forward from the waist, torso and arms dangling outside the window.

I heard cursing in Spanish and an anguished male cry as I turned to run from the house. I'd gotten three steps on the bum ankle when a commanding male voice roared, "Green light! Green light!"

I cradled the boy and hit the deck. Portable floodlights criss-crossed all around as the air filled with the pocking noises of M-16s in front of me and the splintering noises of wood and glass behind me.

FIVE

I was sitting on a hard wooden bench outside the detective bureau in a municipal police headquarters that every force in the state had commandeered.

A sniper from the SWAT team brought me coffee, and I thanked him for the thought, but even if I drank the stuff, I was still too wired to enjoy it.

An EMT had taped my ankle and said I might want to have it looked at back in Boston. I was just about calm enough to see if it still hurt to lift my foot when the detective bureau door opened and Elvin Tyson came out.

He saw me, started toward the bench, then stepped back and closed the door. He made his way toward me again, taking stock from head to toe.

"Elvin."

"They said you wasn't too bad banged up. Glad to see you."

"Same here. You got the cops?"

"I did. Standing back there at my rest stop, freezing in that night air, I realized I didn't care too much for you hollering at me about missing that old Chevy's license plate."

"Sorry."

"So I did the next best thing."

"Which was?"

"I made sure I saw yours."

I closed my eyes and rested my head on the back of the bench. "They swept the streets of towns just off the exits and found my car."

"Took them a while, though."

"It did, but you were still my best chance. Thanks."

"Hell, I didn't do it for you, son."

I opened my eyes and looked at him. "For the child, then?"

"Hell, no. I just hadn't finished with my story."

"Your story."

"Yeah. Like I was telling you, through the tenth, Marvin and the Worm, they was even-steven. But then come the eleventh …"

EYES THAT NEVER MEET

ONE

MARLA Van Dorn owned a condo in one of those bay-windowed brownstones on Commonwealth Avenue. The living room had a third-floor view of the Dutch-Elmed mall as it runs eastward through Back Bay to Boston's Public Garden. The view westward tends toward the bars and pizza joints of Kenmore Square and derelicts on public benches, so most people with bay windows look eastward for their view. As I was.

Behind me, Van Dorn said, "When the leaves are off the trees, you can see straight across Commonwealth to the buildings on the other side. Even into the rooms, at night with the lights on."

I nodded. Ordinarily, I meet clients in my office downtown, the one with "JOHN FRANCIS CUDDY, CONFIDENTIAL INVESTIGATIONS" stenciled in black on a pebbled-glass door. But I live in Van Dorn's neighborhood, so stopping on the way home from work at her place, at her request, wasn't exactly a sacrifice.

She said, "It might be helpful if we sat and talked for a while first, then I can show you some things."

I turned and looked at her. Early thirties, Cosmo cover girl gone straight into a high rise investment house. Her head was canted to the right. The hair was strawberry blonde and drawn back in a bun that accented the cords in her long neck. The eyes were green and slightly almond-shaped, giving her an exotic, almost oriental look. The lipstick she wore picked up a minor color in the print blouse that I guessed was appropriate business attire in the dog days of July. Her skirt was pleated and looked to be the mate to a jacket that I didn't see tossed or folded on the burlappy, sectional furniture in the living room. The skirt ended two inches above the knee while she was standing and six inches further north as she took a seat across a glass and brass coffee table from me. Van Dorn made a ballet of it.

The head canted to the left. "Shall I call you 'John' or 'Mr. Cuddy?' "

"Your dime, your choice."

The tip of her tongue came out between the lips, then back in, like it was

20

testing the wind for something. "John, then. Tell me, John, do you find me attractive?"

"Ms. Van—"

"Please, just answer the question."

I gave it a beat. "I think you're attractive."

"Meaning, you find me attractive?"

"Meaning based on your face and your body, you'd get admiring glances and more from most of the men in this town."

"But not from you."

"Not for long."

"Why?"

"You're too aware of yourself. The way you move your head and the rest of you. I'd get tired of that and probably tired of trying to keep up with it."

Her lips thinned out. "You're a blunt son of a bitch, aren't you?"

"If you don't like my answers, maybe you shouldn't ask me questions."

A more appraising look this time. "No. No, on the contrary. I think you're just what I need."

"For what?"

"I'm being ... I guess the vogue-ish expression is 'stalked.' "

"There's a law against that now. If you go to—"

"I can't go to the police on this."

"Why not?"

"Because a policeman may be the one stalking me."

Uh-oh. "Ms. Van Dorn—"

"Perhaps it would be easier if I simply summarized what's happened."

She didn't phrase it as a question.

I sat back, taking out a pad and pen, to show Van Dorn I was serious before probably turning her down. "Go ahead."

She settled her shoulders and resettled her hands in her lap. "I was burglarized two months ago, the middle of May. I came home from work to find my back window here, the one on the alley, broken. I've since had security bars installed, so that can't happen again. Whoever it was didn't take much, but I reported it to the police, and they sent a pair of detectives out to take my statement. One of them ... He called me on a pretext, about checking a fact in my statement, and he ... asked me to go out with him."

Van Dorn stopped.

I said, "Did you?"

"Did I what?"

"Go out with him?"

"No. He was ... unsuitable."

"Did you hear from him again?"

"Yes. I'm afraid I wasn't quite clear enough the first time I turned him down. Some of them just don't get it. The second time, I assure you he did."

"What'd you tell him?"

"I told him I don't date black men."

I looked at her, then said, "His name?"

"Evers, Roland Evers. But he told me I could call him 'Rollie.' "

"Then what happened?"

"Nothing for a week. I travel a good deal in my job, perhaps ten days a month. When I'd get back from a trip, there would be ... items waiting for me, downstairs."

When I came into her building, there had been a double set of locked doors with a small foyer between them and a larger lobby beyond the inner door. "What do you mean by 'downstairs'?"

"In the space between the doors, as though somebody had gotten buzzed in and just dropped off a package."

"Buzzed in by one of your neighbors, you mean?"

"Yes. The buzzer can get you past the outer door to the street, but not the second one."

"What kind of package?"

"Simple plain-brown wrappers, no box or anything with a name on it."

"What was in the packages?"

"Items of women's ... The first one was a bra, the second one panties, the third ..." Van Dorn's right hand went from her lap to her hair, and she looked away from me. "The bra was a peek-a-boo, the panties crotchless, the third item was a ... battery-operated device."

I used my imagination. "Escalation."

"That's what I'm afraid ... That's the way it appears to me as well."

"You said the burglar didn't take much."

Van Dorn came back to me. "Excuse me?"

"Before, when you told me about the break-in, you said not much was taken."

"Oh. Oh, yes. That's right."

"Exactly what did you lose?"

"A CD player, a Walkman. Camera. They left the TV and VCR, thank God. More trouble hooking them up than replacing them."

"No items of ... women's clothing, though."

"Oh, I see what ..." A blush. "No, none of my ... things. At first I assumed the burglary wasn't related to all this, beyond bringing this Evers man into my life. But now, well, I'm not so sure anymore."

"Meaning he might have pulled the burglary hoping he'd get assigned to the case and then have an excuse for meeting with you?"

Van Dorn didn't like the skepticism. "Farfetched, I grant you, but let me tell you something, John. You've no doubt heard burglary compared to violation. Violation of privacy, of one's sense of security."

"Yes."

"Well, let me tell you. Living in this part of the city, being such a target for the scum that live off drugs and need the money to buy them and get that money by stealing, I've come to expect burglary. It's something you build in, account for in the aggravations of life, like somebody vandalizing your Beemer for the Blaupunkt."

Beemer. "I see what you mean."

"I hope you do. Because this man, whoever it is, who's leaving these ... items, is grating on me a lot more than a burglary would. Than my own burglary *did*. It's ruining my peace of mind, my sense of control over my own life."

"You just said, 'Whoever it is.'"

"I did."

"Does that mean it might not be Evers?"

"There's someone else who's been ... disappointed in his advances toward me."

"And who is that?"

"Lawrence Fadiman."

"Can you spell it?"

"F-A-D-I-M-A-N. 'Lawrence' with a 'w,' not a 'u.'" Van Dorn opened a folder on the coffee table and took out a photo. A nail the color of her lipstick tapped on a face among three others, one of them hers. "That's Larry."

Thirtyish, tortoise shell glasses, that hair style that sweeps back from the forehead in clots like the guys in Ralph Lauren clothes ads. The other two people in the shot were older men, everybody in business suits. "How did you come to meet him?"

"We work together at Tower Investments."

"For how long?"

"I started there three years ago, Larry about six months later."

"What happened?"

"We were on a business trip together. To Cleveland of all places, though a lot of people don't know what that city is famous for in an investment sense."

"It has the highest number of Fortune 500 headquarters outside New

York?"

Van Dorn gave me the appraising look again. "Very good, John."

"Not exactly a secret. What happened in Cleveland?"

"A few too many drinks and 'accidental' brushings against me. I told him I wasn't interested."

"Did that stop him?"

"From the unwanted physical contact, yes. But he's made some other ... suggestions from time to time."

"And that makes him a candidate."

"For the items, yes."

"You talk with Fadiman or his superior about sexual harassment?"

"No."

"Why not?"

Van Dorn got steely. "First, Larry and I are peers. I'm not his subordinate, not in the hierarchy and not in talent, either. However, if I can't be seen to handle his ... suggestions without running to a father figure in the firm, there would be some question about my capability to handle other things—client matters."

"Your judgment. Evers and Fadiman. That it?"

"No."

"Who else?"

"A bum."

"A bum?"

"A homeless man. A beggar. What do you call them?"

I just looked at her again. " 'Homeless' will do."

Van Dorn said, "He's always around the neighborhood. He stinks and he leers and he whistles at me when I walk by, even across the street when I'm coming from the Copley station."

The subway stop around the corner. "Anything else?"

"He says things like 'Hey, lovely lady, you sure look nice today,' or 'Hey, honey, your legs look great in those heels.' "

She'd lowered her voice and scrunched up her face imitating him. In many ways, Van Dorn was one of those women who got less attractive the more you talked to them.

I said, "Any obscenities?"

"No."

"Unwanted physical contact?"

Van Dorn looked at me, trying to gauge whether I was making fun of the expression she'd used. She decided I wasn't. "Not yet."

"You have a name for this guy?"

"You can't be serious?"

"How about a description?"

"Easier to show you."

She stood, again making a production of it, and swayed past me to the bay window. "Over here."

I got up, moved next to her.

Van Dorn pointed to a bench on the mall with two men on it. "Him."

One wore a baseball cap, the other was bareheaded. "Which one?"

"The one closer to us."

"With the cap on."

"Yes."

"Does he always wear that cap?"

"No."

"You're sure that he's the one?"

"What do you mean?"

"Well, it's kind of hard to see his face under the cap."

Van Dorn looked at me as though I were remarkably dense. "I couldn't describe his face if I tried. I mean, you don't really *look* at them, do you? It's like ... it's like the eyes that never meet."

"I don't get you."

"It was an exhibit, a wonderful one from Greece at the Met in New York the last time I was there. There were a dozen or so funeral stones from the classical period, 'stelai' I think is the plural for it. In any case, they'll show a husband and wife in bas relief, her sitting, giving some symbolic wave, him standing in front of her, sort of sadly? The idea is that she's died, and is waving good-bye, but since she's dead, the eyes—the husband's and the wife's—never meet."

I thought of a hillside in South Boston, a gravestone that had my wife's maiden and married names carved into it. "And?"

"And it's like that with the homeless, don't you find? You're aware of them, you know roughly what they look like—and certainly this one's voice —but you never look into their faces. Your eyes never meet theirs."

It bothered me that Van Dorn was right. "So, you think the guy in the cap might be leaving these items for you?"

"He's around all the time, seeing me get into cabs with a garment bag. God knows these bums don't do anything, they have all the time in the world to sit on their benches planning things."

"The items ... The pieces of underwear in the packages, were they new?"

"Well, I didn't examine them carefully, of course. I threw them away."

"But were they new or old?"

"They seemed new."

"And the device."

The blush again. "The same."

"Where would a homeless man get the money to buy those things new?"

"Where? Begging for it, stealing for it. For all I know, he's the one who broke into this place. Fence the CD and such for whatever money he needed."

I looked down at the guy in the cap. He didn't look like he was going anywhere for a while. "Anybody else?"

"Who could be leaving the packages, you mean?"

"Yes."

"No."

"How about a neighbor?"

"No."

"Jilted boyfriend?"

"John, I haven't had a *boy*-friend in a long time."

She looked at me, catlike. "I do have some very good *men*-friends from time to time, but one has to be so much more careful these days."

I nodded and changed the subject. "What exactly is it that you want me to do, Ms. Van Dorn?"

She swayed back to the couch, rolling her shoulders a little, as though they were stiff. "What I want you to do is pay all these men a visit, rattle their cages a little. Let them know that I've hired you and therefore that I treat this as a very serious issue."

I waited for her to sit down again. "It's not very likely one of them's going to break down and confess to me."

"I don't care about that. Frankly, I don't even care who it is who's been doing these things. I just want it to stop because I made it stop through hiring you."

Through her getting back in control. "I can talk to them. I can't guarantee results."

A smile, even more like a cat now. "I realize that. But somehow I think you achieve results, of all different kinds. Once you put your mind to it."

I folded up my pad.

Van Dorn let me see the tip of the tongue again. "You may regret not finding me attractive, John."

"Our mutual loss."

The tongue disappeared, rather quickly.

TWO

I left Marla Van Dorn's building through the front doors, holding open the outer one for a nicely dressed man carrying two Star Market bags and fumbling to find his keys. He thanked me profusely, and I watched to be sure he had a key to open the inner door, which he did. Most natural thing in the world, holding a door open for someone, especially so they could just drop off a package safely for someone in the building.

Before crossing to the mall, I walked around the corner to the mouth of the alley behind Van Dorn's block, the side street probably being the one she'd use walking from the subway station. The alley itself was narrow and typical, cars squeezed into every square inch of pavement behind the buildings in a city where parking was your worst nightmare. I moved down the alley, a hot breeze on my face, counting back doors until I got to the one I thought would be Van Dorn's. There were bars across a back window on the third floor, but a fire escape that accessed it. Before the bars, nobody would have needed anything special to get up and in there, just hop on a parked car and catch the first rung of the escape like a stationery trapeze.

I walked the length of the alley and came out on the next side street, turning right and taking that back to Commonwealth. I crossed over to the mall and started walking down the macadam path that stretched like a center seam on the eighty-foot wide strip of grass and trees. And benches.

The way I was approaching them, the guy in the baseball cap was farther from me than the other man, who looked brittly old and seemed asleep. The guy in the cap was sitting with his legs straight out, ankles crossed, arms lazing over the back of the bench. He wore blue jeans so dirty they were nearly black, with old running shoes that could have been any color and a chamois shirt with tears through the elbow. He was unshaven but not yet bearded, and the eyes under the bill of the cap picked me up before I gave any indication I was interested in talking to him.

The guy in the cap said, "Now who might you be?"

"John Cuddy." I showed him my ID folder.

"Private eye. Didn't think you looked quite 'cop.' "

"You've had some experience with them."

"Some. Mostly Uncle Sugar's, though."

The eyes. I'd seen eyes like that when I strayed out of Saigon or they came into it. "What's your name?"

"Take your pick, John Cuddy, seeing as how I don't have no fancy identification to prove it to you."

I said, "What outfit, then?"

The shoulders lifted a little. "Eighty-second. You?"

"Uncle Sugar's cops."

The cap tilted back. "MP?"

"For a while."

"In-country?"

"Part of the while."

He gestured with the hand closest to me. "Plenty of bench. Set a spell."

"I won't be here that long."

The hand went back to where it had been. "Why you here at all?"

"A woman's asked me to speak to you about something that's bothering her."

"And what would that be?"

"You."

A smile, two teeth missing on the right side of the upper jaw, the others yellowed and crooked. "Miss Best of Breed?"

"Probably."

"Saw you going into her front door over there."

"You keep pretty good tabs on the building?"

"Passes the time."

"You seen anybody leaving things in the foyer?"

"The foyer? You mean inside the door there?"

"That's what I mean."

"Sure. United Parcel, Federal Express."

"Anybody not in a uniform and more than once?"

"This about what's bothering her?"

"Partly."

"What does 'partly' mean?"

"It means she isn't nuts about you grizzling her every time she walks by."

The cap tilted down. "I don't grizzle her."

"She doesn't like it."

"All's I do, I tell her how good she looks, how she makes my day better."

"She doesn't appreciate it."

The guy tensed. "Fine. She won't hear it no more, then."

"That a promise?"

The guy took off the cap. He had a deep indentation scar on his forehead, one you didn't notice in the shadow of the bill. "Got this here from one of Charlie's rifle butts. The slope that done it thought he'd killed me, but he learned he was mistaken, to his everlasting regret. When I was in, I found I liked hand-to-hand, picked up on it enough so's the colonel had me be an instructor."

"What's your point?"

"My point, John Cuddy, is this. You come over here to deliver a message, and you done it. Fine, good day's work. But you come back to roust me some more, and you might find you're mistaken and regret it, just like that slope I told you about."

"No more comments, no more whistles, no more packages."

"I don't know nothing about no packages. What the hell's in them, anyways?"

"Things that bother her."

"What, you mean like ... scaring her?"

"You could say that."

The head drooped, the arms coming off the back of the bench, hands between his knees, kneading the flesh around his thumbs. "That ain't right, John Cuddy. Nossir. That ain't right at all."

THREE

The Area D station that covers my neighborhood is on Warren Street, outside Back Bay proper. The building it's in would remind you of every fifties black-and-white movie about police departments. Inside the main entrance, I was directed to the Detective Unit. Of eight plain-clothes officers in the room, there was one Asian male, one black female, and one black male.

The black male looked to be about my size and a good stunt double for the actor Danny Glover. He was sitting behind a desk while a shorter, older white detective perched his rump on the edge of it. The black guy wore a tie and a short-sleeved dress shirt, the white guy a golf shirt and khaki pants. They were passing documents from a file back and forth, laughing about something.

I walked up to the desk, and the black detective said, "Help you?"

"Roland Evers?"

"Yeah?"

"I wonder if I could talk to you."

"Go ahead."

"In private?"

The white guy swiveled his head to me. Brown hair, clipped short, even features, the kind of priest-like face you'd tell your troubles to just before he sent you away for five-to-ten. "Who's asking?"

I showed them my ID holder.

The white guy said, "Jeez, Rollie, a private eye. I'm all a-quiver."

Evers said, "Can't hardly stand it myself, Gus. All right, Cuddy, what do you want?"

"Without your partner here might be better."

Gus looked at Evers, but Evers just watched me. "Partner stays."

Gus said, "You need to use a name, mine's Minnigan."

I decided to play it on the surface for a while. "You two respond to a B&E couple months back, condo belonging to Marla Van Dorn?"

Evers blinked. "We did."

"The lady's been getting some unwelcome mail. She'd like it to stop."

Minnigan said, "We never made a collar on that, did we, Rollie?"

Evers said, very evenly, "Never did."

Minnigan looked at me. "Seems we can't help you, Cuddy. We don't even know who did it."

"You spend much time trying?"

"What, to find the guy?"

"Yes."

Minnigan shook his head. "She lost, what, a couple of tape things, am I right?"

I said, "Walkman, CD player, camera."

"Yeah, like that. She never even wrote down the serial numbers. That always amazes me, you know? These rich people, can afford to live like kings and never keep track of that stuff."

"Meaning no way to trace the goods."

Evers said, "And no way to tie them to any of our likelies."

"That's all right. I'm not sure one of your likelies is the problem, anyway."

Minnigan said, "I don't get you."

"Van Dorn's not sure it's the burglar who's become her admirer."

Evers said, "Who does she think it is?"

"She's not sure." I looked from Evers to Minnigan, then back to Evers and stayed with him. "That's why I'm talking to you."

Minnigan said, "We already told you, we can't help you any."

Evers said, "That's not what Cuddy means, Gus. Is it?"

I stayed with Evers. "All she cares about is that it stops, not who's doing it or why. Just that it stops."

Minnigan glared at me.

Evers said, "You don't push cops, Cuddy."

"Is that what I'm doing?"

"You push a man, you find out he can hurt you, lots of different ways."

"I'm licensed, Evers."

"Licenses get revoked."

"Not without some kind of cause, and when you stop to think about it, everybody's licensed, one way or the other."

Minnigan came down off the glare. "Hey, hey. What are we talking about here?"

Evers glanced at him, then back to me. "Okay, let me give you the drill. I asked the woman out one time, she says 'no' like she maybe means 'maybe.' Fine. I ask her a second time, she gives me a real direct lecture on why she thinks the races shouldn't mix. I got the hint, you hear what I'm saying?"

I looked at both of them, Minnigan trying to look reasonable, Evers just watching me with his eyes as even as his voice.

I nodded. "Thanks for your time."

Outside the building, I took a deep breath. Halfway down the block, I heard Gus Minnigan's voice say, "Hey, Cuddy, wait up a minute."

I stopped and turned.

Minnigan reached me and lowered his voice. "Let me tell you something, okay?"

"Okay."

"Rollie's going through a divorce. I know I been there, maybe you have, too."

"Widowed."

"Wid—Jeez, I'm sorry. Really. But look, he's just out on his own a month, maybe two, when we answer the call on that Van Dorn woman. And you've seen her, who wouldn't try his luck, am I right? But that don't mean Rollie'd do anything more than that."

"So?"

"So, cut him a little slack, okay?"

"As much as he needs."

Minnigan nodded, like I meant what he meant, and turned back toward the Area D door.

FOUR

When I got off the elevator on the forty-first floor, I let my ears pop, then turned toward the sign that said, "TOWER INVESTMENTS, INC." The receptionist was sitting at the center of a mahogany horseshoe and whispered into a mini-mike that curved from her ear toward her mouth like a dentist's mirror. She gave me the impression she'd hung up however you have to in that kind of rig, then smiled and asked if she could help me.

"Lawrence Fadiman, please."

As she looked down in front of her, a man came through the internal doorway behind her. He wore no jacket, but suspenders held up pinstriped suit pants and a bow tie held up at least two chins. He looked an awful lot like one of the two older men in the photo Marla Van Dorn had shown me.

The receptionist pushed a button I could see and stared at a screen that I couldn't. "I'm afraid Mr. Fadiman's out of the office for at least another hour. Can someone else help you?"

"No, thanks. I'll catch him another time."

As I left, I heard the older man say, "Fadiman's not back yet?" and the receptionist say, "No, Mr. Tice."

The lobby of the building had a nice café with marble table tops over wrought-iron bases that Arnold Schwarzenegger would have had a time rearranging. I chose a table that gave me a good view of the elevator bank servicing floors 25 through 50. I'd enjoyed most of a mint-flavored iced tea before the man in the tortoise shell glasses and clotted hair came through the revolving door from outside. He wore a khaki suit against the heat, the armpits stained from sweat as he checked his watch and shook his head.

I said, "Larry!"

He stopped and looked around. Seeing no one he knew, Fadiman started for the elevators again.

"Larry! Over here."

This time he turned completely around. "Do I know you?"

"Only by telephone. John Cuddy."

"Cuddy ... Cuddy ... "

"Mr. Tice upstairs said I might catch you if I waited here."

The magic word in the sentence was "Tice," which made Fadiman move toward me like he was on a tractor beam.

He said, "Well, of course I'd be happy to help. What's this about?"

As we shook hands and he sank into the chair opposite me, I said, "It's about those nasty little packages Marla's been getting."

Fadiman looked blank. "Marla Van Dorn?"

"How many 'Marlas' you know, Larry?"

"Well, just—"

"The packages have to stop."

"What packages?"

"*The* packages."

"I don't know what—"

"Larry. No more of them, understand?"

He looked blanker. If it was an act, he was very, very good. "I'm sorry, but I don't have a clue as to what—"

"Just remember, Larry. I want them to stop, Marla wants them to stop, and most important of all, Mr. Tice would want them to stop if I were to tell him about them."

Blank was replaced by indignant. "Is this some sort of ... veiled threat?"

I stood to leave. "No, I wouldn't call it 'veiled,' Larry."

FIVE

When I got back to the office, I called her at Tower Investments.

"Marla Van Dorn."

"John Cuddy, Ms. Van—"

"What the hell did you say to Larry?"

"Not much. If he isn't the one who's been sending the packages, he wouldn't have guessed what was in them."

"Yes, well, that's great, but you should have seen him fifteen minutes ago."

"What did he do?"

"He grabbed me by the arm, pulled me into a cubbyhole and hissed at me."

"Hissed at you?"

"Yes. At least, that's what it sounded like. He told me he didn't appreciate my 'goon' accosting him across a crowded lobby."

I liked "accosted." "The lobby wasn't that crowded."

A pause. "What I mean is, I think you've rattled his cage enough."

"He say anything else?"

"Just that if I stood in the way of any opportunities he had here, he'd know what to do about it."

I didn't like that. "Maybe I rattled a little too hard."

"Don't worry about it, I can't say I feel sorry for him. Did you see the others?"

I told her about Evers and the guy in the cap.

"Well, then, I guess we just ... wait and see if the packages stop?"

"I guess."

"Unless you have something else in mind, John?"

"No."

"Well then." Brusquely. "I have things to do if I'm going to be out of here by six."

She hung up. I pushed some papers around my desk for a while, trying to work on other cases, but I kept coming back to Marla Van Dorn. I turned over what I'd learned. Lawrence Fadiman may have confronted her at work, but he wasn't likely to do anything violent there. Her condo was a better bet, and with the back window barred, that left the front entrance as maybe the best bet of all.

The paperwork on my desk could wait. I locked the office and headed home to change.

✳ ✳ ✳ ✳

The guy in the baseball cap was already on the bench with the best view of Marla Van Dorn's likely route from the subway station down the side street toward Commonwealth. Even with me wearing sunglasses and a Kansas City Royals cap of my own above and a Hawaiian shirt, Bermuda shorts, and black kneesocks below, I thought he might recognize me. So I sat with my Boston guidebook and unfolded map on the next bench up the mall, keeping my eye on the side street as best I could, which really meant just from the alley mouth to Commonwealth. I checked my watch. Five-forty.

While I waited, taxis stopped, dropping off some fares and picking up others. United Parcel and Federal Express trucks plied the double-parking lane, moving down a few doors at a time. Owners walked dogs and summer-school students played frisbee and nobody thought to ask the obvious tourist if he needed any help.

Out of the corner of my eye, I noticed the guy in the cap straighten. Looking over to the side street, I saw Marla Van Dorn walking, left hand holding a bag of some kind, hurrying a little as she approached the mouth of the alley, accentuating her figure under the cream-colored dress she wore.

Then one of the UPS trucks entered the intersection, its opaque, beetle-brown mass blocking my eyes for a frame. Before it passed, the guy in the ball cap was up and running hard, crossing Commonwealth toward the side street. As I got up, the UPS truck went by, and I could see the mouth of the alley again. But not my client.

I started running, too.

The guy in the cap disappeared into the alley, and I heard two cracks and a man's yell and a woman's scream. I drew a Smith & Wesson Chief's Special from under the Hawaiian shirt and flattened myself against the brick wall at the mouth of the alley, using my free hand as a stop sign to the people starting to stream down the side street. The two cracks had sounded to me like pistol shots, and both the man and the woman in the alley were still making noise, him more than her.

That's when I looked around the wall.

Marla Van Dorn was on her hands and knees, the front of the dress torn enough to see she was wearing a white bra and white panties. On his back on the ground in front of her was the guy in the cap, but he was bareheaded now, the cap still boloing near him from the hot breeze in the alley. The yelling was coming from Detective Gus Minnigan, whose right arm was pointing at an angle from his shoulder that God never intended, a four-inch revolver about twenty feet away from him.

I came into the alley fast, Minnigan clenching his teeth and yelling to me now. "The goddam bum broke my arm, he broke my goddam arm!"

Hoarsely, Van Dorn said, "This bastard ... was waiting for me ... grabbed me and pulled me into the alley."

Minnigan said, "She don't know what she's saying!"

Van Dorn looked up at me. "He put his gun in my ... between my legs and said, 'What, you don't care about who's sending you the undies and the toy, I don't mean that much to you?' "

I remembered Minnigan in the Area D station, glaring at me when I told him and Evers that.

Minnigan said, "She's lying, I tell you!"

I said, "Shut up or I'll break your other arm."

Rocking back onto her ankles, Van Dorn pointed at the guy lying in front of her. "Then he came out of ... nowhere. He ran right at us, against the gun ... The shots ... He broke this bastard's arm and kicked the gun away, then fell. He came right through the bullets."

I looked down at the guy in the cap. His eyes were open, but unfocussed, and I knew he was gone. Two blossoms of red, one where a lung would be, the other at his heart, grew toward each other as they soaked the chamois shirt.

"Why?" said Van Dorn, staring at the man's face from communion height above his body. "Why did you do that?"

I thought, *eyes that never meet*, but kept it to myself.

SOLDIER TO THE QUEEN

ONE

T he knock from the corridor was so soft, I wasn't sure it was on my door. When I said "Come in," though, the wooden frame with "JOHN FRANCIS CUDDY, CONFIDENTIAL INVESTIGATIONS" on the pebbled glass swung toward me, the woman behind it peeking in.

I said, "Can I help you?"

She looked at me, then at the stencilling on the glass, like I'd offered her my identification and she was trying to be sure I was the genuine article. Black, short and heavyset, she seemed about forty, but the extra pounds bulged her features as well as the summery, print dress, so if someone told me she was five years to either side, I wouldn't have bet against it.

The woman said, "Mr. Cuddy?"

I stood up. "Yes?"

"My name's Georgina Newell. I maybe have a problem you could help me with?"

She said it as a question, a lilt of the Old South in her voice despite the fact that we were standing less than a hundred feet from, and thirty feet above, Boston Common. The name rang a vague bell inside my head. "Please, come in."

Newell came all the way through the door, closing it behind her before moving daintily to one of the two client chairs in front of my desk. The almost mincing walk came from the tiny feet and slim ankles, I think, the small bones giving me the impression that she hadn't always carried the same weight but had gotten used to it.

Sitting down, Newell said, "It's about my boy, Jameson," and reached inside her handbag, fishing around until she came out with a hankie. Not crying yet, but seeming pretty sure she would be soon.

I made the connection. "Your son was driving for Luna McTeague."

A vigorous nod, the hankie dabbing one eye, then another. "Jammy is how I called him, account of when he was a little boy, he love strawberry jam on his bread."

The incident had been all over the news the week before. Luna McTeague was a rock singer, a black woman originally from the Roxbury section of Boston, who was just starting to hit. Her regular driver *cum* bodyguard was on vacation as McTeague was attacked by two masked men in an apparent kidnap attempt. Jameson – Jammy – Newell pulled a gun, wounding one of the men trying to stop them. McTeague was unhurt, the two men escaped, and Newell was DOA at the hospital.

His mother said, "This here is a picture of my boy. His yearbook one."

I took it from her, though I'd already seen it, flashed over the head of the news anchor every time a soundbite on the case had run. His was like any other yearbook photo you've ever known, bright smile, happy eyes, black hair almost shaved, basic-training style. I held the photo longer than I needed to because I thought it would make Mrs. Newell feel better, believing her son was still a substantial part of her life instead of just a part of her recent history.

"Luna, she been real good about everything, good as she can be. Paying for the funeral and all last week, calling me on the telephone, asking me how I was doing."

"Have you heard much from the police?"

She finished with the hankie, at least for now. "They been on the phone to me, too. This one lieutenant, Mr. Murphy, he say you might be somebody I can talk to."

Robert Murphy worked homicide, the only black in the unit. "What is it you'd like me to do, Mrs. Newell?"

"My Jammy, he working for Luna – she a local girl, I knew her mama from when I first move up here – he was so happy. He knew Luna, too, four years behind her in school. Kind of a puppy love for her, I always thought. But my Jammy, he always want to be in the Army, but he get ready to graduate so he go up to the recruitment office, and they say he can't, account of he has this bad knee from football. He wasn't no big boy, my Jammy, just good hands, you know what I'm saying? Wide receiver, caught three touchdowns his senior year for Boston English."

I wanted to bring her back. "How did your son come to drive for Ms. McTeague?"

"Well, she was between gigs – I think that's what you call it – like taking a little vacation before she start on the road again? And so her driver, he take his vacation, too, and she telephone to me, ask if my Jammy can kind of fill in?"

"Your son have any experience doing that?"

"Driving? He have his license for two years now, ever since he seventeen."

"I mean experience driving for someone, acting like a bodyguard."

Newell shook her head, raising the hankie again. "He wasn't supposed to be no bodyguard. Was just supposed to drive her around, run and get her stuff she need so she could enjoy her vacation."

Gently, I said, "Did your son usually carry a gun?"

Emphatic shake of the head. "Nossir. No, my Jammy never carry no gun, never join up with no gang. Never look for trouble from nobody."

"Mrs. Newell, what is it you want me to do?"

"Mr. Murphy, he say maybe I could hire you? Maybe you could poke around some, find out the peoples kill my boy."

That sounded off. Homicide cops, especially good ones like Murphy, don't want or need private investigators mucking up their cases. "What do you think I can do that the police can't?"

Newell clutched her hankie like rosary beads. "Mr. Cuddy, you have any children?"

"No."

"Ever been married yourself?"

I thought of Beth and said, "Not for a while."

"Your wife, she run out on you like my man did on me?"

"She died. Cancer."

I thought that might stop Newell, but it didn't even slow her down. "Well, when my man run out on me, he leave me pregnant with my Jammy. I raised that boy from nothing with nothing, and now somebody gone and take him away from me forever. I want those peoples caught and brought to court and put in prison for the rest of their lives. That's what I want, and I'm sitting here ready to pay you for doing it."

You had to admire her, but admiration wasn't a very solid basis for taking on a client. "Mrs. Newell, I could spend a long time backtracking over what the police've already done. I can't guarantee I'll find something they missed."

"I know that. But there got to be some reason Mr. Murphy tell me to come see you. I can read mens, and I read him and you the same way. You not the kind to cheat me."

She was right about Murphy, and, I hoped, right about me, too. "You have any idea why your son was carrying a gun?"

A shrug. "Like I said, he want to be a soldier, and he just about worship Luna, you'd think she was a queen. His puppy love wasn't nothing but respectful, though. Like them bees."

"Bees?"

"You know, from the TV last month, downtown?"

Got it. In late May, a colony of honeybees was flying through the financial district, God knows why. Some bee expert was interviewed about it on the news broadcasts, saying a downdraft of air from the skyscrapers pushed the bees onto the street. The passing vehicles crushed some of them, including the queen, firefighters having to hose the bodies off the asphalt.

Newell said, "My Jammy, he was just like them bees. They won't leave their queen, even though she dead. The bee-man, he trying to scoop them up in his box, save them from the cars. But they don't care, them bees. Nossir. They like my Jammy with Luna, soldiers to their queen."

The hankie had to go back to work.

✣ ✣ ✣ ✣

A few years ago, the department moved all the homicide detectives from headquarters on Berkeley Street to an old building in South Boston, about a mile from where I grew up. I knocked on the blue door with the blue and white HOMICIDE UNIT sign. A female voice I recognized said, "Come on in, we're always open."

Beyond the door, a woman with brown hair and broad shoulders was sitting on a padded desk chair, doodling on a file. A blocky black man in a hound's-tooth suit stood next to her.

I said, "Two of you at once, an embarrassment of riches."

Cross looked up from her file to Murphy. "Cuddy's here. What a treat."

Murphy spoke to her. "You want to open a window?"

Cross watched me. "We airing the place out, or you thinking of jumping?"

"Sorry," I said, "I was looking for the Comedy Stop."

Murphy used the side of his foot to drag a second swivel chair over for him to use. "What's on your mind?"

I angled one of the straight-backs for conversation and eased into it. "Had a visit this morning from Georgina Newell."

Murphy nodded. I looked toward Cross, and Murphy nodded again, so I figured it was all right to continue in front of her.

"I guess I was wondering how you came to recommend she see me."

Cross handed the file she'd been doodling on to Murphy before he seemed to motion for it. He spread the manila folder on his knees. "Got the call from the uniforms who responded. They did what they could to preserve the crime scene, take down witnesses."

He wasn't exactly answering my question, but I didn't want to interrupt until I saw where he was going.

"Back Bay, Boylston near Arlington. Wednesday last, ten in the A.M.

Lots of closed up stores along there, so the traffic was light. Couple ways to escape in a vehicle, too. Jameson Newell was driving Ms. McTeague east on Boylston when she asked him to stop and double-park, she wanted to look in the window of the Women's Industrial Union there, arts and crafts and things."

I glanced at Cross. "Convenient of her."

Cross shrugged. "Says she does that a lot, one of the reasons she likes to have a driver taking her around. Says she never thought about it as a habit somebody might use against her."

Murphy went back to the file. "According to three sober, neutral witnesses, a sedan pulls up and blocks her car – pink Cadillac, she did a remake of the song couple years back. Masked man exits the passenger side and goes after McTeague, wearing gloves but holding a white cloth in one hand. He's grabbing her as the driver comes out, also masked and gloved. By this time Jammy – that's the dead boy's nickname."

"I know."

"By this time Jammy's up and out of the Caddy. The masked driver goes to take him barehanded, and Jammy produces a firearm and shoots, taking the guy somewhere up top."

I said, "Somewhere?"

Cross coughed. "One of the witnesses says left shoulder, another says right arm, and the third says between the eyes."

"Consistency's not always a virtue."

"Lieutenant said they were sober and neutral. That doesn't make them any good."

"The papers said Newell didn't have a license."

"The papers were right."

"Then what?"

Murphy said, "Everybody agrees Ms. McTeague yelled 'Jammy, no.' "

"In response to him shooting the driver."

"That's right."

"Funny all three witnesses should recognize such an odd name."

Cross said, "They got to hear it a lot, but that's getting ahead of ourselves." She looked back to Murphy.

"Anyway, the masked driver goes down, the other guy, the one after McTeague, drops the white cloth and pulls a piece of his own. He lets fly three from a combat stance, knocking down Jammy with two and knocking out a lamppost across the street. By this time, there's a good deal of running and hitting the deck going on in the general vicinity. The masked shooter runs over to his partner, yelling something about him being hit."

"Exact words?"

Cross said, "Take your pick. We have three flavors, surprise, surprise."

I went back to Murphy. "What then?"

"McTeague starts screaming and runs over to Jammy, who's bleeding out onto the blacktop. The masked shooter gets his driver into the sedan, taking the wheel himself and nailing it. At this point, he either takes a right onto Arlington toward the South End –"

"Or goes straight on Boylston in the general direction of Portugal," said Cross, shaking her head.

"You get a make on the vehicle?"

Murphy shook his head. "Could have been a brown Chevy, a blue Mercury, or – I like this – a black Toyota."

"The white cloth still at the scene?"

"Lab came back positive for chloroform."

"But McTeague never got put under."

Cross said, "No, she just cradled Newell's head in her lap, crying out his name over and over –"

"– How the witnesses all got that right –"

"– and saying, 'Why'd you have to do that, why'd you have to try for?' "

I said, "The chloroform makes it look right."

Murphy nodded.

I stayed with Cross. "Any prior attempts?"

She shook her head. "McTeague says not, and we never got any calls about one."

"Why would you?"

"McTeague lives in one of those highrises at the Prudential Center."

I stopped. "That's only five, six blocks from where she gets out of her car, right?"

Murphy said, "That's right."

"So why does she take a car someplace she can window-shop on foot?"

"Good question."

"And why does the attempt happen when her regular guy is on vacation?"

"Even better. We're trying to talk with the guy, Dennis Giordano, but both McTeague and his brother say he's backpacking somewhere the hell and gone in Maine."

"Giordano's brother?"

"Yeah. His name's Rick."

"There a way I can talk to Rick?"

"Yeah. He's bodyguarding McTeague now."

I stopped again. "Now, but not while Jammy Newell was filling in."

"That's right."

"There some reason Rick couldn't sub for Dennis originally instead of them bringing Newell into the picture."

Cross said, "Not that persuades us."

Which brought me back to the question Murphy hadn't answered. "Why did you send Mrs. Newell to me?"

He closed the file. "After we started on things, Commissioner started getting calls from concerned politicians from Roxbury, Mattapan, and other black – what's the polite word, 'enclaves?' "

"I like that. I grew up in an Irish enclave here, though I can't say I knew it at the time."

Murphy ignored me and spoke to me, all at the same time. "These politicians were very concerned. After the Chuck Stuart case here and O.J. out in the land of LA, they were afraid that the big bad Homicide Unit was going to put their native daughter through the official ringer after what she'd already been through."

Cross said, "Emotionally and psychically speaking, that is."

I looked from one to the other. "So the word rolling downhill from Berkeley Street is ..."

"Look for the bad guys, don't harass the good folks."

They both watched me.

"So I get to harass the good folks."

Neither said anything.

"There anybody else I should know about?"

Murphy handed the file back to Cross. "We'll give you a list of the witnesses names and addresses, you want to run those down. Do us a favor, though. Copy the list in your own hand-writing and then rip up our list."

"No paper trail. That it?"

He said, "There's one more guy you ought to see."

"Who's that?"

"McTeague's manager. Name of Manny Kantrowitz, Park Plaza building."

Cross said, "You can see him, or you can just wait here a while. He calls in every ten minutes or so to yell at us."

❊ ❊ ❊ ❊

I laid the roses diagonally across her grave, the blooms pointing down toward a wrecked dinghy on the shoreline rocks of the harbor below.

It's been a while, John.

"Too long, Beth." I was embarrassed to realize the only reason I was there now was because of already being in Southie at the Homicide Unit.

And you bring me roses to apologize?
"I bring you roses because they're the best."
And so are you, John Cuddy.
"I'll have to be."
What do you mean?
I told her about Mrs. Newell, and the shootings, and what Murphy and Cross had said to me.
A pause after I was finished. *Sounds depressing.*
"Murder generally is."
What I mean is, if you find out an insider had something to do with it, won't that hit his mother even harder?
"Probably, but that might be what she's asked me to do."
Another pause. *I'm glad I don't do what you do, John.*
Glancing down at the wrecked dinghy, I rearranged the roses with no improvement I could measure.

TWO

Luna McTeague's apartment building had a private garage entrance that gave onto Exeter Street and an obese doorman behind a curving white console on the first floor. Using her name got him to telephone up to her, and using Georgina Newell's name got me waved to the bank of elevators.

She was on the fifteenth floor, a door opening to my right as soon as I'd stepped off the elevator. I was pretty sure it wasn't McTeague who came out into the hall, because he was a white male, about six feet, one-ninety and twenty-eight or so. And angry. Very angry.

"You can just get back on and ride back down, man."

I kept walking toward him. "I don't think so."

He didn't wait for me to arrive. Instead he came barreling at me, the walls of the corridor about eight feet wide, or two feet too wide for him. Shifting my whole body, I feinted right, then came in low and under his chest, using the backs of my hands as lifts for his knees. He went ass over teakettle and landed with that satisfying, whooshing sound that meant he'd have all he could do to breathe for a minute or two.

I turned around and bent over him. "I'm guessing you're Rick."

"He is."

I turned back. The woman who was half-in the doorway looked a lot like the shots on TV. In person, McTeague stood about five-six in bare, toe-nail painted feet. She wore stirrup pants under a billowy peasant blouse and geometric earrings over that. Her complexion would remind you of honey, her hair a shade darker except for some blonde streaking here or there that could have come from the gene pool or a Clairol bottle. Prominent nose and lips, jutting chin made for defying a hand-mike, brooding eyes that looked as though they'd spent almost as much time crying as Georgina Newell's.

She said, "Is Rick all right?"

"Ask him."

McTeague watched me. "Rick, you okay, man?"

Giordano grunted something.

McTeague watched me some more. "Can you help him back into the apartment?"

"Probably."

I bent back over him, but he shoved my hand away. He got to his elbows, then his knees, one pair of joints at a time. When his ankles didn't wobble too much, he used them to get himself past me, then past her back into the apartment. I had a feeling he'd be heading to the porcelain facility, and when I joined McTeague in her living room, Giordano was nowhere to be seen.

"Have a seat."

There were plenty to choose from. Burlappy sectional furniture filled the place, each piece arranged to give a different view of the Cambridge skyline on the other side of the Charles River. The coffee and end tables were marble over brass, picking up the major color of the sectionals, issues of Variety, Billboard, and other industry magazines scattered over every horizontal surface. The carpeting was thick enough to hide mice.

McTeague took a sectional five feet across from me and folding one leg under her as she sat down. "Why did Georgina Newell hire you?"

"She thought I might be able to help the police find her son's killer."

"Yeah, but why you in particular?"

"Because I'm good at what I do."

While McTeague worked on that, I noticed a framed photo on one of the end tables. It showed her in a bathing suit with an arm around the waist of an ape-like guy maybe thirty-five years old. McTeague looked better in clothes than in the suit, and the guy looked like an older version of the departed Rick.

I said, "That Dennis?"

She turned, then turned back. "Yes. If he'd been there, none of this would have happened."

"Meaning?"

"Jammy wouldn't be ... dead."

"But wouldn't the rest of it have still gone down, with maybe you being held for ransom somewhere."

McTeague stared at me. "No. Dennis would have stopped them, without getting himself killed."

"Anything like this happen before?"

"No. Like I told the police."

"Then why was Jammy carrying a gun?"

McTeague lost the staring contest. "I don't know. He was real serious about the job, asking Dennis all about driving me around."

"I thought he was subbing for Dennis?"

"He was, but that's what I mean. Jammy wanted to come over and learn everything ahead of time, before Dennis took off and he had to start driving me himself." She seemed to look inward. "Maybe Jammy sensed something the first couple days, maybe somebody watching us or following us. But he never said a word to me about it, and he sure never said he was carrying a gun."

Reaching for a tissue, she seemed sincere. I gave her a minute, then, "Ms. McTeague, you've never gotten any kind of threat?"

Shake of the head as she used the tissue.

"Letter, phone call, over-eager fan?"

McTeague waved with her free hand. "No. You can ask Manny about that, you don't believe me. He's my manager, Manny Kantrowitz."

"Can you tell me what happened?"

"When, that day?"

"Yes."

She took another swipe at her eyes with the tissue, then made both hands go to her lap, like she was punishing them. "He was just driving me to a recording studio we were thinking about using for my next CD. I got to feel right in a place I'm gonna sing, and I wanted to see it before Manny cut the deal. We're going along Boylston, and we slow down for a car coming out of a space, and I see this doll in the window of the store there, so I tell Jammy to pull over."

"Into the space?"

"Huh?"

"Into the space that the other car just left?"

"Oh. Oh, no. There was like another car, waiting on it. So Jammy just double-parked, and I got out and walked toward it. I heard some brakes squeal, and I turned around, like you do, you know?"

I said I did.

"And then all of a sudden there's this dude coming at me in a black mask – ski mask, with gloves and this white rag, coming for my face."

She brought the tissue back into play.

I said, "Did you get any sense of him?"

"Yes. The rag smelled like chemicals."

"No, I mean sense of him. Young, old ..."

"No."

"Black, white?"

A firmer set of the jaw. "No. All's I could see was his eyes."

"No skin around the eye holes?"

"No."

"The mouth?"

Jaw firmer still. "I said no."

Okay. "Then what?"

"Then I heard these shots. And I thought they shot Jammy, account of I didn't know he had a gun. And I hollered at them, screamed at them, 'Jammy. No, no!' "

"Go on."

"Then the man after me, he turns around and pulls out this big gun and shoots at Jammy, and he ... he ..."

I gave her a moment. "Did you hear anybody say anything?"

Through some sniffling, she said, "The one who shot Jammy was saying something to his friend, like 'Hey, you okay, man?' Like that."

"Those the exact words?"

"I don't know. I was worried about Jammy."

"The voice, did it sound young or old?"

"I don't know."

"White or –"

"Look, I told you, I don't know. I was almost hysterical, all right?"

"Ms. McTeague, why'd you call Jammy to drive for you?"

"Because Dennis was going on vacation. I was on vacation, just finished three months of one-nighters." She paused. "Gigs, you know?"

"Yes, but why Jammy in particular?"

McTeague didn't like me mimicking her question earlier. "Account of I knew him, from the old neighborhood. He was a good boy, not into drugs or nothing. I figured I could trust him to drive the car and not crash it on me."

"Why not call Rick instead, have him fill in for his brother."

"Because Rick's a hot-shot, saw Kevin Costner in The Bodyguard. Had him work with Dennis once last year. Nearly broke a guy's arm when the guy just wanted an autograph."

"Like out in the hallway with me."

She nodded. "What I'm saying."

"How much longer will you be on vacation?"

A wariness. "Why?"

"I was just wondering when we could expect Dennis back."

"He's supposed to be back on Friday, account of I have this gig at the Orpheum Saturday. But I'm not gonna make it."

"Make what?"

"The gig. I'm just too ... too ..."

She got a new tissue.

THREE

The wooden plaque screwed into the door frame said EMANUEL KANTROWITZ, MUSICAL AGENT. It didn't look as though it was the first plaque to be attached to the office. I knocked and got a "Yeah, yeah."

Inside, a short, fiftyish man with a ridiculous toupée looked up at me. He was standing behind a desk heaped high with paperwork. There was a telephone receiver pressed to his right ear, the free left hand flicking at his other ear, waving me in like he was annoyed by a bug. The toupée looked enough like a small, sleeping animal that the bug could have been a flea.

Into the receiver he said, "Yeah, yeah, I know all that, but what do you want from my life? ... Harry, she witnessed a murder ... Look, she knew the kid, Harry, he was on the payroll, and he's gunned down like from your desk to the coffee machine, how's she supposed to feel?"

I looked around the office. Framed concert posters, one or two groups I'd vaguely heard of, a stunning one of Luna McTeague implying intimacy with a hand-mike.

"Gimme a break, all right? ... Well, you guys think about that open date in September, maybe the one in early October ... Right, right ... Okay."

Hanging up, he drew his hand down his face like the old actor doing the slow burn, then said, "And what's your problem?"

I showed him my ID, tried not to let him catch me staring at the rug. "I'd like to ask you a few questions on behalf of Georgina Newell."

"Who ... ? Oh, right, right. The mother." He exhaled harshly. "Sure, sure. Why not?"

I sat in a chair whose padding had long ago lost its padness. Kantrowitz sank back into its deskchair mate.

"A tragedy, a real tragedy."

"Did you know Jammy Newell?"

"Just to say hello to. He'd only been driving her like a week, and he was only gonna be around another week, till Dennis got back. You know who Dennis is?"

"Her bodyguard."

"That's what his brother'd like to call it. No, Luna's trending right now, but she's not stratospheric yet. That's why it's such a tragedy."

I was losing him. "How do you mean?"

"This gig at the Orpheum. That was them on the phone just now, me having to cancel and begging them to re-schedule. Took me two years to get that date. Now, at least they're hot to trot with her."

"Because of the shooting?"

"Because of the notoriety. The flash, the sizzle. You name me another rocker's been in the public eye – TV, radio, *Newsweek*, *Time*, you name it – without a drug bust or suicide attempt being the trigger. No, this'll put Luna on the moon, but –"

Kantrowitz stopped cold, then picked up a pencil and scratched on a notepad.

"Mr. Kantro –"

He held up his other hand, finished writing, and dropped the hand and the pencil from the other. " 'Luna on the moon,' get it?"

"I do now."

"You think of something like that, even accidental, you got to write it down, get it to the publicity people, see can they use it somehow."

"They feel Ms. McTeague's going to really make it?"

"Truth is, you never know. I been in this business twenty-nine years. Twenty-*nine*. I go back to Dianna Ross, Dionne, even Tina Turner the first time around. Luna's got the voice, but a hundred girls a year got the voice. Her body's not world-class, but she's got good moves on stage, can sell you the song even when you're not in the market. But she's been building a long time, and that's not so good in this business. Ain't room for too many if they haven't hit it big by twenty-five, and Luna's almost that now."

"So salting the mine wouldn't hurt, publicity-wise."

"Salting the … ? The hell you talking about?"

"There're some aspects of the attempt that make it look a little like a publicity stunt."

"Publicity stunt? What do you want from my life? Didn't I just get finished telling you that I had to cancel the Orpheum because Luna's too upset to go on? She had the place nearly sold out, her biggest single venue yet, and she's gonna do something to queer that, and then, *then*, tell me she's gotta cancel it because the kid's death freaked her out? Gimme a break."

Manny Kantrowitz waved me out of his office, this time not like he was just flicking at a bug.

FOUR

The kid leaned against his rake, grateful to me for pulling him away from the landscape contractor who'd hired him for the summer. "Hey, like is it really cool to be a private eye?"

"Sometimes," but I had the feeling this wouldn't be one of them. He was maybe sixteen. White, skinny, and dense as a post. He wore a Grateful Dead tee-shirt and blue jeans with a tear through the knee that looked carefully executed. His name was Tommy.

"You know, like the rock opera, man."

"The Who."

"I thought you looked the right age, man. The coolest of the cool was the Dead, though, right?"

"And they're still bopping."

"Bopping?"

"That day on Boylston Street?"

"Oh, right. Man, it was a scene. I was on my way up to Tower Records on Newbury, buy some fresh tracks. They're re-releasing all these cool sounds now on CD's. They didn't have those back when you were a kid, right?"

"Not even cassettes."

"You're kidding?"

"No. That day?"

"Oh, yeah. Right. Awesome action."

Tommy gave me the same sequence I'd gotten from Murphy and Luna McTeague. "Only thing was the gunfire sounded bogus."

"Bogus?"

"Yeah. It wasn't like on TV, man. Boom, boom. It was more a crackle, like."

"That's the way real gunfire sounds in the open air."

"Oh. Bummer."

"Could you hear anybody say anything?"

"Yeah, I heard the guy with the mask who shot the kid yell over to his friend, 'Hey, man, you hurt or what?' "

"Exact words?"

"Something like that. I didn't like write them down or anything."

"You get a sense of the voice?"

"A sense of it?"

"Yes. Young, old?"

"Older than me. A guy, not like a kid's voice."

"Black or white."

"Black."

"You're sure?"

A shrug. "Everybody else was."

"Everybody else was sure?"

Tommy looked at me. "No, man. Everybody else was black."

✳ ✳ ✳ ✳

She gestured back toward a woman sitting in a reclined chair with a lot of equipment arrayed around it. "You realize you're pulling me away from a perm?"

"I'll try not to take too much of your time."

"Can't it wait?"

"Maybe not. I'm here about the shootings you witnessed on Boylston."

"Honestly." She said it as a curse. About five feet tall and tubby, she wore a green smock on top and spandex leg-warmers down below. Her own hair was styled in a buzz cut around the ears, the Friar Tuck model bowl-cut above them, but without the bald spot. I wouldn't have let her near my own hair if it was on fire and she had a bucket of water.

The name tag on the smock read "Alice."

"Can you tell me what you saw that day, Alice?"

Same sequence.

"How about what was said?"

"The black singer, she was just screaming. The guy who shot her driver, he was yelling over to his partner."

"What did he yell?"

"I think it was 'Man, you hit,' but Caribbean-like."

"Caribbean?"

"Yeah. The guy's voice, I mean. He said 'man' like it was 'mon.' "

"'Mon.'"

"Yeah, like 'Hey, mon, welcome to the islands,' you know?"

"Did the shooter sound black or white to you?"

"Hey, who am I to know, right? All I do is cut hair, which if you don't mind."

Alice waddled back to the perm.

✳ ✳ ✳ ✳

"I'll be with you in a moment, sir."

"Take your time."

The store manager was in his forties. Sportcoat, tie, and starched white shirt. He carefully slid printer paper, file folders, and a couple of boxes of marking pens into the stationery bag for his female customer. They said good-bye using first names. His was Warren.

"Now, how can I help you?"

"I'm looking into the shootings you witnessed last week."

He closed his eyes. "I hope to never witness anything like it again."

"Can you tell me what you saw?"

"Yes, I was on my way to the bank, so unfortunately I had a perfect view of it, not diagonally the way it would have been through the store windows here."

Warren went through the same scenario as Tommy and Alice. "Did you hear anything said?"

"Well, the young black lady was really upset, calling out the name 'Jammy' over and over again. The killer – the one in the mask who shot the young black man – was more concerned about his confederate, though, and said something to him like, 'Man oh man, you okay?' "

"Exact words?"

"I doubt it. It all happened so fast, really. I didn't get a good look at anything. Probably didn't see any more than the blind man."

"The blind man?"

"Yes, yes." Warren came out from behind the counter and crossed to the store window. "Let me ... no, I don't see ... wait a minute, yes. Yes, there he is."

I followed his pointing finger.

FIVE

The man sat against the exterior wall of an abandoned optometry shop, red-tipped white cane next to him. Sole-worn running shoes with glary, new laces through the eyelets, no socks. Hiking shorts with things bulging past the button-flaps. An L.L. Bean tee-shirt with some stains where you might drop food on the way to your mouth. Amber sunglasses, a surfer-boy braided neckstring connected to each template behind the ear and running down his back. Red Sox baseball cap tilted enough to see his hairline, mostly gray at age sixty or so.

As I walked up to him, he rattled the quarters in the pewter mug in front of him, their clinking muffled a little by the two singles someone or he himself had put into it. I folded a five and slipped it down with its brethren.

A grin, eight or ten teeth missing. "Thank you sir, and have yourself a better day."

"Thanks. I'm hoping you can make it that way."

The grin faltered a bit. "I don't want any trouble."

I squatted down onto my haunches so our faces were on the same level. "I'm not offering any. Just like to ask you a few questions."

"No, I can't see light or fire."

I stopped.

He said, "That's usually the first question, can I make out light or fire. I can't."

"I'm not so interested in that."

He cocked his head. "Then what are your questions?"

"I'm a private investigator, looking into the shootings here last week. I understand you were here then."

No way to read the eyes behind the lenses, even if they were capable of betraying emotions.

"You think anybody in a courtroom'd take my version of what happened seriously?"

"I don't know, but I would."

After ten seconds, he stuck up his hand. "Vince Krushevski."

I shook with him. "John Cuddy."

"What do you want to know?"

"Your version, as you heard it."

"Okay. I'm right here, okay. Some kind of optometry shop's gone under, right?"

"Or moved, maybe."

"No matter, helps with the subliminal guilt, you know? If I was crippled, I'd be outside a sporting goods store, especially if I could find one that's closed. No legs, even the tennis racquets and baseball bats have run away from me."

"No sight, a deserted eyeglass place."

"Now you got it. Anyway, I'm sitting here, and it's a slow morning. Nobody's talking back to me, so I ease off the patter for a while, and just relax. A car pulls up, normal-like, and the door opens and closes. Woman's voice, black but educated – I'm figuring you want this kind of detail, right?"

"That's right."

"Good. Then I hear some brakes on lock-up, and I wait for the thump."

"Of the car hitting something."

"Right. Only I just hear another couple doors open and close on the new car, the one with the brakes. A guy comes running toward her, street shoes but he sounded … I don't know, athletic, crisp-like, a man moving fast and sure. The black woman yells, 'What are you doing?', then she screams 'Jammy, no. Don't.' Then there's a shot, and –"

"Wait a minute. No shot before she screams about Jammy?"

"Uh-unh. Her first, then the shot. Well, actually the first shot, which I hear whump into somebody, and somebody goes down. Then I hear the athletic guy moving quick, then firing three times, more running, and – understand, the black woman's screaming her head off through all this and I've got people diving for cover all around me."

"I understand."

"Okay, then the athletic guy says 'Monk, you hit, man?' and goes –"

"Hold it. The shooter said, 'Monk'?"

"Yeah."

"Any accent?"

"What do you mean?"

"Caribbean, maybe?"

Krushevski laughed. "No. No accent. Sounded just like you or me."

"Meaning?"

"Meaning white male, Boston or at least around here somewhere."

"Go on."

"Well, I hear the doors on the brakes car again, and the black woman sort of stumbles over to the car she got out of, screaming 'Jammy, Jammy, no, no. Why'd you do it, Jammy,' over and over."

"'Why'd you do it, Jammy.' "

"Yeah, but it was more … chant-like almost, like she was saying a prayer for him."

Krushevski let that sit between us.

I said, "Anything else?"

"Just other voices, somebody yelling to call the cops, somebody else calling for a doctor, this one saying I got a cellular phone, and like that."

"The cops talk to you?"

"Yeah, one guy did."

"What did he say?"

"Just, 'Move along now. There's nothing for you to see.' "

As Vince Krushevski gave me another gap-toothed grin, I slipped a twenty into one of the flapped pockets, not trusting the mug to passersby who might be tempted to make the wrong kind of change from it.

* * * *

I thought about what I'd seen and been told. It was thin, but it was the only explanation that covered all the facts. For insurance, I made a phone call. The party I spoke to was pretty impatient but also pretty sure whose nickname it was.

Then I got into my car and drove it the three blocks over to Exeter Street, stationing myself so I could watch the garage exit. If I was wrong, he'd stay there with her all night. If I was right, he wouldn't.

I was right.

About four A.M., a blue Ford came up the ramp, the lamp-post throwing just enough light for me to recognize him. He drove north, Route 1 to 128 to Rockport, forty miles north of the city on Cape Ann. I followed him to a small house five or six blocks up from the water, where he parked and went inside.

Leaving my car on the street, I moved up close to the house, then found an open window. I could hear voices, and I looked in the window long enough to confirm what the voices implied.

Then I made my way back to my car and aimed it south.

❊ ❊ ❊ ❊

The obese man had just come on duty behind the curving console. He told me she wasn't in because he'd just seen her go out. He remembered me, though, and told me that since I looked like a cop, he was pretty sure he knew where she was going, given what she was carrying and all.

❊ ❊ ❊ ❊

It wasn't quite as nice as Beth's hillside across town. The grass was mowed, but this cemetery didn't seem able to keep up with the broken beer bottles and used condoms and other trash that people threw in there. The pink Cadillac stood out like metallic cotton candy against the long, gray ranks of the headstones.

I found her standing over the recent grave, no piece of marble or granite yet marking the place. The air was cool yet at six A.M., and quiet except for a songbird in a nearby tree, so she should have been able to hear me coming, but somehow I didn't think she did.

When her eyes looked up, though, Luna McTeague didn't appear surprised, as though we met like this all the time and she'd just begun wondering what could be keeping me. She'd been pulling the roses from the bouquet one at a time, arranging them that way over the fresh earth. She had three left in her hands, and it took me a minute to realize she was wearing the same clothes as when I'd seen her the day before. It didn't look like she slept in them, just that she hadn't had them off her.

McTeague said, "You know, don't you?"

"Most of it."

She looked back down at the grave. "He was still like a little kid, stars in his eyes about getting to drive for me."

"Which was one of the reasons you picked him, right? You and Dennis."

A nod, barely. "We had it planned just right, you know? Him on vacation, me on vacation. The gig coming up at the Orpheum. Dennis and

Rick just drive up to my Caddy on the street, and Rick makes like to kidnap me, the rag with the chloroform to drop on the street, make everybody realize it's the real thing. Dennis, he knows Jammy'll try to do something, but he's just going to punch Jammy out, make that part look real, too."

"And they take you to the house somebody rented blind up in Rockport, and you manage to escape before the concert and bravely volunteer to go on, the media people giving it the full-court press, Dennis and Rick and maybe a platoon of other guys there to provide security against a second threat when there never was anything but smoke and mirrors about the first one."

"Dennis wasn't even carrying a gun, no need to, and he didn't know Rick had one. I didn't know, either, all the good that does now."

"But after the kidnapping went sour, you had to cancel the Orpheum concert, because Dennis is sitting in the house in Rockport, nursing a wound that wasn't life-threatening but would have been pretty obvious to everybody if he'd tried to show up at the concert with you."

"That's right."

I thought back to the photo of her with Dennis Giordano, looking like an ape, and my phone call to Manny Kantrowitz about the nickname. "Was Rick the only one who called his brother 'Monk'?"

Same kind of nod, acknowledgment more than agreement. "Yeah. Dennis didn't even like him using it around me. You know, black people and monkeys and all."

"We probably ought to be going."

Luna McTeague didn't ask where, just gestured with the roses. "I want to put these last ones on, too."

She bent down on one knee to do it, the queen laying a last wreath at the tomb of her known and faithful soldier.

IN THIS HOUSE OF STONE

ONE

Our Lady of Perpetual Light fit its setting like a lambskin glove. The church rose three stories in gray, pink and blue fieldstone, the white steeple spiring above it visible for a thousand yards as I'd driven through the small business district of Meade, about fifteen miles southwest of Boston. From the driveway, I could see the office annex, two floors of the same stone and connected to the church, nestled against the autumn-fired oaks and maples. The trees stood at the edges of a macadam parking area that surrounded the buildings like a moat.

Over the telephone, Monsignor Joseph McNulty had told me on which side of the annex to park. Very specific directions they were, too, as though he felt it important for my car to be in just the right place. Leaving the Prelude in a diagonal, white-lined space, I could hear the dirge of organ music coming from the church to my left as I walked up to the heavy, wooden entrance of the annex. Pushing a button mounted on the jamb produced a tinkling noise inside, like the sound of canticle bells I'd shaken as an altar boy.

When the door opened, a stubby man with bushy gray eyebrows looked out at me. He wore a priest's reversed white collar, black shirt and black pants. The shirt was short-sleeved despite the October air, the man's arms pale and veined. His face was veined, too, but many of the capillaries had burst, as though my host counted among his faithful the likes of Jim Beam and Jack Daniels.

"Monsignor McNulty?"

"Ah, yes. And you'd be John Cuddy, then. Our private investigator."

He didn't phrase any of it as a question, his voice that combination of brogue and wheeze you hear in men his age, which I'd have put as near sixty.

I said, "Not yet, Monsignor."

"Beg your pardon?"

"I'm not your private investigator until you tell me what you want done,

56

and I agree to try and do it."

McNulty didn't seem fazed. "Well, come in, come in."

I followed him down a corridor that appeared to run the width of the annex, a door similar to the one I'd entered at the other end. A smaller hallway branched left toward the church itself.

McNulty turned into an office on the right, the air smelling of old pipes and old sweat. It reminded me again of my days as an altar boy, the priests not always that careful about laundering their robes and other vestments. The monsignor had a large wooden desk and one wall of exposed stone. His windows were arched rectangles, half the panes around the lead made of stained glass. One window gave a nice view of the parking area and my car in it. The room was hot, and I could understand why my host wore short sleeves.

McNulty noticed me looking at the baseboard heaters. "One of the parishioners installed them, *gratis*. Do a wonderful job of taking the chill off the stone, sometimes too wonderful. Sit, please."

I took a visitor's chair while McNulty turned himself sideways and went behind his desk. He used both hands on the arms of the desk chair to lower himself into it. "So. This being the first time my Church has needed the services of a private investigator, I suppose I don't know where to start. Money?"

"Why don't we wait on my fee until after you tell me why you called me."

McNulty nodded judiciously. "You honestly don't know what happened here at the Church last week."

"I've been out of town for a while."

A sigh. "Last Tuesday, it was. In the afternoon sometime. It's still not …" The words seemed to come hard for him, and he turned to look out his window. "My other priest, Francis Riordan, was struck down and killed in his office across that corridor."

During my trip, I'd heard a throwaway line on a radio news program about a priest being killed near Boston, but no details. "Monsignor, I'm sorry."

Another nod. "Frank – he always preferred nicknames, Francis did, especially his own."

My middle name being "Francis," I could understand that. "Go on."

"It happened sometime between lunch and dinner, because when he didn't come to table that evening, I went to his office. He was lying there, his head in a pool of his own … blood."

"The police have any suspects?"

"The police?" A grunted laugh. "I'm afraid not. They've already stereotyped this. 'Crackhead who panicked.' "

"In Meade?"

McNulty shifted against his chair, making the leather squeak. "Frank Riordan was a fine man, Mr. Cuddy. And I mean a man, not one of those Nancy-boys the seminaries seem to be hatching these days."

I'd never heard the expression, but McNulty flicked his wrist as he said it. I was beginning not to like him very much.

"No, Frank played football in college. Came to his vocation later than some, but for that all the more sure of it."

"Monsignor, what does this have to do with a drug addict attacking him here in Meade?"

McNulty fixed me with a baleful look. "Frank volunteered at St. Damian's House. Do you know it?"

A place for disadvantaged kids in a tough part of Boston. "I know of it."

"Yes, well. Frank thought the lads could do with a look at how the other half lives. So he persuaded Joyce Steinberg – the owner of the health club he belonged to out here – to sponsor a basketball tournament for them. Took a bunch of the boys on a tour of our church buildings as well. The police believe one or more of them came back to rob him."

"Anything taken?"

"His little computer, one of those 'notebook' things, I think he called it. And his chalice."

The goblet Father Riordan would have used to celebrate Mass. "Monsignor, were you here that afternoon?"

"Of Frank's … death, you mean?"

"Yes."

"I was. Sitting right at this desk, going over some budgetary matters."

"Did you hear anything?"

"No, but these walls are thick." Swiveling in his chair and pitching forward, McNulty slapped a palm against the exposed fieldstone. "And following my directions, did you notice anything about the parking outside?"

I thought I saw what he meant. "That the lot winds around the church and annex."

"Exactly. I was sitting here, but someone who knew Frank, and who knew the layout of the buildings here, could have come down the driveway, gone around the other side, and parked near Frank's entrance on the backside of the annex. I wouldn't have seen or heard them come in or go out." Another glance to his window, or to the stained glass within it. "I know, because I didn't that afternoon."

"Have the police questioned the boys from St. Damian's?"

"Oh, they tell me so. The chief here assures me that they've gone through the lot of them, one and all. Nothing."

"Any other possibilities?"

"What?"

Things are usually what they appear to be, but I still asked the next question. "Aside from the burglary-gone-bad, could anyone else have had a reason to want Father Riordan dead?"

McNulty seemed shocked. "What are you saying? You never met the man. He was a saint, genuinely. A Renaissance man with a heart, Mr. Cuddy."

"Then I don't quite see what you want me to do."

"Yes, well." McNulty calmed down. "The truth is, I don't know what you should do. It's clear to me that the police have given up on Frank. They haven't said that in so many words, now, but they've implied as much."

"Monsignor, the police have more resources than I do. If they've canvassed the boys, and you can't give them any other leads, there's not likely going to be some breakthrough because of me."

McNulty frowned, a shrewd look on his booze-weathered face. "Is it the case you've no taste for, or the man trying to give it to you?"

Perceptive. "I don't like taking money with no possibility of result."

"Not what I'd call an answer, but I caught the look on your face when I said 'Nancy-boy,' so enough for now." The man weighed something. "How about if you look into it for a few days? Just give me your opinion as to whether or not it makes sense to pursue."

"I think I already have, Monsignor."

McNulty showed me a sad smile. "My Church has stood on this site for a hundred years, Mr. Cuddy." Instead of slapping the exposed wall, he caressed it. "A round century of tragedy has touched this house of stone, but never so closely, or so deeply. I loved that boy like a father loves a son, and now somebody has taken him from me."

McNulty's eyes welled up, and he sniffed so hard it was nearly a snorting sound. "I owe it to Frank to have someone who's skeptical – and who doesn't much care for me – look into it. Someone whose opinion I can trust. And I feel I can trust you, Mr. Cuddy."

Not liking the man was one thing, not feeling for him another. "I'd have to let the police know I was working for you."

"Why? They told me I could even dispose of his effects, though God knows I haven't had the courage to do that as yet."

"It's still an open homicide, Monsignor. I don't have to get their permission. I just have to let them know somebody's going to be out there, asking questions. They might also be able to help me."

"You ever met the chief here, Smollett?"

"Once. I was hoping he might have retired by now."

Very nearly a real smile from Monsignor Joseph McNulty. "Perhaps you'll be able to push him on his way."

TWO

The only other time I'd been to the Meade police station, the chief's door had been newly painted. It now showed signs of wear, including scuff marks centered at the bottom where somebody seemed to have a habit of kicking it open. The uniform escorting me knocked.

"Yeah," said a gravelly voice on the other side of the door.

I had to push hard to open it, the height of the carpeting in the office creating the problem. New carpeting. Solve one problem, create another.

The chief, sitting behind his desk, made no effort to get up. I didn't expect he would. The old and worn nameplate on his blotter said SMOLLETT, no rank or first name.

"Cuddy. What do you want?"

"Can I sit?"

A wave of the hand to answer me and dismiss the uniform. Smollett's nameplate had stood the test of time better than its owner. The knuckles on the hand were knobby from arthritis, the fingers starting to bend the wrong way.

I said, "I'm here about the Riordan killing."

"We don't have anything new on it."

"How about a look at the folder?"

"Not a chance."

"Why not?"

"I'm supposed to help you and encourage every citizen's not satisfied with our work to go out and hire private?"

Which would just create more work for him. "How about what everybody else knows anyway?"

A explosion of breath. "Look, Cuddy. Simple case. Some crackheads come calling, the good Father knows them, so he lets them in and gets whacked in the temple for his trouble. We didn't find a weapon on the premises, so they came in knowing they were going to hit him. Christ, this Riordan did good deeds among them over at St. Damian's. What the hell did he expect they'd do?"

"Monsignor McNulty tells me whoever did him got his chalice and a notebook computer. Anything else?"

"Not that we're told. The punk fences the chalice though, and he's ours. Real identifiable, according to McNulty, gold with a heavy base."

"They killed him, you'd think they'd dump the chalice and move the computer."

"Maybe they will."

"In which case, why bother to take the chalice at all?"

Smollett just stared at me.

"And," I said, "if they're going to mug him, why not around St. D's instead of in Meade where they'd need transportation and kind of stand out?"

"Stand out? You kidding? Our own kids dress like they watch COLORS on the V.C.R. every night."

"You talk with the people at St. Damian's?"

"One of my detectives did, with a Boston cop as shotgun guard. Nobody knows anything, everybody alibis everybody else. All in bed after saying their prayers."

"Riordan's effects tell you anything?"

"What, you think the crackheads sent him a note in advance or something? 'Hey, Padre-man, try to be in around three so Tyrone and me can axe you a question.' "

My day to let things pass. "Any objection to my going through Father Riordan's things, then?"

"Be my guest. Have them bronzed, all I care."

Another wave of the crabbed hand told me the interview was over.

❄ ❄ ❄ ❄

Winding back through the brick-and-clapboard center of Meade, I saw what Smollett meant about dress code. Baggy athletic pants and oversized sweatshirts, baseball caps worn backward. Only there was a desperately casual note in the way the town's teens wore the clothes and the colors. As though they were trying to be something they weren't but feared.

At the church annex, Monsignor McNulty took me to Father Riordan's office. Same architecture, and for my money, better view, since it looked onto the oaks and maples in the back. It also was more utilitarian and modern, with a fax machine and computer printer to either side of a gap on top of the metal credenza behind the desk.

I walked toward the credenza and pointed at the gap, what looked like fingerprint powder still dusted onto it. "This where Father Riordan kept his computer?"

"When he wasn't carrying it around in that thing."

There was a black vinyl case with a shoulder strap slumped into the corner. Crossing to it, I bent down. A couple of small diskettes, pencils, pen, paper clips. The short version of a manual for the machine itself. No paper copies of anything.

Straightening up, I said, "Where would Father Riordan keep his chalice?"

"Generally in the sacristy, but sometimes here, when he'd clean it properly."

I came back to the desk. "He have an appointment book?"

"Not that I know of. Frank had no head for figures, but a wonderful mind for events and responsibilities. A real people person."

Usually from someone McNulty's age, that label would be sarcastic. No hint of it, though.

I pointed to a photo on the desktop. It showed the monsignor standing next to a husky man of thirty or so, winning smile under a craggily handsome brow and piercing eyes. Both wore Roman collars, the handsome man's arm around McNulty's shoulders. "Is that Father Riordan with you?"

"Yes."

"Good likeness?"

"Taken less than a year past."

There was a large, polished seashell next to the photo. In it were scattered coins, more paper clips, a matchbook, some tooth-chewed pencils, and a set of keys on a tag.

I picked up the keys. "These belong to him?"

"Yes."

On the back of the key tag were handwritten numbers. 219-9256. "This number mean anything to you?"

McNulty squinted at it, angling his face for the light. "What, telephone, is it?"

"Probably."

"No. Not one of our exchanges here in Meade, anyway."

"Your area code's 508, right?"

"Right."

"Can I use this phone?"

"Certainly."

I punched in 219-9256. The nice lady with the atonal voice told me that my call could not be completed as dialed. I added "1" as a prefix, and tried again. Same message. Tried area code 617 for Boston, 401 for Rhode Island, and 603 for New Hampshire. Same each time.

Hanging up, I hefted the keys. "Can I take these with me?"

"I don't see why not."

The matchbook caught my eye. It showed York's Tavern, with an address in Boston. Not far from St. Damian's House, as a matter of fact. "You recognize this place?"

Another squint. "No, but Frank wasn't above a beverage now and then." A weak smile.

I didn't get any smell of tobacco in the office. "You said Father Riordan belonged to a health club?"

"That's right. Meade Health and Fitness, near Route 128."

"He wasn't a smoker, then."

"Never. Wouldn't even let me smoke my pipe in here. Why?"

"Probably nothing." I pocketed the matchbook and the keys. "Can I take that photo, too?"

A frown. "Of Frank and me?"

"Yes."

"But why?"

"I'd like to be able to show it to anybody I speak to."

McNulty chewed on that. "Could you have it copied and returned to me?" A sheepish look. "I'm not sure I have another print."

"Sure."

As I slipped off the cardboard backing, the muted sound of organ music began throbbing through the wall. I realized I hadn't heard it on this visit to Our Lady. "Who's playing?"

"Theresa. Lovely, isn't it?"

"Her last name?"

"T-U-G-L-I-O. I spell it because people want to pronounce the letters 'Tug-*lee*-oh' but she says it '*Tool*-ee-oh.' "

"Did Ms. Tuglio know Father Riordan?"

"Yes." A welling in the eyes again. "I'm afraid his death has left no one untouched."

✵ ✵ ✵ ✵

I told Monsignor McNulty that I wanted to speak to Theresa Tuglio without him. The October sun was bright coming through the high windows, creating shafts of light and shadow, and even though I'd taken the short, inside corridor into the church itself, my eyes still took a moment to adjust. The calliope tubes of the organ soared up the altar's rear wall. From the altar rail, I couldn't see the person playing.

Moving slowly around the railing, I cleared a stout stone pillar. A woman of thirty or so sat on the organ bench, but just barely. Her hands slashed through the air at the keyboard while her dangling feet pumped pedals like a contestant in the Tour de France. Slightly built, she wore her hair drawn back and up into a bun; the cardigan sweater, skirt and shoes were sensible rather than stylish.

At a break in the chords, I said, "Ms. Tuglio?"

The woman jumped, hands off the keys and clasped in her lap, turning sideways in fright to face me.

"I'm sorry if I startled you."

"Who are you?"

"John Cuddy. I didn't see you when I came in."

"You're not supposed to." A shy smile. "The organ itself is tucked away over here so the priest can cue me but the parishioners won't notice me."

Tuglio said the last part as though she were relieved by that. The index finger and thumb of her right hand traced a brass button on the cardigan, a script "T" on it and the other buttons as well. "Can I help you with something, Mr. Cuddy?"

"Monsignor McNulty has asked me to look into Father Riordan's death."

What animation had remained in Tuglio's face from the organ-playing drained from it, and she closed her eyes. "It hurts just to think about Father that way."

"Were you here the afternoon it happened?"

The eyes opened. "Yes. Playing. Practicing, I tell the Monsignor. But really just enjoying. That's part of the tragedy. If I hadn't been making so much noise, perhaps someone would have heard ..." She shook her head. "But I love playing." A hand swept up toward the rear of the altar. "My dad was a metal-worker, like his father before him. My grandfather helped cast those pipes, and my dad maintained them."

"Can you tell me anything at all about Father Riordan?"

A slow intake of breath. "A fine man. Sympathetic, empathetic. Everyone's dream of a young priest."

I got something else from Tuglio's tone of voice. "Any recent changes. Depression, nervousness?"

"No. If anything, just the opposite. What was the word in ... Oh yes, 'ebullient.' Father was generally in good spirits, but that Tuesday, and even the day before, he'd been excited, as though he'd just discovered the secret to life." A pause. "I wish he'd shared it with me."

Secret or life, I thought. Then, from the look she gave me, maybe both.

Reaching into my pocket, I took out Riordan's keys. "Ms. Tuglio, do you recognize these?"

Her head canted a little. "A set of keys? No."

"Monsignor McNulty said they were Father Riordan's."

"Then they must be."

I turned over the tab. "Does this number mean anything to you?"

Tuglio read it, moving her lips. "No."

I tried the matchbook. "Did Father Riordan ever mention this place to you?"

"York's? No, but my brother has."

"Your brother?"

"Anthony. He goes there sometimes, to get a better feel for what his kids have been through."

"His kids?"

"The boys at St. Damian's. He's the executive director there."

THREE

It was a toss-up whether to start at York's Tavern or St. Damian's House. The tavern came up first, on a street with a closed mill and a limping steel fabrication plant.

There was no parking lot for York's, the cars just left half on the street, half on the sidewalk. Outside, the windows were diamond-shaped, too small to crawl through and covered by chicken-wire mesh in a hopeful attempt to block rocks. A short-circuiting neon beer sign hung inside the glass of one, the first and last letters of the brewer's name cut off by the narrowness of the window itself.

The front door had three of the diamond windows. I looked inside before opening it. Nearly full, and mine would be the only jacket and tie. I went in anyway.

The conversation died a bit as I moved through the crowd to the bar, then picked up again when I signaled the keep for a beer. About forty, squat, and balding, he brought a draft of the brand in the window. Reaching under the counter with his free hand, he dealt a coaster to land like a playing card just in front of my elbows, then raised two fingers in a victory sign as he set the mug on the coaster. I laid a ten on the bar, and he went to the register with it, coming back with a five and three ones. As he arranged the change near my glass, I showed him the photo from Father Riordan's desk.

The keep slung a towel over his right shoulder. "You a cop?"

"Private. Just want to know if you've seen either of these men in here."

"The big one, yeah. Wouldn't have thought he was a priest, though."

"Why not?"

"He come through the door in a ski sweater, the other with him wearing this nice navy blazer. I was afraid they might draw a little action."

"For what?"

"For dressing that way. The boys don't like yuppies slumming around their watering hole."

"Like me in this suit."

"Yeah, and you could feel the boys reacting, couldn't you?"

"But not starting anything."

"You look like a cop. And besides, it's early yet."

"What time was it when these two were in here?"

"Early Monday night, last week. I remember account of they kept a table for the football game, then left in the fourth quarter. The other guy got kind of stiff, but the big guy watching the tube, I had the feeling he played somewhere."

"He did. Can you describe the other guy?"

"More like a priest than your friend there, I didn't know better."

"Know better?"

"The other guy's named Tuglio. Tall and skinny, comes in here from time to time. Kind of 'researching' us, I always thought. But he don't usually get slammed, and he does a good job for the kids over to St. D's, so I try and watch out for him."

"With the clientele."

"Yeah. Only one look at your big guy there, and I didn't see anybody messing with them."

"Because of the big guy's size."

"And the attitude, you know? Your priest there, he just carried himself right. A guy with a hard laugh, kind of on edge."

"On edge?"

"Yeah, like he was excited about something, ready to play." The keep looked at me. "Kind of guy could handle himself, he had to."

I told the keep I appreciated his time and left the change on the bar.

✻ ✻ ✻ ✻

"Thank you, June."

The woman smiled and closed the door behind me as the man at the desk sneezed into a hankerchief. "Sorry, this cold. Believe me, you don't want to shake hands, but Anthony Tuglio."

"John Cuddy, Mr. Tuglio."

"What can I do for you?"

"I'm looking into the death of Father Frank Riordan."

Tuglio's features drained of color the way his sister's had of animation. Tall and skinny like the bartender had said, with black, fine hair combed across. His shirt looked pressed and his tie was snugged up to the collar button despite his cold. A tweed sports jacket hung from a hook over files stacked on a low cabinet.

Tuglio said, "Look, I don't want to be rude." Another pass with the hankerchief. "But your people have already gone through this place like Sherman's army, assuming that one of my –"

"Not to interrupt, but I'm a private investigator, not a cop. Monsignor McNulty's asked me to look into this for him."

Tuglio seemed to process that. "Why?"

"He's concerned that the police may have moved Father Riordan's case to the back burner."

A shake of the head, his sister's mannerisms evident in him. "A priest is killed, and even that goes to the 'back burner.' " Tuglio's eyes seemed to wander. "My God."

"Mr. Tuglio?"

He came back to me. "Yes?"

"What can you tell me about Father Riordan?"

"Frank? Salt of the earth, a prince of the Church. We're not part of the Archdiocese here at the House, but we get some funding and a lot of honorable mentions. Well, Frank Riordan put his time where his mouth was. Organized a basketball tournament for the boys, always interested in how they were doing in school. And we weren't even in his parish."

"I understand you saw him the night before he died?"

His sister's shy smile. "Yes. We played telephone tag during the day, and when we finally connected, he said he wanted to have a drink, talk about something."

"What was it?"

"I never really found out. This cold must have been sneaking up on me, because when he suggested York's – it's a tavern just down the street? – I said sure. Well, it's kind of a rough place, but Frank didn't seem to mind. We sat and watched the Monday night game and must have talked."

"Must have?"

"Well, like I said, this cold was creeping up on me, I guess, because the beer really hit me. I remember Frank telling me it was something about the prior weekend, what I couldn't tell you."

"When did you leave York's?"

"I'm not sure. I was so stiff, Frank had to drive me home."

"You live here at St. Damian's?"

"No. Over in West Roxbury. I usually leave my car at the apartment and take a bus to work."

"So Father Riordan drove you home in his car."

"Correct."

"Could he have gone somewhere else after that?"

Tuglio thought about it. "I'd say not. I remember the game going to the fourth quarter at York's, so it would have been pretty late."

I took out the keys. "This number mean anything to you?"

Tuglio read it aloud. "No. No exchange I've ever heard of."

"But a phone number."

"What?"

"You figure it's a phone number."

"Written that way? What else could it be?"

Good point. "When was this basketball tournament?"

"That Saturday."

"Two days before you had drinks with him at York's."

"Yes. The health club woman out there – a Ms. Steinberg? – was very helpful, but said it had to be before the real season started, when her members were still interested more in outdoor tennis and televised football."

"Can I speak to some of the boys who were in the tournament?"

Tuglio gave me a steady look. "Mr. Cuddy, Frank's death has already upset them badly, and the police only made matters that much worse."

"It might help me."

He looked down. "All right, but please, be gentle with them."

"Do my best."

Anthony Tuglio nodded before sneezing again into the hankerchief.

FOUR

"Yo, man, how's it going?"

DeVonne was a solid black kid, maybe thirteen, with the long, graceful arm muscles of an all-around athlete hanging loosely from the sleeves of a rapper's tee-shirt. DeVonne also wore an Oakland Raiders hat, reversed but slightly cockeyed, black vinyl warm-up pants, and scuffed Air Jordans. We sat across from each other in a small room at St. Damian's that was an even smaller cut above a police station interrogation cell.

"DeVonne, my name's John Cuddy, and I'd like to ask you some questions about the basketball tournament you were in at the Meade Health and Fitness club."

"Not *in*, man. We *won* the mother'." A sly look. "You here about the holy man, right?"

"Right."

"Take it to the bank, we didn't have nothing to do with that dude getting chilled."

"Why would I think you did?"

"Aw, come on, man. Who do you think you talking at? Russian mothers' set off a nuke, we'd be the ones get the blame."

"Tell me about the tournament, DeVonne."

He crossed his arms, stretching out in the chair like it was a lounger. "Mr. T loads us on the bus –"

"Mr. Tuglio?"

"Yeah, man. That's what we call the dude, like after Mr. T on the *A-Team*, account of the two mens couldn't be no more different, you know what I'm saying?"

"Go on."

"So, Mr. T, he loads us on the bus, and we ride on out there to the country, and he thinks we're all like gonna be so impressed, we grow up and be good suburban executives. But the club was okay, this foxy chick owner give us sandwiches and stuff. Then we play the tournament."

"Who else was there?"

"The other kids from here, some old priest, and this kind of stale chick, couldn't take her eyes off the holy man got killed."

"The other woman, you know who she was?"

"The stale chick? Heard your holy man call her 'Terry.' "

Theresa Tuglio. "You hear anything else, DeVonne?"

"Holy man, he knew something about the game, account of he was coaching the other team we beat, and he had them playing good against us. Mr. T, he try to coach us, and we try not to hear him so he don't mess up our rhythm, you know what I'm saying?"

"You like Father Riordan?"

A shrug. "He was okay. Acted a little funny sometimes."

"Funny how?"

Another shrug. "I don't know. Always grabbing at you, arm around the shoulder, trying to make you feel like he was your best friend. And I got to admit, for a white honky holy man, he did some good things."

It was the first time DeVonne smiled in the time I'd been talking to him.

✻ ✻ ✻ ✻

I wasn't sure if Estevan had ever smiled. He was a slight, bony Latino kid, fifteen according to Anthony Tuglio, but I thought a ticket-taker at a movie theater might let him in for the under-twelve price. Black tie shoes, white socks, frayed dress shirt with the collar button fastened. Sitting like a West Point plebe at dinner, Estevan kept rubbing his thin wrists under the shirt cuffs.

"I don't mean to make you nervous, Estevan."

"I'm not."

"Can you tell me about the basketball tournament?"

"We went out there. Everybody had to go."

"What do you mean?"

"Mr. Tuglio said Father had gone to a lot of troubles to get this chance for us, so everybody had to go and everybody had to play."

"Father Riordan, you mean?"

Looking down at his shoes, Estevan nodded.

"Do you enjoy basketball?"

He shook his head.

"Why not?"

"Don't like sports. Like books."

"What kind of books?"

Estevan looked up. "Kind Father used to bring to me. All kinds."

Something felt off with the boy. "Are you sorry about him being killed?"

Estevan looked down again, nodding.

"Can you tell me anything that might help find who killed him?"

"No." He shivered and looked back up. "Can I go now?"

"Estevan –"

He got up and left, without turning back to me.

* * * *

Kurt never stopped smiling. If you include grinning and leering.

"So, you want to know about the croaked priest, huh?"

I stared at the grinning blond kid, hair buzzed all around except for a short, braided pigtail at the back. Dressed in a riverboat shirt and jeans, he was maybe Estevan's age, but as aggressive as the other boy was passive. "What can you tell me, Kurt?"

"Hey, not much. I don't even know if Kurt's my real name. Around here, Mr. T takes one look at you, and puts you in the 'proper place.' " Kurt said the last word with a lisping sound.

"You don't like Mr. Tuglio?"

"I don't like faggots. Old ones, young ones," Kurt closed the top button of his riverboat shirt the way Estevan had worn his, then opened it again.

As I wondered how Kurt would get along with Monsignor McNulty, he leered. "Too bad this shirt doesn't have a collar that turns, too."

I stopped. "What do you mean?"

"Hey, forget it, all right?" Grinning again, Kurt began circling the tip of his index finger into his thumb pad. "It's not like you're paying me for all this, huh?"

Lovely boy. "Did Father Riordan ever approach you sexually?"

"Hey, like I said, forget it. I ain't telling you nothing."

"How about the basketball tournament, then?"

"What about it? Big surprise: the niggers won."

"DeVonne's team."

"Right. We could have beaten them, too, we didn't have Es-*te*-van dragging us down."

"How?"

"Your dead priest made everybody play, and Es-*te*-van's worse than having nobody. Four on five, we'd have had a better chance."

"You notice anything else about the tournament?"

"Notice?" Another leer. "Just the way this wannabe babe watched your croaked priest."

"Who was that?"

"He called her 'Terry,' I think. Yeah, Terry. I swear, you'd think she creamed every time he looked her way, much less talked to her. Ugly thing, too, and old. Probably lucky even a priest gave her anything."

"Anything?"

Kurt made the leer harder. "You ever heard of the horizontal Mambo? I think that's what she wanted to dance with him."

FIVE

I left the Prelude in the parking area of the Meade Health and Fitness club and went in the main entrance. Nautilus and aerobics rooms visible in front of me, arrows and signs for locker rooms on the walls.

A striking woman in a long-sleeved, designer jersey and spandex tights turned toward me from behind a low counter to my right. She was five-six or so and trying hard to look only thirty, with a mane of black, curly hair and jangly earrings.

Out came a perky smile. "Hi, help you with a membership?"

"No, thanks. Ms. Steinberg?"

"Yes?"

"My name's John Cuddy, and I'd just like to talk with you about something."

The smile drooped. "Look, we're pretty much full up with personal trainers right now."

"I'm flattered, but it's about Father Francis Riordan."

The whole face drooped, showing her years. "What a way to spoil the day. Police?"

"Private investigator. Monsignor McNulty asked me to look into things for him."

"How about some identification?"

I showed it to her.

"All right, come on in the office." Steinberg motioned a guy in an identical jersey over to the counter, then inclined her head toward a doorway behind it.

Inside the office, Steinberg flopped down on a futuristic desk chair while I took one of the more staid visitor's ones. "Okay," she said, "what do you want to know?"

"Tell me about Frank Riordan."

"Tell you about him. Adonis with a personality, that help? He was Jewish, I'd have tied him to a bed until ..." She bit off the next phrase. "Sorry, that was just the way ..." A wave of the hand, enough like Chief Smollett's that I noticed it.

"How did the basketball tournament come about?"

"Talked me into it. Personality, charm, Frank had it all. I should have had my head shrunk for listening to him, but it was good for the heart. Seeing the kids, I mean, watching them feel important. And what did it cost me? Some food, some drinks, an afternoon of electricity for the lights and the scoreboard. Thanks to God no one got hurt, or the insurance company would have fried my ..." Another bite.

"Ms. Steinberg –"

"Joyce."

"Joyce, did anything happen during the tournament?"

"Happen? Happen. No, I just told you, we got through it without –"

"I don't mean injuries. I mean, did Father Riordan seem different to you, anything like that?"

Steinberg put an elbow on the arm of her chair, cupping her chin in her hand. "Well, he seemed pretty excited about the tournament."

"Excited."

"Yes, that everything went so well, everybody played, everybody had a good time. More so on Tuesday, if that's possible."

"Tuesday?"

"The day he got killed. He was here in the morning, to work out. Said, 'Hi,' seemed on top of the world." Steinberg made a face. "That boss of his, though, the Monsignor? He was kind of a wet blanket during the tournament, looked more worried than I was about the kids breaking something or getting hurt."

"Was there anybody else involved?"

"Involved? Involved." Steinberg nodded. "Yes, now that you mention it. There was this woman, kind of parched-looking, sort of standing off to the side. I went up to her, see if she wanted something, and Frank called her over. 'Terry' was the name he used."

"And?"

"And she stayed by him most of the rest of the time. She had it bad for the guy."

"Bad."

"Bad, bad, bad. But I don't think Frank really noticed." Steinberg smiled at me, a little coy. "Lots of the really good ones don't, you know."

I took out the set of keys. "You recognize these?"

"What, keys? Keys are keys, right?"

"These belonged to Father Riordan."

"So, it's some surprise to you that Frank had keys?"

"How about this number on the tag?"

Steinberg looked at it. "Sure."

"Sure?"

"Sure, I know what it stands for. Frank had no head for numbers."

"And so?"

"And so, all the changes of clothes the man had to go through, I told him he could have one of his own. I tell you, though, the other –"

"One of his own what?"

"I'm telling you, all right? We got over nine hundred members here, I can't have one for each, so there's three hundred in the men's and another hundred in the women's – they don't like to change as much in front of each other – but if word got out that Frank –"

"– had his own locker."

Steinberg looked at me like I was a very slow learner. "Of course, his own locker. Number 219."

"And the other four numbers?"

"His combination. Right-nine, left-twenty-five, right-six. The man was just terrible with numbers, like I told you."

"Ms. Steinberg –"

"Joyce, remember?"

"Joyce, can I see his locker?"

"Sure." The coy smile. "Of course, I can't come with you."

✳ ✳ ✳ ✳

At number 219, I spun the padlock's dial a few times, then tried the combination. The hasp clicked ajar, so I pulled off the lock and opened the door.

Musty air of sweat and fresh tang of deodorant. Tee-shirt, gym shorts, jockstrap. And next to his running shoes, a red envelope the size of a birthday card, but somewhat heavier as I picked it up.

The envelope was addressed simply "T.T.," and inside it was a card. The cover read, "Thank you ..." and opening it, the greeting continued, "... For the Time of my Life!!!" After the signature "Yours always, Frank," was a P.S.: "The enclosed came off just 'before,' but I stuck it in my pocket and didn't remember it till I was changing at the club. Can I help you "stick it" back on?"

I hefted the enclosure in the envelope. It was a bright brass button with a scripted "T" on it.

Just like the one on Theresa Tuglio's cardigan sweater.

SIX

Getting out of the Prelude, I could hear muted organ music coming from the church, so I went to it instead of the annex. Inside the doorway, deep chords pounded and bounced around the empty, cavernous space. Given the cover of sound, Theresa Tuglio again wasn't aware of me approaching her.

I said, "Ms. Tuglio?"

She turned as she had the first time, startled, a different sweater on today, her hands clasped in her lap. "Mr. Cuddy? What is it?"

Reaching into my jacket pocket, I said, "There's something here you ought to see. From Frank Riordan's locker at the health club."

I handed her just the envelope containing the card. She noticed the initials on the outside, then opened it and took out the card. Mouthing the words, she stopped, shook her head, and glanced down at the bottom. More shaking, then a bewildered look up at me. "That's Father's signature."

"Yes. This was the 'enclosure.' "

I held up the button.

"But ..." Tuglio glanced down at her sweater, even though it didn't have any buttons on it. "But, I'm not missing any of mine."

"Any of yours?"

"Yes. My dad made those for both ... Oh. Oh, no."

The expression on her face made me realize the same thing she did.

✳ ✳ ✳ ✳

"What ... what are you doing here?"

"The House said you were home sick today, Mr. Tuglio."

We were on the third floor of a three-decker in West Roxbury. He sneezed into the handkerchief. "Yes, I'm afraid this is getting worse instead of better, so I thought I ought to stay here, try to beat it. Don't know when the last time –"

"Can I come in?"

A hesitation, then, "Certainly."

The living room was tastefully decorated. Furniture, prints on the wall, some small sculptures on end tables and mantel.

Tuglio gestured toward an easy chair as he perched on the edge of a couch cushion. "How can I help you?"

"I should have seen it, Monsignor McNulty telling me Frank Riordan loved to use nicknames. That'd make you 'Tony,' right?"

Tuglio stiffened. "What are you talking about?"

Handing him the envelope and card, I palmed the button. As he read, I held out my fist, turning it up and opening my fingers.

Seeing the button, Tuglio closed his eyes, his head going left-right-left, slow motion. "Oh, Frank."

"Can you tell me about it?"

Tuglio kept his eyes closed. "I could always sense something about Frank, a pent-up energy that verged on anger. I thought I knew what it was, and I was right. But just before his damned basketball tournament, I got the results back from a test." Tuglio now looked up at me. "An anonymous test."

I said, "Blood test."

A tiny nod. "HIV-positive. I don't know why it took me so long to tumble to it. I hadn't been feeling well for a while, but you don't want to know, not after you've had so many friends ..."

Tuglio shook it off, spoke with more juice. "Anyway, Frank was on the edge of coming out, to himself, I guess, and he made certain ... overtures during the tournament time we spent out at the health club. I agreed to meet him for a drink Monday night." Tuglio looked away from me. "I was going to ask him about ... try to get some advice, some guidance, but he was in such a buoyant mood, I couldn't bring myself to bring it up."

"So you two watched the football game at York's."

"And I got drunk, and Frank had to drive me home. I'm not ... I'm not sure what happened how after that. Here, I mean. I do know we had ... unprotected sex, a lifetime of built-up desire on his part, with me as the focus. I swear to you, I never ...I didn't think about the possibility ..." Tuglio's voice trailed away.

"But the next day, you decided to tell him."

"I had to, and I did. I drove to work that Tuesday morning because with the hang-over, I was late as it was. At lunch, I slipped out of St. Damian's and drove to Meade. From the driveway, I could hear Theresa practicing in the church itself, so I parked around back by Frank's office in the annex. I went in, he seemed so glad to see me. He was … he was packing up, putting some things in a box on his desk."

"Things like his chalice."

Tuglio flinched. "Yes. I asked Frank what he was doing, and he said, 'Getting started on a new life. Here.' He showed me the draft of a letter he'd done on his computer. A letter of resignation, saying he'd decided to 'follow his spirit elsewhere,' with me."

"I'm genuinely sorry, Mr. Tuglio."

"Thank you." A hesitation, then, "I tried to tell Frank slowly, indirectly, but it wasn't working, and his face grew … Oh, it was like implying to him that he'd made a huge mistake, that Frank was wrong about 'us.' And I couldn't stand that, so I told him flat out, that I … that he might have become … infected."

"And what did Father Riordan do then?"

Tuglio brought the hand with the handkerchief up to his eyes. "He went berserk, tried to choke me. I was bent over his desk, fading out of consciousness and scared. Oh God, I was so scared. I reached and felt something heavy and just swung it, to knock Frank off me. But I caught him hard above the ear, and the base of his chalice was so heavy, his eyes just rolled up into his head, and he just …went down …"

"So you had to take the chalice."

"And the computer. I didn't know his system, and anyway I couldn't take a chance on what else he might have 'written.' So I threw everything including the draft letter into the packing box and just got out of there."

"Where's the box now?"

"In the basement here. I have a storage area."

I leaned forward. "How do you want to handle this?"

"My life's as short or as long as it's going to be, Mr. Cuddy. But I don't think I can stand a trial. I'll just –"

"Maybe there won't be any prosecution."

Tuglio searched my eyes. "What do you mean?"

"I mean, the police have no suspects, including you. If I bring Father Riordan's box back to the church, it'll be up to Monsignor McNulty to do something about it."

Tuglio was trying to process what I'd said. And meant. "Won't the … that is, the police –"

"Will be coming or not, depending on what my client does. But I need for you to give me the box of Father Riordan's things."

Anthony Tuglio sat back in his couch, trying to decide what would make the rest of his life better. Or worse.

* * * *

When Monsignor McNulty opened the annex door, I went through it, carrying the closed box in front of me.

"Mr. Cuddy, what's going on?"

I moved into his office and set the box on the chair I'd used during my first visit there. "How do you mean?"

"Theresa was here not an hour ago. Beside herself, crying so hard I couldn't make sense of her."

"Better sit down, Monsignor."

"What's all this?" he said, indicating the box.

"Please. Sit."

He went around his desk and lowered himself into the seat.

I opened a flap of the box, and with a hankerchief of my own, lifted out the chalice.

McNulty started out of his chair. "Frank's ... ? It is, my God in Heaven, where –"

"Let me tell you." And I did.

McNulty sagged halfway through, burying his face in his hands by the end. "No. No, Frank, no, no ..."

"What do you want to do?"

"Do?" McNulty dropped his hands to the desktop. "I want the killer punished. Or I did. But this, this ... abomination. It's unbelievable."

"I believe it, but you're the client."

McNulty seemed lost. "Meaning?"

"Meaning no matter how bad it looks or will sound, I think it was self-defense. And everything will come out. Or be whispered about via the media and word-of-mouth."

"But, but I've never ... What should I do?"

"Sleep on it. Call me tomorrow."

Turning, I left the office and went through the annex door to the outside world. On my way, Monsignor Joseph McNulty had begun to cry, and I wasn't sorry when the closing door sealed that sound within his house of stone.

TURNING THE WITNESS

ONE

Riding the elevator alone to Steve Rothenberg's floor, I finished reading an article in the Boston *Globe* about the lame-duck governor of New York and the dead-duck mayor of its largest city, the latter committing political suicide by crossing party lines to endorse the former. We don't have those kinds of problems in Massachusetts. No, our electorate votes overwhelmingly in favor of term limits on the Commonwealth's pols, then on the same ballot returns Teddy Kennedy to continue his fourth decade in the Senate. You figure it out.

When the elevator stopped, I tucked the paper under my arm and walked down the corridor to Rothenberg's door. He shared space with six or seven other attorneys, the individual names on wooden cross-bars, each done by a different artisan. The overall effect would remind you of a primitive, vertical xylophone.

Inside the door was a cluttered, shabby waiting area, but I didn't need the receptionist. Rothenberg already stood by her desk.

"Steve."

"John, I'm glad you're here."

"Client getting a little nervous?" I said.

Rothenberg just ran a hand through his thinning, graying hair. The beard was a shade darker, his tie already tugged down from an unbuttoned collar, even though my watch read only nine-thirty A.M.

"Come on back," he said, shrugging out of his suit jacket.

As we entered the office, a man in his thirties rose from one of Steve's client chairs. About six feet tall and sturdy, he had curly, black hair and blue eyes that might have gained some sparkle from contact lenses. His complexion was ruddy above the collar of an oxford shirt and repp tie, the herringbone suit looking custom-tailored.

Hanging his jacket on a battered clothes tree by the desk chair, Rothenberg said, "Rick Blassingale, John Cuddy."

78

Solid handshake, but he also placed his left hand over our joined right ones. "Mr. Cuddy, I really appreciate your coming down on such short notice."

The voice was gravelly, and I placed him from the media coverage of his wife's killing. "Mr. Blassingale –"

He released my hand. "Rick, please."

Rothenberg said, "Why don't we all sit down?"

Settling back into his chair, Blassingale said, "I guess the first issue would be confidentiality here."

I remembered the newspaper describing him as an investment advisor. "You have any law school, Rick?"

A modest smile. "Graduated but never practiced. You?"

"One year, nights. Steve didn't tell you there's a confidentiality provision in the licensing statute on private investigators?"

"He did. I just wanted to be sure we were all aware of it."

I was beginning not to like Blassingale very much, and I wondered why an apparent high-roller would be represented by a hand-to-mouth criminal lawyer like Steve Rothenberg.

Blassingale let out a breath. "As you've probably heard, the police think I killed my wife. We were separated, and the Probate and Family Court was in the process of cleaning me out, but good. The police say that's plenty of motive, since Libby had no other living relatives, which means everything comes back to me."

"If you're acquitted."

A very steady "Yes" with a glance toward his attorney. "And the bail bond just about tapped me out of what I did have left."

Meaning he had to go with a low-rent lawyer and keep his fingers crossed. I looked to Steve. "Where do I fit in?"

Rothenberg twiddled a pencil on the desk top. "The evidence against Rick is completely circumstantial. Libby Blassingale was still living in their marital home, a condo on upper Marlborough Street. Nothing missing from the apartment, and she was bludgeoned to death, weapon not found."

"Suggesting premeditation," I said.

Rothenberg nodded. "No sign of forced entry, either, and time of death is a wide bracket, six P.M. to sometime around midnight on Tuesday, November 15th. The body wasn't discovered 'til the next morning when the decedent didn't meet a neighbor for coffee as scheduled."

Blassingale said, "Libby was a platinum blonde, John, very flashy. She could have picked somebody up, or just let them in."

"What makes you think that?"

"It's how we met." He let that sink in some. "I've learned my lesson, though. Strictly brunettes for me now."

A poor joke, and I couldn't remember the last time I'd heard somebody actually use the word "brunette" in a spoken sentence.

Blassingale mistook my silence and grinned, man-to-man. "You married, John?"

I thought of Beth, lying in her hillside overlooking the harbor in South Boston. "Used to be."

"Then you understand what I mean."

I looked at Rothenberg, who in turn looked out his window at the Boston Common across Boylston Street.

I said, "My wife died, Rick."

"Oh." He shifted in his chair. "Jesus, I'm sorry, huh? What I meant was, Libby was crazy enough to try anything, anybody, even in these times."

I turned back to Rothenberg. "What else does the prosecution have?"

"Rick's fingerprints all over the apartment."

"Hey, it used to be my place, too."

I said, "Any other forensics?"

"Fibers from her carpet on a pair of Rick's shoes." A glance to his client. "Her new carpet, laid down after Rick moved out. And some blood of hers on the top of those shoes."

I looked at Blassingale, who said, "I was over there after I moved out. September, two months before Libby was killed. We were talking about trying to work something out on the settlement – the divorce stuff – and she got nervous, pulled a hang-nail. It must have dripped blood on my shoes when we said good-bye at the door."

A hang-nail. "How hard did you hit her, Rick?"

Blassingale opened and closed his mouth. Then, "She never reported it, but that coffee friend of hers saw the mark, and told the cops about it when they questioned her."

From the tone of his voice, Blassingale thought that awfully unfair of the friend. I said, "Didn't the papers say something about an eye-witness?"

Blassingale just looked at me, but Rothenberg said, "Two, actually, the night of the killing. One was a woman walking her dog, says she saw a man wearing a Celtics warm-up jacket on the right block about eight P.M. that night."

Within the bracket. "She identify Rick as the man?"

Blassingale said, "Couldn't pick me out of the line-up, but the guy she described was close enough to me."

I turned to him. "You have that kind of jacket?"

"Had."

"What happened to it?"

"I don't know. It was old, and I must have left it somewhere."

I didn't say anything.

Blassingale grew more earnest. "You know, all the warm weather we had back in October? I must have taken it with me some place and just left it. I don't remember where, but give me a break, huh? Everybody and his brother has one of those."

To Rothenberg, I said, "Sounds like enough for the DA to get to the jury."

"It is, but the second witness is what you're here for."

"Go ahead."

"This second witness is named Claire Kinsour, K-I-N-S-O-U-R. She lives on the next block of Marlborough in-town from Mrs. Blassingale." Rothenberg drew in a deep breath. "Ms. Kinsour came forward a few weeks ago, just after the prosecution said it was going to trial against Rick. She says she saw the man in the Celtics warm-up jacket that night of the 15th, too, only it was about eight-thirty. And she saw him running east down the block, away from the decedent's building."

I said, "Where do you live, Rick?"

Blassingale shifted again in his chair. "Waterfront." A grunt. "Like I'd walk two miles to Libby's place in my own jacket to kill her."

"Where on the waterfront?"

"Where I live, you mean?"

"Yes."

He gave me the name, one of the chi-chi wharf buildings that stick out into the harbor. "Only about a mile and half, Rick."

"That's not the problem."

Rothenberg said, "The problem is, Ms. Kinsour definitely identifies Rick as the man she saw that night."

"How can she be so sure?"

Blassingale said, "Claire and I used to work together."

Great. "Go on."

"She was a trainee at Goff Searle, this brokerage house I worked for until I went out on my own three years ago. Claire had the hots for me then, and I wasn't interested."

"And Ms. Kinsour just happens to live down the street from your wife?"

Rothenberg said, "Moved in a month before Mrs. Blassingale was killed."

"Did they know each other?"

Blassingale said, "I don't know. I sure never took Libby to any Goff

Searle events when Claire was there."

"You have an alibi for the night in question?"

"No. I was home, reading. I even pulled the phone out of the wall jack."

I shook my head.

"Hey, I do that sometimes, get some peace and quiet. Claire's lying. She's going to commit perjury to get even with me, and Steve here says there's nothing he can do about it."

I couldn't remember a perjury indictment for the past ten years. "What kind of plea bargain did the prosecution offer?"

Blassingale's face got ruddier, the color high at the cheekbones. "That seems pretty damned defeatist, don't you think?"

Rothenberg made a calming gesture with his hand. "Before Ms. Kinsour came forward, twenty and change. Afterward, *nada*."

I thought about it. "And Ms. Kinsour comes forward only after the news hits about Rick going to trial."

"Yes."

"Why?"

Rothenberg smiled. "One of the many questions we'd like you to ask her." Then the smile died. "We have to impeach her, John. The other stuff I can deal with on cross of the Commonwealth's witnesses. The blood on the shoes through the coffee friend and the abuse incident –"

"I didn't abuse her, for Chrissake! I slapped her, once."

Another calming gesture. "But Ms. Kinsour sinks us, John. We have to turn her as a witness, or the jury sees this thing only one way."

I looked to Blassingale. "Any other help you can give me on that?"

A shrug. "I don't know. Claire had a girlfriend at Goff Searle, another trainee. Gina Ferro – that's F-E-R-R-O – was her name, but we checked the phonebooks, and she's not listed anywhere."

"Might the brokerage know?"

"Might." Blassingale brightened. "Yeah, they might. I should have thought of that."

Yes, he should. "Anybody still there who I could contact?"

"Try Mike Oldham. Ferro worked with him the most."

I watched Blassingale. "One more thing?"

"Shoot."

"You seeing anybody now?"

"Seeing … ?" Blassingale looked down at his shoes. "Yes."

"She with you that night?"

Blassingale looked up. "No."

"You sure?"

"I said, no. Besides, she's married."

"And brunette?"

The flesh around the cheekbones got ruddier again.

TWO

Marlborough Street stretches east to west for nine blocks from the Public Garden through Boston's Back Bay neighborhood. The buildings are three- and four-story townhouses in brownstone and brick, some still single-family. Most are divided into condos and apartments, though that doesn't diminish the imitation gaslamps and residential parking restrictions or the red-bricked sidewalks, frost-heaved into stumble-humps. The trees whose roots helped with the heaving were bare of leaves and stark against the sun on the north side of the block where Claire Kinsour lived.

At the front entrance, I walked up the stoop and pushed her buzzer. Getting a tinny "Who is it?" from the speaker, I asked if Ms. Kinsour could speak with me about a court case. Two minutes later, the massive formal door opened, and an ash blonde in her late twenties looked out coyly at me. Kinsour was slim but big through the chest under a cotton cowl sweater, and she cocked her hip straining some bleached jeans.

"And who might you be?"

I showed her my identification.

Kinsour took the folder, holding it up to the light. "John Francis Cuddy." She looked from it to me, using her free hand to tap the index fingernail against her lower front teeth. "Irish, right?"

"At some point."

Kinsour handed back the ID. "What's this about?"

"I'm working for the lawyer representing Rick Blassingale."

"And you'd like to ask me some questions, help to trap me later on in court."

"Something like that."

A coy smile joined the look. "Well, at least you're honest, which is more than I can say for Rick." She canted her head. "The prosecutor said I didn't have to talk to anybody if I didn't want to."

"And you don't."

"But you're cute enough to spend some time with." One tap of the nail. "And I don't have anything else to do, so come on up."

As Kinsour climbed the central stairs ahead of me, I said, "It's good luck to find you home."

"Not really. I'm unemployed. Those of us out of work spend a lot of time at home." She half-turned. "Or hadn't you heard?"

"Heard what?"

"About the latest decline in the securities industry. First there was Black Monday in 'eighty-seven, and then came just the slow torture of the last year or so."

We reached the second floor, and a door stood open around the corner of the landing. Kinsour beckoned me over the threshold into a front unit with nice sunlight streaming from the bay window onto an oriental rug. The furniture was tasteful and fairly new, an elaborate stereo system arrayed under the window.

"Nice place for being unemployed."

She laid a hand on the back of an easy chair, then made for the one opposite it. "I wasn't out of work when I landed here."

We sat. "Which I understand was just early October?"

Kinsour became a little defensive. "That's right."

"Did you know Libby Blassingale?"

"Before she died, no."

"But you're sure you saw Rick Blassingale the night of the killing."

"That's right."

"From this room?"

"It was only about eight-thirty, but I wanted to turn in early, so I was in the bedroom." The coy smile. "Alone. Then I came out here to be sure the CD player was off, and I saw Rick across the street."

I got up and walked over to the bay window. "From here, then?"

"Right where you're standing."

I looked through the panes of angled glass. Sqeaky clean, and a nice view for one block east and another west. "And where exactly was Mr. Blassingale?"

"Rick was on the other side of the street – his wife's side, it turns out. Running toward the Public Garden."

Meaning eastward. "Wearing?"

"One of those shiny green Celtics jackets? You know, that kind of off-green you see everywhere on St. Patty's Day." A pause. "No offense meant."

"None taken." There were two gaslamps across the way, and the trees would have been bare by then, even with the warmer weather we'd had. "Was he carrying anything?"

"Some kind of bag, like for gym stuff."

Which could have held the weapon. "Hat?"

"Wearing one, you mean?"

"Yes."

"No. I got a good, clear look with the streetlights, and I recognized him."

"Because you two once worked together."

"That's how I'd describe it. Rick, though, he wanted it to be more than that."

I turned to her, came back to the chair. "How so?"

Kinsour rotated her neck on the shoulders a little, then tapped again with her index nail against the teeth. "Sex so."

"Anything come of it?"

"I was a trainee at Goff Searle. I wasn't about to cut my own throat, so I didn't make any sort of complaint."

Which wasn't exactly what I'd asked her. "Were you and Blassingale ever intimate?"

Kinsour puffed out a breath. "Only in his dreams."

"Why were you so late in coming forward to the authorities?"

"Identifying him, you mean?"

"Yes."

"Simple. All I saw was Rick running down the street that night. No big deal, right? Then the next morning, I had a dawn flight to Seattle. That's why I was going to bed so early."

"Seattle."

"Yes. Job interview, and I stayed with a friend of mine from college for a few days. So I guess I left before her body was found, and all the TV stuff about Rick had died down by the time I got back."

"Then what led you to contact the police?"

"There was this thing on the news about Rick going to trial soon, and I just kind of freaked. Then I said, 'OhmyGod, I bet they could use me,' so I called them."

"To get even with Rick."

"That's why I called them." Tap, tap. "But that's not what I saw or why I saw it that night."

"And you remember it was that night −"

"November fifteenth, because my flight was the sixteenth. I didn't get the job, but check it out with the airline, you want to."

"Thanks, I will." I rose, and she did too, slowly, even languidly.

"One other thing," I said. "Have you heard from Gina Ferro recently?"

"Gin ... ?" Tap, tap. "What does she have to do with this?"

"Maybe nothing. I'd just like to speak with her."

"Well, I don't know how'd you'd reach her."

"No idea at all?"

A theatrical shrug. "She got married, I heard. Don't know about the name."

"Her husband's name?"

A patient look. "No, her name. If she changed it, I mean. A lot of women still do, you know?"

THREE

"Law Offices."

"Steve Rothenberg, please. John Cuddy calling."

"One moment, please."

A click and a burr, then, "Steven Rothenberg."

"Steve, John Cuddy."

"How does it look?"

"Bleak, if Claire Kinsour is on the level."

He paused. "Well, that's the question, isn't it?"

"I know, Steve. But Kinsour says your client's the one who made the move at the place they worked."

"You believe her?"

"I'm not sure I want to believe either of them, but a jury would like her more than Blassingale, I'd say."

"Oh, that's just ducky." Again a pause. "On the other hand, whether he rejected her or she rejected him, either way I can show Kinsour's biased." A third pause. "You going to the brokerage house next?"

"Unless you have a better idea."

"If I did, I wouldn't have hired you, right?"

✽ ✽ ✽ ✽

The receptionist at Goff Searle & Associates led me deftly to a rear, corner office. Plaques recounting good deeds and photos displaying hearty handshakes occupied every available square foot of wall space. The desktop was covered by two different computer systems and God knows what else to support them. Michael Oldham seemed nearly buried behind the equipment. Even when he stood to greet me.

About five-three and slightly bowlegged, Oldham reminded me of a miniature Dick Van Dyke from the old TV show as he dimmed the screens he'd been studying. Half-glasses on the end of his nose over a bowtie and suspenders, Oldham was very old-school and pushing fifty, but not showing an ounce of fat doing it. "Have a seat, Mr. Cuddy."

"Thanks."

Oldham signaled to the receptionist, who withdrew and closed the door behind her. Taking off the glasses, he said, "Now, just what can I do for you?"

I told him.

The stockbroker's face looked as though the market had just hit the "dive" button. "Distasteful business."

"I agree. But that doesn't get it done."

His expression turned to normal. "No, you're certainly right there. Very well. What do you want to know?"

"What was the relationship between Rick Blassingale and Claire Kinsour while they worked here?"

"Relationship?"

"How did they get along?"

Oldham knew that wasn't what I meant. "Claire was a trainee. I matched her up with Rick. My fault, really."

"What was?"

"There was some kind of tension between them. Friction. You could almost see it jumping off their bodies whenever they were together."

"Sexual tension?"

"As I said, distasteful business." A snort. "I'd guess possibly, but I never saw or heard anything that would confirm such a thing. Rick was married at the time, but I take it you already know that."

I nodded. "Any sense that one of them was being jilted."

"No."

Oldham's reply brooked no further discussion. "How about Gina Ferro?"

"Ah, Gina. Wholly different person."

"From Kinsour?"

"From both of them." Oldham seemed to warm up a little. "Rick was always a bit too ... positive for his own good. Arrogant, even. I don't mean just ego, either. Ego you need in this business, along with nerve and judgment. Rick had all those, but his arrogance kept him from reconsidering his own decisions over time, and over time that failure can pummel a portfolio, simply pummel it."

"And Claire Kinsour?"

"Awfully aware of her good looks. And more than a bit too deferential. Waited for others to move before she would. Insufficient initiative, I'd have said. But Claire didn't stay long enough to gauge that for certain."

"Blassingale have anything to do with her leaving?"

"No. At least, I don't believe so. Claire simply moved on to another house. I couldn't say if she's still there or not."

"And Gina Ferro?"

"Would have made a fine broker, but she didn't really enjoy it. The thrill of the game just wasn't there for her. Pity, too. Fine mind, excellent at analysis, projections ... ah, but you hate to lose the best of the younger ones."

"You have any idea where Ms. Ferro is now?"

"She left the industry entirely. Married, settled down. A pity, but ..." Oldham shrugged.

"Would you happen to have an address on her?"

"Home address, you mean?"

"Or any way I could get in touch with her."

The frown. "Don't know that I would have her married name, but ... wait a minute." Oldham brought up one of the screens, clacked away a minute, then traced his middle finger down the screen. "Yes. Yes, Gina sent me an announcement when she had her baby, and I made a note of the address. Day Boulevard. All the way over in Southie, I'm afraid."

It had been a while since my last visit. "Not a problem."

✼ ✼ ✼ ✼

I wouldn't have thought they'd still have tulips, this time of year.

I looked down at her headstone, Elizabeth Mary Devlin Cuddy. "Mrs. Feeney said they weren't from Holland, but that was all she knew."

Well, they're beautiful, John. Special occasion?

"I've never needed one before."

I just stood there for a while, watching a boat from the Boston Police Harbor Unit rise and slap against the chop as it patrolled the water below her hillside.

What's bothering you?

"A case. Husband accused of killing his wife, maybe abusing her, too. Some possible hanky-panky at the office when both sides weren't willing. And I don't know who to believe out of it."

Would the case be any easier if you did?

I smiled. "Not necessarily."

Maybe you just haven't found the right person yet.

"The right person?"

The one you can believe.

We talked about other things for a while after that. Old friends and older times, back when we were together and the world seemed easy.

Then I noticed the police boat's running lights were on, and I figured it was time to say good-bye.

FOUR

The address Michael Oldham gave me turned out to be an expansive two-decker just west of the L Street Bath-House on Day Boulevard. The woman who answered the bell was holding a little boy between the ages of one and two. Her eyes were chocolate brown, as was her hair, in a pageboy flip, like she took care of it. About the same height as Claire Kinsour, she was a little bigger all around, as though she might not yet have shed the extra pounds child-bearing had imposed on her.

"Yes?"

"Gina Ferro?"

A smile. "Not anymore." Then a cautious look. "Wait a minute. How did you get this address?"

"I'm helping Rick Blassingale's lawyer, and I was able to track you down."

Still cautious. "You have some identification?"

I showed her my ID. After reading it, she pointed to the name laminated under the buzzer I'd pushed. "I'm Gina Shukas now. My husband's folks are from Lithuania."

"It would be a help if I could take a few minutes of your time."

"Sure, I guess. Come on up."

The second floor was sunfilled, even in the December afternoon. Spacious living room, modestly furnished but beautifully kept, despite the time burdens the child must have created. Gina Shukas took the couch, allowing the little boy to crawl off her lap onto the cushion. I sat across from her in a rocking chair.

Mother patted son's rear end, causing him to giggle. "Arthur Junior."

"Fine-looking boy."

"He has his daddy's eyes, but his mommy's hair." A different tone. "Now, what do you need to know?"

"Whatever you can tell me about Rick Blassingale and Claire Kinsour."

"If you're helping Rick's lawyer, why do you need to know about Claire?"

Neutrally, I said, "She might be a witness at the trial."

"Oh. Well, I haven't really followed the case, so I don't know what to tell you. When we all worked together at Goff Searle, I know Claire thought he was kind of cute."

"She did."

"Yeah, but I don't know if it went anywhere. I mean ... you know what I mean. When I saw in the paper that he was accused of killing his wife, I thought about calling her back – Claire, I mean – but I just never got around to it."

"Calling her back?"

"About his wife getting killed that same night. Like I said, I haven't really followed the case and all, but how many people do you know have ever been charged with murder?"

When I didn't say anything, Shukas said, "Oh, right. For a minute there, I forgot who you … Well, never mind. I didn't get a chance to call her after we had dinner."

I was still confused. "Dinner?"

"Yes. Claire called me in early November, said she was going out of town for a while, and did I want to get together with her. I thought it was kind of funny, but I said, sure, why not. I mean, the baby's kept me kind of home-tied for over a year now – they say you can watch TV and all? Don't believe it, especially when Art – my husband, I mean – is out of town."

"Ms. Kinsour called, and you thought it was 'kind of funny'?"

"Well, yeah. I mean, Claire and I weren't exactly close at Goff Searle, and she left before I did. But you know, once you leave a place, you lose touch with the people, especially if you aren't working somewhere else. Claire said she wasn't working either and was flying to Seattle, maybe to move there, and 'Why don't we get together around seven,' you know? So I said sure."

"And so you did?"

"Yes." She ruffled her son's hair, and he giggled again, kicking his leg sideways. "I got Art's mom to babysit – she isn't too keen on me going out when he's gone, tell you the truth, but that's just her way. So I met Claire for a drink, and we talked about her new job possibility and Arthur Junior here. One drink turned into two, and two turned into dinner. Just pasta and salad, but it was nice. Kind of reminded me what I liked about working downtown."

"And when was this?"

"When we went out? The night before her flight."

"Wait a minute. The night Libby Blassingale was killed?"

"Like I said. Of course, I didn't hear about it right away – Arthur Junior keeps me pretty occupied, don't you?" More ruffling, and the boy plodded around, like a cat coming back to be scratched. "But I remember saying to Claire at dinner, 'Girl, you're gonna be dead on your feet tomorrow, you don't get to bed early,' and thinking later how weird it was that Rick's wife got killed, probably around the time I was saying that. But Claire wouldn't hear of cutting the evening short. Said how often would we ever see each other, and she had a good point there."

Very slowly, I said, "What time did you and Ms. Kinsour finally part company?"

"Oh, ten, ten-fifteen? I know it was ten-thirty before I got home, because Art's mother was in a funk over how late I was out with my 'girlfriend.' "

Two hours after Claire Kinsour supposedly stood in her apartment, seeing

Rick Blassingale running down Marlborough Street. "Where did you eat?"

"This little place on Beacon Hill. It wasn't very expensive, but even so Claire insisted on treating me."

"She did."

"Yes. Said, 'So long as I have plastic, I can't be broke, right?' I felt kind of bad, her being out of work and all, but she gave the check and her card to the waiter before I knew what was happening."

Which meant a receipt and maybe even ... "Ms. Ferro, do you remember the name of the restaurant?"

FIVE

The weather had finally turned to winter by the time of Rick Blassingale's trial in a ninth floor session of Suffolk Superior Court. At Steve Rothenberg's request, the female, fiftyish judge allowed me to sit inside the bar enclosure at counsel table with him and his client. What a treat.

The courtroom itself was old-fashioned. High, almost church windows over mahogany wainscoting and scarred oak furniture. Fifteen years ago, the jury would have been three housewives, three retired people, three welfare recipients, and three postal workers. Now, with the "one-day, one-trial" system, almost everyone was subject to jury duty, even lawyers and judges, and the men and women staring back at us seemed as close to a cross-section of society as one could draw.

The prosecutor was a guy about Blassingale's age, and the case for the Commonwealth went in smoothly, a tide building from the jury box against the defendant. On cross-examination, Rothenberg chipped away at each witness where he could: getting the dog walker to admit she couldn't pick the defendant out of a line-up, the coffee friend to venture that the mark on Libby Blassingale's face might have bled a little, the forensic expert to concede that the blood stain on Rick's shoe might have been left there months before the killing.

The prosecutor saved Claire Kinsour till last. Her ash blonde hair was pulled back into a conservative bun, her suit a dark blue that complemented her coloring. Kinsour was composed, even compelling. I could feel the tide from the jury rising to a wave against Blassingale.

When the prosecutor passed the witness to Rothenberg, Steve rose and requested permission to approach the bench. When he got there, he asked the judge if "this item" in his hand could be marked as Defendant's Exhibit No. 5 for Identification. After the court reporter scribbled on it, Rothenberg showed it to the prosecutor, who did a good job of not fainting. Then Steve requested and received permission to approach the witness.

At the stand, Rothenberg said, "Ms. Kinsour, it was your testimony a few minutes ago that you saw Rick Blassingale running eastward on Marlborough Street about eight-thirty on the night of his wife's death, is that correct?"

Kinsour didn't have to think. "Yes."

Nodding to the jury, Rothenberg handed her the "item" and said, "I show you now Defendant's Exhibit Number 5 for Identification and ask you if that's your signature at the bottom."

Kinsour said, "Yes," and then her eyes bugged as they moved up the restaurant receipt to the top.

Rothenberg lowered his voice. "And what is that exhibit, Ms. Kinsour?"

"It's ... it's a charge card ..."

"The exhibit is a charge card receipt you signed at a restaurant half a mile away from your apartment on the night in question, is it not?"

"Yes."

"Please note the computer time-stamp under the name of the restaurant and tell the jury what it says."

"It ... it ..." Claire Kinsour rubbed a hand over her face. "I can't ... Oh, God, I can't believe this." She turned to the jury. "I lied. I was attracted to Rick when we worked together –"

The jurors all came forward in their seats, some with mouths open.

"Objection, your Honor!" cried the prosecutor.

The judge started to say something, but Kinsour just rode over her and the prosecutor both, voice carooming around the courtroom. "I didn't see Rick that night at all. At ten-thirty I did see a man running down the block, carrying a bag and wearing a green Celtics jacket like I knew Rick had."

"The witness will please –"

"– When I heard Rick was going to trial, I went to the police and lied. The man I saw, and saw clearly that night, was not Rick Blassingale."

Steve Rothenberg moved back to the defense table. The judge told Claire Kinsour that her next unresponsive sentence would leave her open to contempt of court, but you could tell the judge's heart was barely in it.

In disgust, the prosecutor said, "No questions. That's the Commonwealth's case, your Honor."

The judge looked over toward us. "Mr. Rothenberg?"

"I don't see the need for any defense witnesses, your Honor."

"Yes, well, why don't you keep your editorial comments to yourself. Ms. Kinsour, you are excused."

As the witness left the stand, eyes down and almost trotting out of the courtroom, the judge turned to the jury. "After I hear some motions by counsel, we may have closing arguments tomorrow morning." Then she told them when and where to report and excused them for the day.

After the last juror had filed out and the court officer closed the door, Rick Blassingale threw his arms around Rothenberg, then extended his hand to shake mine, again closing his left over our two hands, saying warmly, "All I could ask for, John. Thank you, thank you, thank you."

For some reason, I felt sick.

✻ ✻ ✻ ✻

Usually cases are hard. Occasionally they're easy. Virtually never is one served up on a silver platter, and so dramatically.

Leaving the courthouse, I went back to my office and sat with my eyes closed, going over in my head what I'd learned and how I'd learned it. Blassingale giving me Claire Kinsour, Michael Oldham, and Gina Ferro. Kinsour telling me Rick was after her, not the other way around, but also mentioning that Gina might have changed her name after getting married. Oldham not knowing that new name, but having a new address in his computer. Ferro remembering the date and time of her dinner with Kinsour, who paid for it in a way that produced a time-stamped receipt. Almost like I was following directions.

At the cemetery, I'd told Beth that I didn't know who was telling the truth. If what Claire Kinsour said from the stand after seeing the receipt was reality, then Rick Blassingale had been honest with me in Rothenberg's office. Ferro might have mentioned over dinner that she wasn't keeping up on the news, given the baby and all. But if Kinsour wanted to nail Rick as vengeance, why not just say she saw him running down the street at ten-thirty, not eight-thirty, which was still within the time-of-death bracketing? Especially when Kinsour had to know that Ferro, if found and interviewed, could destroy the eight-thirty version?

There was only one complete explanation, and I just hoped Michael Oldham's take on the players was right enough to help me prove it.

✻ ✻ ✻ ✻

Dressed in dingy work pants, a sweater torn at the neck, and an old parka with the stuffing peeking out, I put a liter bottle of Sprite in a brown paper bag and crimped the paper at the top. Then I drove down to the waterfront, parking three blocks from Rick Blassingale's building on the wharf. I walked to the building, a little unsteadily, and slumped down against a wall across from the main entrance, taking a slug now and then from the Sprite as though it were something stronger.

Nobody was on duty inside the door, which didn't surprise me. People came and went, several on entering having some trouble getting their keys to turn in the lock. Then a brunette appeared, her back toward me, walking toward the front door. Her hair was done in a pageboy flip, the long, winter coat bulky around her body, making it hard to gauge weight.

She had trouble with the key, too. Then she held it up to the light, tapped with her index fingernail on her lower teeth, and tried the key again, this time getting it to work.

She disappeared inside, and I watched an upper floor light come on, then go off. Shortly afterward, what might have been a living room light dropped to a romantic level.

Oldham was right. Arrogance on the one hand, and deference on the other.

Leaning over, I poured out the rest of the Sprite and went home.

✻ ✻ ✻ ✻

Steve Rothenberg said, "John, thanks for coming, but we really don't need you for the closings."

I looked at both of them, people bustling around us in the corridor outside the courtroom. "The judge denied your motions?"

Rothenberg glanced confidently at Rick Blassingale beside him. "Yes, but I expected that. Without the Kinsour woman's testimony, there was still barely enough for the prosecutor to carry his burden of production, so the judge is letting the case go to the jury. But after what she did yesterday on the stand, I'm not worried about this one."

"You should be."

Rothenberg darkened as the color ripened in his client's face. "What do mean?"

I pinched Blassingale's arm gently at the elbow. "Why don't we go over here, where it's a little more private."

In the dead-end alcove, they stood while I sat on the stiff bench and crossed my arms, leaning back. "I'm going to give you my own closing here, guys. Tell me what you think of it."

Neither of them said anything.

"Rick Blassingale is going through a bad divorce but has a new – or not so new – girlfriend. It'd be great to be a widower, he thinks. Unfortunately, though, he'd be the prime suspect, a role he'd rather not play. Then he sees a way to get what he wants without having to duck the role."

Blassingale said, "You don't know what you're talking about."

"It gets better. Rick has his girlfriend move into an apartment almost across the street from his wife's place. Using that as a base of operations, he ventures forth on the night of November 15th around 8:00 P.M. in a fairly common jacket that was expendable. Unfortunately, a woman walking her dog spots him, but that alone isn't fatal. He uses his old key to get in his wife's building, then gets her to open up the apartment door on some pretext, maybe more talk or 'I have a make-up present in the bag, Libby.' "

"You're nuts," said Blassingale.

Rothenberg said quietly, "Let him talk, Rick."

I nodded toward the client. "You get back to Claire's place pretty quickly, leaving her the weapon, the Celtics jacket, and probably everything else you were wearing that night in the bag, to take to Seattle with her and dump safely. You're homefree, except you forget to throw away the shoes you wore in September, the night you hit Libby, the shoes that had her blood on them as a result. Bad luck, but then, you can't be expected to think of everything, right, Rick?"

No response.

Rothenberg said, "But then why have Kinsour come forward at all?"

"She doesn't, Steve, not until after the lab tests on the shoes, together with the other evidence, give the DA enough to go to trial. That's when Rick's reserve plan has to kick in. Not a great plan to a practicing attorney, but it must have seemed awfully clever to somebody who only graduated law school. Have the witness, with an apparent motive to get even with the defendant, testify against him, then be turned by an incontrovertible piece of evidence, like the restaurant receipt or Gina Ferro's testimony on timing that night."

Rothenberg shook his head. "So that Kinsour first implicates, then exonerates, Rick as the killer?"

"Exactly. Otherwise, she just testifies that she saw the definite Ricker here at ten-thirty, leading to no impeachment of her testimony by receipt or Ferro."

I fixed Blassingale, who was breathing badly and looking worse. "And you used me to set it up for you, Rick. Knowing that the system wouldn't bother prosecuting Claire for perjury, you led me by the hand to Kinsour, Oldham, and eventually Ferro and the restaurant. Neat, but a little too neat."

Blassingale managed to say, "I told you, I swore off blondes."

"Not based on what I saw last night, at your building's front door, with her own key. A brunette to the outside world, an ash-blonde inside your apartment?"

Blassingale clenched his hands into fists and took a step toward me on the bench.

I said, "Keep coming, Rick. You'd look great to the jury with a broken nose."

Rothenberg turned to Blassingale. "Calm down. I need to know whether John's just blowing smoke here."

The ruddy face pushed toward the lawyer's. "You don't need to know anything. You just need to go back in that courtroom and argue to the jury what they heard from the stand."

I shook my head this time. "Sorry, Rick. No go. I seem to remember the DA offering you a plea bargain of twenty and change before Claire Kinsour came forward. I have a feeling the prosecutor would jump at that if you were to tell him through Steve here that the offer looked good, that you didn't want to risk what the jury might still do."

Blassingale stared. "You're asking me to send myself to prison?"

"Rick, it's plead out, or I go to the prosecutor myself with what I know, and hang you in front of this jury or the next one."

Blassingale's face looked like it was about to explode. "No way! That's double jeopardy."

I looked to Rothenberg, who said, "Not until the verdict comes back, and we haven't even closed yet. With what Cuddy has, the judge could declare a mistrial and start you in front of a whole new jury."

His face back to me, Blassingale started to dissolve. "But you promised me confidentiality. I'll go ... I'll file a complaint ..."

"That's just a license, Rick. This is murder. I lose my ticket, I lose it. But one way or the other, you're going to pay for killing your wife. And I have a feeling that after I talk with the other side, the twenty and change won't make it back onto the bargaining table."

Tears actually started from Blassingale's eyes, rolling down his ruddy cheeks, spotting his collar and tie. "What are you doing to me?"

I stood up. "Just turning the witness, Rick. That's the problem with the technique, though. Sometimes they turn back on you."

Steve Rothenberg and I walked away from Rick Blassingale, to give him time to make up his mind.

BODY OF WORK

ONE

I looked from the client to her lawyer and said to him, "How about if we start with why you contacted me?"

Martin Fodor stroked the left side of his mustache with the pad of his right index finger. "As a private investigator, you mean?"

"That's what I mean."

Fodor resettled himself in the chair. Squat and barrel-chested when he'd stood from behind an impressive teak desk to shake hands a minute ago, the graying hair was combed across a skull that had weathered fifty or so years better than its feathery covering.

Fodor said, "I knew a bit about the good work you did for Craig Abbot up in Beacon Harbor."

Abbot was a domestic relations (read: divorce) attorney I'd helped with a homicide in the coastal town north of Boston. "And he told you I could keep my mouth shut."

Fodor permitted himself a small smile. "Craig's exact words were, 'John Cuddy will tell you the truth, whether you want to hear it or not.'"

"So what do I call you?" said Patricia Tsoris.

I turned to her, seated in the other chair in front of Fodor's desk. Tsoris was about five-six, with light brown eyes and lustrous black hair flared like a fashion model with a wind machine behind her. Dressed in a plain gray suit and bright print scarf, she gave the impression of a woman in charge of the situation, except that the cuticles around the fingernails had been chewed on worse than a baby's teething ring.

"Your money, your choice," I said.

Like her lawyer, Tsoris barely smiled. "How much of my money are we talking about, John?"

I tried not to picture the unpaid bills next to my checkbook at home. "That'll depend on two things."

"Namely?"

"What you want me to do, and whether I decide to do it."

Fodor cleared his throat. "Perhaps we're getting a bit ahead of ourselves. Why don't I provide some background, and then we all can make rational decisions."

I squared toward him in my chair. "Go ahead."

The lawyer opened a file on his desk, though he spoke without referring to the papers it contained. "Last week, a rather well-known local artist was killed at his home in Beacon Harbor. You knew of Elton Wix?"

"Not before I read about his murder."

Another clearing of the throat. "A little deeper background, then. Elton was African-American, one of the baby-boomer phenoms in the art world. A bit reclusive, but brilliant. His specialty was the collage." Fodor looked at me rather carefully. "You know what a 'collage' is?"

I thought about the one my wife Beth had made from photos of us, the year before she died. "Central character or theme, with fragments of image or words around it."

"Yes. Only Elton had a rather unique approach. He would use great symbolism in his work."

"What's unique about that?" I said.

Tsoris leaned into the conversation. "Elton was illiterate, John."

"Completely?"

"Functionally." Having gained my attention, she leaned back in her chair. "He grew up in the Caribbean – a peasant village, to hear him describe it. English was his first language, but he never learned to read and write. Symbols, on the other hand, fascinated him."

"Symbols of what?"

"The dollar sign for 'money,' or the ghost-busters circle/slash for 'prohibited.' Elton loved symbols that stood for whole concepts."

I said, "How do you know so much about him?"

Tsoris nibbled on her left thumb. "For the last five years, I represented him."

"You're a lawyer, too?"

"No, no. I was his agent, for the artwork. Without me, Elton would still have been cutting and pasting for peanuts."

Tsoris' tone carried equal parts of arrogance and derogation.

Fodor might have sensed something about how I was reacting. "In any case," he said, "Elton was just reaching some local pinnacles, and was poised – thanks to Patricia – for national, even international, acclaim."

"Why?"

A stroke over the mustache. "Why?"

"Yes. What was so special about the collages he did?"

"Nothing, really," said Tsoris. "It was all in the marketing, you see."

"Not yet."

Tsoris descended to my level. "Who has the money to dabble in art right now? The baby-boom generation. What appeals to them? Things that remind them of being young. Music, as in 'classic' rock, not 'oldies.' Hot cars, as in the return of the 'rag-top' from Detroit and everywhere else. Etc., etc."

"Including," I said, "the elevation to 'great art' of the posters they had hanging under fishnets in their college dorm rooms."

Tsoris cocked her head, spoke a little more normally. "Exactly."

"For which they're now willing to pay a tad over two-ninety-eight."

Now Tsoris gave me a coy smile, showing some teeth. "A tad."

"How much 'tad' are we talking about?" I said.

"Five to ten thousand."

Jesus. "Sounds like enough for some kind of motive."

Fodor said, "We hope not."

I looked at him. "What do you mean?"

He stared down at his file now. "Elton was found by his next-door neighbor in Beacon Harbor, though I understand 'next-door' to be a euphemism, since something like a quarter-mile separates the two houses. He'd been shot, relatively close-range according to the police."

"Sounds like means instead of motive."

Fodor glanced up at me, then at Tsoris. He said, "There were two finished collages in the house –"

"– More like a shack, John –"

"– and neither had been taken."

I thought about it. "Could there have been others that were?"

"No," said Tsoris. "He'd just been finishing those up."

"How do you know?"

She looked out the window. "I'd been there – a week *before* Elton died – discussing things with him."

"Things."

Fodor said, "I believe that what's material to the murder is that the police found Patricia's fingerprints at various places in Elton's hou – shack."

"That's something, but not much. How about the murder weapon?"

"Apparently it was a handgun Elton kept by his bed."

"Apparently?"

"Right caliber for the bullets … the wounds in his body, I'm told, but it's missing."

I nodded. "Why do I get the feeling that I haven't heard everything yet?"

Tsoris said, "Martin, the way you're telling it, we'll be here forever." To me, "I don't have an alibi for the time of Elton's death."

No surprise there. "Go on."

"As his agent, I'd visit him in that shack, the last time a week before the killing, like I said. The police claim that the lipstick found on a glass there matches the kind I started using *after* that last visit. It's called 'Black Panther.' Only supposedly this glass had been 'washed' and wiped of fingerprints. Now, I ask you, do I look the type who'd kill somebody and then forget to clean my own lipstick off a glass?"

No, at least to the cleaning part. "How many people knew about this new lipstick?"

"Everybody. Elton asked me about it at his opening."

"An art opening?"

"Yes, a gallery on Newbury that specializes in works like his."

Newbury Street is the chi-chi shopping drag in my neighborhood of Back Bay, but I've never spent much time – or money – in its galleries. "Name of the place?"

Tsoris gave me the coy smile again. " 'Collage,' what else?"

Easy enough to remember. "When was this opening?"

Tsoris attacked her left ring finger this time. "The night before he was killed."

"A minute ago, you said 'everybody' knew about your lipstick?"

"Elton was incredibly self-centered, even for an artist. One of his less endearing habits was that after asking you a question, he'd always boom out your answer, so that it would appear the information was actually coming from him."

"Got it."

"Well, three others were around in Collage that night. The gallery owner, Rex Noel. Elton's girlfriend, Lucie Son – that's S-O-N, some kind of oriental."

Fodor winced.

Tsoris said, "And, of course, George Hetherington."

"Who's Hetherington?"

Fodor rustled some papers. "The neighbor who found Elton's body. I understand they didn't get along."

"They didn't get along, but this Hetherington shows up for the opening?"

"That's one of the things we'd like you to look into."

Tsoris raised her voice. "Not to mention the girlfriend, who calls herself a 'media' journalist but doesn't give a damn about art. Has her own column for the newspaper up there, though. 'Sonrise.' Get it?"

"S-O-N-R-I-S-E?"

"Exactly."

"And Mr. Noel?"

Tsoris looked to Fodor, seeming to seek guidance for the first time as she nibbled on her left pinky. Three fingers out of five, and another hand to go yet.

Facing me, he said, "Rex told Elton how much he'd gotten for one of the collages."

"So?"

"Well, a gallery sends the check to the artist's agent, who then deposits it, taking out the commission and forwarding the balance to the client."

When nobody said anything more, I thought about it. "And while Mr. Wix was illiterate, he wasn't ... innumerate."

Tsoris looked out the window again. "I was in a cash bind. I would have made up the difference on his next piece."

"Did Mr. Wix confront you about it?"

"We. ... talked it over, the night of the opening. I'd smoothed things out with him."

"Do the police know about this?"

Fodor stroked both sides of his mustache. "So far as we're aware, not yet. But they have all the pieces, and if they ask for bank records and computer ledgers, well ..."

I sat back. "So, you want to hire me before the other shoe drops."

"Yes," said Tsoris.

"One problem with that. For a homicide, I'd have to check in with the local police up there, and that'll make them wonder why you've hired a private investigator."

She looked at me. "Can't you just tell them it's confidential or something?"

"Yes. But all they have to do is ask around to everybody about retaining me, and eventually your name will stand out."

Fodor cleared his throat a third time. "Perhaps by then you'll have determined who really killed Elton."

I returned to him. "This amount of foresight's pretty unusual. Why not just wait for the other shoe to drop?"

"For an indictment, you mean?"

"Yes."

"I'll tell you why, John." Tsoris bared her teeth this time, but nothing like a smile. "People in the trade would understand me killing a client, particularly a self-centered bastard like Elton. They'd never accept me cheating one."

I thought I could see another reason why Fodor wanted to head this off at the pass and avoid a trial. "You told me who knew about the new lipstick. Who else knew about the gun?"

Tsoris blew out a breath. "Everybody, too. Elton used to brag about it all the time. 'Got dis gun beside my bed, y'know? I'se one tough nigger, mon.' "

Fodor winced again. He had to keep Patricia Tsoris off the stand because a jury couldn't miss her attitude, blowing any hope of acquittal sky-high.

TWO

I laid the roses diagonally across the grave, so that the blossoms pointed toward the last few letters of ELIZABETH MARY DEVLIN CUDDY on the stone.

Roses. Somebody must be feeling flush.

"Just picked up a new case, Beth. Killing of an artist, with his agent afraid she's a prime suspect."

Why?

"Apparently she kind of unilaterally increased her commission."

You don't like her, do you?

I looked down the cemetery's slope, toward the blue bay water at its foot. "Not especially."

How come?

"She's arrogant, and probably more than a little racist, and she cheated a client when she needed money."

But you still took her on.

"Yeah. Because I needed money, too."

A pause. *With one major difference, John.*

"I'd like to hear it."

You wouldn't cheat a client to get what you needed.

"Not so far, anyway. But she probably felt like that at some point, too."

Another pause. *Where was this artist killed?*

"Up in Beacon Harbor."

Well, at least the case will be picturesque.

I looked down at Beth, and then to her water view again. I didn't ask if "picturesque" helped.

❊ ❊ ❊ ❊

"Hey, Cuddy. What're you doing back here?"

Detective Sergeant Joe Patrizzi sat behind his desk, feet up on the

secretarial pull-tray, Beacon Harbor having bought its department desks long
before computers and work-stations came into vogue. A nice view of a tree-
dotted hillside through the window framed his narrow head and thin
shoulders in the plaid shirt, tie knotted but pulled down. Patrizzi had told me
in the past that he didn't like to be called "sergeant," as it reminded him of
his days in uniform, which he didn't ever intend to wear again.

"I wanted you to know I've been hired to look into a homicide up here."

"You gotta mean *the* homicide, right? Our own little Picasso?"

"That's the one."

Patrizzi pursed his lips. "We don't have anybody charged yet. Who're you
representing on this?"

"Confidential, for now."

A shake of the narrow head. "So, what, you're just going to muck around
some?"

"Not without letting you know first."

"Courtesy ain't dead." Patrizzi brought his feet down to the floor. "Okay,
you let me know."

"I was wondering if I could maybe talk with you some, too."

"Talk with me, but not about who's paying your freight."

"Yes."

Another shake. "I'll say this, Cuddy. You're so upfront, it's like
disarming, you know?"

"Thanks."

"Take a seat."

I did. "What've you got?"

"What I've got is a state trooper attached to the DA's office who couldn't
find the ocean from the beach. But I went over this one with him, and I
maybe can't blame the guy much."

"Why?"

"Well, we've got the crime-scene analysis, which tells us that our Mr.
Wix was coming out of his kitchen into the living room when somebody
greeted him from about ten feet away with six shots."

"Six."

"Yeah. Thirty-eight caliber. Five hit him, three having the good
manners to lodge in his soft tissues where we could recover them. Ballistics
won't bet the farm on it, but the markings suggest a Smith & Wesson barrel,
and the decedent was known to keep a revolver around the house."

"Any reason for Wix to be afraid?"

"Hey, a black guy, living by himself out on the moor there?"

"I haven't been to the house yet."

"Yeah, well, it was me, I'd have an assault rifle under my pillow."

"Any history of racial things against him?"

"None. Beacon Harbor's pretty tolerant that way. Of course, it's also ninety-seven percent white, so it can kind of afford to be."

"I'm told a neighbor found the body."

"Yeah. One George Hetherington. Retired lawyer. If only they all would decide to hang up the spikes."

"What was Hetherington doing in the victim's kitchen?"

"Body was found out back, on the water side of the house."

"This Wix owned waterfront property?"

"Given to him a few years ago by some 'patron of the arts.' I guess Hetherington's nose's been out of joint ever since, account of he thought him and the former owner had a deal that Hetherington could buy it himself."

I didn't want to lose the sequence here. "So you figure that Wix got shot in the house. Then what?"

"Blood trail tells us that he probably staggered out the back door onto his deck, and then down into his junk before kissing the ground and expiring."

Seemed like a lot of effort for a man hit five times and carrying three thirty-eights inside him. "What do you mean, his 'junk?' "

"Wix kept a lot of stuff in the backyard, I guess for 'his art' or whatever. Pieces of lumber, old bent metal, all kinds of junk, like I said. Probably another reason the neighbor wasn't too thrilled about him."

"You turned the house over to the relatives yet?"

"No, but only because there aren't any."

"So nobody's claimed the body, either."

"Girlfriend – Lucie Son, as in 'father and son' – wants to cremate him, but she's a reporter, thinks she knows all there is in this world."

"Meaning?"

"Meaning she's screaming that the Medical Examiner ought to have DNA tests done first."

"DNA?"

"Yeah. I told her, 'We don't have anything in the house to match up with a perp.' But she kept at it, so the M.E. drew some blood and tissue samples from Wix that we'll hold for elimination purposes, we ever arrest somebody."

"Any physical evidence beyond the slugs?"

"Yeah."

I waited, but Patrizzi just smiled.

"Any chance of me seeing the inside of the house?"

He pursed his lips again, kind of theatrically this time. "Sure. What else do I have to do?"

❊ ❊ ❊ ❊

I followed Patrizzi's unmarked sedan in my car, so that he wouldn't have to bring me back to the station. We drove out of the town center and over a few miles of rolling country lanes before turning east onto a gravel driveway. It forked pretty quickly, Patrizzi taking the left prong as I looked back toward the right, which led to a nice, two-level Cape saltbox perched on a bluff overlooking the water.

The left fork ended at a tumble-down one-story house with mismatched shingles as siding and what appeared to be strips of green felt for a roof. Patrizzi killed his engine and got out, some dust swirling around his feet.

As I joined him, he said, "Pretty humble, huh?"

"So far."

Patrizzi had a key to the front door and led me inside. There was really just one large room containing a lot of ratty furniture, with a double bed in an alcove on the right and the doorway to a closet-sized bathroom on the left. Behind the living room was a double-wide doorway with no door leading toward a kitchen that, facing east, would probably have the nicest water view in the place.

"I don't see any artwork."

Patrizzi shrugged. "Agent – name of Patricia Tsoris, don't ask me to spell it without the file in front of me – said it was important to be sure they were protected, so she got permission to take them away."

"But they're still being here kind of rules out a burglary gone sour."

"Oh, yeah. Plus what we found in the cabinet."

"Cabinet?"

"Kitchen. Come on."

We walked back into the kitchen. Through the window above the nineteen-fifties sink, I could see the junk in the yard and the ocean beyond.

Patrizzi pointed over the counter. "Cabinet." He opened the door to it. "See these wine glasses?"

There were a half dozen or so, sitting upside down, as though to drain the water from the bulbs. "I see them."

"Well, turns out that two of them were still a little wet when we came on the scene, and there was a half bottle of white wine in the fridge."

I looked over to the refrigerator, about the same vintage as the sink and everything else, then back out to the living room. "Suggesting that maybe Wix was entertaining somebody."

"Right. Only we talked to everybody, and they all claim they weren't here."

"Any alibis?"

"Hey, Cuddy, you never see those outside the movies."

I thought about it. "Didn't you tell me the neighbor – Hetherington – was here?"

"Uh-unh. I said he's the one found the body. Hetherington was supposedly out jogging when the deed was done."

As casually as possible, I said, "You get anything off the glasses?"

Patrizzi grinned. "I knew it. The agent, Tsoris, am I right?"

May as well tough it out. "I don't get you."

"Fine." Still grinning. "We got no prints, but there was some lipstick on one of the wet glasses that we matched up with the kind Tsoris just started using."

I said, "But no gun."

"Hey, the way the ocean carved up the shore around here, we got over three miles of coastline in this town. I had the divers check for two hundred yards north and south out to fifty yards east, but there's a limit, you know?"

He was right about that. I moved back toward the living room, stopping in the doorway. "Is this where Wix would have been?"

"Or close to it, the stains on the floor there and the spatter marks on the wall and jamb."

I looked down and up. A drab brown now, the way blood always dries.

"And after he's shot in the front, he turns," and I did, too, "and goes out the rear door here."

"Yeah," said Patrizzi, opening it for me. There was a planked deck maybe fifteen feet square. "Then he goes down these three steps to the grass, and gets maybe forty feet toward the water before he falls."

Fifteen feet of deck plus forty through the grass. Hell of a distance to run from a gun that, if it was his, he'd have to know was already empty.

"Cuddy?"

"Just thinking about something. Can you show me where he was when Hetherington found him?"

"Not exactly. Guy moved the body some."

"Moved it?"

"Rolled Wix over first, see what was wrong."

"That would have been pretty obvious."

"Not while the decedent was still lying on his stomach."

"Well, can you show me about where he was?"

"Yeah, but why not get it from the horse's mouth."

"I don't follow you."

Patrizzi gestured toward the neighboring saltbox. "I'm not seeing things, that's Hetherington himself, watching us with a pair of binoculars."

THREE

"Originally, I purchased these for the birds."

George Hetherington waggled the binoculars. We were sitting on his own deck in a pair of wicker peacock chairs with fanny cushions, Joe Patrizzi having driven back to the station. Hetherington faced north toward the Wix house, me more easterly, "so you can enjoy the view while we talk."

In addition to being solicitous of his guest, Hetherington was about six-one in running shorts and a light vinyl warm-up jacket. His features were weathered and his short hair bleached almost white, like he spent the warmer weather in the sun up here and the colder weather in the sun down south. His legs had that defined but wizened look that comes from aging to roughly seventy while you train and pay heed to your diet at the same time.

I said, "You're a bird-watcher, then?"

"Oh, yes. Fine hobby for the retired, so long as that's not all one does. But I keep fit by jogging every day between four and five P.M., with occasional tennis or golf at the club. That way I can enjoy the more pastoral aspects of living here without feeling guilty about them."

Somehow Hetherington struck me as the sort of man who'd never felt guilty about anything. "Is that how you were able to see Mr. Wix's body?"

"Not exactly. I'd been out running – three-point-six miles, that afternoon. Upon my return, I began warming down on the deck here. Stretch the old muscles, that sort of thing. I certainly didn't hear any shots, but I noticed Wix had his back door open."

"Which was unusual?"

"Well, I certainly hadn't noticed it before. Though with all that flotsam and jetsam in his yard, I suppose I shouldn't have been surprised by it."

But he was. "What did you do after you noticed the door?"

"Well, I picked up the field glasses here, and I focused them on his door. I thought I could see a reddish stain there. The man fancied himself an artist, so I thought at first it might be just paint."

Fancied himself. "You didn't think much of Mr. Wix's work?"

"Work? Well, perhaps you could call it 'work.' But one certainly couldn't call it 'art.' Just pasted up any old thing around a photo of some celebrity's head. Not exactly Van Gogh in my book."

"Yet you went to one of his openings."

"Yes. The man invited me as a goad, knowing I wouldn't attend. So I decided I would, just to goad him back."

"You two didn't get along, then."

"No. And not because of the obvious."

"The obvious?"

"Something racial. No, that property had been promised to me by its prior owner, you see, who then let it go to wrack and ruin. However, I held my tongue and stayed my hand. As an attorney, I knew an oral promise to convey real property wasn't enforceable – Statute of Frauds and all that – but I believed we had a gentleman's agreement. Then the prior owner became enamored of Wix's 'art' and decided to donate the place to him for a studio. Which Wix promptly turned into a junkyard."

"Not exactly in keeping with the … ambience."

Hetherington fixed me with soul-less eyes. "You think to mock me. The unfortunate fact is that Beacon Harbor had no land-use restrictions that applied directly to what Wix was doing. And, to be frank, I couldn't really see the junk from here. Just knowing it was there, however, was galling enough."

Galling enough to … "Mr. Hetherington, I wonder if you could show me how you found Mr. Wix."

"I just described it to you, didn't I?"

"Over in his yard, I mean."

Hetherington seemed to consider that. "Very well."

We walked north across the high moor grass to the rear of Wix's deck.

Hetherington stopped. "I was about here, just ready to walk up the steps. I'd been keeping my eye on that door – swung open then, as I said before – and the reddish stain on it, noticing that the color was running down the wood, even pooling some on the planking of the deck. That's when I suspected foul play."

"Foul play."

"Precisely. So I turned and looked around, and that's when I saw his body."

"Can you show me?"

"Well, it was over here." Hetherington moved forty feet or so toward the water, past hunks of corroded metal and rusty artifacts like an egg-beater, a toy train, and so on. He stopped again, this time at a piece of one-by-four lumber maybe three feet long. "Yes. Yes, that's the spot. Do you see the blood stains?"

More dried brown, seeped into the wood. "And Mr. Wix was on top of that?"

"Yes. On his stomach, head toward the water. The wood was approximately halfway up his thighs, at the perpendicular."

"At the perpendicular."

"Yes. His legs were close together, as though he'd pitched forward with his arms out in front of his head, you see."

"To break his fall?"

"No, no. More as though – oh, this is rather silly for such a serious matter – but more ..." Hetherington lifted his own arms above his head, elbows bent, fingertips on each hand just touching, like a ballerina.

"And that's how you found him?"

"Yes." Hetherington dropped his arms. "He looked so unnatural, I said, 'Are you hurt? Can you hear me?' And when he didn't respond, I took hold of his right elbow and rolled him over, onto his back. That's when I saw ... the wounds ... I ..." Hetherington looked east, as though the ocean could relieve something. "I practiced corporate law, never handled anything remotely criminal or ... violent."

"After rolling Mr. Wix over, what did you do?"

"I ran back to my house and called the police, of course."

"You didn't go inside this place?"

"Certainly not. God knows what I might have found."

"Any idea who might have done this?"

"None. But Wix was one of those you see nowadays."

"One of those?"

"Blacks who have a chip on their shoulder, always assuming racism in a foul-mouthed manner before it's proved."

"And do you think it could have been proved here?"

A smile without any more soul than his eyes.

FOUR

"I'd like to see Lucie Son."

The woman behind the counter at the *Beacon Harbor Weekly* was about thirty, with blonde hair and a kinder face than her profession should allow. "Let me take you back."

She opened a swinging gate in the counter, and I followed her past a clump of occupied computer terminals before we reached a couple with empty chairs.

My guide looked at a closed door in the opposite wall and cupped a hand to her ear. "Oh, no."

"What's the matter?"

"Lucie's been sick ever since her ... for a couple of weeks now."

Concentrating, I could pick up that sound of the dry heaves, muffled by the wall but unmistakable. "Sorry to hear that."

"Just be understanding if she has to rush off on you."

"I will."

The muffled sound of flushing, too, and soon the door opened, a young woman with Asian features coming out. About five-three, she wore no make-up, the wan cast of her face not covered by the color of her skin. The long, black hair was pulled back into a pony-tail, and Son wore hiking boots, plain jeans and the kind of hippie blouse you used to see as the uniform in Harvard Square twenty-odd years ago. She walked unsteadily at first, then perked up a little.

"You okay, Lucie?" said the woman next to me.

"Better, Helen. Thanks."

"This gentleman wants to see you."

By the time Son reached me, Helen was almost back at the counter.

A gesture toward the next work-station. "Pull up a chair."

I dragged the computer swivel over to face Son's, and we sat simultaneously.

"And you're ... ?"

"John Cuddy." I showed her my identification holder.

"Private investigator." She handed it back to me. "What's this all about?"

"I'm looking into the death of Elton Wix."

The wan face hardened. "Who hired you?"

"I'm afraid that's confidential."

"Then I don't think we'll be talking much further."

"Would you reveal one confidential source as a condition of interviewing another?"

It was a moment before Son said, "Why do you want to talk with me?"

"I thought you might be able to tell me about Mr. Wix, maybe something that would help find out who killed him."

Another moment. "You know that Elton and I were seeing each other."

"Yes."

"Okay." Son seemed to be organizing things in her head. "I met Elton about four months ago. He was just starting to 'hit' in the Boston art circles, which made him quite a celebrity up here. I wangled an interview with him for my column."

"Wangled?"

"Elton didn't like to mix with people much. Oh, he'd do the artist turn for the gallery stuff, but he believed that too much socialization warped or blurred his 'vision for the work.' " A wan smile. "I'm afraid I never really understood how he did what he did. That may be why we got together."

"Because you didn't understand his art, you were no threat to it?"

"Something like that, I think." A distant look.

"The police said you wanted them to take DNA samples."

Son snapped back to me. "I want them to find his killer."

"Do you have anybody in mind?"

A little relenting. "His neighbor didn't like him. Real WASPy guy, I think he resented a mixed-race couple next to him."

I stopped. "You were living with Mr. Wix?"

"Oh, no. No, I have my own place. But I'd be over there enough, he could have thought that."

"The neighbor."

"Right."

"Did you know about Mr. Wix's gun?"

"Like, who didn't? Elton always bragged about that, kept it next to his bed. 'Kill me a Klanman, he come looking.' "

"There any reason one would?"

"Not that I know of. But then I don't think it was racial."

I was feeling a little confused, but the woman was also feeling a little sick. "How do you mean?"

"Elton told me either his agent, Patricia Tsoris, had stolen from him, or this gallery owner, Rex Noel, had lied to him."

"And that made Mr. Wix mad?"

"Mad? No. No, it was more like …" Son appeared to be organizing things again. "Like he wanted to believe Rex, because that meant he'd caught Patricia, had power over her. Could kind of expose her, I guess."

Tsoris seemed afraid of roughly the same thing. "Did Mr. Wix say he was going to do anything along those lines?"

"Not in so many words. He was kind of mysterious about it, actually."

"Mysterious?"

"Yes. He just said, 'I'll get mine over this. Yes, I will.' "

"Anything else you can tell me?"

"No. I haven't been feeling too well, so I was working on a column at home the day he was killed."

Which wasn't exactly what I'd asked her.

FIVE

"And how can we help you, sir?"

"Rex Noel?"

"Yes." The man stepped from behind the cash register disguised as reception desk on the left-hand wall of Collage and folded his hands below his belt in roughly a figleaf manner. The belt was distressed leather, holding up double-pleated pants under a loose fitting polo shirt and above tassled loafers. About five-eight and a hundred-forty including any coins in his pockets, Noel had sandy hair so short that the part must have been razored into his scalp.

"I'm interested in seeing pieces by Elton Wix."

A beaming smile. "Seeing we can arrange. Buying will be slightly more difficult."

"Why is that?"

"Well …" He glided toward the back wall, textured plaster with three framed and subtly spotlit pieces on it. Each frame bore a little blue sticky-dot on the lower left corner. "As everyone knows, an artist's body of work increases in value after his death."

"Because that's the end of the supply."

"*Exact-a-mont.* Once the news broke last week, so did the ceiling on the prices that Elton's pieces could command."

"And the blue dots … ?"

"Connote 'sold' works. I'm sure more will come onto the market, but they'll simply cost the earth."

I looked at the three pieces on Noel's wall. Each had a news photo, laminated, of a well-known person. Donald Trump, Whitney Houston, Pope John Paul. Radiating around Trump were the silhouette of a tower; neon dice and poker chips; a high, blonde wig; and dollar signs and cent symbols drawn large and small, thin and wide, in all the colors of the rainbow. Around Houston were microphones, CD cases, and musical symbols like G-clefs and notes. Around the Pope were fragments of stained glass; a tall, gilded headdress and staff; and more dollar signs, some with crosses super-imposed over them.

"Stunning, no?" said Noel.

"Different."

"Very intuitive of you. Anyone can patch together some shards of glossies from a magazine and call it a collage, but not many had Elton's exquisite sense of composition, unified by the perfect selection of themes and symbols to accentuate – no, to incomparably *cap*ture the essence of the subject involved."

"How much did these 'essences' go for?"

"I'm afraid I'm not at liberty to say. But, if you'd like, I could take down your name and advise you of any new pieces that trickle through the pipeline."

"I was thinking more about a rumor that some old pieces trickled out of here for more than Mr. Wix might have thought."

Noel sniffed. "Police, is it?"

"Private investigator."

"Then I don't think I've anything further to add."

As he turned, I said, "Did Mr. Wix believe what you told him?"

Noel hesitated, then turned back to me. "What *I* told him?"

"About his agent maybe shorting him on his share."

A very visible swallowing. "I believe I need to ask you to leave now."

"And I'll go. But when I come back, the police may be with me."

"Look, pal," said Noel. "What's going on?"

Very little of Newbury Street in that last question. "I was hoping you could tell me."

"All I know is that somebody snuffed a rising star who might have gone *mega*. Elton's agent was savvy enough to place his work here, where my customer base is the perfect self-selecting audience, and I was glad to have the pieces, despite how bitchy Elton could be in person. But this gallery is a legitimate operation, and I don't want to be tarred by the same brush as some others who dealt with him. Is that clear enough?"

"For now. I appreciate your time. And the art lesson."

"Both wasted, I'm sure."

❊ ❊ ❊ ❊

Maybe not. Wasted, that is.

Back in my office overlooking Boston Common, I tried to piece together my own collage. Not very artistic, granted, but sometimes just seeing everything in front of you at once can help.

I took out one of those pads of three-inch square paper. From my notes, I lifted buzz words, and wrote one on each piece of paper. Last names like "TSORIS," "HETHERINGTON," "SON," and "NOEL." First names of "PATRICIA," "GEORGE," "LUCIE," and "REX." Even things connected to them, like "COMMISSION," "BINOCULARS," "COLUMN," "GALLERY," and a dozen more. Then I drew a little stick figure of Elton Wix lying on his stomach in the yard, as George Hetherington had described him. Putting the stick figure in the center of my desk blotter, head pointing toward twelve o'clock, I laid the other pieces of paper around it. Not exactly "stunning," to borrow Rex Noel's phrase.

I began rotating the other pieces clockwise around the stick figure. Nothing. Then counterclockwise. Same. Then I began rotating the stick figure itself. A frustrating way to pass the time.

It wasn't until I had the head of the stick figure pointing to the piece of paper with "JUNK" on it that I remembered the three-foot section of 1x4 under Wix's legs. Why did Wix, who must have been in agony and fading fast, push himself onto his deck and forty feet into his yard to fall with a piece of wood under his thighs? Maybe coincidence, but I drew the lumber in at the right place, and suddenly the next rotation of the stick figure pointed to three o'clock and what I thought was the answer.

❄ ❄ ❄ ❄

Helen-of-the-kind-face just let me in through the swinging gate this time. As I approached Lucie Son's computer terminal, she looked up at me.

Her eyes flickered, and I knew I was right.

Son looked back down at her screen. "I'm a little pressed just now, Mr. Cuddy."

"Putting the finishing touches on a column?"

She clacked two keys at once, which made the machine burp and bleep. Then she stared up at me. "Yes."

"The one called 'Sonrise.' "

"Only one I write."

"And you never really understood Mr. Wix's art."

Son tried to pull off baffled, fell a little short. "What are you talking about?"

I sat in the same empty chair I'd used on my earlier visit. "You heard Patricia Tsoris in Collage, telling Mr. Wix about her new lipstick."

"Everybody did. Whatever Elton wanted to know, he always repeated. Loud."

"But you don't wear make-up yourself, so no chance of any 'Black Panther' you applied to one of the wine glasses being connected to you."

Another flicker. "What?"

"And no problem with weapon, either. Mr. Wix provided nicely for that, telling everybody he had one, even where he kept it. All you had to do was get rid of the gun afterwards."

"Are you flipping out on me?"

"No, but I'm guessing that's what Mr. Wix did."

"What Elton did when?"

"When you told him you were pregnant."

Son dropped the staring contest.

I said, "He didn't want a baby, did he?"

Very quietly, she said, "I couldn't figure out what was wrong with me. I mean, I never get the flu, and besides I didn't have any other symptoms except the … morning sickness, and then it hit me. And I just wanted to burst, I was so happy."

"But Mr. Wix wasn't."

Son's distant look. "I told him the night of the opening, after we got back to his place. I thought it would be perfect, you know? Kind of the crowning glory of his night, of his ... life up till then. But he got enraged, telling me he wanted no part of a 'brat' now, now that he was about to ... make it as an artist. He pushed me out the door, saying that when he blew the whistle on his agent, the publicity would shoot him to the stars."

"Was that when you got the idea?"

"The – oh, to shoot him, literally?" Son nodded abruptly. "Yes. I knew about Patricia cheating him, and the lipstick, and the gun. And that neighbor of his who always jogs the same time everyday. So I stayed home from work, and I went over to Elton's, telling him, 'Let's just break it off cleanly, have some wine and forget it.' So he said, 'Sure,' and went into the kitchen and I heard the refrigerator door and I went over to the bed and he must have heard me because he came back into the living room without any glasses and I shot him and shot him and shot him ..."

The run-on sentence ran out of gas. "Because Mr. Wix didn't want your baby."

"*Our* baby. But I did."

"And that's why you were so insistent with the police on the DNA testing."

A slow nod this time. "I don't understand much about art, but I knew Elton's collage pieces would get more and more valuable after he ... was dead. The baby was entitled to that money, Mr. Cuddy, and I wanted to be sure I could prove Elton was the father."

"By matching the baby's DNA with the samples from Mr. Wix that the Medical Examiner would be holding."

"Yes." Her distant look again. "I watched Elton. After I shot him, I mean. I watched him turn and stagger to the back door, and then watched through the kitchen window as he went down the deck steps and into the yard. I didn't know what to do – I'd shot all the bullets in the gun. But then Elton finally stopped and fell."

Son focused on me once more. "You know, finally telling somebody all ... this. It actually makes me feel better."

"Not for long, I'm afraid."

"What do you mean? You can't prove any of it."

"Don't be too sure, Ms. Son."

"Why not?"

"A minute ago, you said you watched Mr. Wix fall."

Wary now. "Yes?"

"Down to his knees, like he was praying, maybe. Then forward, his arms above his head."

Warier. "So?"

"Mr. Wix knew you didn't understand his art."

Now just confused. "What?"

"The collages. The symbolism in them. He kneeled down out in the yard so he could fall onto a board, perpendicular to his body at the thighs. And pitching forward, Mr. Wix used his arms to approximate a circle as best he could, the whole symbol –"

"Symbol? Symbol of what?"

"Circle on top of a stick with a crosspiece halfway down the stick. The medical symbol for 'female.' "

"Female." Her voice sounded hollow.

"And pointing eastward."

The eyes did a little shrug. No comprehension.

I motioned at her computer. "The sun comes up in the east. 'Sonrise.' "

Her eyes closed.

Then, barely audibly, Lucie Son said, "Why couldn't Elton have cared as much about people as he did about his art?"

I had no answer for that one.

CHOU'S GAMBIT

I t was one of those sunny, late-April Mondays that actually made you believe winter had finally released its grip on Boston. Walking at a leisurely pace from my apartment in Back Bay to my office on Tremont Street, I'd worn only a business suit. However, the older man standing in the corridor next to my door evidently didn't share my view of the weather.

He wore a cotton turtleneck under a V-neck sweater and a light, loose-waisted parka. The colors were pastels you'd associate with Florida, the man's deep, leathery tan complementing the image. His hair showed equal amounts of brown and gray, the eyes bright and sharp. I put his age around seventy-five, depending on whether the tan was hiding or adding a couple of years. About five-ten and stocky, he turned to the door and pointed at "JOHN FRANCIS CUDDY, CONFIDENTIAL INVESTIGATIONS" stencilled on the pebbled glass.

"You're Mr. Cuddy?"

A slight accent, German or Polish. "That's right."

"Henry Silverberg." Instead of shaking hands, he looked down at his wristwatch. "Nine-fifteen."

"I'll take your word for it."

"I've been waiting here already twenty minutes."

"If you'd let me know you were coming, I'd have arrived earlier."

Silverberg said, "When I got here, I knocked, but your secretary didn't answer."

"I don't have a secretary." I put my key in the lock and turned the tumbler, swinging the door wide for him.

"What, nobody opens up for you?"

"Uh-unh."

"In my practice, I always had a receptionist, welcome the patients." We entered the office, me going behind the desk, Silverberg moving toward one of the two client chairs in front of it. "A lot of people, they tell me, 'Henry, you're a dentist, you don't need a receptionist,' but I liked the way it made the first-timers feel comfortable, coming to see me."

"Can I take your coat?"

"No, thanks. I just got back from Lauderdale – I'm down there December till last week, the Tennis Club condominiums – and after five months in that sunshine, this today still seems kind of cold to me."

"Dr. Silverberg –"

"Not 'Doctor' anymore. Somebody even your age calls me 'Doctor' or 'Mister,' it makes me feel old, and believe me, seventy-nine is already old enough to feel."

"So, 'Henry,' then?"

"And 'John,' that's all right with you."

"Fine." As we both sat down, I brought a legal pad and pencil to the center of my desk. "What can I do for you?"

Silverberg suddenly looked less comfortable than his former patients probably were with the receptionist. "I got a problem."

"Involving?"

"This friend of mine, Chou."

"Chew?"

"C-H-O-U. Chinese gentleman I play chess with in Brookline."

The town just west of Boston. "He lives there?"

Silverberg seemed confused. "What?"

"Mr. Chou lives in Brookline?"

"Oh, no. I live there, when I'm not in Florida. Chou – and it's just that, no 'mister' for him, either. He's the one first gave me that line about feeling old enough already."

Okay. "And Chou lives ... ?"

"Chinatown, above his convenience store, seven blocks from where we're sitting in this office."

"Seven."

Silverberg now looked a little sheepish. "I measured it off."

"Why?"

"Because I wanted a private detective close enough to him to see what was what, and fast."

"Henry, maybe if you told me what the problem is?"

"You're right." A decisive nod. "I don't think I need the coat now."

I started to rise, but Silverberg waved me down, easily shrugging out of his parka without getting up himself. "This is the beauty of playing tennis, John. Keeps the old body fit, just like chess does for the mind." Laying the parka over his knees, he fixed me with the bright eyes. "Let me give you some background first, so you'll understand the problem, that's all right with you."

I set my pencil on the desk. "Whatever's easiest."

Silverberg's face said it wasn't going to be easy at all. "I come to this country from Germany, nineteen-thirty-four. The 'government' they had in those days explains that, but my brother didn't believe things were going to get so bad. Jacob was two years older, already in his business, so he decided to stay. My leaving was hard – and not just because of leaving him. America had quotas then on Jews. Oh, Roosevelt and everybody else would deny it, they were still alive to argue the point, but the real rules weren't so different from today."

"Today?"

"The new immigration stuff. We hear a lot about it down in Lauderdale, account of all the Latinos working there. Now these great United States aren't going to take anybody from somewhere else hasn't got a 'sponsor' here who already makes twenty thousand a year, because Washington's afraid all these new immigrants are going to sign up for welfare. Twenty thousand, that would have bought a mansion when I come over in 'thirty-four."

"Henry –"

Another wave. "No, no. You're right. I'm getting off the point. Only let me finish the background, so you'll know."

"Go ahead."

"All right, so where ... Jacob, right. Well, I come to America, and Jacob goes to Auschwitz, but I don't even know that for sure until after the war, when I try to get him traced. And that's the end of that."

Silverberg cleared his throat. Over fifty years, and you could still sense the pain.

"So, I'm here, and I work my way through college and dental school. My practice prospers to the point I don't need it anymore. After I retire, though – you married, John?"

I thought of Beth, lying on her hillside in South Boston. "Widower."

"Oh. Oh, I'm sorry." Silverberg shook his head. "But maybe you'll know what I mean, then. Myself, I never married, and after I retire, I realize I'm pretty lonely with no wife. You see, I miss the patients. And the problems in their mouths they'd bring me to fix. The tennis is fine for the body, like I said, but I'm looking for something to do with my mind, and I come back to what Jacob taught me in Germany but never had time for while I was a dentist."

"Chess."

"On the button. There's this park where I play in Brookline, the boards are engraved on concrete table tops, with little chair-benches for the players to sit. All kinds of people, which makes it different. And good intellects, too, which makes it challenging." Silverberg cocked his head. "You play, John?"

"No."

"Pity. You should learn. We have younger ones, too. They're on their lunch breaks, so they play speed chess, just five minutes per player, ten minutes for the whole game. But Chou and me, we like to … linger over our moves, the way my brother and me used to back in Germany. Jacob was the one who told me about the great Jewish champions, like William Steinitz and Emanuel Lasker. Later we had Boris Spassky and Bobby Fischer, but Steinitz and Lasker, together they were international champions for fifty-five years in a row. Can you imagine?"

"Henry –"

"Chou even plays like Jacob. Loves the gambits."

"Gambits?"

"Oh, sorry. I forgot you don't know the game. The beginning in chess is called the 'opening.' Me, I've always liked the 'Ruy Lopez,' which is named after this Spanish monk. There are all kinds of defenses, too. The French, the Sicilian. But Chou goes for the gambits, like the Bishop's or even the King's, where you risk sacrificing a minor piece to gain a positional advantage for the others on the board."

"Does your problem with Chou come from the chess games?"

The uncomfortable look again. "Not exactly."

"Then what is it?"

Silverberg brought a hand to his face, using the thumb and index finger to massage his eyes at the nose. "I think somebody's killed him."

Uh-oh. "In that case, you should be talking to the police, Henry, not a private –"

"No." The hand came down abruptly. "No, John. I take this story to the cops, they're going to say all the right things, but they're going to think, 'senile old buzzard, fried his brains in the sun too long.' "

"What story?"

"What … oh, right. Well, last week, like I said, I get back from Florida, and Tuesday the weather's nice enough – like today – the players are in the park, at the chess tables. So I go over there, only no Chou. Now, you have to understand, John. Chou loves his chess, come over from his store two days a week to play, Tuesdays and Thursdays. Like clockwork."

"But you haven't been in the park since December, right?"

"Right, only it's been the same every year for the last three, ever since I met Chou there the first time. Once, when he was sick, he even called me, let me know he couldn't make it. You see, we're a lot alike, Chou and me. I had a brother in the old country, same for him. We both come to this country with nothing and got citizenship. Each of us our own business, our love of chess." Another wave of the hand. "Oh, there were differences, sure. I never married, Chou married late. His wife died way before I met him, but they had two kids first. In college now, Lily and Peter. Themselves, they never came to the park, but Chou gave me their picture once."

Silverberg dug into a pocket of the parka and produced a couple of photos. One was a posed portrait shot of two children with Asian features, maybe twelve and fourteen, the girl younger, the boy older. The other photo was a candid, showing Silverberg and an Asian man smiling at the camera from an outdoor chess table. A tattered baseball cap shadowed most of the Asian man's face as he reached a right hand to move one of the chess pieces, a sign behind him reading "TOWN OF BROOKLINE, CHESS HERE FOR ALL."

Silverberg said, "That's Chou with me, there."

"How old is he, Henry?"

"Sixty-four when that picture was taken, last October."

I handed the photos back to him. "Why do you think your friend is dead?"

"Not just dead, John. Killed."

"Killed, then."

A deep sigh. "When Chou wasn't at the park last Tuesday, I asked some of the other regulars. They said they hadn't seen him since this one nice day during the January thaw, which worried me. I mean, even with the winter and all up here, there's some good weather, right?"

"Right."

Silverberg darkened. "When he wasn't there Thursday, I couldn't sleep that night. Well, it was either go to the public library and read through three months of death notices, or go to his convenience store and try to see what was what. So, last Friday, I went over to Chinatown."

That sounded wrong. "Why not just call him?"

Sheepish again. "I didn't know his number."

"What?"

Uncomfortable now, waving at me. "I know, I know. It sounds stupid to you, imagine how it would sound to the cops. But even after three years seeing him twice a week when I wasn't in Florida, I never had reason to call the man. When I looked last Thursday in the White Pages, there were fifty, a hundred people last name 'Chou,' and I didn't even know the name of his store."

"Henry –"

"No." He held up a palm in the "stop" sign, then dropped it. "I'm sorry, John. I don't mean to be rude. You see, Chou always just referred to his business as 'my store,' and we were only 'chess' friends, not 'social' ones. Understand?"

"I'm not sure."

"All right, let me put it this way." Silverberg took a breath. "I'm a rich, old dentist. Chou, from the way he dressed and all, didn't have two nickels to rub together. In Lauderdale, it's like that, too. You have tennis friends, the ones you play with because they're your ability level, and then social friends, who have the same interests in the theater or concerts and the means to enjoy them. See now?"

I thought so. "You've never really met Chou outside the chess park."

"On the button."

"Then how did you find his store last Friday?"

"Chou told me it was in Chinatown, between a Korean restaurant and a petshop. So I walked the streets there till I found the right block."

Silverberg grew solemn. "Well, I go in the store, and there's his daughter behind the counter – oh, she'd changed some from that picture I showed you, but it was her, no question in my mind. She was standing with an older gentleman – Chinese, too, who seemed kind of … disabled, like you see stroke victims? So, he's smiling a little goofy, counting out change from the cash register real slow for this woman who's just buying a bottle of spring water. After the woman leaves, I walk up to the counter."

Silverberg shifted in his chair. "I say to Chou's daughter, 'I'd like to see your father.' She says to me, 'This is my father' – pointing to the older gentleman – 'but he has suffered a stroke.' And I look at him and say, 'What?' And she says, 'He cannot talk. I told you, he has suffered a stroke.' So I look from her to him again, John, and you know what I say next?"

I thought I did. "'This man's not Chou.'"

"On the button. She tells me he is, and I tell her he isn't. And I have to get out of there. Already, I can't stand even to be in the store." Silverberg came forward in his chair. "John, I won't pretend to you that I'm some kind of expert on Chinese faces, and except for being older, this guy did resemble Chou. But you don't sit across from a man over a chess board for three years without noticing things. A mole, the creases by the eyes. And for me, his teeth."

"His teeth?"

"I was a dentist, remember? This goofy-smiling older gentleman the daughter's trying to pass off had his own teeth, and they weren't Chou's."

I watched Silverberg. I didn't think him crazy, but his story certainly was, and no police detective with file cabinets full of obvious crimes would have listened long enough to separate the man from the tale.

"What do you want me to do, Henry?"

Silverberg worked his hands a little on top of the parka. "All weekend, I been thinking how I always felt bad about Jacob. I couldn't do anything to stop what the Nazis did to him, except trace him after he was gone. I told you Chou reminded me of Jacob, right?"

"Because of the way he plays chess."

The retired dentist in the pastel clothes nodded, then straightened in his chair. "John, I want you to do for Chou what I did for my brother. I want you to find out what's really happened to him."

I told Henry Silverberg that if he'd give me the address of the convenience store, I'd start right after lunch.

❊ ❊ ❊ ❊

Carrying the white, waxy bag in one hand and a camp stool in the other, I made my way up to her row. When I reached the right headstone, I opened the stool's legs until they formed an "X," then sat with the bag on my lap. Below us, a few hardy souls sailed across the harbor, the air having to be at least twenty degrees colder on the water. I took out the roast beef sub first, followed by the Dr. Pepper, and finally the tin-foiled two ounces of potato chips.

Her voice said, *Irish health food.*

I looked down at the lettering chiseled into the marble. ELIZABETH MARY DEVLIN CUDDY. "I haven't learned much over the years about nutrition, Beth."

So long as you've learned about other things.

"Like living without you?"

No answer for that one.

I said, "A man came to me this morning about an odd case."

Odd in what sense, John?

Summarizing Henry Silverberg's story for Beth didn't make it seem any more likely.

After I finished, there was a pause before, *What are you going to do?*

"Silverberg already asked around at the chess park, and his visiting the convenience store probably blows any chance of surprise there."

Agreed.

"So, I thought I'd try a flanking attack."

It kind of pleased me that Beth took a minute to figure that out. Of course, after you're alone long enough, you learn how to exist on small pleasures.

❊ ❊ ❊ ❊

As I walked into Chinatown, the streets narrowed and the air widened, the tang of exotic spices filling every breath I took. A garbage truck was making the rounds of the back alleys and crowded sidewalks, its rear hoist lifting trash that somehow seemed more basic than what I saw in the dumpster behind my own building. Boxes of cardboard or wood slats, with scant remains of vegetables and fruit in them. Not much wasted paper, either, even though there were more people in business suits than anywhere else in the city but the financial district. A couple of festive banners arced overhead, many of the store signs displaying both English lettering and Asian characters.

I say "Asian," because the area – lying east of Washington Street and west of Atlantic Ave – that everybody still nicknames "Chinatown" should now more accurately be designated "Asiantown." A lot of folks from Mao's old mainland call the neighborhood "home," but Thai, Cambodian, Vietnamese, and so on all struggle there for a decent slice of the American pie.

I saw a modest marquee for the Korean restaurant first. I figured to start with it and then skip over the convenience store to the other flanking business, the petshop.

A slim, middle-aged Asian man in a cuff-linked shirt and conservative tie met me at the door of the restaurant. Maybe twenty small tables were arrayed behind him, only three of them still occupied by dawdling customers. Smiling with bad teeth that included a pair of gold canines in the top row, the slim man said, "One for lunch?"

I stepped inside and slightly past him. "Thanks, but I've already eaten."

The smile faded. "What you want, then?"

There might be greater cooperation if he thought I was official rather than private, so I didn't show him any ID. Instead, and gesturing with my right hand, I said, "I'd like to ask you some questions about the man who owns the business next door."

The smile seemed not just to be gone, but running hard away from him. "Chou is sick. Old, have bad stroke." A respectful mimicking of a right arm that hangs uselessly at the side of the body.

"Someone who knows him is worried about him."

"His children take care for him. No one should worry."

"Maybe if –"

"I am busy. Very busy. Cannot talk now."

But when the slim man turned from me and walked back into the restaurant, he passed all the tables and went through a door that looked more office than kitchen.

* * * *

I crossed the street diagonally away from the convenience store and used the opposite sidewalk, looking into the businesses there rather than the eventual target. After I was far enough along, I recrossed the street diagonally again so as to come up on the petshop fairly blindly.

No one met me at the threshold, but a tiny woman who could have been Laotian stood behind the front counter. She wore a scarf around her hair and was just returning a telephone receiver to its cradle on the wall behind her. Beyond the front counter were stacked aquaria with fish of all hues, the fins of all filigrees. Lizards the size of river rats lay inert on gravel behind glass walls while large, flamboyant birds that I didn't think were parrots did a trapeze act in their cyclindrical, wire-mesh chimney.

As soon as the tiny woman looked up at me, she frowned. "Yes?"

Thinking of the slim man in the restaurant, I tipped my head toward the telephone. "Let me guess. You don't think I'm interested in the iguanas today."

"What you want here?" came next, the voice a little more shrill.

"I want to know what you can tell me about the man who owns the convenience store," this time gesturing with my left hand.

"Chou good man, but he very sick. Bad stroke." She let her right arm flop to its side.

"I see."

"His children take care of him, good care."

"Other than that, nothing is wrong?"

"Nothing. You go now."

I decided to see if I could be in Chou's store before the petshop lady could finish calling, too.

* * * *

There was no name in the small window, but it did display samples of the merchandise. Wheat crackers and radio batteries, oranges and facial tissues. When I came through the door, an Asian woman perhaps in her late teens and an older Asian man were behind the cash register. The woman let her black hair fall onto the shoulders of a green blouse, the man wearing a threadbare flannel shirt and just setting down a closed pocket knife with his left hand, the right dangling loosely at his side. Even if I'd brought Henry Silverberg's photos with me, I'm not sure I could have confirmed the man as being – or not being – the one depicted at the chess park, but I felt pretty confident the woman was a later version of the daughter in the portrait shot.

With a brave smile, she said, "You have an idea what you want?"

Unlike the people in the restaurant and petshop, no accent, except for a little dash of Boston making the "a" in "idea" an "er" sound. "Is this Mr. Chou?"

The woman nodded, and the older man followed her lead.

I said, "A friend of his is very concerned about him."

She kept smiling. "I'm his daughter, Lily. Could I see some identification, please?"

I took out the holder with the laminated card and opened it for her.

Lily Chou said, "You're a private investigator?"

"That's right."

Another nod. "Then we have nothing to say to you." She closed the holder and passed it back to me. "Please leave."

"If you don't talk to me here, we may all end up having a conversation with the police."

The brave smile never faltered. "I don't think so. My father is old and sick." She turned to him. "He has suffered –"

"– very bad stroke, I know. How about the name of his doctor?"

"That's none of your business. Now please leave before I'm the one to call the police."

It was their store, and I had no right to stay, but I also had the feeling Henry Silverberg would be disappointed in me.

❊ ❊ ❊ ❊

Or maybe not.

I noticed the tail two blocks away on Washington Street, where the pedestrian traffic begins to thin out before reaching the large stores that constitute Downtown Crossing. A twentyish Asian guy, he was dressed in a crewneck sweater and baggy jeans. When I turned casually at a corner, lolling my head as though loosening a crick in my neck, he stopped to read thoroughly the posted menu of a coffee shop. At the next corner, he was still behind me, amateurish enough that I caught the guy staring in my direction when he didn't realize I could see him in a window's reflection.

Or recognize him, for that matter. From the portrait shot with his sister.

It wasn't hard to turn Peter Chou. I just popped into Filene's at the Summer Street entrance and took the up escalator. From the next level, I could watch him, walking first slowly, then quickly around the ground floor, looking for me. Eventually he stopped, shoving his hands into the side pockets of his jeans and going back out the same door we'd both used.

I got on the down escalator and followed, even though I was pretty sure where the trail would lead.

❊ ❊ ❊ ❊

From the corner of his father's block, I saw Peter Chou go in the front door of the convenience store. I went around back.

There was no one in the alley behind the Korean restaurant, Chou's store, or the petshop. Moving to the middle door of the three, I put my ear to the jamb. Talking on the other side, occasionally rising to bursts of shouting.

A small, barred window was at head height next to the door. I looked through it.

Around a table that seemed to function as a desk, Lily Chou sat with the older man while Peter Chou paced and harangued at them. Happily, he used English, and enough carried through the glass to get more than the gist of his one-sided conversation. Of even more interest was the way the "stroke victim" passed the time as he seemed to ignore Peter's lecture.

The older man whittled with that pocket knife I'd seen, grasped now in his left hand while the right did just fine holding a hunk of wood securely.

I tried the back door quietly. Unlocked, probably to put trash out for the garbage truck I'd seen earlier.

Well, nothing ventured …

They were not pleased to see me. Peter picked up a sawed-off baseball bat, brandishing it more like a nightstick. The older man stood abruptly, the knife poised for close-in work.

Only Lily Chou stayed still, speaking first and briefly in Chinese, then in English. "Peter, put that down."

"This guy's got no right –"

"Peter," her voice resigned now, "it's over."

I said, "Not necessarily," but waited until Peter lowered the bat and the old man, at Lily's tugging on his sleeve, sat back down.

The young woman looked up at me, her head tilted to the side. "What do you mean by 'not necessarily?' "

Leaning against the wall, I said, "Your little charade. It may not have to stop."

Peter Chou didn't want to give up his bone. "You followed me back here, didn't you?"

"That doesn't matter now," said his sister. Then, to me, "How much do you know?"

"Enough, from standing out there while Peter laid it out in lavender."

Her brother didn't like that, but at least he didn't say so.

I came off the wall slowly, rolling my shoulders to take the fight-or-flight tension out of them. "Okay, here's what I do know. Sometime in the last three months, the owner of this store had a stroke, a massive one that left him functionally paralyzed."

Lily beat her brother to the punch. "People recover."

"But, unfortunately, your father didn't. He died."

"That's not true," said Peter. "He's right here."

I looked at both males. "I saw a photo of your father, Peter. He was moving a chess piece, a very careful thing for him, I suspect, especially when he knew someone was aiming a camera at him."

"So?"

"So he was using his right hand, and this nice gentleman with the knife is lefthanded."

The daughter shook her head.

I said, "Before he died, your father told you what he wanted to happen."

"He couldn't." Lily Chou looked back up at me, wearily. "After the stroke in February, our father couldn't talk. His mind was still there, but the stroke took away his ability to speak as well as move. All he could do was blink. Once for yes, twice for no. It took nearly a week of asking him questions before we could figure out what our father wanted us to do."

I glanced at the older man. "Does he have English?"

"Just a few words," said Lily.

Which made a "stroke" the perfect cover for not speaking. Or even understanding what people might say to him. "Who is he?"

"Our uncle."

I remembered something Henry Silverberg told me. "Your father's brother?"

"Yes. He stayed in China when our father came here. Uncle worked hard, saved his money. Our father wanted him to join us in the States for years, but Uncle wouldn't hear of it. Until this January, when things got really bad in his province and he wrote our father from China."

Peter chimed in again. "I went to the Immigration Service at the federal building here, to get information about it. They said under the new regulations, our father had to be earning over twenty thousand dollars a year in order to 'sponsor' our uncle." The son laced the word "sponsor" with contempt. "I was already a junior in college, and Lily a freshman. No way our father could show that kind of income from this little hole-in-the-wall."

The daughter said, "Our neighbors thought that was who you were."

"I'm sorry?"

She motioned toward the walls. "The people from the restaurant and the petshop. We had to tell them what we were doing, and they rehearsed what to say if an Immigration officer ever showed up."

And I hadn't shown the neighbors any ID to dispel that impression. "But while your father didn't qualify as a sponsor, he was already a citizen himself."

"Yes," said Peter Chou. "And proud of it. So, after his stroke, he came up with a plan."

Lily over-rode her brother. "It was simple, really. Uncle had enough money to get here illegally, by boat. And he did, last month. Then our father …" She shook her head again.

Peter had to swallow, hard. "Our father decided to die, to give his brother his identity and therefore his citizenship, too, the chance here that 'our government' wouldn't provide."

I recalled Henry Silverberg's comment about quotas on Jews wanting to immigrate to America in the 'thirties. "I think once my client hears the whole story from me, he'll leave you in peace."

Lily Chou spoke as though she hadn't heard me. "After the stroke, our father willed his own death. He literally sacrificed himself so that Uncle could improve his position in life."

Looking into her eyes, I thought, "Chou's Gambit," but kept it to myself.

VOIR DIRE

ONE

Bernard Wellington, Esquire, had that mournful look of an old dog betrayed by incontinence.

I watched Bernie ease himself into the highbacked swivel chair behind his desk, a muzzy twilight through the wide bay window silhouetting both man and furniture. An inch taller than my six-two-plus, you'd have pegged him an inch shorter, almost four decades spent bent over law books stooping his shoulders and spoiling his posture. A widow's peak of black hair coexisted peacefully with the fringe of snow at sideburns and temple. Wellington's face and hands were disproportionately long, his voice a baritone burred by the long-term effects of good scotch. Descended from a Boston Brahmin family, he'd betrayed his heritage in choosing criminal defense work coming out of Harvard lo those many years ago.

That fine October Monday, though, Bernie had left a message with my answering service around lunchtime, asking me to meet him in his office at 5:00 P.M. Meaning after court.

As I took a client chair, the nail on Wellington's right middle finger began picking at some leather piping on the arm of the highback. "John Francis Cuddy, it's been a while."

I hadn't seen him since doing the preliminary investigation for one of his armed robbery defendants three months earlier. "What've you got, Bernie?"

"What I've got is Michael Monetti."

The *Globe* and the *Herald* both had run third-page stories when Monetti, a career hood, was indicted some months back for the attempted murder of an overweight "business associate" on some scam.

I said, "The trial ought to be coming up soon."

"We impanelled the jury last Friday afternoon. Which is why I've asked you here."

A little late in the game to be bringing in a private investigator. "Go ahead."

130

"I will, John. But first, indulge me a moment?"

"It's your dime, Bernie."

Wellington cleared his throat, the way I'd seen him do in the courtroom to focus attention on himself without having to raise his voice. "As I believe you know, the Commonwealth of Massachusetts has been one of the few states in the Union not permitting attorney voir dire of prospective jurors."

"But you can ask the judge in advance to submit questions for them, right?"

"Right. However, without personally forcing individual jurors 'to speak the truth' before being impanelled, I don't get much information or guidance toward exercising peremptory challenges on them. The typical juror questionnaire provides me just generic data such as occupation, marital status, and children's ages. That's the reason for this new experiment."

"Experiment?"

"Our esteemed legislature passed a bill establishing a pilot project in three counties. Under the project, each attorney has up to thirty minutes to question jurors on bias, temperament, et cetera, et cetera."

I thought about it. "Fairly helpful when you're representing somebody as mobbed up as Monetti."

Wellington seemed hurt. "My client is not 'mobbed up,' John."

"I don't recall any esteemed judge letting him out on bail."

"And a travesty, that, especially when his extended family has been in the front row of the courtroom audience every minute of the trial. The proud father is a former brick mason, the doting mother a retired school teacher. Michael's older sister prospers as a registered beautician, and he once shared with me the career of a second cousin who does stand-up comedy, like that chap Rich –"

"Bernie?"

A pause before, "What?"

"Save the 'he comes from a good family' argument for the sentencing phase of the case, all right?"

A stony look. "All right."

"I still don't see why you want me to come in now."

The look softened, and Wellington leaned back into his chair's headrest, the leather bustle depressed and cracked from the countless times he must have pondered knotty problems of strategy and tactics. "I'm troubled by one of the jurors, John."

"How do you mean?"

"Our case falls under this new pilot project, and I had a truly splendid sequence of questions to include in my voir dire. But, for all the prospective male jurors called to the box from the pool, Michael insisted I use his questions instead."

"His questions?"

"Correct. My client wanted to know if they'd ever been in the armed forces, or arrested, or even if they'd worked in a 'strategically sensitive' industry."

Didn't make sense to me. "I can maybe see the 'arrested' part, Bernie, but what do the rest of Monetti's questions have to do with his attempted-murder charge?"

"Nothing, John. And worse, Michael's approach squandered the opportunity to use the individual voir dire as a way of warming up the jury for him."

"So what happened with them?"

"The male jurors, you mean?"

"Yes."

"Two had in fact been arrested, and the prosecution used peremptory challenges on both."

"Meaning Monetti's questions actually helped the other side decide who it should ding?"

"Correct again." Wellington seemed to sour at the memory. "Of the remaining potential males called from the pool, one had been in the Army, the other the Navy. Michael had me challenge both."

"Why?"

"He didn't say."

And I didn't see Monetti's strategy. "What about the rest of the jurors?"

Wellington closed his eyes for a moment. "One had worked at a defense think-tank on Route 128, and my client wanted him off, too. However, the three who answered negatively to all of Michael's questions were eventually seated."

"Because neither the prosecutor nor you challenged them."

"That's right," said Wellington. "But believe me, I wanted to knock off one of the three, a Mr. Arthur Durand."

I thought about it. "I'm guessing he's the juror who's 'troubling' you."

A nod. "I didn't like him, John. The juror questionnaire said Mr. Durand was unemployed, never married, no kids. In person, he also had this tendency of scratching his nose and squirming in his seat." Wellington caricatured both. "Plus, the man's hair and clothes weren't terribly neat, and he had rather a dopey cast to his eyes."

"I don't know, Bern. This Durand sounds like perfect juror material for your guy Monetti."

Another hurt look. "Except for Michael's hundred-dollar razor cut—courtesy of the talented older sister – and thousand-dollar suits. Anyway, I just didn't like Mr. Durand, but my client insisted on keeping him."

I shook my head. "Bernie, what aren't you telling me here?"

Wellington sighed. "We finished impanelling Friday afternoon, Mr. Durand being the last one seated. Then the jury was excused for the weekend and went home."

"No sequestration order?"

"Not for 'just' attempted murder, John." A deeper sigh. "So, we reconvene this morning, and guess what?"

"I'm drawing a blank, Bernie."

"All the jurors show up, including our Mr. Durand. However, it being just the first day of testimony, I didn't really know them very well yet."

"Know them?"

"Yes. After a few days of trial – even without attorney voir dire at the beginning – the jurors become burned into your brain by face and seat number."

"Because you're looking at them while the prosecutor is at bat with a witness?"

"Or while I'm cross-examining. But the first morning of a new case, I probably couldn't pick five of the jurors out of a line-up."

"Except for this Durand."

Wellington came forward in his chair. "Yes and no. I look over at him, and I notice he's gotten a haircut. The clothes are about the same, but when I move around the courtroom, his eyes are following me, like Mr. Durand is now actually paying attention. Oh, he still fidgets in his chair and scratches his nose, but something … I don't know, bothers me."

I shook my head some more. "Bern?"

"Yes?"

"What else aren't you telling me?"

Wellington leaned back again, now swinging his chair in a slow, twenty-degree arc. "I've represented Michael on and off for the better part of two decades, John. Despite my Herculean efforts on those earlier occasions, his past record combined with another conviction this time around would carry a life sentence."

"And?"

A nearly glacial sigh now. "And once before – years ago – Michael had two of his loyal employees seek to 'influence' someone supposedly in the Commonwealth's 'Witness Protection' program."

"That was bright of him."

"I'm afraid my client learns a lesson hard, John."

I chewed on it. "Meaning you're afraid Monetti may have had his muscle pay a visit to the non-sequestered Arthur Durand."

Wellington closed his eyes. "That other time Michael tried it, the whole case nearly blew sky-high. Fortunately, the witness called me instead of the prosecutor."

"Called you?"

"To request a 'cash consolation' for his 'mental anguish.'"

I thought I knew Bernie better than that. "You didn't pony up the money."

A shocked expression. "Of course not. But as a result, we had to take a plea bargain thirty-percent worse than the deal originally offered by the prosecution. I told Michael, 'never again,' or I was through representing him."

I didn't envy Wellington his ethical stand. "So, what do you want me to do?"

He leaned back into the cracked headrest, his fingernail picking at the leather piping some more. "I don't know, John. Perhaps you could come to court tomorrow, watch Mr. Durand for a while in the jury box, and then follow him afterward. That might give me some sense of whether Michael's stepped over the line again."

"Bernie, you want a private investigator shadowing a current juror?"

"Unless you've got a better plan."

Frankly, I'd meant that I was thinking about turning down the assignment altogether. But the return of the mournful, hang-dog look on Bernie's face kind of took that option off the board.

I said, "Would tomorrow after lunch be all right?"

"You can't make it any earlier?"

"There's somebody I want to visit in the morning."

Bernard Wellington, Esquire, started to ask me who, but remembered just in time to catch himself.

TWO

There really aren't any trees on her hillside to turn yellow or orange in the autumn, but the grass does what it can by exchanging summer's green for a salt-bleached brown. And the breeze off the harbor water is bracing enough, the gulls shrieking as they scavenge in that part of South Boston where Beth and I grew up, got married, and still spend time together.

In a manner of speaking.

I drew even with her row, opening the little campstool I carry now to spare my bad knee too much standing. The headstone reads as it always has. ELIZABETH MARY DEVLIN CUDDY. No easier to look at, though.

John, why aren't you working?

Smiling, I squared my butt on the stool. "What, you don't think your enterprising husband could have a cemetery for a client?"

Beth paused. *Something's troubling you.*

"No man could ever fool a good wife."

Never kept you from trying. Want to talk about it?

I found that I did.

As always, she listened patiently. Then, *So what's really the problem for you, the client or the case?*

"A little of both, I guess. Bernie Wellington's just fine. I even admire him for that stubborn way he clings to his ethics. But I don't like working for Michael Monetti, and I really don't like risking my license by following a current juror in a felony case."

But you're working for Wellington, not Monetti, right?

"Technically."

Literally. And whatever you find out might make the system work better, not worse. So, you really aren't doing anything wrong.

I didn't have a counter-argument. "Will you represent me should the system disagree?"

Another pause, but this one more like the time it takes to force a smile. *Would that I could, John Cuddy. Would that I could.*

As a gull wheeled overhead, somebody said, "Amen."

❊ ❊ ❊ ❊

Back in my office on Tremont Street across from the Boston Common, I called a friend named Claire who had the computer access of a Microsoft billionnaire. She answered on the third ring, and I asked her to run "Durand, Arthur," through what she calls her "data bases." Claire said she'd have to get back to me, and I told her to leave a message with my service. Then I locked up, went downstairs, and crossed over to the Park Street Under subway.

❊ ❊ ❊ ❊

Michael Monetti had attempted the killing of his associate in Cambridge rather than Boston, so the trial was being held at the relatively modern Middlesex Superior Courthouse across the Charles River rather than our dilapidated Suffolk County one. A Green Line trolley carried me to Lechmere Station in East Cambridge, and I walked the three blocks over to the tall, gray-stoned building. After clearing metal detectors at the lobby

CUDDY PLUS ONE / 136

level, I rode an elevator to the sixth floor.

The courtroom itself had hush-colored carpeting, polished oak benches, and a domed ceiling. From earlier experiences, I knew that dome gave the space the acoustics of a concert hall, ostensibly so no one in the audience outside the bar enclosure would have to strain in order to hear testimony from the witness stand next to the judge's bench. In reality, though, so much as a whisper from anywhere in the room, including counsel tables, could be heard clearly everywhere.

Given the lunch hour, I was able to get an aisle seat in a row on the prosecution side of the audience. On the first bench across the aisle sat the people I took to be the Monetti family. An older man with scarred hands and an older woman with a stern demeanor were sandwiched around a fiftyish woman whose face shared characteristics of each apparent parent. Other people in the second row comforted them by nodding in unison or squeezing a shoulder.

Suddenly, a side door near the front of the bar enclosure opened, and Bernie Wellington came through it. He was followed by a slick, well-dressed guy in his late thirties, two bailiffs – one male, one female – leading him into the courtroom. I recognized Michael Monetti from the media coverage of his indictment. He shared the family features, but whereas the other members looked stalwart, Mikey resembled a killer whale somebody had shoe-horned into a suit.

As Bernie Wellington made eye contact with me, Monetti sat down at the defense table, then turned in his chair toward the front row of his cheering section. Smiling, he told them not to worry. The jail food wasn't so bad, he'd had worse, how was their lunch, and so on. The dome's acoustics carried every syllable back to me.

After the stenographer moved toward her seat and the court clerk toward his kangaroo pouch in front of the bench, the judge appeared from her chambers door, everyone rising. She was African-American and fairly young. When we were all settled again, the female bailiff who'd escorted Michael Monetti into the courtroom went to another side door and knocked. Seconds later, the jurors began filing through and into their rectangular box against the wall. Once they were seated, too, the bailiff took a chair near the telephone table at our audience end of the jury.

Then Wellington stood and asked the judge if he could have a moment. She granted his request, and he came through the gate of the bar enclosure, walking down the aisle to me.

Leaning over, Bernie brought his lips to within an inch of my ear, his voice as delicate as a lover's kiss. "Thanks, John. Durand is in seat number

Twelve, closest to you and that court officer."

I nodded, but waited until Wellington arrived back at the defense table, Monetti tugging on Bernie's sleeve as he wrote something on a pad. After that decent interval, I looked over to the bailiff seated at our end of the jury box. Just past her in the last seat of the front row was a skinny man scratching his nose with his left index finger. He had dark hair which indeed looked freshly cut, a suit jacket with lapels ten years old, and a collared shirt without benefit of tie. Suddenly, the skinny man shifted a little in his chair before cupping the scratching hand over his mouth and whispering to the young female juror on his right. She rushed one of her own hands toward her teeth, stifling a laugh.

The judge glared at the two of them in a way that told me it wasn't the first time she'd done so. Then the prosecutor – a red-haired and freckled-faced lad who could have passed for twelve at a movie theater box office – recalled one of his witnesses to the stand.

A police lab tech, she waxed eloquent about various fibers found at the scene of the crime. I tuned her out and glanced occasionally toward the jury. To the naked eye, Arthur Durand was paying attention, all right.

After the lab tech, the prosecutor put on a male ballistics expert, who testified that the three bullets removed from the victim's ample soft tissue came from the nine-millimeter Sig Sauer carried by Michael Monetti in violation of this statute and that. I left the courtroom just as the ballistics witness stepped down off the stand, because I wanted to be outside the building and in position to follow juror Durand on foot, by cab, or via public transportation.

* * * *

Public trans' it t'was.

At a little after five, Durand made his way through the courthouse door, his shoes making the clacking noise of a cheap computer keyboard as he walked to Lechmere Station. Instead of the subway, though, he hopped an Arlington Heights bus, and I climbed on very casually with a bunch of "other" transferring commuters. The bus made stops through East Cambridge and then Somerville, Durand getting off in a decaying neighborhood about half a mile before the Arlington town line.

I followed him down the bus's steps and out the door, crossing the street so as to parallel his route of march. He passed a couple of alley mouths with dumpsters slightly overflowing. At a wider side-street, Durand turned. When I reached the intersection, I saw a block of wooden, three-story houses.

I waited until he stopped at the stoop to a house painted a hardware-sale shade of lavender. If Durand hadn't turned his head toward the car parked diagonally across and up the street, though, I'm not sure I would have spotted them.

Two men, sitting in the front seat of a beige, white-walled Ford, the Crown Victoria model. The guy at the wheel was sipping through a straw from a big, fast-food cup. His partner on the passenger side was motionless except for a single tug on his ear lobe, the way Carol Burnett used to end her monologue.

Then Arthur Durand went up the stoop and into the lavender three-decker. I kept walking, but only around the block.

The Crown Vic was now halfway down the street from me. Unfortunately, I couldn't see its rear license plate because of a truck between us. On the other hand, I'd certainly known a lot of vehicles like it over the years.

The favorite unmarked car of plainclothes police everywhere in the state, though usually with only black-walled tires.

I couldn't see why Arthur Durand would be getting special protection unless Michael Monetti's stupid move on the earlier-case witness had gotten around. However, best to invest some time and be sure.

I moved to the other side of the street, which let me see the back of the two men's heads but still not their registration tag. The driver stopped sipping his drink and turned to his partner, saying something. The wheelman had straight, sandy hair, the other dark, curly hair, which was about the extent of description I could get without becoming obvious enough to be made by them.

I found a quiet doorway and waited.

It was nearly midnight – and me nearly starving – when the driver turned to his partner again, the other nodding and tugging on his ear some more. Then finally the Crown Victoria started up and pulled away.

But not so fast I didn't get their tag number.

THREE

A groggy, "Who the ... ?"

Into my end of the phone, I said, "Claire, this is John Cuddy."

"What time is it?"

"By my watch, seven A.M."

Her voice grew an edge. "Seven? You call fucking farmers at seven, Cuddy. Cyber-wizards, we like to sleep a little more toward noon."

"I've got a lot to do today, Claire, and I didn't pick up your message until after twelve last night."

"Yeah, well, hold on a minute."

A bonking noise came across the wire along with a distant, muffled, "Shit."

Then Claire's voice got closer and clearer. "Goddam phone. I should get a speaker thing, one of you guys ever paid me half what I'm worth for finding all this stuff for you."

"Your weight in gold, Claire."

"That some kind of crack?"

"No, it –"

"I mean, I lost five pounds in the last month, and I don't take kindly to –"

"A compliment, Claire."

"What?"

"It wasn't a crack, it was a compliment. As in, 'you're worth your weight in gold.' "

"Yeah, well, remember that when you're writing my check." A rustle of paper. "Let's see ... let's see ... 'Durand, Arthur,' right?"

"Right."

"Okay, with no middle initial, I wasn't sure how many I'd turn, but I've got three out by Springfield, two north of Worcester – probably a father-and-son thing – and just the one in our own Slummerville."

"Unkind, Claire. Give me the Somerville listing."

"That's Durand, Arthur 'G.' as in 'George.'" More rustling. "Let's see ... No service record, no arrest record."

So, Durand had told the truth answering those questions.

Claire said, "He does have a driver's license, but no current car registration. Social Security is – you want the number and all?"

"Not necessary. Has there been any activity on the account?"

"Nothing from job withholding. Just a ... yeah. Yeah, he's been collecting unemployment for about three months now."

In other words, a man who might be vulnerable to a bribe offer. "And before that?"

"Worked in a video store."

"Any time in 'sensitive industries?' "

"What, you mean defense contractors, that kind of thing?"

"Yes."

"I think you overestimate our Durand, Arthur G."

"How about bank records?"

"Simple savings and checking," said Claire. "No real activity beyond depositing his unemployment and writing his rent checks."

"You have a payee on those?"

"Yeah. 'Stralick,' that's S-T-R-A-L-I-C-K, Rhonda, M."

"Address?"

"Same as your guy shows in Somerville."

A resident landlady. "Any credit cards."

"Negative."

"Bank loans?"

"Also *nega-tivo*, though I gotta tell you, Cuddy, I can't see how this Durand could qualify to finance anything beyond a tattoo."

"You turn up much else, Claire?"

"No records of marriage, divorce, or birth of child. The guy's your basic loner/loser."

"I can ask if he's available?"

"I'm not that fucking desperate, thank you very much. Let me just total your tab here."

"Hold it, Claire."

"Why?"

"I've got a license plate I'd like you to run."

"Jesus, Cuddy, you have any idea how much of an uproar the Registry of Motor Vehicles is in about this new federal law?"

"Which law's that, Claire?"

"The one's supposed to keep 'stalkers' from getting computer access to the home addresses of any sweeties they see driving by. But, if the Commonwealth doesn't pass its own statute, we're –"

"Claire?"

"What?"

"Just this one tag, please. And today, if possible."

A grunt. "Why not? You got me up at the crack of dawn, I'll have plenty of time to fucking *carpe diem* and get the registration for you, too."

❊ ❊ ❊ ❊

I waited until after court would resume at nine to walk down to my old Honda Prelude behind the apartment building. Going to Arthur Durand's place by car would be a lot more direct than trolley-and-bus, and in seven hours the night before I'd seen all of two cabs cruising the drag at the foot of his street.

I made my way to Somerville using the Western Ave bridge and Central Square in Cambridge. Turning at Durand's corner, I did a drive-by of the lavender three-decker but didn't see any Crown Victoria staking out the block. I did find a parking space near the next intersection, though, and took it.

Walking back to Durand's building, I studied its exterior. If you could forgive the color, the clapboard facade was fairly well maintained, especially compared to its neighbors. I climbed the stoop, three bells mounted next to the door having just unit numbers rather than names below them. Figuring that an owner would live on the first floor to enjoy the backyard, I started with "1."

I was about to press the button again when the door huffed open, a piece of rubber insulation making for a pretty tight fit against the jamb. The woman on the other side was trying a little too hard to still look forty. Her platinum blonde hair was spun around her head like cotton candy, biggish ears not quit hiding under it. The facial features pushed through make-up applied in layers, and even a nice manicure couldn't hide the veins bulging on top of her hands. She wore a sweatsuit the color of the clapboards and fuzzy bedroom slippers.

"And who might you be, luv?"

A slight English accent. "John Cuddy."

Hooding her eyes, she canted her head. "Well, now, John. You're the cute one, aren't you?"

Ah, but consider the source. "Ms. Stralick?"

A wariness now crossed her eyes. "You know my name?"

" 'Stralick, Rhonda M.' " I showed her my identification.

"A private investigator, is it?"

"That's right."

"I don't know nothing about anything."

"You don't have to. I'm just here for an employer who's thinking of hiring one of your tenants."

Wary became surprised. "Arthur?"

"Probably. I have 'Durand, Arthur G.' "

Stralick didn't seem convinced. "Who wants to hire him?"

"I'm afraid that's confidential. But what I have to do won't take very long."

Another change of expression. "Good. That'll give us more time to get acquainted, won't it?"

Said the spider to the fly. "Could I come in?"

With one of her arms, the spider made a sweeping gesture.

Stralick led me along a short corridor to an apartment entrance, just past the base of a staircase that would serve the upper two floors of her house. "Please excuse the mess, John."

That would take some doing. In the living room, television trays functioned poorly as magazine racks, some daytime talk show splayed but muted across a wide color screen. Three teen-aged girls – one white, one black, one Latina – sat awkwardly on a stage, an older man sporting evangelist hair roaming the audience with a handheld mike. The brightly printed caption at the low left of the screen read, "Step-daughters pregnant by their step-fathers."

I thought, *And the mothers who loved them both.*

"What was that, luv?" said Stralick, behind me.

I must have thought out loud. "Nothing."

There was a flower-print armchair with the bulbous design of a 'fifty-two Chevy. I went to it as my hostess took the matching couch, near enough to me that our knees almost touched.

Then she trotted out the hooded-eyes trick again. "So, what do you want to talk about?"

"Mr. Durand indicated on his job application that he was currently unemployed."

"Three months worth," said Stralick.

"I'm sorry."

"No need to be sorry, luv." She licked her lips. "What I meant was, he hasn't come up with the rent for the last little while."

"I see. Before that, though, was he prompt in his obligations to you?"

"Money-wise, yes."

"How about 'otherwise'?"

A shrug. "Arthur helps me out with the storm windows, the snow-shoveling, that sort of thing." A smile Stralick probably thought was coy. "But for real 'otherwise,' he's not exactly the life of the party."

"Fine with my client."

"You don't understand, John. After I divorced the mound of shit who lured me to your fine country, I got a little lonely. But Arthur, he's quiet as a churchmouse, he is. Man's got the third floor, my bedroom's on the second."

Stralick paused, my chance to jump in, no doubt. When I didn't, she made a face before saying, "Weeks can go by, and I won't even hear him, much less see him. No taste for fun, Arthur." Another wetting of the lips. "If you get my drift."

"Sober, responsible types make better employees."

Stralick's eyes narrowed to slits. "I hope you're not as dull as your client, luv."

I gave her an ingratiating smile. "Any reason you can think of why Mr. Durand shouldn't be hired?"

"Only if it'd mean you'll visit with me longer."

A bulldog, Ms. Stralick. "I wonder, then, could I get a look at his apartment?"

Now wary again. "Why?"

"I just like to see the place where a prospective employee lives. Helps me put a little flavor into my report, maybe even turn it into a full-blown recommendation."

"God knows that'd be a help, what with him in arrears on his rent the way he is."

"And it would also be good if my visit today could stay our little secret, okay?"

"I like 'secrets things' as much as the next girl, luv, but I do have a question first."

"What's that?"

Back to coy. "If you know Arthur's unemployed, what makes you think he's not up there now?"

"Because Mr. Durand advised my client he'd be on jury duty for a while."

Stralick finally seemed convinced. "Right, then. Only I have to go with you, of course."

"Of course," I said, neutrally.

❊ ❊ ❊ ❊

"Kind of captures him, if you get my drift."

Rhonda Stalick had managed to rub or bump against me three times during our trip up the staircase. Arthur Durand's apartment consisted of a living room with bay window in front, bedroom next, kitchen and bathroom in the back. The worn, faded furniture seemed to be the only furnishings, and the rooms gave off a spic-and-span sensation. Which didn't tell me much.

What wasn't there told me something, though. No knickknacks, keepsakes, or even photos. More like a large, spartan motel room.

At least until you got to the kitchen.

"Damn him!" Stralick went to the sink, using a paper towel from a cylindrical dispenser to crush three or four cockroaches scurrying over a dead pizza box on the counter. There were beer cans and other take-out trash here and there. "Arthur's usually neat as a pin, he is."

"Maybe Mr. Durand had somebody over last night and forgot to clean up."

"Not a chance. No family, no visitors, no personality. That's Arthur, to a tee." She began to lift the box by its edges.

"You might want to leave that where it is."

Stralick looked at me. "Why?"

"So Mr. Durand won't know you let somebody in to see his apartment."

"Oh. Right you are, luv." She let the box drop back onto the counter, then made a ritual of wiping her hands across the thighs of her sweatsuit. "I hope this business with the bugs doesn't ruin our nice little mood."

Seeing my out, I took it. "Afraid so. Delicate stomach."

"Just my luck." Stralick tried to put on a happy face. "Well, then. Next time you're in the neighborhood, you'll stop and visit a while, won't you?" Now the hooded eyes again. "If you get my drift."

More like her tidal wave, and I managed to make it down the stairs before Rhonda Stralick could guide me in her own touchy-feely way.

❈ ❈ ❈ ❈

I'd just put the key in the Prelude's doorlock when the beige Crown Vic turned onto the block. I ducked my head a little, but I couldn't do much to disguise getting into the car and pulling out of the parking space just up from the lavender three-decker.

Glancing in my rearview mirror, I saw the sandy-haired driver had slewed his vehicle to the curb. He was squinting in my direction and talking to the dark-haired ear-tugger, who himself was writing something down.

Probably the letters and numbers on my license plate, but there wasn't much I could do about that, either.

FOUR

Back in the office, I dialed Bernie Wellington's number. His secretary told me that, not surprisingly, he was still in court on the Monetti case. I asked her to have him return my call as soon as possible.

I considered trying Claire again, too, but twice in one day seemed to be skating over the edge of her good will. Paperwork on other cases occupied me until almost three, when the phone rang.

A sound nearly as shrill as her voice.

"John Cuddy."

"You own a pencil?"

"Ready, Claire."

"All right, let's see ... let's see ... Yeah, the tag belongs to a rental agency."

That felt wrong, though it explained the white-walled tires. "You sure?"

"I'm insulted. But not as much as if I was the one actually running the plate."

"Give me that again?"

"I told you about this new federal crackdown on computer access, right?"

"Right."

"Okay, so I had this friend of mine over at the Registry do the search for me. He says the tag belongs to a Ford Crown Vic – some ridiculous color that amounts to 'beige' – and the car belongs to, and I quote, 'Best-Ride Car Rentals, Inc.,' over by the airport. Here's their address."

The name meant nothing to me. Writing it down – along with the number and street Claire gave me – I said, "You ever hear of this outfit?"

"No, but my friend at the Registry has."

"In what context?"

"In the connected context."

Uh-oh. "A mob launderette?"

"Or maybe just a captive business the wiseguys turn to when their own wheels ought not to be involved. Help you any?"

"Maybe, maybe not. But thanks, Claire."

"Hey, Cuddy, do me a favor, huh?"

"What's that?"

"Mail my check before you pay these 'Best-Ride' people a visit, okay?"

Couldn't blame her for asking.

❊ ❊ ❊ ❊

After leaving two more messages for Bernie Wellington and not getting a return call, I locked up for the night at five-fifteen and went downstairs to the parking space behind my office's building. I got in the Prelude and crawled with the rush-hour traffic to a tavern in South Boston called the "Jack O'Lantern."

The beginning of West Broadway near L Street is undergoing a general – if not quite gentle – gentrification. A lot of the old blue-collar, shot-and-a-beer joints are being squeezed out, their liquor licenses bought up by fern-and-butcher-block places for the new condo crowd. With orangy lights shining through tooth-gap windows and an oval bar inside a walking moat before the tables start, "the Jack" is a kind of a compromise: a good place for an after-work dinner with the wife and kids, then a watering hole for serious barflies from nine or so onward.

Maybe the early hour was what surprised me.

I'd just finished a steak platter with two Harp lagers, expertly drawn by Eddie Kiernan behind the bar. About five-eight and skinny as a rail, Eddie had been as good a spray hitter in his prime thirty years ago as anybody Southie had produced in this century. Crashing into a stanchion after a foul ball once, though, he'd separated his shoulder badly, so he came back to the neighborhood and opened the Jack. Most of my dinner had been spent listening to Eddie grouse about the competition from his chi-chi new neighbors – "the wormy bastards" – and the skyrocketing rates for liability insurance they'd brought like a plague along with them.

Checking my watch, I saw it was nearly seven-thirty, so I got up to use the men's room and try Wellington one last time before driving home. As I made my way between the bar and the tables, a guy getting off a stool slammed into me, then staggered back. A little theatrically, I remember thinking at the time.

Maybe six feet tall and solid, with sandy, straight hair and an oft-broken nose, he glared at me. "The fuck is wrong with you, asshole?"

I took in half a breath. "I believe you're the one who bumped into me."

"The fuck he is," said a voice standing at the bar.

I turned. Same size and build, but black, curly hair and standard nose. He tugged on his left ear once, and I began to get the picture.

Sandy stepped up first, throwing a right cross at the left side of my face as I stayed turned toward his partner. I parried the sucker-punch, looping my left arm over Sandy's right and catching the fist under my armpit. With the heel of my left hand braced under his elbow, I lifted up, hard. I could feel more than hear the joint dislocate, but I heard more than felt Sandy's scream of pain as I released the hold.

Curly had swung his left just as I hunched my right shoulder up to protect my head and neck, but he'd had the time to realize that his first had to count. It rocked me into a table of four, who had pushed back and stood up as the fighting began. Sandy was on the floor now, cradling a floppy forearm, facial features squinched up, voice down to a keening moan. When Curly stepped in to follow up with a right, I used the table to support my own bad left knee. Then I side-kicked out with my right foot aimed at his left shin, all his weight having transferred forward onto that leg.

This go-around I did hear the cracking sound, Curly toppling like a felled tree with about as much noise. By this time, Eddie had come out from behind the bar, a Louisville slugger in his hands. I was about to initiate appropriate inquiries of the two on the deck when Eddie jabbed me in the solar plexus with his bat as though he were doing bayonet drill.

I joined the hamburger plates on the party of four's table. By the time my breath started returning to me, Sandy had struggled to his feet and gotten Curly up as well, the combined three good arms and three good legs carrying both of them through the Jack O'Lantern's door and out into the October night.

Eddie was standing over me, the bat at half-mast.

I said, "Why ... me?"

"I was scared shitless you were going to maim the wormy bastards. My liability premiums would shoot out of sight."

I forced some air into my lungs. "Then how come ... you didn't ... hit them first?"

He gave me a jaundiced look. "I said I was insured, John, not insane."

As Eddie Kiernan promised the table of four he'd bring them new meals, I decided I couldn't blame him, either.

✳ ✳ ✳ ✳

When I was able to breathe in for a count of eight without cramping, I left the tavern and made my way to the Prelude. Nobody had touched it. I got in, drove home, and climbed the stairs slowly, thankful of not having worse wounds to lick.

Once in the apartment, I checked with my answering service for the office. A message from Bernie Wellington, asking that I reach him the next day before court.

I went to the CD player, choosing on some soft and soothing soprano sax, courtesy of the late Art Porter. Then I lowered myself onto the couch and stretched out, trying to make sense of a situation that was anything but soft and soothing.

Then I tried some more.

✳ ✳ ✳ ✳

I started awake, the pain above my gut keeping me from sitting straight up in bed. I'd been having a dream – about Rhonda Stralick, I'm embarrassed to admit – but a throwaway line of hers from my "visit" that day clicked into place. And suddenly something Bernie Wellington had mentioned joined it.

If I was right, Michael Monetti's odd-ball voir dire questions made perfect sense. I even thought I could see why the two guys staking out the lavender three-decker had rousted me at the Jack.

But I needed to confirm one more piece of the puzzle to be certain, and I came up with a method I thought would work.

FIVE

That next Thursday morning, I took considerable care leaving the apartment building for two reasons. First, my solar plexus was still a tad ginger, thanks to Eddie's bat. Second, Sandy and Curly – or their replacements – might also have a friend at the Registry who could have run my plates and come up with a home address for me.

In the parking lot, I got down on hands and knees, examining the Prelude's undercarriage to be sure no "after-market" options had been added to the ignition system. Starting up, I decided to avoid my office, since that was for sure where the muscle boys had been waiting before following me to the Jack O'Lantern.

It could have made for a long day, but our Museum of Fine Arts on Huntington Avenue had a great photographic exhibit by Herb Ritts to go with its other, usual wonders. About eleven A.M. – and knowing Bernie Wellington would be in court – I used a payphone near the coatcheck alcove to call his secretary. I left only a blind message with her for him to try me at the office the next morning.

No sense in risking Bernie's license, too.

❊ ❊ ❊ ❊

Later that same Thursday, I drove from the museum across the Charles to East Cambridge. Parking the Prelude a few blocks from the Middlesex County Courthouse, I loitered discreetly outside the main entrance. At four-forty, Arthur Durand appeared in a stream of people too randomly dressed to be lawyers and too jaded to be anything but "citizens summoned to serve." That same young woman from the jury box was walking beside Durand, and he seemed to exaggerate some mannerisms of head and hands as he said something to her. She laughed again, this time not covering her mouth as in the courtroom, and they waved a casual good-bye, Durand scratching his nose with his left index finger.

I watched him move off toward the Lechmere Station. When the woman turned the other way, I fell in behind her, half a block away and across the street.

❊ ❊ ❊ ❊

Sometimes you get lucky.

At the corner, she got into a waiting station wagon, one of those Subarus you see Australia's Paul Hogan hucking on TV. There was a man about her age behind the wheel, and a toddler strapped into a plastic restraint bucket against the rear seat.

The lucky part was that a taxi had just pulled to the curb in front of me, dropping off an elderly couple who'd already given the driver their fare.

The young family entered the stream of traffic, my cabbie and me trailing.

❊ ❊ ❊ ❊

"Marjorie, come on, huh? You want this family package or that one?"

"Hey, Phil, give me a break, okay? I've been listening to witnesses and lawyers since Monday. It doesn't look like we're anywhere near finished, and this Monetti guy isn't exactly O.J. material, you know?"

Phil wouldn't let go of his bone. "Yeah? Well, try picking up Troy each afternoon from daycare."

"Like every other week of our lives I *don't*?"

We were all shuffling our way along the cafeteria line of a Boston Markets franchise, the operation that was lucky to survive changing from the successful marquée name of "Boston Chicken." The charming Marjorie and Phil still hadn't made up their minds which of the many dinner options – including turkey and ham – to choose. Their toddler, Troy, seemed to me the best behaved of the three, but then I don't have any kids myself, so it's easy for me to judge.

Marjorie finally went for the turkey combo, and Phil paid at the cashier before helping carry the trays of food and drink to a nearby booth for four. Across from an empty table for two.

As I ate my own fresh ham, husband said to wife, "So, you still can't talk about the case?"

"Not until the judge okays it, like after we vote and everything. But I'll tell you this. If it wasn't for Arthur, I'd be stir-crazy by now."

Phil wisely let that last part lay. "He's the other juror you sit next to?"

"Right. The judge already had to tell him twice to stop saying things during dead spots in the testimony or whatever, account of how he was, like, breaking me up."

I thought back again to Rhonda Stralick's evaluation of her tenant as Phil said, "Jokes? During a murder trial?"

"Attempted murder." Marjorie took a slug of her Pepsi. "But really, without Arthur and his impressions keeping all us jurors loose, I'd don't know where we'd be."

Phil pushed some turkey to the side of his mouth. "Impressions of what?"

"Not of 'what.' Of 'who.' Arthur can do Jimmy Stewart and Kirk Douglas –"

"From the movies, Mommy?" said boy Troy, until now content to wile away the meal smearing mashed potatoes across his face.

"That's right, honey. From the movies." Then back to Phil with, "And Arthur has this wicked Johnny Carson, too, even better than that guy used to do."

"What guy?"

"Oh, you know. Rich-somebody-or-other."

"Rich who?"

"The one who did that great Nixon. C'mon, Phil, you have to know who I mean?"

Her husband claimed he didn't, but I was pretty sure I did.

❊ ❊ ❊ ❊

"Wellington."

"Bernie, it's John Cuddy."

"Good Lord, John," came the voice from the other end of the line. "Where have you been?"

"Kind of busy, Bern."

"*You're* busy? The Commonwealth expects to rest tomorrow, which means I'm supposed to open the defense case Monday, and I've been trying to reach –"

"It's a long story, and you might be better off not hearing all of it."

A hesitation. "How bad, John?"

"Let me ask you something first."

"What?"

"When you were impanelling the jury for Michael Monetti, did anything odd happen?"

"Odd? You mean, other than those questions he made me ask?"

"Right. Specifically with Arthur Durand."

"Well, yes." Another hesitation. "Not odd, so much, though. More coincidental."

"Tell me what you mean."

"Okay." On the other end of the line, Wellington seemed to gather his thoughts. "After I asked the last of Michael's questions to Mr. Durand during voir dire, I came back to the defense table to confer with my client about challenging him. Just then, one of Michael's family in the audience sneezed rather loudly, and everybody in the room laughed. It was about the only comic relief in the whole process."

"And that's when Monetti told you to keep Durand on the jury."

"When Michael said not to challenge him, right. And I don't mind sharing with you that it still feels wrong to have that chap in the box. I mean, defense attorneys are getting sued all the time now for 'ineffective assistance of counsel' when they fail to use all their peremptories and the jury comes back 'guilty,' and here's my own client basically ordering me not to –"

"Bern?"

"What?"

"I'll get back to you."

"John –"

SIX

The next morning, Friday, I got up at six A.M., my solar plexus barely twinging. I dressed in old clothes and drove the Prelude across the Western Ave bridge and through Central Square, eventually reaching the foot of Arthur Durand's street. No sign of anybody surveilling the lavender three-decker, but that didn't mean the overall plan wasn't still on.

I left my car and walked into the mouth of the nearest alley. Taking ten more steps, I hunkered down behind its dumpster.

To wait.

At seven-forty, I heard the distinctive clacking of a certain person's dress shoes coming from the direction of Rhonda Stralick's three-decker. I moved back to the mouth of the alley again. When the thin man who scratched his nose and shifted in his chair crossed the opening in front of me, I clotheslined him with my left forearm.

He went down hard, but not quite out.

I grabbed his collar and dragged him quickly behind the dumpster before he was focussing well again. Propping his butt and torso into a sitting position against the brick wall of the alley, I squatted down, waiting until his eyes registered me in front of him.

"What the … ? The fuck is going on?"

"My friend, we need to have a little chat before court resumes this morning."

He tried to make his hands work, palms pushing at the ground toward scrabbling back up.

I laid my own hands on his shoulders, calm him down. "You find yourself in deep weeds, boyo. Very deep weeds."

"The fuck are you –"

"First I talk, and then maybe you talk. Understand?"

He didn't say anything to that.

"Michael Monetti's career is going south on him. One more felony conviction, and he never sees the sun outside of exercise time in a prison yard. But he's also about to be tried for attempted murder, and so something has to be done. Mikey once had his muscle tap a state-protected witness, but that didn't work out so well for him. Then he has a brainstorm about his current situation."

I looked down into the man's eyes. "Specifically, you."

"I don't know what –"

"Be patient, I'm not done yet. Mikey made it easy for you. Sit with the rest of the family in the front of the courtroom's audience that first afternoon of trial last week, sort of hide in plain sight. Then watch as the jury's selected. If somebody answered Mikey's voir dire questions the right way, you'd pay a little closer attention, to see if it was also the right kind of somebody. Male, slim, some mannerisms maybe that were easy to mimic."

I had my subject's undivided attention now.

"Arthur Durand turns out to fit the bill nearly perfectly. So that night – a week ago today – Michael's enforcers follow him home to Rhonda Stralick's three-decker around the corner while Mikey's sister the beautician goes to work on you. A fresh haircut, maybe even some make-up. Your rough resemblance to the guy and considerable talent can do the rest, particularly for people like the other jurors who'd never seen Durand before that afternoon."

"I'm ... I'm Arthur Durand."

"You're not listening to me, my friend. The enforcers take Durand out of the three-decker, remove any photos of him, and put you in his place. Bingo. The next day of trial – Monday morning, now – there's a juror among the twelve who's eventually going to vote his second cousin 'not guilty' for sure. Maybe even make a few friends on the jury during the course of the trial, what with some snappy patter and a knack for impressions of famous people. Like that great comic, Rich Little, used to do. It wasn't Durand's personality, but you might get a couple of other votes to swing with you so the 'hung' jury looks good. Hell, even an acquittal wouldn't be out of the question, enough of the other jurors take a shine to you."

"I'm telling you. I'm Arthur Durand."

I shook my head. "You're a little nervous, now, right?"

No answer.

"Right?" I repeated.

A grudging, "Right."

"Okay. Only problem is, you've been forgetting to scratch your nose the way Durand does. Or more accurately, did."

A glimmer of something beyond nervous. "What are you talking about?"

"Let me guess. Mikey told you they were just going to snatch Durand, then put him back into his life after the trial, right?"

"I'm not saying."

"Fine. Just listen then. The juror questionnaire covers things like job, family and so on. Guess what? Durand has nobody. On the surface, great for your cousin's plan, because there's no one to miss Durand while he's 'gone' for the course of the trial. Mikey even has his enforcers camp outside the three-decker, probably to babysit you so your winning personality doesn't go off romping at night and maybe piss in the stew somehow. And think about the questions your cousin had his lawyer ask those certain jurors, including Durand. Armed forces? No. Arrest? No. Sensitive employment? No. Tell me, what do all those things carry with them?"

Nothing.

"Okay, time's up. I'll have to answer for you. All those experiences require the person involved to be fingerprinted, boyo. I'm guessing you've never been printed, either, am I right?"

The second cousin swallowed hard, maybe seeing where I was heading.

"The medical examiner is pretty good about figuring out time of death. Not to the hour, but weeks instead of days? No problem. Now, here's the stumper: If Mikey's enforcers have been sitting outside the three-decker, probably babysitting you to be sure your winning personality doesn't go out romping at night, and –"

"But they never showed up last night."

"That's right. They spotted me nosing around the block, found out who I was, then set me up for a barroom beating."

"But ... but you don't look like they –"

"I was able to discourage them."

He just stared at me.

"Let's get back to my question, okay? If your cousin's enforcers have been babysitting you since they snatched the real Durand, and the rest of the Monetti clan – including even you – has been sitting dutifully in the courtroom, who does that leave to look after poor Mr. Durand, shut up in a room somewhere?"

"I don't ... I ..."

"Let me clear it up for you, then. Durand is dead, my friend. When the trial is over, that leaves you as a pretty embarrassing loose thread, wouldn't you say? You were the life of the party in the jury room, but not with your landlady. Your fellow jurors are going to remember you that way, and sooner or later you'd run into Rhonda Stralick face-to-face, maybe when she knocks on her tenant's door for the next month's rent. If I'm Michael Monetti, I don't think I can afford that level of risk. But then, you know your cousin better than I do. What do you think he'd do?"

"You're saying ... you're saying Michael's gonna kill me? His own blood?"

"I'm betting Michael sees it more as your life or his future. And I don't think I'd lose. But even if I'm wrong about that, I blow the whistle on your little charade here, and you're up for conspiracy in the murder of the real Arthur Durand."

He looked down, eyes flicking left-right-left, then back up to me. "The fuck am I gonna do?"

"Come with me to the courthouse this morning. We go to the judge and the district attorney."

His eyes got wide enough to see white all around the pupils. "What're you, nuts? If I wanted to fucking die, ratting out Michael would do it."

"You tell the authorities about what he's pulled here, and they'll get you into the witness protection program."

"Yeah, and how safe am I gonna be in that? Michael's guys already broke the thing once."

"That's not all they broke."

"What?"

"The two of them are in body casts by now."

"So, Michael sends two more. What are my chances then?"

"Better than they are now."

He looked down again. Coughed out a couple of breaths while a tear trickled down from each eye along that nose he was no longer scratching.

The next words were spoken toward the ground next to the dumpster. "Basically what you're saying is, I gotta go in and tell the truth."

"They call it 'voir dire.' "

He looked back up. "Huh?"

"Skip it," I said.

LEGACY

ONE

I t was a cold day in Boston, one of those with a crust of refrozen snow on the ground and still early enough in December that you couldn't even begin to think of the temporary reprieve Christmas might grant to the situation. Walking down Boylston Street with the Common on my left, I turned into Steve Rothenberg's building, taking the elevator – working for once – to his floor. The door to the office suite he shared with a rotating cast of other attorneys still had the vertical xylophone of names on different wood plaques next to the jamb, Rothenberg's appearing by patina to be oldest.

Which wasn't necessarily a status symbol.

Inside the door was a waiting area, the receptionist *cum* secretary sitting behind her desk and in front of a computer monitor. She had orange, spiky hair over a pair of small earphones, her shoulders rocking to something other than dictated correspondence.

When her head turned toward me, probably by accident, I said, "John Cuddy for –"

"Hey, Steve?" she yelled. "That investigator's here."

A South Boston accent, the neighborhood where I grew up.

Just seconds later, Rothenberg's head came around a corner, almost like a clip from the Marx Brothers. "John, come on in."

As we entered his office, he waved me to one of the client chairs in front of a scarred and cluttered desk.

Sitting down, I said, "Your treasure with the orange hair. What's her name again?"

"I can never remember either."

Rothenberg lowered himself into the swivel chair backed by a drafty window. He was wearing his suit jacket for a change, the tie snugged up to his collar, probably more a function of the weather than any sense of decorum. The departing hair and fuller beard, both salt-and-pepper, even gave an illusion of frost to his features.

155

"So," I said, "you called my answering service?"

"I've got an interesting matter, John. A first-timer for me."

Rothenberg had been a criminal defense lawyer for most of his career, which is how I'd met him while doing a favor for a Boston Police lieutenant. But lately Steve had been dabbling in other areas of legal endeavor.

He called it "diversification."

I looked at him. "Not a divorce case?"

"No."

"I don't do divorce, Steve."

"I know that, John."

"Okay, shoot," I said, leaning back in the chair.

Rothenberg did the same in his, swinging a little on the swivel point. "This woman named Dalia Looney came back north about five months ago with her two kids, a boy and a girl."

"That's 'D-A-H-L-I-A,' as in the flower?"

"As in the flower, but she's Lithuanian, and they drop the 'H'."

"Where does the 'Looney' come from?"

"She took her husband's name when they got married. He moved back up here, too. Works construction with his father over in Charlestown."

Another neighborhood of Boston. "And where's Mrs. Looney?"

"Your old stomping grounds."

"Southie?"

"Just off West Broadway. Dalia and the kids are living in her mother's house."

Husband with father, wife with mother. "Steve?"

"Yeah?"

"This is sounding suspiciously like a divorce case."

A smug smile and a shake of the head. "Already happened."

"What did?"

"The divorce. After the wedding, they lived up here for a while, him working with his dad. Then there was some kind of fight between Senior and Junior over how to run the construction business, right around the time the newlyweds' son was born. So Junior packs his family off to somewhere around Atlanta, for the building boom down there. Then to Florida for a while, and even Alabama before they end up in a little town with 'ville' at the end of it. Husband and wife got divorced, southern-style, citing 'irreconcilable differences.'"

"Then why do you need a private investigator?"

Rothenberg came forward in his chair, hands spreading on top of his desk. "The court down there ordered Junior to pay child support, and he did. For a while. When the money stopped coming, though, Dalia had a tough time trying to get an enforcement order, and I guess she never really liked that part of the country. So, she moved with their kids – the daughter was born during the 'Florida period' – back up here."

"And now Mrs. Looney wants a Massachusetts court to order her husband to pony up."

"All eight months arrearage, and a continuing obligation to –"

"Steve, this is a divorce case."

"Uh-unh." Rothenberg put a little passion into his voice. "All the real 'divorce' work's been done for us."

Us.

"I'm a little hazy on the details, John, since this is my first time 'registering an out-of-state judgment.' But based on what I've read about it, I just file a complaint with the Probate and Family Court up here, attaching certified copies of the official papers from down there."

"And what do I have to do, Steve?"

The passion in his voice was replaced by a twinkle in his eye. "A simple asset search."

"The husband's squirreling money?"

"Has to be. They were doing fine down south, financially speaking, anyway. Then once Junior's a bachelor again, he decides to stop paying child support and heads home to happier hunting grounds."

"Steve, the husband's such a good wage-earner, how come he's working with the father he had a fight with?"

"Cover."

"Cover?"

"My client's positive her ex brought a pot of gold north with him, and is working with his father just as cover for the money he's hiding."

"Sounds like you need an accountant more than an investigator."

"That might be too late. Once I file my complaint with the court, I can force formal discovery. But meanwhile, they'd be on notice that Mrs. Looney is coming after them, and might just bury the stuff deeper."

"Steve, there are computer outfits that can search for assets on-line a lot faster than I can on-foot."

"And we might use one. But I'd like your take on things first, because I trust your judgment."

Compliments are something private investigators rarely receive. I glanced down at my left wrist, the watch an old Timex with real hands on a face of twelve numbers.

Rothenberg said, "You have another appointment?"

"No. It's just that I'm paid for the hours I put in, Steve, and so far, I don't quite see where my fee's coming from on this."

"John" – a note of disappointment in the voice now – "these are needy people. A single mother with two small children."

"Living with grandma, Steve. I don't have that luxury."

"Meaning?"

"Meaning, I pay my own rent, apartment and office, my own –"

"John, I smell money here."

"The husband's 'pot of gold.' "

"Yes."

"Which is where my fee would come from, if at all."

Steve Rothenberg sighed deeply. "Tell you what. I'll pay you out of my own pocket for the time it'll take to drive to Southie and meet these people. If you still decide against working the case, no hard feelings."

I thought about Rothenberg's making things easier for me when I did that favor for Robert Murphy of the Homicide Unit. It also had been a while since I'd visited my wife, Beth.

Sleeping in her hillside in Southie, overlooking the harbor.

Rothenberg said, "John?"

"You have an address for the grandmother?"

TWO

It was a three-decker on a block of them within walking distance of the Lithuanian Club, where the fathers of some kids I went to grammar school with would hang out on their days off. The house itself had stonework around the front door and aluminum siding replacing the original wood, but some of the paint skin on the siding was peeling, and the front stoop's cement steps were crumbling, as though the owner hadn't stopped the damage when she could have.

Leaving my car at the curb, I walked up a solid part of the stoop. Three buzzers over the mailbox, but only the top and bottom ones showed slots for names, and only the bottom one actually had printing on it. VALECKAS.

When I pressed the button, I heard a bumblebee sound inside the house. I was on the verge of pressing it again when the door opened on what I at first thought must be an unusually strong spring.

Until I got a look at the person doing the opening.

She was maybe five-two, skinny rather than slim, with short, curly hair shading from blonde to gray. I'd have pegged her age at mid-sixties, but the sunken eyes, hollow cheeks, and sagging flesh told me I couldn't rely on a first impression, because I'd seen all three aspects before.

In Beth, when she'd had her cancer.

I said, "Mrs. Valeckas?"

"It is pronounce Vah-*las*-kuss."

"My name's John Cuddy."

The eyes might be sunken, but they glowed now. "You are from my Dalia's lawyer?"

"Yes."

"You come in, out of the cold."

She had trouble with pulling the door wider, so I pushed a little to help.

"Thank you," said Valeckas.

The foyer had a staircase leading up to what would be a second and then a third landing, some sepia photos on the walls of people with a healthier version of my greeter's features standing around farm equipment.

"The land of my father, outside Vilnius. We have thirty hectares of potatoes, with orchards of cherries around our house. And a big cross of wood, tall as tree, to protect us."

"It looks like a pretty place."

"Then, yes, before the Soviets." Valeckas walked toward the first floor door on the left. "My *dukra* waits in the parlor."

"Your ... ?"

"In Lithuania, '*dukra*' mean daughter. After you talk to her, you come see me in my kitchen, yes."

Valeckas didn't phrase that last as a request, and I took it as an order. "I will."

After going through the door – opening onto a dining room – she pointed left but walked to the right. I followed her finger to a bay-windowed parlor that would have been filled with sun in the summer but at four-thirty on that wintry day lay shadowy, the only light a floor lamp. The rug and furniture were threadbare, an old and heavy walking stick like a squared-off shillelagh mounted over the couch.

Where three people were sitting.

One was a woman around thirty, with curly blonde hair not yet graying and a full-cheeked face like Mrs. Valeckas must have had at her age. A little stolid from child-bearing, Dalia Looney looked up at me and held the stare as I crossed the small room to her. She was flanked by a boy around seven and a girl maybe four. Both had looked up, too, when I came into view, then both looked down at the floor, as synchronized in their movements as an Army drill team.

I didn't think the kids should have been there. "Mrs. Looney?"

"Yes." She took my hand, a brief, clammy shake. "This is Michael and Veronica."

A slight twinge of the south mixing with the Southie in her voice. The two bookends looked up again and down again, the girl rubbing one arm with the other hand, the boy coughing in a way my own mother would have called 'the croup.'

I said, "Maybe it'd be best if we talked alone."

Looney nodded, then glanced left and right. "Michael, Veronica, y'all go into the kitchen with Gram, okay?"

Each looked at her, looked at me, and stood up. They were still small enough to walk abreast through the doorway. From a few rooms away, I heard Valeckas say, "My *anukas* and my *anuke*. We have currant cookies and milk, yes."

Then the sound of the boy coughing again before a swinging door creaked to a stop, closing him off.

As I took an armchair across from Looney, she said, "My mother's always baking cookies. Currants – both the black kind and the red? – are just real popular over there."

"In Lithuania."

"Uh-huh."

A test. "Steve Rothenberg asked you to have the children with you for me, right?"

Looney hesitated, then nodded, almost enthusiastically. "He said you told him you might not want my case, but that Michael and Veronica ought to convince you."

"I just don't like to waste anybody's time, Mrs. Looney."

"Could you ... Would it be all right if you called me 'Dalia'?"

"Did Steve tell you to do that, too?"

Looney looked hurt, and I regretted my words – and the edge in my voice – as soon as they'd hit the air.

She said, "Nobody told me nothing. I keep the 'Looney' name for the kids' sake, but I just don't much like to hear it tied to me any more."

"I'm sorry, Dalia." Give her a chance to convince. "Steve said you thought your husband –"

"Ex-husband."

"– ex-husband was hiding assets?"

Another enthusiastic nod. "When we were down south, he was doing just real well, every place we lived. The judge even said so, when he ordered Johnnie to pay the support."

First time I'd heard his given name. "Can you spell that for me?"

She did.

I said, "So, this judge ordered child support?"

"Uh-huh. And insurance, too. Medical for me and the kids, and a life policy on him, so we'd be okay in case anything happened. Then, after the divorce and all, Johnnie moved again – back to Florida – and I tried just real hard to make a go of it, but I couldn't once he stopped sending the checks. Mom kept up the insurance, account of the companies had to let us know that he wasn't paying them any more, either. And that's when I came back home."

"To Southie."

The enthusiastic nod.

"You didn't pursue your husband in Florida?"

"No way. Never liked living there, and without the support, I couldn't afford to, anyways ." Another hesitation. "Besides, there was his gun, too."

Swell. "Which gun is that, Dalia?"

"Johnnie – back when we still lived up here? – bought this revolver. He had a permit and all, so it was legal. Said we needed one in the house account of the Castle Law."

Massachusetts has a home-defense statute, allowing someone to use deadly force if they fear an intruder means them severe bodily harm. "And he kept the revolver when you moved?"

"Wherever we moved. Down there, the states don't seem to care so much about people having guns."

"You think your husband would use his?"

"Johnnie was always kind of a hot-head." Looney blushed. "That was what attracted me to him in the first place, back when we were in school here. But he's also a drinker, and I don't know what all Johnnie would do if he got it into his head that I was coming after him with a lawyer."

Or a private investigator. "Dalia, how do you think your ex-husband is hiding his money?"

"I don't know that, either." A weak smile. "I guess if I did, I wouldn't need Steve or you, huh?" Even the weak smile disappeared. "But Jake's been in the business a long time, and it was him doing funny things with the books that started them fighting in the first place."

"Jake being Johnnie's dad?"

"Uh-huh. Looney Construction, over in Charlestown." A shiver. "And if Johnnie can scare you, Jake's a lot worse."

This just got better and better. "Has either of them ever threatened you?"

"No. Fact is, Johnnie and Jake haven't even been by to see Michael and Veronica. Can you imagine that? A father and grandfather, and they don't care about their own kin?"

"If they feel like that, what do you think I can do?"

Dalia Looney shrugged, not just with the shoulders, but her whole body.

And then the tears began running down each side of her nose. "Help us, maybe?"

❊ ❊ ❊ ❊

"Mrs. Valeckas –"

"My name is Izabel, with the 'Z.' And this is not milk."

An amber bottle shaped somewhere between a pint and a quart stood in front of her on the kitchen table of stamped tin painted white. Sitting with her hands out of sight in her lap, Izabel Valeckas had sent her grandchildren back to their mother as soon as I'd come through the swinging door from the dining room. There were two more doors off the kitchen, in Southie probably a pantry and a half-bath.

"Sit, sit. We have some *suktinis*."

"Sook-teen-as?"

Valeckas brought her right hand up and to the bottle, pouring a dram of liquid a little paler than amber into each of two jelly glasses. "It mean a dance like the polka, where the man and the woman spin around and around. You spin like that, too, you have very much *suktinis*."

I tasted it. Fiery, but with flavors of honey and … clove? "Excellent."

Valeckas said, "In English, the drink is call 'mead.' As old like beer from my country."

And "only" fifty percent alcohol, according to the label on the bottle.

I set down my glass. "Mrs. Val –"

"Izabel. I just tell you, remember?"

"I remember."

"And you. There is a business card I can see?"

I took one out, put it on the tin in front of her. She used the pinkie of her right, drinking hand to drag it closer to her.

"John … Francis … Cuddy." Valeckas looked up. "I thought at my front door you have the same name as my Dalia's husband. But since he leave her, I do not like that name no more, so I call you 'Mr. Detective.' "

"Izabel, why did you want to see me?"

She tossed her *suktinis* off in one gulp, returning the glass to the table and her right hand with my card in it to her lap. "You take my *dukra*'s case, yes."

"I don't know."

"Why not?"

"What Dalia – or her lawyer – wants done is very difficult with no information."

"How much of the 'information' you need? You see she have two babies and no man to work for her family."

"Izabel, I can't just walk up to Dalia's ex-husband and say, 'Where are you hiding your money?' "

A smile of triumph. "So, you too think he hide it."

I shook my head. "If he's any good at all, he can bury his assets so deep nobody could find them."

"Bury." Valeckas dipped her head, the wattles under her chin shaking. "Soon, my *dukra* must bury me."

When I didn't respond to that, Valeckas looked back up, the eyes aglow as they had been at the front door. "You know much about the cancer, Mr. Detective?"

"Some."

A change fluttered over he eyes. "I think more than 'some.' But you do not have to know much to see I have it. And bad. The last doctor say I have six months, and then I am with my husband again. In the parlor, his walking stick I keep over the couch still. My Kazimieras is name for the patron saint of Lithuania. Dead five years now, my husband, but there is not one day, one hour, when I do not think of him."

"Izabel, I know how that can be."

Her turn not to respond.

I said, "But as far as helping your daughter is –"

"Legacy."

I stopped for a moment. "Legacy?"

"The lawyer word, for what we leave to our children. In Lithuania, there is no tax on the land, so my father could leave our farm to us, if the Soviets do not come. That is why he bring us to America, to give us the chance. I marry my Kazimieras here, and we work hard, buy this house. Then God bless us with Dalia, and now Michael and Veronica, too."

I looked around the kitchen. "Your daughter and her children will get this place, then."

"No." A weary shake of the head. "No, I pay the insurance when her Johnnie stop, but not the insurance for me."

"What about Medicare, or –"

A tight smile now. "How old you think I am?"

"I hadn't thought about it, Izabel."

"Do not play stupid with me, Mr. Detective. You think about it outside, when I open the front door and you see the cancer in my face." She waited a moment. "I am only fifty-three years, and I cannot get the Medicare."

When I didn't respond again, Valeckas said, "So, I call the bank, and the nice man there give to me a 'reverse mortgage.' You know what is this?"

I wished I didn't. "The bank sends you money each month in exchange for owning the house when you die."

"Just so. The doctors find the cancer two years ago. I think the reverse mortgage is a good idea, because my *dukra* has a husband who can take care of her, of my *anukas*, Michael, and my *anuke*, Veronica. My Dalia is a *gulbe* – a swan, Mr. Detective – but that 'Johnnie' treat her like a crow. And then he divorce them. So now I have no legacy to leave except the walking stick of my Kazimieras, this bottle of *suktinis*, and the bill for my funeral."

"Izabel –"

"I have met my Dalia's lawyer. Steven Rothenberg is a good man, but he cannot upstand to that 'Johnnie' like could my Kazimieras or my father." The eyes softened. "In Lithuania, my father a great hunter. We have the heads – the horns – of deer and elk and moose on the walls of our house, what he takes with his gun." The eyes hardened again. "You carry a gun, Mr. Detective?"

"Occasionally."

Now the eyes glowed angrily. "When my *dukra* comes home with her children, I help them to put away their clothes and things. Some are in boxes, and in one, I find these."

Valeckas brought her left hand in a fist up from her lap and over the table before turning her wrist palm down. When she opened her fingers, five cartridges fell to the tabletop, making a jarring rattling sound on the stamped tin.

Valeckas said, "What kind of man would leave bullets from his gun where his children could find them?"

I had no answer for that one.

She leaned over the table and toward me, her breath foul but laced with the honey-and-clove flavor of the mead. "The lawyer man cannot upstand to Johnnie or his father. But you can, and you must, yes. For my Dalia, my Michael, my Veronica."

Valeckas then squeezed her eyes shut, and I could see a spasm wrack her body nearly off the chair.

When her eyes opened again, Izabel Valeckas said, "And for me."

❊ ❊ ❊ ❊

My feet made a crunching noise on the icy path, the folks who maintain the cemetery doing a little better job of mowing the grass in summer than shoveling the snow in winter. When I got to her row, the wind began coming up from the water, stinging my face even before I laid the roses longways to where she was.

The stone still read "ELIZABETH MARY DEVLIN CUDDY," although the lettering seemed more worn than the last time.

When was the last time?

John, it's too cold for you to be here.
"It's never too cold, Beth."
A pause. *Why do I feel it's not just the weather that's bothering you?*
"Maybe because I just met your match today."
Another pause. Then, *Someone you're interested in?*
"Interested ... ? Oh, no. I meant your match in knowing how to handle a certain Irishman."
Tell me.
I went through it, from Steve's office to the grandmother's kitchen.
You told this Valeckas woman you'd help, didn't you?
"Worse than that. I promised her."
But what are you going to do?
The wind really began howling now, the stinging sensation superseded by a nearly ripping one, as though I were strapped into one of those astronaut accelerators that simulate Mach 5 or –
John, you still with me?
"Still here, Beth."
Well?
"How am I going to help the family?"
That's what I mean.
"Actually, Izabel Valeckas gave me the idea herself."
She did?
"Sort of," I said, deciding to leave the details 'til the following morning.

THREE

Just over the bridge from the old Boston Garden – now replaced by the Fleet Center – lies Charlestown. The people who live there call it simply "the Town" and themselves "Townies." The neighborhood was best known recently as the home of the poor white family in the late J. Anthony Lukas's book *Common Ground*, his version of Boston's school desegregation/busing crisis during the seventies.

But Charleston is a mixed bag today. It provides a berth for the U.S.S. Constitution – "Old Ironsides" – at a wharf on the water. It supports the Bunker Hill Monument – "Don't shoot 'til you can see the whites of their eyes" – on the mound of the same name. In between, you have everything from tough housing projects bordering auto yards to spanking new condo complexes bordering the harbor.

And, on one of the main commercial drags, the headquarters of Looney Construction, Inc.

Sitting in my Prelude near a mom-and-pop convenience store, I went over what could loosely be called a strategy. Izabel Valeckas really had been the inspiration for it, by triggering my statement about not being able to just ask Johnnie Looney where he'd hid his money. Standing over Beth's grave the night before, doing exactly that seemed my best bet for getting the informal assessment Steve Rothenberg wanted.

When my watch read 9:00 A.M., I got out of the car and walked a half block to the freestanding, brick building that once might have been a small branch of the local savings and loan. There was a postage stamp of a parking lot on the side holding one passenger car and two blue pickup trucks with room for maybe a couple more. Going in the front doors of the building, I nearly collided with a stumpy guy about my age in charcoal jeans, an Army field jacket, and powder-blue hardhat with "Spence" stenciled across the crown.

"Help you with something?" he said, a black hand going up to mop a line of sweat on the broad forehead despite the temperature outside hovering in the teens.

"I'm looking for Johnnie Looney."

"I ain't him."

"Mr. ... Spence?"

The eyes rolled northward, as though trying to read the stencil from the inside. "That's me, I guess."

"You know where I can find Johnnie?"

Spence took a half-step backward, sizing me up. "You the law?"

"In a manner of speaking."

A nod. Not a happy one, just an acknowledgement to himself that, unfortunately, he'd gauged me right. "Johnnie ain't here."

"When's he due back?"

"Can't say, man."

"I'll settle for Jake, then."

Spence spent a moment gauging something else, then said, "First door on the right."

As Spence left the building, I moved into the hallway. The door to my right stood open, a man looming over a drawing board as he clipped a blueprint to the corners of it. His complexion was ruddy enough from the weather – or the booze – you'd have called it blotched. He wore a maize chamois shirt, sleeves rolled above burly forearms. On top of his head was a toupée so thick and so badly matched to the fringe of carrot hair around his ears that it made me embarrassed to think we swam in the same gene pool.

"Jake Looney?"

He looked up. "Happens every time."

"What does?"

Looney gestured toward an empty desk on his left near the door. "Send the girl for some decent coffee, and I get interrupted by a guy's gonna make trouble for me."

"What makes you think I'm trouble?"

"You're wearing a suit, bucko, and I don't recognize your face. Maybe you're a new inspector from the city, maybe you're somebody's lawyer, maybe you're just a guy thinks he can sell me something without even needing samples to show."

"None of the above, though you were warm with the middle one."

Looney regarded me a minute. "Lawyer?"

I took out my identification holder. "Working for one. John Cuddy."

He glanced at the laminated copy of my license. "What's this about? I haven't had a guy injured on the job for going on a year now."

"It's about your son."

"Johnnie?"

"And his obligations."

Looney squinted at me now, the toupée inching down bizarrely, as though extending his hairline by manifest destiny. "What obligations?"

"To his wife and children."

"Oh, that's just what I need." Looney made a face like he'd bitten into a sour lemon. "Tell you what, bucko, let me save both of us a lot of time. Sit in the girl's chair, and I'll give you the straight skinny."

I moved over to the empty desk as Looney went behind a bigger one against what might have been the bank's drive-up window. He said, "First off, Johnnie shouldn't never have married that broad. Don't work you mix the bloodlines like they did."

"It's okay to hire them, but don't let them date your sister."

Looney squinted at me again, the toupée reaching toward this eyebrows again. "You making fun of me, Cuddy?"

"Yes."

A gruff laugh. "You ran into my house nigger on your way in, right?"

"I'd rather you didn't use that word."

"Or else what, you'll kick my ass?"

"Into next week."

Looney squinted a third time, but this time the toupée stayed put. "You and me are headed for troubles, bucko."

"Almost certainly. Which would waste our time instead of saving it the way you were hoping a minute ago."

The eyes opened halfway, and he blew out a breath. "Okay. I got to hire the blacks – and the Chinese, for that matter, they decide to turn in their chef's hat for a hard one. Otherwise, I got the state and the feds all over me. But that doesn't mean I trust them, any more than I trust the Lithuanians like that shrew of a grandmother over in Southie."

I got a slight impression of "He doth protest too much" from Looney's tone, but I shelved it. "You know Mrs. Valeckas then?"

"From the wedding, where we didn't exactly hit it off, you might say. Turned up her nose at us like we were some kind of peasants and she was the fucking lord of the manor. Or 'lady,' whatever. Well, her daughter – who meets Johnnie on account of busing, by-the-by."

"Busing?"

"Yeah. When old Judge Garrity decided the neighborhood schools didn't work right. My son was going to the Eddie – the Edwards Middle School – only it was getting bad, and Charlestown High worse. So I dug deep and sent him to Catholic school, which is what the Lithuanian shrew decided to do with 'her Dalia,' too. Wasn't for Garrity and those goddamned buses, none of this ever happens."

"None of what?"

"The daughter wouldn't ever have met Johnnie, much less be able to do her best to get knocked up by him. And – surprise, surprise – along come two little yard-apes."

"Your grandchildren."

"You'd think so, wouldn't you? Only their momma and her momma poisoned them against my side of the 'family' from the word go, made them move down to the land of cotton and 'Negro spirituals.' "

"I understood the move south had more to do with Johnnie and you having a falling out."

"See, that's just what I mean about the poisoning stuff."

"A falling out over financials."

"Financials, huh? Well, let me set you straight, Cuddy. Johnnie and me had our differences, but it was more the father/son competition thing. Two years out of school, and the boy could see exactly how the old man was 'mismanaging' the company. The same general contractor that rebuilt half of Chelsea for the Jews after that fire. And half of the Town here, once the new lady executives found out they could walk to the State Street skyscrapers and even walk home without getting yanked into an alley for twelve angry inches of black salami. So, I told Johnnie, Look, you want to run things, start your own company. And – give the Devil his due – he goes down to Georgia and does just that."

"And did well, from what I've heard."

"And the word 'did' is the important – no, what the fuck do they call it?

Yeah, yeah, the 'operative' word. Johnnie did fine for a couple of years during the boom when any bozo with a hammer in his hand and nails in his mouth could make a fortune. Then the boom goes bust, and he's gotta move on. And on. Well, pretty soon the lovely blonde bride becomes a fucking palomino horse, and the boy realizes he's made more than a few mistakes I warned him against. So Johnnie comes back north with his tail between his legs, realizing he can learn from his old man while he earns enough to live on."

"But not enough for his family to live on, too."

"Christ on a crutch, Cuddy, you know how the courts work. The judge looks at a couple of financials and listens to a couple of lawyers looking to feast off the fucking corpse of the marriage, and before you know it, the poor husband's supposed to be supporting his wife and kids in the fucking Taj Mahal."

"What happened to all the money your son made down there?"

"What happened to it is Johnnie likes to drink. They tell you that over in South Lithuania?"

"Yes."

Looney seemed a little surprised. "They also tell you he hit a kid with his car when he was over the limit, both booze and speed?"

Jesus. "No."

"I didn't think so. Way my lawyer here tells me, Johnnie would have been better off, he killed the kid. No 'established earning power yet' or some fucking mumbo-jumbo. Anyway, the kid's never gonna walk again, and Johnnie's insurance wasn't enough to cover the verdict. So that means everything he worked for is up in smoke. My son's gotta move back north, come on bended fucking knee to the old man."

"I assume he's got all the paperwork on this."

A shifty look. "Paperwork?"

"On the accident case."

"Beats me." Very casual now. "I think they sealed it or something, so nobody can get at who agreed to pay what."

Convenient. "You realize your son hasn't even been to visit his children since they've been back?"

Looney stood bolt upright from his chair, fists on the desktop in front of him. "You realize that fucking shrew won't let him in her house?"

"What?"

Grandma Vel-las-kus or however you pronounce it. She told Johnnie he don't pay the support, he don't get to see his kids. She's even called here, asking me – me – to send her money I don't have."

I closed my eyes, reminded of why I didn't do divorce cases. "Mr. Looney, there's talk your son has a gun."

"A gun? He did, it'd be pawned by now. I'm telling you, Cuddy, Johnnie doesn't have a pot of gold. Fuck, he doesn't have so much as a pot to piss in. The poor kid drives a ten-year-old pickup and eats day-old bread. He lost his watch and can't even afford to buy a new one, tell him what time to be at work."

"Meaning he's late this morning?"

"Meaning you and I are finished talking. I hope I saved us both some time, but you want to settle this another way, there's lots of empty alleys in the Town."

"I'm already looking forward to it."

❉ ❉ ❉ ❉

Going out the front door of the building, I saw Spence standing by one blue pickup truck as another bounced hard into the side lot, jerking to a halt across two of the precious spaces. The man who came out the driver's side stumbled a little on the running board. When Spence called him over, I got a pretty good look at the face. Replace the rug with natural hair, and you had Jake Looney at age thirty or so.

Which would make the man walking unsteadily toward Spence son Johnnie. I decided to join them.

Spence was speaking low and quickly, based on how fast his lips were moving. Looney shook his head constantly, using his palms to push away at the other, older man.

Kind of awkwardly missing him, truth to tell.

As I drew within earshot, Spence pointed toward me, and Looney turned. His eyes were bleary, and the first words out of his mouth rolled a cloud of whiskey fumes into my face.

"The fuck you want?"

"Johnnie Looney?"

"I'm the one doing the asking here."

"Johnnie," said Spence, "be cool, man."

"Fuck you, Harry. I'm gonna settle this here and now."

Spence glanced from his face to mine and back again. "I don't think that'd be too good an idea, Johnnie."

Apparently Looney didn't like the tenor of Spence's advice, because he threw a roundhouse left at me. The punch took about an hour arriving, so I just sidestepped it. Junior's second effort was a straight right, with enough weight behind it to do some damage. But even at twice the hand speed Looney was showing, his son Michael could have blocked it. I just parried the punch with my own left palm, letting Junior follow through. Then, swiping my right foot at his right ankle, I unbalanced Looney enough to send him face down toward the macadam.

He landed so heavily you could hear the air leave his lungs in a whumping rush.

Spence watched me – probably making sure I wasn't going to follow up my advantage – then knelt down next to Junior, grabbing him by the belt near the buckle and lifting up and down slowly and smoothly. "Johnnie, you got to breathe, man. In deep and out, or you'll plain pass out."

It took a minute, but Looney finally managed to gain his feet in a four-count movement, thanks to some levitation help from Spence. After two steps, though, Junior shrugged off the other man's hand, choosing instead to stagger toward and eventually through the doors of his father's brick building.

Harry Spence watched the boss's son until he disappeared inside, then turned to me. "Talk with you a minute?"

❇ ❇ ❇ ❇

"Johnnie, he got himself a significant drinking problem."

We were standing next to the poorly parked pick-up, the words 'LOONEY CONSTRUCTION, INC.' on the dinged and faded driver's door, some jokester having scratched out the 'E' in the name.

Which actually captured Junior rather well, I thought.

Spence waited for me to say something. When I didn't, he lowered his own voice. "I'm in the program myself, so I seen a lot of Johnnies, up close and personal."

"How long you been sober?"

"Two years, eight months, twenty-nine days."

"What's the longest Junior's been on the wagon?"

I thought Spence might take offense at my nickname, but he just said, "Need a stop watch with a good second hand, man."

"He usually get physical like that?"

"Not usually. But I been where he's at, so I can identify with the boy. You hear what I'm saying?"

"I think so."

"Back in my drinking time, I chased away a pretty fine wife, too. She up and took off with our three kids. I never did find out where to."

"Your point?"

Spence rubbed his chin. "Maybe you could see your way to cutting Johnnie a little slack here, account of he so fucked up right now."

"Not my call."

"Maybe you can, like, persuade the one whose call it be."

"Maybe, if I was convinced Junior was really dead broke."

Spence grinned, a little theatrically. "Man, what's past 'dead' in the 'broke' department? Johnnie, he don't got his own pot to pee in. He driving this old truck, eating –"

"– yesterday's bread."

Spence dropped the grin, his voice growing a burr. "Maybe you oughta forget about 'persuading' anybody about this thing, man. Maybe you just oughta butt out, like Johnnie told me to do over there."

"Unfortunately, I'm not very good at doing what other people tell me to."

"Might want to learn." Harry Spence sized me up the way he had when we met at the building entrance. "Be seeing you."

My turn to watch somebody walk toward the front doors of Looney Construction, Inc.

FOUR

"Claire, John Cuddy calling."

"Hey, Cuddy," came her voice from the other end of the line. "What time next month do you need whatever it is you want?"

"Claire, your computer can't be that backed up with traces."

"No, it's not. But I am, and you may not believe this, Cuddy, since you don't know shit from Shinola when it comes to the ethernet, but the computer can't work unless I enter stuff into it."

"I thought it was called the 'Internet'?"

"Only by the uninitiated."

"Claire?"

"What?"

"This is a case for a single mother with two little kids."

"She should have thought of that before letting the guy duke –"

"Her ex-husband's a boozer, quasi-violent, who hasn't paid child support for eight months now."

"Cuddy, you got to stop. My heart's already bleed –"

"And the woman's own mother, who took the family in, is dying of cancer herself."

A silence at the other end. "You wouldn't shit me about this, Cuddy."

"No."

"I mean, this isn't something you cribbed off *Queen for a Day* or –"

"My hand to God, Claire."

Another silence. "Your wife died of cancer, right?"

"Right," I said, as evenly as possible.

"My dad, too. Shitty way to go."

"It is that."

"Almost makes you nostalgic for the good old days, when people just dropped dead from heart attacks."

"Claire?"

"Now what?"

"I'm in kind of a time bind here."

A third silence, followed by a sigh like the air leaving Junior's lungs on the parking lot's macadam. "All right. What've you got?"

"Asset check. Start with 'Looney, John, Jr.' "

"This the deadbeat dad?"

"Yes."

"Any AKAs?"

"Try Johnnie, double 'N' and 'I-E' at the end."

"Should run it with double 'N' and 'Y,' too."

"Claire, I trust your expertise like no other's."

"Asshole," came over the line, but behind it the sound of computer keys clacking.

"I'm not coming up with much, Cuddy ... Car registration on a – Christ, some ten-year-old clunker of a truck ... Rent checks to a realty trust in Charlestown ... Balance in the account ranges between low three figures and overdrawn."

Silence, except for the clacking of keys.

"Claire?"

"I'm trying, Cuddy, but I think we're in blood-from-a-stone territory."

"How about John, Sr., AKA 'Jake'?"

"The deadbeat dad's own father?"

"Right. And 'Looney Construction, Inc.' over in the Town as well."

"Wait one ... I'm doing the corp' first, on the – Christ. Great group of people you're giving me."

"What've you got?"

"Looney Construction's up to its limit in bonding capacity. Unless they finish a project and get the surety company to let them off the hook, John the Elder won't be starting a new one before the millennium."

"Anything unusual in the corporate holdings?"

"Holdings? Let me check the Secretary of ... yeah. Yeah, here we go. Security interest filings on a backhoe, a few small trucks – Christ, John the Elder seems to do all his buying on credit, Cuddy. Even some gasoline generators are on the float."

"Not much owned outright, then?"

"His hardhat, maybe a screwdriver or two. And worse on the guy personally."

"How do you mean?"

"I've got a back door into the Commonwealth's corrections records. Seems your construction exec did two stretches in a secure hotel with three squares a day."

"Charges?"

"One fraud, one assault with a deadly."

Dalia Looney wasn't kidding about Senior being scarier than Junior. "What about assets, Claire?"

"Showing a four-year-old car, checking balance between a thousand and two. Nothing like a gold mine or paid-off saltbox on the Cape."

I thought about it. And about Harry Spence's protective attitude toward the boss's son despite the father's overtly racist attitude toward the employee.

"Hey, Cuddy, you still drawing oxygen there?"

"Try 'Spence, Harry' or variations."

"Wait one more." Clacking, sighing, more clacking. Then, "Whoa, would our man be African-American?"

"He would."

"Win the lottery, maybe?"

"Not that he mentioned."

"Well, 'Spence, Harold' has deposited twenty to thirty large, each month since August."

Bingo. Maybe. "Any indication of the source?"

"That'd be in the paper records, not the electronic. And you'd need a court order for it, not that you shouldn't for what I've already –"

"Claire, print out what you've got anyway. And if you find anything else, call my answering service, leave a message."

"On the print-out, you finally join the twentieth century with a fax, or should I messenger it over?"

"Use the bicycle folks."

"Cuddy?"

"Yes, Claire?"

"What kind of gun you carry, a flintlock?"

✳ ✳ ✳ ✳

"Steven Rothenberg speaking."

"Steve, about that receptionist."

"You have something for me on Looney?"

"I mean, she's chewing gum when she answers your phone, the muzak starts as soon as she picks up, and I don't think *Twisted Sister's Greatest Hits* is exactly the image you want to –"

"John, please. It's been a long morning already. Tell me if you've got something."

I told him.

Rothenberg said, "I knew I smelled money."

"Only we don't know where Harry Spence got it from."

"Has to be the Looneys."

"Agreed. The father painted the man as just affirmative-action window dressing, but Spence's loyalty to both of them seemed to run deeper than the bans of mere employment. However, there's still the problem of which Looney's money he received."

A pause before, "I'll file the enforcement action tomorrow, maybe seek an ex parte attachment of –"

"Steve?"

"Yes?"

"You need me for anything else?"

"Just that print-out of the asset search."

"It's being messengered over to me, and I'll hand carry it to you."

"John, thank you. From both me and my client."

❊ ❊ ❊ ❊

I dropped the print-out at Rothenberg's within half an hour of receiving it. Returning to my own office, I sat down thinking that, all in all, it's been a pretty good day.

At least until 4:47 P.M.

I lifted my receiver on its third ring. "John Cuddy."

"Mr. Detective," the voice hushed. "You know who is this?"

"Mrs. Valec – Izabel?"

"Just so."

"What's the –"

"There is outside my house a car up the street."

"A car?"

"A little blue truck. What do you call them?"

Pickups. "Is anyone inside it?"

"I think yes. Then, when I look again, I think no."

"Izabel, where are Dalia and the children?"

"They are out, but they come back soon."

"Call nine-one-one, then get out of there, too."

"No," she said, still in the hushed voice, then louder. "No, he does not scare me from my own house."

"Izabel –"

"Please, you promise me you help us. Come, come quick."

"First call –"

"And please, bring your gun, yes."

❉ ❉ ❉ ❉

With the crosstown traffic, it took me half an hour to reach the head of Valeckas's block in Southie. Leaving the Prelude, I could feel the butt of my Smith & Wesson Chief's Special ease off the right kidney area enough to save me massaging back there. The swirling winter wind whipped across my cheeks and nose as I closed the door and did a quick survey of the street. About half the parking spaces were filled, one by a blue pickup.

If there was lettering on the truck's door, I couldn't see it from where I was standing, even with the high stoop light from a nearby house shining on it.

Slowly, I moved down the sidewalk opposite the pickup. Drawing even with it, I caught the Looney Construction lettering, the "E" still scratched off.

Junior's truck.

Two minutes later, I was knocking softly at the rear door of the Valeckas house, and ten seconds after that, Izabel opened it for me.

"Come in, quick, quick."

I slipped through the door, Valeckas wearing an apron over heavy pants and a sweater, her father's walking stick leaning against the wall. When she reached for the stick, Valeckas held it in two hands like a club rather than one hand like a cane.

"I think I hear something back here before you knock, so I take the walking stick of my Kazimieras off the wall."

"What did you hear, Izabel?"

"The sound of glass, like somebody break it."

"Dalia and the kids?"

"Still gone."

I nodded, then put my fingers to my lips. She nodded back.

Easing the Chief's Special from its holster, I held it tight to my right shoulder, muzzle toward the ceiling. I checked the stairway to the cellar first, hoping not to get my feet shot out from under me as I descended the steps. Oil burner and tank. Hot-water heater. Boxes that might have contained her family's things as they moved back north.

I checked behind everything Junior could have used as a hiding space. Zero.

Back upstairs, Valeckas was standing by the doorway like a sentry in a castle, the walking stick at port arms.

I leaned into her ear. "Rear room now."

She nodded again.

The room faced the small backyard and wasn't much more than a closet with a window. All the panes seemed intact, though, and nobody there, either.

Valeckas came even with me.

I said, "Rest of this floor first, then upstairs."

A third nod.

There were three more doors off the kitchen. One was the swinging door to her dining room, the second probably the pantry, and third her half bath. The latter two were both closed, and each was at right angles to the other on different, short walls forming a corner.

Meaning no way to open both at once while covering each.

I pointed to the door on my right, and Valeckas moved against it. As I opened the one in front of me, a light came on overhead, surprising me and a pair of cockroaches, intent on some breakfast cereal.

A worse surprise was the sound of the other door opening, Valeckas yelping in pain.

But by the time I turned, the stars were already rising across the back of my head, and I felt my left wrist turn awfully funny as I landed heavily on it.

FIVE

"He wakes."

I didn't recognize the voice, though I had the feeling my eyes had vaguely registered her face. I concentrated on keeping both lids open at once, then focused on the woman standing next to my bed.

She was all in white, a nametag on her left breast pocket under some pens and little medical tools. I couldn't read the tag from where I was lying, and I couldn't even think about getting up.

She said, "I thought it might be a concussion, so we held you overnight. The wrist is just sprained."

I let my eyes loll over and down, seeing a soft cast on my left forearm all the way to the hand. "Peachy."

The woman reached into the nametag pocket. "However, I'm afraid your watch wasn't so lucky."

As she laid it gently on my night table, I could see the crystal cover was broken.

"Oh, and you have a visitor. If you're up to seeing him."

"Let me guess," I said. "He draws his salary from the city and he's smiling."

"Chuckling, I'd call it, but still not a bad prediction. Maybe you should play the lottery this week."

"I've the feeling I already have."

❊ ❊ ❊ ❊

"Okay, Cuddy, how many fingers am I holding up?"

Just the middle one. "Not funny, Lieutenant."

He laughed a little anyway, pulling over a visitor's chair. Robert Murphy, appointed to Homicide in the long ago when a city councillor mistook surname for race, was around six feet tall and carried twenty more pounds of rumpled flesh than either his wife or the department's doctors preferred. His tie was knotted neatly, the fashionable pattern one of those I can't keep track of. A collar stay held the points of his shirt in formation, a small pad and gold pen contrasting against the black hands holding them.

Murphy's eyes closed to little slits in a Buddha-like face. "Lucky for you that gramma was riding shotgun."

"I don't remember anything after hearing the bathroom door open."

"How's about you fill me in on what happened before that?"

I went through it for him, from the time I first spoke with Steve Rothenberg in his office two days earlier.

Murphy said, "Must be close to record time for you, Cuddy. Most folks don't decide to kill you till after a week or so."

"What went down after I did?"

"There's only one version of that, but I'll give it to you anyway. Mrs. ... just a second ... yeah, Val-*las*-kus. Mrs. Valeckas says that as you opened that pantry door, this Johnnie Looney banged through the half-bath one, knocking her over. She assumes he hit you because when she looked up, Looney was standing over you, then started yelling at her for where his kids were."

"First time he'd shown any interest in them for a while, financially or personally."

"Be that as it may, Looney rampages through the first floor, then gramma hears him climbing the stairs. She told me she wasn't too worried then, account of she knew her family wasn't home yet. So Mrs. Valeckas moves over to you, see if you're okay. She sees you're still breathing, then notices the butt of your gun sticking out from under your right arm."

I thought, Looney didn't take it?

Murphy flipped a page in his pad. "Anyway, Mrs. Valeckas figures she'd better put the gun in her apron, which she does. And that's when ex-son-in-law comes stomping down the stairs and back into the kitchen, still demanding to know where his kids are. Gramma said she could smell liquor on his breath."

"You confirm that?"

Murphy looked at me, then flipped another page. "Yeah. One of my team talked to a Spence, Harold, who works at the father's construction company."

"We've met."

"Which?"

"Both Spence and Looney, Sr."

"Anyway, Spence says Looney, Jr. gets a telephone call. Apparently your

Johnnie's half in the bag already, but he tells Spence there's some emergency and takes off for parts unknown."

"Southie."

Murphy nodded. "Another guy on my team talked to a bartender two blocks over from the Valeckas house. Says Looney came in, stayed about an hour while tossing down four whiskies, straight up. Man must've had an aversion to ice and water, I guess. Oh yeah, and he kept asking the bartender what time it was."

"What time?"

"Yeah. Seems our construction worker didn't wear a watch."

I thought back to what his father had said about his son losing the watch and not being able to afford a new one.

Murphy went back a page. "So where … right, right. Looney's in gramma's kitchen with booze on his breath, telling her she doesn't come up with where the kids are, he's gonna put bullets in you till she does."

"And Valeckas stonewalls him."

"Tough little lady. Well, Looney turns and aims at you – one of your legs, she thought, but wasn't too sure, since she was more concerned with getting your piece out of her apron. Gramma yells at him to stop, and he swings around, his gun no more than two feet from her in that kitchen. Looney shoots once, and Mrs. Valeckas empties your Chief's Special into him. By the way, the techies recovered only four rounds at the scene."

"That's all I load, keep the chamber under the hammer empty."

"Old-fashioned, with the new half-cock safety."

Back to the point. "Lieutenant, all Looney's wounds were through and through?"

"That range? You bet. Left most of his vitals sliding down gramma's walls in the corner there."

"And how is she?"

"Looney's slug took her just below the ribcage. Mrs. Valeckas is in a room down the hall and around the corner, though she's not in much better shape than him."

"Looney made it?"

"Dead at the scene, dead in the ambulance, dead on arrival." Murphy closed his pad. "In fact, you and gramma were real lucky about the timing yourselves."

"I don't get you."

"By six, enough of the traffic's gone so your ride to the hospital got here in less than ten minutes, door-to-door."

"Six o'clock."

"Yeah. Of course, the Castle Law applies no matter what time of day, though I've always thought that once it's dark out, the homeowner should get even more benefit of the doubt." The lieutenant rose from his chair. "You got anything else to add?"

"Let me sleep on it," I said, but as soon as Robert Murphy left my room, I reached over to the nightstand.

Shit.

I closed my eyes, maybe for an hour. Or at least until I was pretty sure I'd worked things out as best I could on my own. Then I creaked out of bed and into the shirt and pants somebody had hung in my closet.

❊ ❊ ❊ ❊

She was only seven rooms away from mine.

I looked through the little diamond window in her door. I could see Izabel Valeckas lying in bed, apparently zonked. Her daughter perched on a chair by the side of it, holding her mother's left hand in both of hers.

I didn't bother to knock.

Dalia Looney spun around, nearly dislodging the braid of tubes running into the older woman's arms and up her nose.

I said, "Sorry if I scared you."

Looney took a breath, the sound almost as ragged as her mother's was raspy. "I thought ... I thought it was Jake, coming to take revenge on us."

"You ask for a policeman outside the door?"

"Yes, but that Lieutenant Murphy said he couldn't spare one for you and one for her, so he's just got an officer down in the lobby with a photo of Jake." Looney paused. "I guess they had some mugshots of him?"

"I guess they might have." I inclined my head toward Valeckas. "How's your mom doing?"

"She's trying, trying so hard, but I ... I ..." The tears started coming, more rapidly and harshly than in the parlor of the Valeckas house two days before.

I said, "We need to talk, Dalia."

She cupped her hands, using the heels to dam some of the tears. "About what?"

"I think maybe we talk first, yes."

Both of us looked toward the bed.

Izabel Valeckas, eyes now open, said, "Dalia, you will not sleep, go to get some coffee, so at least you stay awake better."

"Mama, I –"

"Go, my *dukra*. Mr. Detective and me are fine together."

When Looney glanced in my direction, I said, "It might be best."

Once her daughter had closed the door behind her, Valeckas pointed shakily toward the empty chair. "Come, sit with me."

I went over, using my right hand to lower myself into the chair.

"That crazy man," she said, "he break your arm, too?"

"My wrist got sprained when I fell."

What passed for a nod from the pillowed head. "He try to shoot you, and me too."

"And you shot him, to save both of us."

"Just so."

"No, Izabel."

The eyes blinked, her features contorting under the facial tubes. "What you say?"

"You set Johnnie Looney up to be killed."

The eyes closed. "Mr. Detective, you are crazy man, too."

"I think I've got most of it worked out, but feel free to correct me if I botch something. Your daughter comes back to live with you, because her husband has divorced her and isn't paying child support any more for their children. Problem is, Johnnie's a drinker, which probably doesn't help him hold a steady job, and definitely doesn't help him when he hits a child down south while under the influence and speeding to boot. Whatever money Johnnie did accumulate went toward satisfying the accident verdict."

"He lie about that."

I thought back to my first talk with Valeckas in her kitchen. "So, you did know Johnnie had the accident."

A small, grudging smile. "You take advantage of me, a poor woman, shot in her own –"

"Fortunately, though, you'd kept up the premiums on insurance, especially health policies for Dalia and the kids, if not yourself. Oh, and that over-the-rainbow possibility of Johnnie dying young."

"What is 'over-the-rainbow'?"

"Watch *The Wizard of Oz*, next time it's on TV. Only problem is, while Johnnie Looney's back up here and therefore within reach, he isn't coming around to see his children, and you're a little too sick to go hunting for him in a manner that'd let you get away with killing him."

"I am too sick for listening to you."

"So you need to set a trap. You convince your daughter to go to a soft-hearted lawyer, who in turn brings in a soft-headed private eye. Nobody tells either of us about Johnnie's accident trouble down south. But you know from your daughter that Looney, Senior hasn't always been on the up-and-up regarding his bookkeeping. So, you maneuver me to go stir things up over in Charlestown, riling them while diverting me from your real plan."

"I got no plan."

"You didn't just find those bullets when you helped your daughter unpack. Drunks often misplace things, like watches, for example. Well, Johnnie left the bullets and the gun together – probably forgetting where – and you found both."

"Why do I want his gun?"

"Because the police might not believe someone your size, weakened from cancer, could wrest a weapon away from a man who worked construction. A much better version would be Johnnie having his gun, and you having mine."

A deep sigh, and the grudging smile was back. "Very good, Mr. Detective. Very good."

"I know how you got me to come to your house last night. How did you lure Johnnie to your block and send him to sit in that bar?"

The smile stayed put. "Johnnie like to drink, and the bar have liquor."

"But getting him to Southie in the first place?"

"My Dalia is in the bathroom, making ready to take Michael to doctor for his cough. I call to Johnnie at his father's business. Michael is coughing bad then, and I say on the phone, 'Your son is very sick, you can hear him, yes.' And Johnnie say Dalia should take him to doctor. And I say she cannot, he must come because I am scare for my *anukas*. And Johnnie finally say he will come."

"And when did he arrive?"

"Dalia and Michael and Veronica, they are all at doctor. I tell Johnnie, 'Go off to bar, come back in one hour.' I see him at his truck – to get money, maybe – then walk for the bar."

"Which is when you called me."

"Just so." A different smile now, that one of triumph Valeckas first showed me at her kitchen table. "I put the fear in my voice, I hear same in you. Then I get the walking stick of my Kazimieras and wait for you to come."

"In order to lead me around the kitchen. Then you faked the bathroom door hitting you and rapped me with the stick."

"I would use the gun, but I think maybe I cannot hit you hard enough with my one arm only."

"And when Johnnie came back from the bar, you let him in."

"I tell him everyone is in kitchen. When we get there, he see you, he bend down. I yell at him, Johnnie turn around, and I shoot him as many time as you have bullets in your gun. When he is down on the floor, too, I kneel on my legs beside him, and I put the gun I find in my *dukra*'s pack box in his hand. I hold my arm away from my body, and I point the front of the gun at my side. I push on Johnnie's finger to shoot me once." The smile of triumph again. "It doesn't hurt so much as I think before. Then I call the police for ambulance to take us to here."

"You thought of everything, Izabel."

"Just so."

"Maybe not quite."

Valeckas dropped the smile. "What you mean now?"

"When 'Johnnie' hit me, he 'forgot' to take my gun?"

"He is drinker, and drunk men not think so good."

A gambit. "When Johnnie got the phone call from you, he told one of his co-workers you'd called him."

"It is like I say. Johnnie is drunk man. He lie to worker, or worker lie to you." The smile came back. "Or maybe even you lie to me, Mr. Detective, yes."

"This is no lie, Izabel. The police can trace through the phone company that a call was made to Looney Construction from your phone at that exact time."

"So? I call to the boss father, ask him for money to feed his grandchildren. I do this several time before already. But yesterday, I get his crazy-man son, who come after me in my own house."

"Speaking of time, you called my office at four-forty-seven."

"If the phone company will say that, too."

I took out my ruined watch, dangling it by the strap in front of her eyes. "This broke when I hit the floor in your kitchen, after you hit me. The hands are frozen at five-twenty-three."

Valeckas blinked at the watch face.

I said, "It shows I was down and out over half an hour before you called the police about Johnnie supposedly hitting me, then threatening to kill the two of us."

"I already tell police Johnnie threaten to kill only you. This I remember. And your watch?" She managed to sniff derisively, even with the tube up her nose. "It is cheap and old. Maybe it stop before six o'clock yesterday for many reasons."

I stood up. "You think you have all the answers, Izabel, and you might be good enough to pull it off. But I'm going to try and stop you."

"The police?"

"Yes."

"They talk to my doctor, they do not bother."

I stared at her.

"My doctor, he say to me that the bullet through my side go too close to the liver, already weak from my cancer. I would not live to see the trial you want for me."

"Then I'll turn to the insurance company that wrote the policy on Johnnie's life."

A troubled look now. "So they do not pay my Dalia the money?"

"That's right."

"For what purpose, Mr. Detective? Johnnie is dead, I will be dead, too. Together we leave a legacy to my *dukra* and her children, the money to have a real chance at life in this country."

"Because you killed your former son-in-law."

The glow rekindled in her eyes. "You promise to help us. In my kitchen, the first time you come two days ago. You call to insurance company with these little things you say, maybe you look very bad to the other detectives."

I stared down at her. Valeckas might not know chapter and verse, but she was as wise as anybody I'd ever dealt with.

Or been up against.

I rose and turned to leave the room.

"So, Mr. Detective, you come to my funeral, yes."

I yanked on the door handle. "Don't wait for me."

Izabel Valeckas said, "I know these are your words before they come out your mouth."

Without looking back, I could picture the smile of triumph on the grandmother's lips.

WHAT'S IN A NAME?

ONE

Harry Mullen said, "John Francis Cuddy. You want to sit behind your old desk?"

I looked past Mullen to the high-backed swivel chair he'd inherited from me at Empire Insurance after my wife, Beth, had died and I'd gone private. "The one in front of the desk is fine, Harry."

I sat down as he waddled around our shared piece of furniture. It was mid-October, and Mullen had put on even more weight since the last time I'd seen him. Also, the smell of stale cigarette smoke in the office seemed stronger than it should have been from just wafting off his clothes.

"You still hooked on the nicotine, Harry?"

Sinking into the high-backed chair, he sniffed, then frowned. "That bad in here?"

"Like you'd hosted a poker game last night."

"Jeez." Mullen waved his hand ineffectually in front of him. "Did I tell you last time, they catch me using my smoke-catcher in here, I'm canned?"

I pictured his little black appliance with the grill and humming motor. "You told me, Harry. Why not just go outside like everybody else in Boston?"

His waving hand made a pass over the desk top cluttered with manila file folders. "Who's got the time?"

I nodded toward the file closest to him. "That the one you want me on?"

"Yeah." Mullen opened it, leafed through the first few pages. "Life policy. Insured was one Mah-*goo*, Brian D."

I took out a pad and pen. "Spelling?"

"Capital 'M,' small 'c,' capital 'G-e-o-u-g-h.' And 'B-r-y-a-n,' not 'i'." Mullen looked up at me, smiling with teeth as yellow as the keys on an old piano. "But, what's in a name, huh?"

"This countryman of ours fresh off the boat?"

"Uh-unh. Born here, along with his brother, Matthew. Looks like their mother came over from Dublin, though."

"How do you know that?"

185

"She's the one took out the policies on them."

So the mother's place of birth would be in the file, too. "Where's she now?"

"Dead three years, but her will provided for future premiums to be paid ten years after."

I remembered a few arrangements like that from my time at Empire. "Meaning Mom wasn't too sure of her boys' futures?"

"And with reason. Bryan, our decedent, was kind of a ne'er-do-well, used his small inheritance from the old lady to buy this ramshackle cottage up in Beacon Harbor."

I'd had a few cases there. "Old lobsterman's place?"

"According to the investigating officer."

"Who is?"

"Patrizzi, sergeant on the municipal force."

"I know him. He's good."

"Then maybe he won't have a problem with your looking into things."

I shifted in my chair. "Looking into exactly what, Harry?"

Mullen riffled more papers in the file. "Seems Mom was primary beneficiary, the boys reciprocal alternates."

"So, Bryan dies, Matthew gets the proceeds."

"Or the other way around, which now ain't real likely."

"And you think Matthew might have hastened his beloved brother's departure?"

"Could be," said Mullen. "The face amount's only twenty-five thousand, but people have been popped for less."

"Bryan was shot?"

"Uh-unh. 'Bludgeoned' to death with a piece of firewood, apparently during a botched burglary."

"And something makes you think the brother."

Mullen smiled, the yellow teeth absorbing any light that tried to glint off them. "Matthew spent a hard three in Walpole for burglary."

Our state prison, now called "Cedar Junction" by the Commonwealth's more euphemistic correctional officials. "Three years for simple B&E?"

"Talk to Patrizzi about it. But all Empire cares is whether brother did brother."

"In which case, you get to keep the twenty-five."

A hurt look from Harry Mullen. "Not me, John. The company."

TWO

Two brothers, John?

"And Irish, too." Kneeling on the close-cropped cemetery grass, I arranged the tulips so the heads pointed toward her gravestone. ELIZABETH MARY DEVLIN CUDDY. The name on the granite's growing fainter, but not the memories of the wife who lies beneath it.

You shouldn't stay on your knees like that this time of year. The dampness seeps up into clothes and bones, both.

I got to my feet. "Yes, Mom."

I could feel Beth smile as a freighter lugged through the choppy water below her hillside in South Boston.

John, you were always enough of the little boy that you needed a woman who was both spouse and mother to you.

Something caught in my throat as I said, "I know I needed you, Beth."

And now you're muddling through without me. As you'll continue to do.

"But not forever."

You've only the one life to live, John. Make it count for something more than visiting a grave.

I nodded, though without completely agreeing with her.

❄ ❄ ❄ ❄

Beacon Harbor's a twenty-mile drive north of Boston, but the fall foliage muted the traffic, and besides, Empire Insurance was paying portal-to-portal for my time. I found the police station again, nestled near the wharves before the town ever knew such sites would be worth top-dollar to developers some day.

As I got out of my old Prelude, I saw from the back a man walking toward the water. Narrow head, thin shoulders, plaid shirt over khaki slacks.

With a sandwich bag in his hand.

"Patrizzi?"

The man turned and smiled, then raised the bag to chest level. "Hey, Cuddy, you eat yet?"

❄ ❄ ❄ ❄

"I figure, the taxpayers in their infinite wisdom don't grant us a raise in four years, may as well enjoy the view, right?"

I said, "Right," around the bite of sandwich in my mouth.

After I'd told Patrizzi why I was there, he'd steered me to his favorite deli in the quaint, cobblestoned old-town before settling on a public bench. Just out of the sea breeze, we overlooked some of the cabin-forward wooden boats bobbing at white, poker-chip moorings.

Patrizzi took a sip of iced tea from a bottle shaped like a split of red Bordeaux. "Pretty soon, these lobstermen aren't gonna be able to operate out of here." A gesture toward the finger of land with a lighthouse topping it. "They're building condos there on the point, and the real smells of a working harbor won't be what the high rollers'll want coming over their cedar decks at cocktail hour."

"I understand this Bryan McGeough lived in a lobersterman's shack?"

"Yeah. Remember the one I showed you, the time you were up here on that dead artist guy?"

"I do."

"Well, the artist's place was a fucking castle next to the shithole McGeough lived in."

"The brothers local boys?"

"Unfortunately. Bryan was the older, the kind of loser gets more belligerent the more booze he puts away. But Matthew's been in and out of trouble, too, since he was old enough to throw a stone through window glass."

"My contact at Empire thinks Matthew might have graduated from stones to firewood."

Patrizzi chuckled with his mouth full. "Yeah, that hunk of birch was real convenient. Goes great with the botched-burglary story."

"Especially since Matthew did serious time for a … prior transgression."

"The stupid shit. Hits a house in the daytime, doesn't check to see a ten-year-old's sleeping in a back bedroom."

The light dawned. "Which kicked a simple B&E up to 'Home invasion.' "

"And got Matthew his stretch in state instead of county."

I chewed awhile. "You wouldn't think he'd make the same mistake twice."

Patrizzi gave me a sideways glance, then went back to watching the boats. "Glass in the rear door was broken, outside in. Television, boombox, crappy little camera taken."

"What wasn't?"

"Stash of cash Bryan kept under one of the many loose floorboards in his bedroom."

I thought about it. "And Matthew claims he knew the cash was there."

"Right. Which, despite his proven specialty in the field, makes him not likely to be the burglar this time."

"He says."

"You're right. Cash counted out to two-hundred-nine. Not much of a call bet to rake in a pot of twenty-five large on Bryan's policy."

"Matthew the only heir?"

Patrizzi nodded. "So he'd eventually get even the two-oh-nine back from his brother's estate."

"Unless Matthew was convicted on a murder charge."

Patrizzi gave me another look, then decided he wasn't that interested in the harbor after all. "I'll tell you, Cuddy. I got motive, I got means, I got opportunity. Only I talk with this Matthew, and it don't feel right, you know what I mean?"

I remembered Patrizzi as a good cop, but he was maybe better than I remembered. "What does the state police investigator think?"

Another chuckle as the last of his sandwich disappeared. "She's a wizard on the computer, but this is her first assignment that comes close to the street. All she sees is the circumstantial shit, not the people."

"Meaning there's more than just Matthew on the scene?"

"Last month, our Bryan filed a criminal assault complaint."

"Against who?"

"His brother's boss."

"Matthew's boss?"

"That's right," said Patrizzi. "Contractor named Ish Torenstein."

"Spelled 'I-s-h'?"

"You got it. Short for 'Isaac.' Ish goes about six feet, two-twenty. He somehow felt that Bryan was hitting on his wife."

"And so Torenstein starts hitting on Bryan."

"At the company barbecue, no less."

"Wait a minute," I said. "How come Bryan's at an employee thing thrown by his *brother's* boss?"

"Ask Ish. Or Matthew. Or better yet, both."

I watched Patrizzi for a minute. "You really have a bad feeling about this, don't you?"

He crumpled his wax paper and dropped it back into the bag. "Our Bryan autopsied out with a blood alcohol content of point two-oh."

"Staggering drunk."

"Probably, though he hit it hard enough generally that maybe he was still somewhat functional."

"Like at the picnic?"

"Talk to Bryan's neighbor, too. She's the one found the body. Or her dog did."

"Her dog?"

"Yeah. Neighbor's name is Greene, Renée, both with three 'e's.' She's new in town, subbing at the elementary school. Kind of horsey for my taste, but supposedly she's magic with the kids, so the board's gonna offer her a full-time slot come January."

"Can you take me out there?"

"Don't need to. We've released Bryan's house as a crime scene, and with that back door busted, you won't have any trouble getting in."

"How about Ish Torenstein?"

An odd smile from Patrizzi this time. "His company office is out on Route 1. They can probably tell you where he's working today."

Patrizzi rose from the bench and hook-shot his paper bag into a trash can. "Cuddy, whoever did Bryan McGeough oughta get a medal instead of a cell. But you shake anything loose, let me know, okay?"

I watched him walk back up the cobblestones toward the station, whistling a happy tune.

THREE

Bryan McGeough's house was a little closer than Ish Torenstein's office, so I drove first to the murder scene. Both sides of the street were lined with small cottages on postage-stamp lots. Some of the buildings had been added to and fixed up, appearing now to be year-round homes. The address I'd gotten from Harry Mullen fell more in the "before" than "after" category.

Patrizzi never told me which abutting shack belonged to the neighbor who'd found McGeough's body, so I started with the one on the right. A Boston Whaler lay cradled in its trailer off the driveway, but there was no answer at the door, and nothing in the mailbox. The house on the left had a small Japanese compact occupying its drive, but nobody answered my knock there, either. Its mailbox held four pieces of mail, however. Two catalogs were addressed to "R. Greene," one local utility bill to "Renée Greene," and an envelope with a veterinarian's return address—forwarded from Yelverton, Iowa—to "Pooky Greene."

Gruff barking began behind me a breath before a smoky voice yelled, "Can I help you?"

I turned and saw a tall woman coming toward the cottage, a German shepherd with some hound in its family tree lunging on a stout leash. Detective Patrizzi's "horsey" might have been unkind, but, on first impression, it was descriptive. A big-boned blonde in her thirties, Greene had striking features that once would have been called "handsome." Dressed in a heavy sweatshirt and jeans, she strode purposefully up the little flagstone path until her dog was a growling, straining two feet away from me.

"Renée Greene?"

A cock of the head. "And you'd be just who?"

"John Cuddy." I handed Greene her mail and took out my license holder, opening it for her to read. "I've been asked by an insurance company to look into the death of Bryan McGeough."

Green stared at my ID, curling her lower lip so that she looked peculiarly like her dog. "Pooky, that's enough."

The words, plus a forceful yank on the leash, resulted in the dog sitting back on its haunches, whining faintly.

Greene said, "What kind of insurance?"

"A life policy on your former neighbor." I put the holder back in my pocket. "Matthew McGeough's the beneficiary."

"That's Bryan's brother, right?"

"Right."

Greene blew out a breath that lifted the bangs off her forehead. "I was the one who found Bryan."

"Detective Patrizzi told me."

"Which is why you're here?"

"Yes."

"Okay." Another breath. "I guess I can go through it one more time."

Greene tucked the mail under her free arm, then led an unconvinced Pooky in a safe circle around me. She unlocked the door and waved a "come-in" with her key case.

The interior of the cottage was neat but spare, as though Greene had cleaned the place out but hadn't quite moved in herself.

I said, "Have you lived here long?"

"Arrived just over a month ago."

"From Iowa?"

Greene looked at me sharply as she shooed Pooky into a—probably *the*—small bathroom and closed the door. "How did you know that?"

"A piece of your mail. Or your dog's."

"My ...?" She took the envelopes from under her arm and flipped through them. "Oh, the vet's notice. They do that in Iowa. Call pets by the owner's last name, I mean."

"Nice touch."

Greene grinned, but not in a friendly way. "You buttering me up for something?"

"I'd just like to hear your version of what happened."

"Well," said Greene, moving to a loveseat that substituted for a couch in the miniature living room, "I don't really know 'what happened,' but I can tell you what I saw."

I took the old rocker opposite her. "That'll do fine."

Greene folded her arms into the folds of sweatshirt under her breasts, maybe something she'd learned to hide biggish hands. "It was like today."

"How do you mean?"

"I'd gotten home from school – I'm subbing?"

"Detective Patrizzi told me that, too."

A nod. "It was about two-thirty, and I changed clothes. The police asked me if I noticed anything odd about Bryan's house then, but I didn't. I just came in my front door there and put on jeans like today and took Pooky for a run along the beach." Greene tried a tentative smile. "She loves that, and we don't have too many beaches in Iowa."

"That why you moved here?"

Greene seemed to hesitate. "To the area, anyway. My mother was French-Canadian, but grew up in Massachusetts on the ocean. After both my parents died back home, I decided to make a fresh start near the water."

"Fresh start?"

Greene frowned. "You ever live in Iowa?"

Point taken. "So that day, you went walking with Pooky."

"Running, actually. She gets kind of antsy cooped up in this place all day. But it was all I could afford in Beacon Harbor, and I still owe a lot of sweat equity before winter."

I looked at the walls. Not yet insulated.

Greene said, "Well, when we got back from the beach, Pooky started growling and straining at her leash, like with you before. She wanted to go over to Bryan's in the worst way."

"Was that unusual?"

"Pooky and Bryan didn't get along real well."

"Any reason?"

"I think Pooky could sense he wasn't a man of honorable intentions."

A quaint way to put it. "Did Mr. McGeough ever make ..." I searched for a matching phrase, " ... unwanted advances?"

"Just once." Greene screwed up her features so they looked even more mannish. " 'Renée, I've never had a girl your size before. Oughta be a real challenge.' "

"His words?"

"Every one of them. That was the last time Bryan ever set foot in this house."

"He was here?"

"I tried to do the neighborly thing, like we do in the Midwest? Invited him in for a drink. He'd downed the first one before I turned around."

"Mr. McGeough liked the stuff?"

"I'd hear him once in a while, coming home late next door. Banging into things, you know. Some nights, I was amazed he didn't wrap his pickup around a tree."

"If we could go back to the day you –"

"Right, sorry." Greene blinked a few times. "Well, like I said, Pooky was hell-bent to get over there, so I went along. I thought maybe she was playing Lassie, you know?"

"That Mr. McGeough might have been hurt ..."

"... and Pooky wanted to rescue him." Greene closed her eyes. "But it was a little too late for that."

"How do you mean?"

"As soon as I was around the back of his house, I could see the glass in the door was broken. When I looked through where the pane'd been, I could see the smashed pieces – what do you call them?"

" 'Shards'?"

"Yes, yes the shards were all over the floor on the inside. And, because of where Bryan ... where the body was, I could see his hand and arm, so I tried the door, and it opened."

Greene hesitated again. "When I got to him and could see his head ..." One of the large hands went to her mouth, and she closed her eyes. "It was all bashed in, and there was this bloody piece of firewood next to the body. Well, I knew anybody looking like that just had to be dead, so I got out of there real quick and called the police from here."

"You ever meet Matthew McGeough?"

"Only just. I was leaving the house for work one morning, and Bryan yelled over to me from his driveway. 'Hey, big girl, this is my brother, Matt.' " I never did talk with the man, but I got the impression from Bryan that he'd been in some kind of trouble."

"Matt had been."

"Right, but that Bryan had gotten Matt into some other kind of trouble, too."

"And what kind was that?"

Renée Greene rolled her lower lip under again. "I think it had to do with somebody's wife?"

FOUR

After leaving Greene to liberate Pooky from the bathroom, I did a walk-through of Bryan McGeough's cottage. "Shack" really was more like it, the inside maintained pretty much as you'd expect a drunken bachelor to keep house. There were still some blood and police-tape marks that were consistent with what Greene had told me about finding her neighbor's body.

I went back outside to the Prelude and looked for an access road to Route 1.

✳ ✳ ✳ ✳

Torenstein Construction had a sandwich-board marquée at the far end of a strip mall that looked to be dying of starvation. The company's office was a free-standing concrete bunker with a front door like a tavern might need in a bad section of town: black metal except for a double-glazed, diamond-shaped window reinforced with chicken wire.

The door was unlocked, though, so I just pulled on the handle to get inside.

The first thing I heard was a woman's voice saying, "Well, why the fuck aren't they there?"

As I cleared the doorway, I could see a counter to my right. A woman with big, chestnut hair was turning toward me, a portable telephone squeezed by her jawbone against her collarbone. She wore tight green slacks and a gold lamé blouse that showed some cleavage. Her hands were going through the yellow copies of multipart forms, the fingernails longer than a gull's beak.

I sparked a smile, though, as she said into the phone, "Look, asshole, the purchase order says we put it through your guy on the twenty-seventh, which is three weeks ago … I don't care he was on vacation then, you gotta have somebody backstopping your … When? … No, no good. Ish needs them onsite by tomorrow noon … Well, then maybe he comes by and helps you 'break them loose.' You want that? … I didn't think so … Yeah, call before … Oh, love you, too, Donna."

The woman pushed a button on the phone. "Suppliers." She looked me up and down, then leaned over the counter, stressing the lamé some. "Why do I get the feeling you aren't in construction?"

"John Cuddy, Ms. … ?"

"It's Torenstein, but I like first names. Mine's 'Layla.' "

I guessed her to be late twenties. "After the Eric Clapton song?"

"Yeah," said Torenstein, her eyelashes actually fluttering. "But I'm more the 'heavy metal' than the 'unplugged' version, if you know what I mean?"

I let my ID holder fill the gap in the conversation. Torenstein looked from the laminate back up to me, even though there's no photo on it.

"Private eye?" she said. "We haven't had an onsite accident in two years."

"I'm not here about an accident. I've been asked by an insurance company to look into Bryan McGeough's death."

The only color left on Torenstein's cheeks came from her rouge. "Bry?"

"Yes. I understand you knew him?"

"Kind of." Torenstein went back to her yellow multiparts. "His brother, Matt, works for us."

"Was the company picnic the first time you met?"

Her face came up sharply. "Who told you about that?"

"Police records of an assault complaint."

"Oh, that wasn't anything." Torenstein gave me a smile. "Ish thought Bry was moving on me."

"Was he?"

"Yeah," she said, a little coyness in the lilt of her head. "Bry thought he was irresistible."

"Was he?" I repeated.

Torenstein leaned back across the counter. "He was cute in that Irish way you guys have."

"But your husband didn't quite agree."

She frowned. "Look, Bry has a few beers, he starts putting his hands here and there," Torenstein demonstrating on me as best she could given the two feet of Formica between us. "Ish spots it, comes over and belts him one across the mouth. Bry's a real man, he laughs it off. Instead, the weasel goes formal with the complaint thing."

"And what happened at the courthouse?"

Torenstein got coy again. "Thought you told me you knew all this?"

"Just that the complaint was made."

"Well" – another lilt – "some legal clerk talked Bry out of pushing it, so everybody made nice-nice. Hell, Matt's still working for us, that oughta tell you something."

"Can you tell me where he's working?"

"Matt? The big condo site we're doing out by the lighthouse on the point."

What Patrizzi had been smiling about during our lunch at the harbor. "Thanks."

As I turned, Torenstein said behind me, "You know, John, I seem to have this weakness for the whole Irish gene pool."

I looked back at her.

Layla Torenstein's tongue came out to wet her lips. "You got any more ... questions?"

"No," I said, and reached for the door handle.

❖ ❖ ❖ ❖

"Cuddy, can I put you on hold there?"

"Carla, I'm calling from a payphone."

"What, you don't have a cellular yet?"

"It's on order with my fax machine."

"Look, don't get me started on you and the twentieth century, all right?"

"Just come back to me quickly?"

I heard a click, then mercifully no Muzak. Carla operated a computer information service for nebbishes like me who couldn't work one ourselves, but she was no-frills when it came to the amenities.

I'd waited two minutes, twenty-three seconds when I heard another click and "Okay, Cuddy, where's the fire?"

"I have some names I'd like you to run."

"What're you looking for?"

"Anything interesting. It's an insurance/death case."

"Let's have them."

I gave her all the people I'd seen that morning except Harry Mullen and Patrizzi, having to spell most of them.

Carla sighed. "Christ on a crutch, Cuddy. 'Ish.' 'Renée.' 'Layla.' This 'Matthew's' the only one sounds normal."

"Can't always tell a can by its label."

"Me, I try to look on the bright side that way."

"Which is?"

"Screwy names like these, it'll make the search go faster."

FIVE

Speaking of names, Torenstein's could have been "Jonah" instead of "Isaac," because his construction site looked like the skeleton of a huge whale.

Most of the posts, beams and joists were erected and tied in, like a ribcage with forty-five degree bends in its cartilage. I pictured a realtor's brochure: "The waterfront units perched over a smashing surf enjoy cathedral ceilings and wrap-around windows from which views of both the lighthouse and ocean abound."

I asked a Latino guy working at a table saw for Matt McGeough. He pointed past two African-Americans carrying an eight-by-eight on their shoulders toward a guy in his twenties banging away with a nail-gun. I walked over, waiting until the blacks had left before I said anything above the firecracker noises.

"Matthew McGeough?"

The man stopped and turned. "Boss sees you without a hardhat, he's gonna go ballistic."

"I hear it wouldn't be the first time."

"Huh?"

"That Ish Torenstein went ballistic." I got to within three feet of McGeough and stopped. "John Cuddy. I'm investigating your brother's death."

McGeough squeezed his eyes shut for just a second, and I felt a little tug in my gut as he said, "Cop?"

"Private."

"Then I don't got to talk with you."

"Learn that at Walpole?"

A barely noticeable nod. "They like us to call it 'Cedar Junction' now. Soothes the visitors."

"Your brother come by often?"

Another flinch from McGeough's eyes, and another little tug behind my belt buckle. "Yeah, he did. Bry stood by me the whole time, man. 'That's what family's for,' he'd say."

"I heard Bryan didn't respect some other 'families' quite as much."

"Look," the eyes hardening, the nail-gun shifting in his hands, "you're not getting anything out of me about Ish. He hired an ex-con when a lot of other people wouldn't. So the guy shows some temper. Bry had it coming at the picnic, behaving like that when I got him invited in the first place."

"Maybe Mr. Torenstein didn't think the lesson took."

"I don't know what anybody else thinks but me."

"Then what do you think about the insurance policy on your brother's life?"

"That's why you're here?" A bitter laugh. "Look, I forgot Ma even took those things out. And I never thought they were for us."

"Even after she died?"

That same flinching blink, and I was leaning toward Detective Patrizzi's view of McGeough as suspect.

"Let me tell you something, man. I'm not getting rich working construction, but I'm working. I did my time on the home-invasion thing, and I'm doing my time with Ish. Maybe people wanted to hand Bry money, but I work for what I get."

"Hand him money?"

McGeough didn't laugh this time. "The night before ... before Bry dies, we're over at his place drinking beers, and he's talking about coming into some easy cash. 'Like that *Dire Straits* song, Matt,' he says to me. 'Get your money for nothing, and your chicks for free.' Then Bry laughs like crazy."

"About what?"

"Who knows? Like I said, we were drinking, and he was probably just pissing in the wind."

"But it seemed to you like the cash was going to be –"

"The fuck you doing on my site without a hardhat?"

A voice like rolling thunder, and I turned to meet the boss.

❀ ❀ ❀ ❀

Ish Torenstein was in his forties and, at the six feet and two-twenty that Patrizzi had pegged, a little shorter and heavier than I am. It felt like his right forearm alone made up the difference in weight as he led me by the elbow out from under anything that could fall from the framing.

"Mr. Torenstein –"

"I gotta pay workers' comp and liability insurance, I gotta deal with OSHA inspectors, I gotta listen to a town hall guy don't know a carpet tack from a railroad spike. And then a suit like you thinks he can just stroll onto my site and not get bounced for it?"

"Mr. Tor –"

He used his strong grip to spin me by the elbow. "I got a good mind to kick your ass all the way back to that little car's gotta be yours over there."

I glanced toward the Prelude fifty yards away. "That would take some doing."

Torenstein flared. "What, you think I can't?"

Very casually, I reached over to his free elbow, finding the nerve bundle inside the bone notch and pressing the pad of my index finger against it.

Torenstein coughed, then sagged a little at the knees.

I said, "I've no desire to show you up in front of your crew here, so why don't we both let go and just talk this out, okay?"

A ratcheting nod from his head as he breathed raggedly and released my elbow just a fraction before I released his.

Hoarsely, Torenstein said, "What the fuck do you want?"

I explained about the policy on Bryan McGeough's life.

Torenstein flared again, but without getting physical. "And you think I had something to do with that? The guy was an asshole around my wife, so I squared it right there."

"And your message got through?"

"Hey, I married a younger broad, you know? Layla's spirited."

"I meant your message as applied to Bryan McGeough."

Torenstein ran his good hand down his face in a now slow burn. "Look – Cutty, is it?"

"Cuddy, with two 'd's.' "

"Cuddy, this Bry was an asshole, but his brother's a good carpenter. Use your eyes on my crew. I got a regular 'rainbow coalition' working for me, but not because I'm some kind of liberal. Uh-unh, it's that guys from different backgrounds see things different, can make suggestions on the job that the fancy-schmancy architect never even thought about. Improvements that make the owner happy, and the building better, something you can bring your family out to show them, say, 'I built this fucking place, and it's better than it would've been with anybody else on it.' "

"Great speech, but I lost track of your message to Bryan McGeough."

Torenstein still simmered. "Let me tell you, then. If I caught Matt's brother moving on my Layla again, would I have rapped him another good one? You bet, maybe two or three, knock a coupla teeth out of his shit-eating grin, make the point. But I'm sure as hell not gonna brain him with a piece of firewood when I got something like Matt's nail-gun over there, riddle the guy like he was a pincushion and get myself some real pleasure from it."

One decisive nod this time. "Now, why don't you walk back to your little car and drive the fuck off my site so we can get some work done here?"

Without waiting for an answer, Ish Torenstein turned away and lumbered back into the empty bowels of his ascendant whale.

SIX

Arriving at my office in Boston, I checked with the answering service. Seven messages in all, three on the McGeough case.

I returned Carla's first and got a busy signal.

Detective Patrizzi's number was next. Out on the street for a while.

Then Carla again. Still busy.

Harry Mullen's message was the third, and he picked up after three rings.

"Hey, John, how're we doing?"

I could hear a little whirring sound in the background. "Shouldn't smoke on the phone, Harry."

"Jeez, how could you tell?"

"That black box has a motor, and your phone's—"

"Christ, thanks." I heard a scraping noise from his end. "That better?"

"I don't hear the whirring any more."

"Maybe I shouldn't worry about the cigarettes so much," said Harry. "Just go up to the Head of Boston Office, blow a few smoke rings in her face, and quit before she can fire me."

"Not until you hear what I have to say."

"I'm hearing you, John, but so far you ain't telling me anything I want to know."

I reviewed my stops in Beacon Harbor and shared my evaluation of Matt McGeough as a suspect.

Mullen said, "Same thing that detective up there thinks, huh?"

"Patrizzi and I seem to agree that the circumstantial stuff points in the wrong direction, only we don't have any other likely candidate."

"Don't matter to Empire. If the beneficiary's legit, we cut the check."

"Well, I'm still waiting to hear on some computer data searches. Give it two days, and if the searches don't turn anything, I'll submit a report advising that you can give brother Matt his money."

"Sounds good, John. And thanks for hopping on this one so quick."

"Thanks for thinking of me, Harry."

✻ ✻ ✻ ✻

I did paperwork on other cases the rest of the day, trying Carla twice more with busy signals both times. About nine-thirty the next morning, my phone rang.

"Cuddy, I got something for you."

"What you should get is call-waiting."

"Don't bullshit me this time, okay?"

Her voice seemed odd. "Carla, you all right?"

"It's just that sometimes … Well, you're the one deals in the real world with this shit, and I just pull it off a screen, but that don't mean I don't feel something, too."

"What are you –"

"Okay, okay. You got a pen?"

"Yes."

"It's about your 'Greene, Renée.' Took me a while to access things out in Iowa, had two modems cooking all yesterday afternoon."

"So what's the story?"

"You gotta drop the third 'e,' " said Carla in a tone I now recognized as subdued.

My pen hovered over the last letter in "Greene" before I spoke. "I think you're wrong there. I've seen four pieces of correspondence with her name on them, all from different places. Each showed her as 'Greene' with an 'e' at the end."

"Cuddy," in the subdued voice again, "I'm talking about the other third 'e.' "

SEVEN

It was pushing eleven by the time I arrived at the little clumping of shacks on Greene's street. Her car was in the driveway, but again no answer came to my knock, so I began walking in the direction she and her dog had appeared from the prior day.

After three blocks, the road petered out to gravel and then just packed sand, some trashcans nearly filled by people still staunch enough to brave the almost-winter wind but conscientious enough to deposit their litter. The beach in front of me was more gradual and sandy than the promontory where Torenstein and his crew were erecting condos. Here driftwood angled along the tideline in pieces as large as telephone poles or as small as the stick Pooky carried between her teeth as she pranced along.

I spotted Renée Greene a little farther on, half standing and half sitting on the stump of an uprooted tree. As I approached, she saw me, then called out to her dog.

Reaching Greene half a beat before the growling Pooky, I said, "No school today?"

She looked up at me. "Didn't need a sub, anyway."

"But, come January ..."

Greene looked harder for a moment before wresting the branch from Pooky's mouth and bringing it behind her head like a tomahawk.

I said, "Should I be worried about what you can do with wood?"

A grunt, then she let fly with the stick, sending it a ways and causing Pooky to tear off after same, paws spewing rooster-tails of sand.

Greene said, "I thought it'd be easier to have her running back and forth like this, so she doesn't pick up on your tone of voice."

"Like she did with Bryan McGeough?"

Greene sighed this time, then rested her rump back on the driftwood stump. "Just what are you thinking?"

"I'm thinking that you were known in Yelverton, Iowa, as a big sports fan, great host at tailgate parties."

Greene's head snapped up. "How did you ... ?"

"Computer search. It picked up a local newspaper article on a football game."

Greene shook her head now, and I had the feeling she was shaking off the pose as well. "Overcompensation."

"What?"

"Overcompensation," she said. "We do that, you know."

"I didn't, but I also found out that back home, your first name was spelled 'R-e-n-é.' "

"We do that, too." Another sigh, more resigned this time. "Easier to 'fudge' things if you can keep a name people often misspell."

"Ms. Greene, what's the term I should be using?"

"My, aren't we polite." Then a sniffle. "Sorry, you *are* trying to be polite." The large hands wrestled each other in her lap. "Okay, term for the condition: 'gender dysphoria,' a deep and abiding sense that you're a woman in a man's body. Or vice versa. Term for the person involved: Lots of them to choose from, but I prefer 'transsexual.' "

Pooky came back with her prize. Greene hurled it out a little farther this time.

I said, "Have you had the ... operation yet?"

"No. I've been through months of daily estrogen therapy, though. And weekly electrolysis, too – I'm lucky, with blond hair the beard doesn't show as much, but of course it isn't only the five-o'clock shadow we worry about, appearance-wise."

"You mentioned taking estrogen?"

"It gives me these breasts." Greene looked down her front. "B-cups, and quite attractive. The drug also shrivels the genitalia." She shuddered. "But not quite enough."

"That how Bryan McGeough caught on?"

"He chatted me up the first few times we saw each other. Bry was a pretty cute guy, and I was … flattered, to be honest. That what I'd dreamed about in Iowa for almost thirty years seemed to be coming to pass here."

"So you had him over for that drink."

"And before I knew it, he had Pooky closed up in the bathroom, and Bry was all over me." Greene looked up just as her dog arrived back with the branch. "As a guy all my life, I just didn't have the … instinct to sense what was happening until he had a hand up between my legs."

I kept quiet.

Pooky whoofed twice, and Greene sailed the stick, but only about half the distance of the last toss. "Bry started to laugh, the bastard. He knew I'd been subbing at the elementary and was approved to be hired on full-time next semester." Greene glanced up. "That was going to be how I'd afford my operation and the time off to recover. Earn the money January through June, have the surgery in early July, and be back in the classroom by Labor Day with no one any the wiser."

"Except for Bryan McGeough."

A pained smile. "I begged him not to say anything. After the way I had to … 'live' in Iowa, I wanted a fresh start here, like I told you before. A fresh start in leading the new, real life I was always meant to live."

I thought about Matthew's comment at the job site. "Bryan asked you for money."

"A hundred dollars a week, two hundred once I got on full-time at the school. I tried to explain to him I needed that money for my surgery, for the convalescence. But Bry just laughed. 'Hey, big girl, how do you think the parents'll like their little kids' teacher waving a dick under her dress?' And … and he went on from there."

Pooky came back, whoofing again as she dropped the branch at Greene's feet.

I said, "What did you do?"

"Walked over to Bry's house the next day, after I thought he'd maybe calmed down. I knocked on the back door, but got no answer, so I went in. Bry was passed out on the couch, probably drinking from the time he'd left my place. I must have surprised him, though, because he came at me, violent-attack mode. I tried to fight back, but Bry had my arm and was bending it – real pain – and so I picked up the log and swung it. Unfortunately, he was stepping that way – into the log, I mean – and he … he just went down."

Pooky whoofed some more. I reached toward the sand and tossed the stick end over end maybe forty yards away. The dog got the hint and tore after it.

"Thanks," said Greene, then closed her eyes. "I looked down at the pool of Bry's ... blood seeping out from under his hair, and ... and I got out of there before any stained my shoes. I went back to my house, settled my nerves, then waited till the next day to walk Pooky over there and kick in the glass. I took his television and a few other things to make it look right before I called the police."

I watched Greene sniffle again, then wring the big hands in her lap. "It just doesn't seem fair. All I want to be is what I feel I am, a woman who loves teaching the children who love her." A hesitation. "But now that's all wrecked."

"Not necessarily," I said.

Greene's face jerked up. "What?"

"I was hired to find out whether brother killed brother. I'd become pretty sure of the answer before learning about you. My report to the insurance company doesn't need the extra boost."

Greene blinked rapidly. "I ... I don't understand what you're saying."

I let my eyes rove down the beach, Pooky loping back with her prize. "The proceeds from the policy on Bryan's life can be paid in all good conscience since Matthew had nothing to do with his brother's death."

"But what ... ?" Green blinked some more. "Where does that leave me?"

I thought about my talk with Beth at her grave. "Make your 'fresh start' count for something beyond fixating on somebody who's already dead. Be good to the kids you teach, Ms. Greene, and put all this behind you."

"You're just going to let me ... go?"

"No. I'm going to let you stay."

Walking away from the water, I could hear Pooky whoofing louder and louder. It almost covered up the other sound, the crying one, but even that faded into the October wind whipping around the place where Renée Greene liked to run her dog.

HODEGETRIA

ONE

The woman who had knocked on "JOHN FRANCIS CUDDY, CONFIDENTIAL INVESTIGATIONS" opened the pebbled-glass door and entered my office tentatively. "You are Mr. Cuddy?"

An accent, Italian maybe. "I am."

"My name is Carmen Viola. There was a telephone call made to you about me, yes?"

Just after lunch, by an old friend from my days as an insurance investigator. "I've been expecting you. Please, come in."

Viola was a slim five-three walking toward me in conservative, two-inch heels. Thirtyish and pretty, she wore a black blazer and matching skirt, a leather attache case hanging from her right shoulder by a strap. The dark hair was short, kind of a mushroom shape on top, nearly shaved around the ears and neck. Up close, her eyes were bright blue behind wire-rimmed glasses, and a slight pong of tobacco came off her clothes as we shook hands.

I said, "Take a seat."

Viola chose the lefthand client chair, turning her face slightly against the September sun streaming across the Boston Common and into the office from the window behind me.

Settled, she said, "My superior was met with your friend from a prior claim against one of our ships, but I do not know how much he tells you about our current situation."

I brought a legal pad and pen to the center of my desk. "Just that an employee had died under suspicious circumstances, and your cruise line felt it might need a Boston-based investigator for some reason."

"Some reason, yes." Viola looked as though she needed a cigarette.

I said, "If you'd like to smoke, I don't mind."

"Thank you. Truly, but I am trying not to use the cigarettes when I am in America. As practice for quitting them when I return home."

"And home is?"

"Italy. Rome. Our company is headquartered there, but of course the ships go here and everywhere."

Viola might mangle an idiom, but her voice was musical even if her manner was all business. "How can I help you?"

"One of our employees, Mr. Daniel Boyle, died on his ship, the Star of Genoa. You know of it?"

"No."

"The Star is in the middle of our fleet. Not too big, not too small, not too old, not too new. Mr. Boyle, age thirty-four years, was an entertainment specialist."

"Entertainment … ?"

"… specialist, yes? The player of a piano in the lounge of our casino."

"I think I can picture that."

"Well, he embarked on this last cruise of the Star to the Caribbean. One day before its first stop in the islands, he is found dead …" Viola swiped an index finger under both eyes.

"You knew Mr. Boyle?"

"I hear him play the once, on a cruise I took with the ship for its inspection of the year."

"As part of your job?"

"Yes."

"Which is?"

"My job?"

I nodded.

Viola pursed her lips. "I was trained in the university as a lawyer, but I am used by our company as – how you say it, 'a troubleshootist'?"

"'Shooter.'"

"Ah, thank you so much."

"And Mr. Boyle's death is the current trouble."

"Yes." Another swipe under the eyes. "I have seen the pictures of him dead on his bed. Not a good thing."

"What did he die from?"

"When he was found, there next to him was a hypodermic needle. After the Star reaches its first port, we have an autopsy and analysis by laboratory of the needle holder." Viola paused. "Heroin."

"Mr. Boyle died of an overdose?"

"Of too much too pure, yes. When his body is examined, the island doctor there found evidence of drug injection on the feet between the … ?"

Viola wiggled her fingers at me.

"Toes?" I said.

"Ah, of course. His toes."

I turned things over. "Long-term?"

"Long ... ?"

"Had Mr. Boyle used drugs for a long time?"

"From the doctor's report, yes."

In Boston, heroin had gotten swept away by the avalanche of another white powder and its smokable alter-ego. But I'd heard horse was making a comeback against cocaine and crack in some circles. Even so, a long-term addict – especially one controlled enough to be regularly employed – ought to be pretty in tune with his dosage limits.

"Mr. Cuddy?"

"Sorry. Was your company aware of Mr. Boyle's condition?"

"That he was addict to the drug? No. We never hire him if we know, we fire him if we find out."

"And he would have known that was your policy."

"Our rule," Viola said firmly.

I gave it a beat. "I don't quite see why you need me."

She drew in a breath. "Because Mr. Boyle breaks our rule, my company must be sure now the problem is with him only. We do not wish to prosecute any person officially. But we do wish to know what happen so we can prevent the same thing in the future."

"And where do I come in?"

"Mr. Doyle when he is not on the ship lives here in Boston. The house of his mother in a neighborhood that is not so good. My superior thinks it better for me to work with an investigator who knows this city."

I focussed on the dead man's name. "And maybe one that is Irish-American also?"

"I believe that was for my superior a consideration, yes."

Direct, anyway. After I quoted my retainer and fee schedule, Viola accepted it, taking a leather case from her attaché and writing a check I was pleased to see drawn on a Boston bank. "You have offices in the city as well?"

"Not as such, 'offices.' But the Star is sometime in port here for minor repairs, so it is helpful for our company to have a relationship with a local bank. In fact, I am seeing you today because the ship lies now at dock in your East Boston."

"And her crew?"

A brightness came into Viola's eyes. "So you can talk first with those who knew Mr. Boyle?"

"Yes."

"I have arranged them to be available."

As troubleshooters go, I thought Carmen Viola might do nicely.

TWO

"The Star of Genoa," said Viola as she paid the cab driver who'd brought us to the waterfront in East Boston.

I'm not sure what the thing would look like next to a battleship, but standing dwarfed on the wharf, I thought of one. Painted white instead of gunmetal gray, though, with portholes like large pixels dotting her hull and the red "trim" halfway north turning out to be a deck level lined by lifeboats.

As we began walking toward the gangplank, I said, "How long is she?"

"Almost two hundred meters."

"And how tall?"

"The height of your Statue of Liberty less one floor."

Viola showed some kind of ID to a security guard near the base of the gangplank, then led me up a succession of metal treads like construction crews use to cover trenches in roads. At the top, a second guard admitted us onto a deck deserted except for a dozen men and women in green maintenance jumpsuits.

I said, "Anybody entering or leaving the Star gets checked like that?"

"You mean by the guards?"

"Yes."

"We try always, but no system is perfect."

Viola opened a hatch door, and I thought we'd entered a tower branded with the name "Trump". A three-floored, escalatored atrium of brass and glass sporting see-through elevators and strategically placed observation balconies. Not to mention arrowed signs or visible fixtures for a jewelry store, beauty salon, library, theater, ice cream parlor, tennis –

"So you will understand the investment our company has to protect, yes?"

I returned Viola's gaze. "Yes."

She pressed a button for one of the elevators. "Because it is his ship, we must see first the Captain."

❊ ❊ ❊ ❊

"Good day to you. I'm Captain Sjeng Rippen. And you, sir?"

That almost-German accent, but with a little hoot-owl on the vowels that I thought signified Dutch.

Viola said, "May I present Mr. John Francis Cuddy, who will investigate for us the death of Daniel Boyle?"

Rippen nodded gravely, shaking hands with fingers nearly half-again as long as mine. About an inch shorter than my six-two-plus, his fringe of hair and mustache were as white as his uniform, the latter with black epaulets and buttons on the short-sleeved tunic. The hair made judging age difficult, but I'd have said somewhere between fifty and sixty, with the body of a tri-athlete if the forearms were any indication of overall fitness.

After seating us in – appropriately – captain's chairs across from his chrome desk, Rippen looked once around the chart-walled and book-shelved room before focussing on me. "I must tell you, I never cared for this man."

"Mr. Boyle?"

"Yes. Oh, not for any offense, mind you. More the way he exploited his disability."

I turned to Viola. "Didn't you tell me the company was unaware of Mr. Boyle's addiction?"

Rippen answered for her. "Oh, I do not refer to that … poison, Mr. Cuddy. I mean the man's use of his cane."

"Mr. Boyle had an injury?"

"Indeed he did. And while I recognize that the days are long past when I could insist on only able-bodied seamen among my crew, I still do not have affection for ones who take advantage of their circumstance."

I could sense more than see Viola cringe, both at "able-bodied" and I thought "sea*men*" as well. "How did the injury happen?"

"Not on my ship," said Rippen. "It was from his schoolboy days, the reason he took up the instrument in the first place."

"The piano."

"Or so he said, frequently. That's what I mean, Mr. Cuddy. The man traded on his infirmity instead of dismissing it and surmounting it."

A great vocabulary in an at-least second language for Rippen, but while the words might have impressed the V.I.P. passengers seated at his table for dinner, I wondered how well he was able to mask the arrogance behind it.

Viola said, "Captain, we would like for Mr. Cuddy to tour your ship and interview the crew who knew Mr. Boyle the best, yes?"

A coolness pervaded the room. "If that's what the company thinks appropriate."

"It was my superior's specific suggestion," replied Viola.

"Well, then, Carmen," said Rippen, a degree or two chillier despite addressing her by first name. "Since we're not at sea, I suppose that is what will happen. However, even in port, I am quite busy. May I suggest you start Mr. Cuddy with the room where our 'entertainment specialist' met his coward's end?"

❊ ❊ ❊ ❊

"Not the easiest man to spend time with," I said.

"No, the Captain is not that."

We'd reached what Viola had advised me was called "B-deck." The shopping-mall spaciousness above had given way to dimensions more like those you'd see in a submarine movie. "This is the level where the crew is quartered?"

"Yes. The next door here was the berth of Mr. Daniel Boyle."

Viola produced a key and used it to open a metal hatchway that revealed a small stateroom with twin beds along each of the long walls. "Long" might be deceptive, as even those were only ten feet against the eight-foot width. Just room enough for a night table under a window – hibiscus-print curtains drawn – and a single lowboy bureau before the door to a closet bathroom.

"Cozy," I said.

"I am sorry?"

"Never mind. Mr. Boyle was found where?"

"The one there," Viola pointing to a bedspread in the same pattern as the curtains, but stained brown and yellow, probably from the release of Boyle's control muscles after death. "We have changed nothing. Except of course to take away the body and the hypodermic needle."

Even so, there wasn't much in the way of evidence that someone had lived in the room. I saw the cane Captain Rippen had mentioned, resting upright against the nightstand separating the two beds. It had the usual curved handle, a brass ring like a cigar band where the handle joined the shaft.

I pointed to the closed curtains. "Was that window open?"

"I would be surprised." Viola crossed to the night table, then pulled back the curtains to reveal just an additional expanse of wall. Smiling at me, she said, "This is an 'inside' stateroom. Our passengers who can afford more money prefer the 'outside' ones."

Afford more ... "Meaning, some passengers might stay in the rooms on this deck?"

"In the season, yes, when the bookings are like so." Viola raised her palm above her head. "But in the hurricane time, we have discount specials for the better berths, so these lesser ones are not sold."

I turned that over as a color photo on the nightstand caught my eye. "In the high season, then, the crew often sleeps two to a room."

"I am sorry?" said Viola, more cautious than confused, I thought, as she let me slide past her.

"Sometimes two crew members must share the same room?"

"Ah, 'share.' Of course."

I picked up the photo, an old five-by-seven in a horizontal, Lucite frame. It showed a young, red-haired woman and a baby boy with even redder, curly hair, the tail-lights of a '63 Ford visible behind them. The infant was cradled in the crook of his mother's left arm, her right arm gesturing outward. The expression on the baby's face was serene, almost maturely resigned, but the woman's features were etched with worry as she seemed not to quite make eye-contact with the lens.

Behind me, Viola said, "Hodegetria."

I turned to her. "What did you say?"

"It is from the Greek, I believe. 'Hodegetria' describes the pose and the … look the Byzantines showed in their painted icons of the Madonna and Child. We are to think that Mary and the tiny Jesus can see into the future, the suffering the Savior will endure for us all."

"Is this a photo of Mr. Boyle and his mother?"

Cautious again. "I assume so, yes."

Not the best omen for him, as things turned out. "May I go through the drawers?"

A canting of her head.

I pointed to the night table and bureau.

"Ah, of course."

From top to bottom: underwear, socks, shirts, a Polaroid camera, Ace bandages, back issues of Playboy and Penthouse. Nothing unusual in the bathroom, either. Just a stall shower and miniature basin next to the hopper, a dopp kit with typical male toiletries in it.

I said, "How about the roommate?"

"The roommate?"

"Can I speak to the person who shared Mr. Boyle's room during the high season?"

"Ah, yes. I bring you to him."

❄ ❄ ❄ ❄

"Arne, this is Mr. John Francis Cuddy. Please, you will answer any questions he has?"

I thought, Carmen Viola knows the crew on a first-name basis, then remembered she'd cruised once on her inspection trip.

As Viola moved off to one of the coral-colored barrel chairs in the empty cocktail lounge, Arne turned to me. He was in a tee-shirt and canvas shorts, standing on a stool as he held a clipboard near some liquor bottles on the secured shelves over the perimeter of the bar. Maybe five-eight when he hopped down off the stool, Arne had sandy hair, green eyes, and no facial hair, though his sideburns were worn a little long and flared toward the nose like miniature mutton-chops.

"Mr. Cuddy," he said, extending a hand to shake. "I am Arne Nyquist."

An engaging, sing-song accent. "From Sweden?"

"Stockholm, before I choose the sea and the Star of Genoa choose me." A practiced smile.

"Doing inventory?"

He looked back at the clipboard. "Inventory, yah. We must be full up with liquor for our next cruise. Food we can run out. Liquor, never."

I nodded. "The company has asked me to look into the death of Daniel Boyle."

Nyquist's face fell. "Danny, Danny, Danny. 'Tragedy' is what you call it."

"How long had you known Mr. Boyle?"

"Almost two years? Yah, he come aboard with us three years after me."

"And you roomed with him during those two years?"

"In the high season, when we are full up with passengers. Danny is no trouble, however. He sleeps like the dead, and ..." Nyquist closed his eyes. "I did not –"

"Don't worry about it. But you shared the room he died in?"

"Yah, yah."

"Why did you move out?"

The eyes opened. "Why? Because in the low season, we are not so full up with passengers."

"Yes, but you were the more senior employee. Why didn't he move to another room while you stayed in that one?"

"Oh, yah. Yah, now I see you. It was his leg."

"Because he had a disability."

"Not so much 'disability.' But with the ... with his leg, it was harder for him to move his stuff than me."

"So you moved instead."

"To have my own berth."

"When you roomed with Mr. Boyle, did you ever see him use any drugs?"

"No." Then a little louder, I thought to reach Viola in her chair. "No, against company rule. Never."

A mite hard to swallow. "You roomed with him. Saw him undress or come out of that shower, yet you never saw any track marks?"

" 'Track marks?' "

I used myself as an example. "Marks of a needle, on his arms or his legs."

"No. No, never."

I motioned toward my shoes. "How about between his toes?"

"I not look at Danny's feet. Why would I?"

A fair question. "Tell me, when you moved to a different room, what did you do with your key to the shared room?"

"Do? I keep it." Nyquist dug into the front pocket of his shorts, came up with a ring of keys. "This one it is."

"Anyone else Mr. Boyle was ... friendly with on board?"

Nyquist looked away, at first I thought toward Viola in the barrel chair. Then he pointed past her to the baby grand on a tiered stage. "Danny played the piano. Friendly with everybody."

"Anybody in particular?"

Nyquist came back to me, then stole a definite glance at Viola this time, lowering his voice to say, "Genna Drake."

✣ ✣ ✣ ✣

"She is another specialist, in our 'ShipShape Spa.' "

"Your what?"

Carmen Viola led me toward a staircase, the sign next to it reading "Sports Deck" under an upward arrow. "The Spa is our exercise lounge on the Star."

We climbed to the next level, Viola showing me a glass-walled room maybe twenty-five feet square. It was crammed with Nautilus and Cybex exercise machines, some treadmills and StairMasters sprinkled in. Off to the side was a reception counter, a blonde woman with a gymnast's body stretching her neon-chartreuse Spandex sheath as she did toe-touches.

"Genna Drake," said Viola as we entered the room. "This is Mr. John Francis Cuddy."

Drake straightened, hands going to hips. "Can you spell that for me?"

Midwestern inflection to the voice. Approaching her, I said, "C-U-D-D-Y."

She huffed out a breath. "For some reason, I can remember names better when the person spells it."

Drake had a nice blush to her cheeks, with maybe a little more facial hair than she'd like creeping over them near her ears. The hands and arms gleamed with a sheen of perspiration that had already drenched the Spandex.

Plucking a hand-towel from a stack of them on the counter, Drake began to mop her brow. "I'd ask you to sit, but there's no real comfortable machine."

"Genna," said Viola, "Mr. Cuddy is investigating for our company about the death of Mr. Daniel Boyle."

Drake blinked at her, then at me. "The poor piano guy?"

Awfully casual. "Somebody mentioned that you knew him pretty well."

Drake looked back to Viola, who said, "I must do a small errand. Mr. Cuddy, I will meet you here after fifteen minutes, yes?"

"Fine."

Drake waited for Viola to close the glass door on her way out. "Arne, right?"

"Arne?"

"Okay, you don't have to tell me. But if I were you, I'd have talked with Danny's roommate before the one he wanted to room with."

Sharp lady. "Mr. Boyle was interested in you romantically?"

A huffed laugh now. "Romance wasn't Danny's strong suit, believe me.

Aside from that piano of his. You've heard the expression, 'He talked a good game?' "

"Yes."

"Well, Danny 'played' a good one." Drake seemed to go inside herself. "He could make the damned piano cry till it nearly broke your heart." Then she looked at me again. "But that was his only talent. The musician was fine, the man left a lot to be desired."

"How well did you two know each other?"

More mopping with the towel, up and down the arms. "You mean, how far did Danny get with me? Some hand-holding, a little grab-ass. I could have fended him off, but hey, with that leg he couldn't dance, so I figured, cut him some slack, right? Only thing, with Danny it was give him an inch, and he'd take a mile."

"So you never became ... intimate?"

"No. No way." Now she used the towel on her neck and chest. "I worked hard for this body. I wasn't about to risk its future."

"I'm not sure I understand."

Drake tossed the towel into an open hamper behind the counter. "After a particularly good set he played in the lounge, I brought him a drink, and we ended up in his room. But Danny made the mistake of taking off his socks before he turned off the light."

"And ... ?"

"And I saw the needle marks. The pig shot up down there with whatever it was made him happy."

"To your knowledge, did he use drugs with anyone else?"

"No. Never even talked about it, the way some will."

"Some?"

"Some druggies I've had the bad luck to hook up with."

I thought about what Arne Nyquist had told me. "The track marks on Mr. Boyle's feet. Visible enough for anybody to see?"

Genna Drake went inside herself again. "Well, with his leg and that pale Irish skin, he never hung around the pool, but if somebody saw him undressed, I suppose, yeah." She glanced at the clock over the counter. "Hey, I've got to shower, and I'd like to do it here instead of my room so I don't steam everything up."

"I'll wait for Ms. Viola outside."

A different look in Drake's eyes now. "Or you could wait for me?"

"Thanks, but no."

"How come?"

"I'm sort of spoken for."

Genna Drake huffed out a final breath. "These days, show me a good one who isn't."

✻ ✻ ✻ ✻

I was on the other side of the Spa's glass wall for only a couple of minutes before Carmen Viola came up to me.

"Mr. Cuddy, I am sorry to be late."

"I was early."

"There is no other person on the Star I know for you to speak to."

"No problem. I think I'd like to try Mr. Boyle's Boston connection next."

"His 'connection?' "

"Do you have his mother's address?"

"Ah, of course." Viola dipped into her attaché case for a slip of paper. "Here it is. You would like me to come with you, yes?"

I looked down at the number and street. South Boston, where I'd grown up. Which would let me make a little visit afterward.

"Mr. Cuddy?"

"I think I can find it on my own."

✻ ✻ ✻ ✻

The address belonged to a matchbox single-family, the runt of the litter on a block of three-deckers off West Broadway. Even with the Massachusetts bottle-deposit law, the remains of quart-sized Bud and Schaefer beers lay in shards all over the sidewalk in front of the house. Its ocher paint was peeling like an onion, its cement stoop crumbling at the edges and corners. After ringing the doorbell three times, I got no answer to the bumble-bee buzz inside.

I went around to the side entrance. The screened door was closed, but the inner, wooden one stood ajar. I knocked on the aluminum jamb and heard a tired voice say, "It's open."

The doors gave onto an empty kitchen, the kitchen onto a small dining room and then a proportionately sized living room. Dust motes floated through stale air, the worn rug supporting a scarred coffee table centered before an old sofa against the wall.

A woman sat on the sofa. Or sagged on it.

She raised her eyes to me, but not her face. The eyes were veined, the cheeks and nose as well. Her reddish hair had sprigs of gray, no attempt at style that I could see. A house dress was as shapeless as the body it covered, the flesh puffy at wrists and elbows. Her mouth hung open, less like she wanted to speak and more that she couldn't quite muster the strength to shut it. You'd have to look very hard to see even the troubled young woman in the shot from the stateroom's nightstand. She held another photo in her lap, though, hands clutching the sides of the frame.

"Mrs. Boyle?"

The mouth stayed open, the lips flaccid. "Yes."

"Mrs. Boyle, my name is John Cuddy." I unfolded the leather identification holder, moving it to eye level for her. She glanced at my license, but not long enough to have read much of the printing on it.

I put the holder away. "I'm a private investigator."

No response.

"I've been asked to look into your son's death."

"Danny."

"Yes. Your son, Danny."

"My only child. First I lose his father to the drink, and now him to ..."

Her face went back to the photo in her lap. This wasn't going to be easy.

"Mrs. Boyle, I'd like to ask you a few questions."

No response again.

"Could I maybe see Danny's room here?"

"Upstairs."

"Thank you."

"The one that isn't mine," said her mouth without using its lips.

✻ ✻ ✻ ✻

There were only two bedrooms on the second floor, and not much doubt which was whose. Danny Boyle hadn't taken down his boyhood posters of sports stars from the seventies. Havlicek shooting a jumper, Yaz looping a home-run swing, Esposito scooping a puck past an opposing goalie. Some trophies, apparently from musical competitions, decorated the top of the oak dresser, "Daniel X. Boyle" engraved on flaky bronze captions.

Thinking of the bureau on the ship, I started with Boyle's dresser. Top drawers of socks and underwear, though not much of either. Same quantities of shirts and sweaters in the next two. His bottom drawer functioned as a memento box, with more back issues of "men's" magazines, some old newspaper clippings, and three photo albums. I skimmed the clippings, mostly short articles paralleling and expanding upon the music trophies. Then I flipped through one of the photo albums, finding an empty space where I thought the "mother-and-child" shot might once have been mounted before going onboard with the son depicted in it.

As I went to return the album, some loose Polaroids tumbled out the back. Gathering them up, I noticed the first showed an apparently surprised Asian woman, shying off from head-on while she pulled a bedsheet up to her chin. I caught the hibiscus print of the curtain in Boyle's stateroom behind her pillow, so I thumbed through the rest of the photos. The array included two white women and a black, all similar candids in the same setting, all anonymous until

I reached number five.

Carmen Viola, her wire-rimmed glasses visible on a corner of the stateroom nightstand, she herself not quite as quick with the sheet as the others.

Putting the album back in the bottom drawer, I pocketed the Polaroids.

❄ ❄ ❄ ❄

"Mrs. Boyle?"

Same position on the sofa, and nearly the same posture, staring down at the photo in her lap. I moved over to where I could see it, too.

Another shot of her son, but an 8-by-10 head-and-shoulders portrait. Probably high school yearbook, given the shaggy hairstyle and the sepia texture of the print.

"Mrs. Boyle, I need to show you some other photographs, okay?"

"Others?"

"I need you to tell me if you recognize any of the people in them."

She looked up at me.

I shuffled the photos to make Viola's next to last, then cropped each with my fingers so only the face was visible. Holding up the Asian woman first, I said, "Do you know her?"

"Know her? No."

Same for the next two, and then Carmen Viola as well. When I showed Boyle the black woman, though, she said, "Colored."

"You recognize this one?"

"No, but they're what did Danny in."

I returned the photos to my pocket. "How do you mean?"

Boyle spoke to the yearbook portrait in her lap. "The liberals with their busing, they brought the colored."

Boston had barely survived a terrible time in the seventies over forced integration of its public schools. Black kids were bussed into Southie, white parents not just protesting but actually throwing rocks and bottles through the windows behind which terrified children from other parts of the city thought they were riding toward a more equal education.

"My Danny never knew about drugs till then. And he swore to me that he never used them himself. Swore it on his father's grave."

I didn't say anything, hoping she'd just keep going, when Boyle looked back up. "Danny couldn't play sports because of his leg. Car accident when his father was …" Back to the portrait again. "During the busing, Danny got friendly with this colored football player. He's the one got my son started."

"Started on what?"

Boyle's face actually snapped up at me, impatience the first emotion crossing her features. "Smuggling the drugs on his ship, what do you think? My Danny never met that Tuggle boy, none of this would've happened."

She looked down at the photo of her son.

"Mrs. Boyle, do you know Mr. Tuggle's first name?"

"Of course I do. He had one of those names the colored give their kids. 'Vardell.' Vardell Tuggle. Danny would say, 'Ma, they're people, too.' But I knew better."

I couldn't see moving Boyle off her fixation, but she'd helped me, so ... "Do you have somebody checking on you?"

Her face stayed fixed on the photo. "What?"

"Is anybody coming to see you. A neighbor, a priest?"

"Just my son."

"Your son?"

Her eyes never left the frame in her lap. "My Danny. He visits with me every hour of every day."

I made sure the wooden side door closed and locked on my way out.

❊ ❊ ❊ ❊

Given it's a poor neighborhood, I think the cemetery people do a pretty fair job of maintaining appearances. The grass gets mowed regularly, and once a month somebody whacks the hard-to-reach weeds with one of those portable machines spinning stiff fishing line. But a little gardening can't do much to disguise a place you'd never mistake for any other. And it can't do anything for the freeze-thaw effect of Boston winters, reducing the lettering on a headstone while different forces of nature reduce what lies beneath.

Arriving at the granite reading ELIZABETH MARY DEVLIN CUDDY, I paused for a moment before speaking. "I picked up a tough one today, Beth."

Tough how, John?

I told her about Daniel Boyle. Then the people on his big ship, and the woman in her little house.

So, what are you going to do?

I looked off, down the slope and toward the twilit harbor. A couple of crows were playing keep-away with a much larger gull. The scrap of unidentifiable food would dangle from one black bird's mouth as the gull wheeled and dived. When the larger bird got too close, the carrying crow would drop its treasure, the other snatching the scrap up again before the gull could react.

John?

"Sorry, kid. Kind of winking out on you. Your question?"

What are you going to do about the new case?

"Wait till tomorrow, then make a call and pay a visit."

To whom?

I told her.

John, I don't think that's such a good idea.
"Frankly, neither do I."
At least, be careful.
I caught myself before offering the same advice back.

FOUR

The next morning, my call went to a police detective in the Narcotics Unit who owed me a favor. His computer popped out several addresses, and I got lucky – in some sense of the word – at the first.

It was in the African-American neighborhood called Roxbury, on a main drag displaying a lot of plywood windows. Stencilled above the entrance in place of a street number were the words "PRIVATE CLUB," a Boston euphemism for any place that could serve alcohol to its "members," a group that in turn would be loosely defined regardless of the dominant ethnicity of the men drinking there. Coming through the door, I was the only white I saw.

The room was humid despite the brisk fall air outside, some aftermath of liquor spilled making the atmosphere heavier than it had to be. The chairs and tables were mismatched, mostly cast-off dinette sets salvaged from alleys on trash day. All talk stopped the moment people looked up at me, a guy going six-five in a Chicago Bulls singlet and dungarees coming over right away.

He said, "Use your eyes over the door, you see 'Private Club.' "

"And I'm not a member."

"And ain't never gonna be."

"I'm looking for somebody who might sponsor me, though."

Almost a laugh. "Sponsor you for what?"

"Kind of a guest pass." I took out a twenty-dollar bill from my pants pocket. "Just for the day."

I hadn't exactly extended the bill, and the Bulls fan didn't exactly reach for it.

He said, "You smell like the Man, but don't no cop be flashing money at the get-go."

From one of the dinette tables, a man in his early thirties with good shoulders called over to us. "Dude buys me a round, he can sit for a while."

My tall greeter half turned to him. "Vardell, ain't you got enough whitey friends?"

The words that came back were just, "Man can't have too many friends, Kenneth," but the tone was, "Step aside," and Kenneth did just that, shrugging in a face-saving way as he ambled loose-jointedly toward the makeshift bar on the other side of the room.

I walked toward the man who'd interceded for me. He ran somewhere over six feet himself, close to two-thirty with a developing beer belly. His hair was cut short, sharp furrows razored down to the scalp in a V-pattern. The green polo shirt had a teddy bear logo on the breast and a stain from dark tea or dried blood below that. The eyes were the color of chocolate, but the look in them made you wonder if all God's killer whales stayed in the sea.

I said, "What are you drinking?"

"Establishment don't serve but one kind." Light, bantering tone, now. With a pump-sneakered foot, he pushed a chair away from the table for me. "Only somehow I get the feeling you ain't here to drink anyways."

I sat down, then laid the twenty on the table. "Still happy to stand treat, Mr. Tuggle."

He reached over, slid the twenty toward him under the middle finger of his right hand. "Way you dealt with Kenneth up there at the door, I figured you for the real thing. Hell, you just walk in here all by your lonesome, there got to be some cards in your hand besides that Southie accent in your voice." The twenty slipped under the table, the bantering tone disappearing with it. "You know my last name, you come here for me. Why?"

"I've been hired to find out about Daniel Boyle."

"Danny Boy?"

"He died from an overdose of heroin. I'm not talking prosecution, not even a lawsuit. I just want to know what happened to him and why."

"What and why, huh?" The bantering tone again. "You find me before I hear somebody looking, that mean you got connections on the police. Private eye?"

I showed him my ID, and Tuggle nodded once.

As I put it away, he said, "Also means you know about my principal means of support."

"Probably, but enlighten me."

A little rumble noise from his chest that didn't make it past his teeth. "Now you sound like old Danny Boy. First day I met that carrothead – was during the busing time?"

"I'd moved on before that."

"Yeah, well, lots of folks in your neighborhood, they still there then. The shit we had to face ..." Tuggle's eyes left me for a moment, a little fear flickering in them. Then he seemed to come back. "First time I met Danny was the first day we in that South Boston school. Nobody except a couple of the girls talk to us, but old Danny Boy, he read the newspapers, knew about me and the football."

"Which he couldn't play on account of his leg."

"Which his father fucked up for him in a car accident, drove his clunker straightways into a lightpole when he dead drunk behind the wheel. Well, I guess Danny figure he could use a body guard, even a homeboy nobody else'd hang with." The rumbling sound again. "Shit, Danny Boy was all right, but that momma of his? He actually apologize to me one day, account of he saw her throw this brick at my window in the school bus." The eyes went funny again. "Imagine that, the carrothead figure we tight enough he can actually admit his momma like to take my face off."

"You were friends with him."

"I suppose."

"So, what was the story?"

"The story?"

"About why Danny Boyle was shooting up on that ship."

The hard tone again. "Why the fuck should I tell you?"

"Because I've been hired to find out, and if you tell me, then maybe I won't have to ask a whole lot of other people the sort of questions that might bounce back on you."

Tuggle thought about it. "Cop-type people, you mean."

"Probably."

He looked casually around the room, as though checking to see if another guest had finally arrived for the party. Then Tuggle leaned forward in his chair, voice low. "My man, I hear from folks that what I'm about to tell got around, you be having to find yourself a new town. You know what I'm saying?"

"I know."

Tuggle stayed forward, voice still low. "Okay. Your connections on the police must of already told you about me and the smack."

Heroin. "Just a little."

"Well, they's kind of a 'boutique' market for the junk now, and I kind of fill it. Danny Boy, he know this, account of him and me talked about it over drinks one time he back in town off that big boat of his. Well, next time Danny on dry land, he want to know can I give him a little product."

"A piece of your action?"

"Right, right. So I say to the man, 'Shit, why you want to get into the smack for?' And he tell me, 'Vardell, you would not believe the coke and shit come north from Colombia, but the beauty is, the Customs people and all only watching for the nose candy coming north, not anything going south.' And Danny got some friends on the islands, they pay plenty for just an itty-bitty taste of the Old White Horse."

"So Mr. Boyle wanted you to give him some heroin to smuggle down there aboard the ship?"

"Yeah, yeah. Chump change for me, man. But to Danny Boy, it like twice his salary, you hear what I'm saying? And with that cane of his, ain't no real risk, neither."

"His cane?"

"What he use to hide the smack in. Danny hollow out the wood, then he take these little plastic bags, and he slide them down inside. That Danny Boy limp the product right past everybody, account of they know he play the piano on the boat."

I thought about it. "You know he was using, too?"

"Uh-unh. Man showed no signs of it. Besides, anybody dealing smack know better than to use it. Pretty soon, you shooting the money oughta be in your wallet up your arms instead."

"I was told Mr. Boyle injected between his toes."

Tuggle looked at me carefully. "Danny, he really shooting up regular?"

"According to the autopsy report."

A shake of the head. "Well, then, that explains it for you."

"How do you mean?"

Tuggle lowered his voice some more. "Say you dealing with these buyers in the islands, but you know they ain't real familiar with the product itself. So, before you give it to them, what you gonna do?"

"Step on the heroin a few times, make it go further."

"Right, right. And once the product down there, these customers step on it some more. Shit, they probably step on it so many times, you get a better hit from orange juice. But say these buyers, they ain't completely dumb, neither. So, before they give you the cash, what they gonna do?"

"Test the heroin somehow."

"Right on. So what Danny Boy told me he did, he keep this near-pure bag at the top of his cane, the first one in by the handle. That way, the island customers want to do a test, he give them that one."

"Bait and switch."

"Say what?"

"Show the buyers the pure, but sell them mostly the diluted stuff."

"Right, right. So, that's what must of happened on the boat."

"I don't get you."

"Listen what I'm saying to you." Tuggle slowed down, as though tutoring a poor student. "If Danny Boy on the shit like you telling me, can't be he was real heavy into it, account of I'da noticed the signs in him. So he just a dilly-tant, probably use the stepped-on product he selling on the way down there for his own recreation purposes. What happen must of been he got confused."

"Confused?"

"Yeah. Danny cook up some shit from the wrong bag – the pure one – and shoot it into himself."

It made more sense than anything else I'd been told. "Thanks for the ... enlightenment."

Vardell Tuggle smiled, but the eyes were as hard as his earlier tone. "Just don't be expecting no more."

FIVE

I'd asked for her at the gangplank. Five minutes later, she walked down it. "You wish to come back on the Star?" said Carmen Viola.

"Yes."

She got me past both security guards. As we started toward the atrium elevators, I said, "Let's sit a minute first."

Adjusting her glasses, Viola looked at me oddly, but led the way to a cushioned bench like a hotel lobby might provide. We sat side by side, and I took out the Polaroids, showing them to her in the same order I'd used with Boyle's mother.

Viola didn't jump at the fourth one quite as much as I expected. "Why do you show me this thing?"

"I found these at Mr. Boyle's house. In his bedroom bureau. Why didn't you tell me you'd been intimate with him?"

She glared now. "It was not your business."

"That the company's troubleshooter and the man whose death she's hired me to –"

"It was the 'shipboard romance,' yes? Only the one time last year on my cruise to inspect. And I know before Danny Boyle takes this picture that I will not see him again."

"Why?"

A self-possessed shrug. "He was better at his piano than he was in his bed."

Direct again. "You were that close to him, you didn't realize Mr. Boyle was using drugs?"

"Never while I am with him."

"And the track marks on his feet?"

Another shrug. "I do not see them."

"His feet?"

"The marks." Viola removed her glasses. "Before the plastic lenses, these were very thick. I am nearsighted, I do not see things without my glasses unless they are close to me, like so." She held her palm six inches from her eyes. "And Danny Boyle's feet never so very close."

"How about his cane?"

Now just a confused look.

✣ ✣ ✣ ✣

We were inside Boyle's stateroom, me unscrewing the handle of his cane at the brass cigar band. When the handle came off, I held the open ends up to the light, then turned both shaft and handle upside down before shaking them.

Nothing.

Viola said, "Why do you do this?"

"I have reason to believe Mr. Boyle smuggled heroin in the hollow of his cane."

"*Narcotraffico?* On the Star of Genoa?"

A little disingenuous, I thought. "You said when Mr. Boyle's body was found, the syringe was still there."

"Yes. He died from the overdose."

"Were there any bags or packages of drugs as well?"

"Not in the report."

"Whose report?"

✣ ✣ ✣ ✣

Genna Drake looked from Carmen Viola to me. "What's the big deal?"

"The big deal," I said, "is that you found Daniel Boyle dead."

She leaned her elbows on the Spa's counter near the hand towels. "I thought you already knew that when you came to see me yesterday."

"I didn't."

"Yeah, well, maybe you should have."

I found myself conceding Drake the point. "You told me then you wanted nothing more to do with Mr. Boyle."

"Nothing sexual. He could still play the piano, though."

Viola said, "You went to his stateroom to ask for him to play for you?"

"Not for me. I was off-shift, just sitting there in the casino bar, and Arne said, 'Hey, Genna, Danny's late. Can you go get him up here?' "

I waited for Drake to finish.

She did, by saying, "And when I got down to B-deck, the stateroom wasn't even locked, so I pushed in the door, and – yuck, was I glad I never slept with that jerk."

I didn't look at Carmen Viola, and she didn't look at me.

✣ ✣ ✣ ✣

"There's a reason I asked Ms. Viola not to come up here with me."

Arne Nyquist busied himself rearranging glassware that looked fine where it had been. "Yah, and I should be interested?"

"Probably. You knew Daniel Boyle pretty well."

"Just because I share a room with –"

"Probably some sense of his … love life?"

Nyquist wouldn't meet my eyes. "Some."

"That he was fairly successful with women?"

A pause before another, "Some."

"Well, that says to me that you wouldn't send Genna Drake down to Mr. Boyle's stateroom to check on him when he was a little late." I beckoned Nyquist closer across the bartop. "What I think you'd do is go down yourself, give your friend a break in case he was bedding the lady *du jour.*"

Now Nyquist didn't know where to look. "All right. I go down there first, yah."

"And when Boyle didn't answer your knock, you used your key to open the stateroom door."

A nod.

"And found him."

Another nod. "It was … horrible. His face, and …" A violent shudder.

"But most important of all, you took away the heroin."

Nyquist decided it was time to look at me. "I see his cane open at the top, and I do not understand. Then I look inside, and shake out the … I do not know what the powder was. Just that it … must be drugs, and Danny …"

"And Danny what?"

"The company fires him for such if he is still alive, so I take the drugs and throw them into the sea."

I wasn't sure I bought that, but I said, "And you left the stateroom door unlocked, and then in the bar asked Ms. Drake to go down and 'get' Danny."

"Yah, yah. I did not know what else to do. Danny was always telling me about his mother, how hard the life is for her. Arne Nyquist ran out of steam. "I thought so much drugs lie there with his body, it can be worse for her. And maybe this way, the company pays her something, yah?"

It sounded so stupid, I found myself believing him.

SIX

I left the Star of Genoa and went back to my office. Looked across the Common at the gold dome of the State House. Watched the tourists flocking like swallows for our foliage season. And thought about how I'd spent my last two days.

The piano player, with his job and his friends, his cane and his smuggling. And, most of all, his death. Such a bizarre mistake for …

Then I thought of a question I hadn't asked. And though I wasn't sure I wanted the answer, I owed it to myself to find out for sure.

❊ ❊ ❊ ❊

The screened door at the side of the house was still just clicked shut, but the inner, wooden one that I'd closed and locked remained that way. When knocking didn't work, I mentally devoted some of my fee from Carmen Viola's company to fixing any damage I might cause.

The third time I put my shoulder to the inner door, the lock cracked out of the jamb, and I was inside the kitchen. No lights, no sound. I moved very slowly to the dining room and through it into the living room beyond.

Boyle was still in the same place on the sofa, but now the yearbook photo was on the coffee table instead of her lap, as though she must have gotten up at some point since I'd left her. The room was mostly in shadows, some slats of half-light dimly striping her features.

I took a threadbare chair across from the sofa. "Mrs. Boyle, I'll pay for your door."

"My door?" Her mouth stayed open, the lips still not contributing much.

"When I was here yesterday, we talked about your son, remember?"

Boyle spoke to the photo. "Danny's my only child."

"You told me. You also told me about how Vardell Tuggle got Danny involved with drugs."

"Colored. Colored did that to him."

The question I hadn't asked. "When your son talked with you about the drugs, did he describe how the deals were done down in the islands?"

Boyle looked at me now, the head swaying stolidly, like a cow watching a car go by on the road outside its pasture. "Danny thought he was so smart. He knew how to fool those people he sold the drugs to, fool them with that one pure bag he'd show them. 'My calling card, Ma,' he'd say to me."

"And you were afraid for him?"

"Afraid?" She looked back down at the photo of her son. "No, I wasn't afraid. I just didn't want my only child doing that colored thing there."

"I'm sorry?"

Back up to me again, but now with the impatience in her voice. "Selling drugs, the way the colored do." Then a softening. "But I was smart, too. Smarter than Danny. I figured out a way to get him out of it."

Jesus. "To get him out of dealing drugs?"

"Right. I waited till the day before he was going back to his ship again. When he was asleep – Danny was always a sound sleeper. Slept through the night from the time he was seven months old."

"Mrs. Boyle?"

"Yes?"

"The night before your son went back on the ship ..."

"... he'd already packed and everything. So, I went into his room upstairs, and I took that cane of his, with the colored drugs already in it. Then I opened the handle part and switched the first two bags around."

What Vardell Tuggle had suggested to me. "So the pure bag wasn't on top anymore."

A nod. "The people on the islands – Danny's customers, they wouldn't want to buy from him anymore." The head went back to her coffee table before a sigh like a skyscraper collapsing on itself. "Danny swore to me."

"That he didn't use drugs himself."

"Swore on his father's grave." Then Boyle reached down with her right hand, picking up the yearbook shot and cradling it, face out, in the crook of her other arm. "This is Danny. He's my only child."

Recalling Carmen Viola's explanation of "hodegetria," I left Boyle on the sofa with her son.

A BOOK OF KELLS

ONE

The Irish-American Heritage Center was located in a red-bricked building three blocks off East Broadway in South Boston. Growing up in the neighborhood, I remembered the structure as a public elementary school, but when the city fell on hard times in the seventies, the mayor and council sold a number of municipal properties to keep real estate taxes from rocketing skyward. As I parked my old Honda Prelude at the curb, I got the impression that the Center was doing a lot better by the building than the school department ever had.

The main entrance consisted of three separate doors, the one to the left having a sign in gold calligraphy reading, "Try This One First," which I thought was a nice touch. Inside the lobby area, the same ornate lettering adorned the walls, including a virtual mural with the homily:

> May your troubles be less,
> Your blessings be more,
> And nothing but happiness
> Come through your door.

Returning to reality, on my right was an office complex, probably where the principal used to hold court. A woman sitting behind a reception counter rose when she saw me and slid back the glass over a piece of burnished oak that I doubted could be original equipment.

"Can I help you?" she said.

"John Cuddy, here to see Hugh McGlachlin."

"Oh, yes." Her expression shifted from concerned to relieved and back again. "Please, come in."

A buzzer sounded, and she opened the door nearest her counter. Instead of making me cool my heels like a recalcitrant student, though, the woman showed me through a second, inner door immediately.

She said, "Hugh, Mr. Cuddy."

227

A voice, with just a lick of the brogue, said, "Thank you, Grace. And hold any calls, if you would, please."

Grace nodded and closed the inner door behind me.

The man rising from the other side of the carved, teak desk was about five-nine and slight of build, wearing a long-sleeved dress shirt and tie. His hair was gray and short, combed a little forward like those busts of Roman emperors. Despite the hair color, his face was unlined around the blue eyes, and his smile shone brightly enough for a toothpaste commercial.

A woman occupied one of the chairs in front of McGlachlin's desk, but instead of standing as well, she turned toward me while twisting a lace handkerchief in her lap. I pegged her as middle forties, with florid skin and a rat's nest of red hair. She wore the drab, baggy clothes of someone catching up on her housework, a canvas tote bag that had seen better days at her feet.

The man came around his desk and extended his right hand. "Hugh McGlachlin, Executive Director of the Center here. Thanks so much for coming so quickly."

I shook with him, his grip the vise that comes from holding tools a lot.

McGlachlin turned to the seated woman. "This is Nora Clooney."

She swallowed and shook hands with me as well, hers trembling in mine.

"Well," said McGlachlin, tapping the back of the other chair in front of his desk, "I'm not sure of the protocol, but I think I'd be most comfortable using first names."

"Fine with me."

He and I sat down at the same time.

McGlachlin studied me briefly. "I didn't tell Michael O'Dell why we needed a private investigator."

O'Dell was a lawyer in Back Bay who'd fed me a lot of cases over the years. "Probably the reason he didn't tell me."

The toothpaste smile again. "Michael is a member of our Advisory Board. And he assured me you were the soul of discretion and someone to be trusted."

"I'll be sure to thank him."

McGlachlin leaned back in his chair. "I think you may be just the man for the job, John."

"Which is?"

He pursed his lips. "How much do you know about the Heritage Center?"

"Only what I've seen so far this morning."

Hugh McGlachlin rose again, picking up a nine-by-twelve manila envelope from the corner of his desk. "In that event, I think a brief tour might prove instructive. Nora?"

Clooney preceded us out the inner door.

❋ ❋ ❋ ❋

"We incorporated as a non-profit institution in seventy-five," said McGlachlin, "and the Center moved into this building four years later. I don't mind telling you, John, the city left it quite the mess." He made a sweeping gesture with the envelope. "But, with the help of Irish-American tradesmen generously donating their time and talents, we've been able to renovate the interior a bit at a time and rejuvenate the community we serve."

I sensed that the operative word for me was "donating."

The three of us were moving down a hallway festooned with the various crests of the thirty-two counties of Ireland, that signature gold calligraphy naming each. On the left, double doors opened onto a large and beautifully rendered countryside room sporting an exposed-beam ceiling, slate floor, and a massive fieldstone fireplace on the shorter wall. In the hearth was a cauldron suspended by metal bars over an unlit fire, an iron milk jug bigger than a beer keg to the side.

I said, "Hugh, what exactly is the Center's problem?"

McGlachlin just stopped, but Clooney seemed to freeze in her tracks.

He looked up at the crests over our heads. "Would you know where your forbears hailed from, John?"

"County Kerry on my father's side, Cork on my mother's."

"Ah." McGlachlin pointed first to a shield with a white castle and gold harp. "Kerry ..." Now a crest with a galleon sailing between two red towers. "... and Cork, there."

Then he took a step onto the slate floor of the countryside room. "In both places, John, they would have broken their backs hoisting jugs like that one onto a pony cart to carry their cows' milk to town, ladling it out to those with the money to be buying." McGlachlin fixed me with those blue eyes. " 'Tis a marvelous thing that we who emigrated are more fortunate, don't you think?"

"Hugh?"

"Yes?"

"Until I know why you called Michael O'Dell – and probably why Nora seems nervous as a wet cat – I won't be able to tell you whether I can help the Center for free."

McGlachlin grinned this time, but without showing any teeth, and I had the feeling that despite being six inches taller and fifty pounds heavier, I'd hate to meet him in an alley.

He said, "Yes, I do believe you're the man for our job. This way, please."

We got on an elevator and exited at the second floor. As I followed McGlachlin down the hallway, I tried to stay abreast of Nora Clooney. No matter how I adjusted my stride, though, she always stayed a step behind me.

McGlachlin stopped again, this time outside a large classroom where the chairs and tables were shoved against the walls. Perhaps a dozen girls and young women were moving in a circle, their hands joined but held high.

He said, "We have step-dancing classes in here, though we also host Lithuanian folk-dancing for our neighbors of that extraction. The 'Nimble Thimbles' teach needlework over there, and every Wednesday we have instruction in Gaelic for both beginners and intermediates in the native tongue."

I just nodded this time.

Another toothey smile. "All right, then. The next floor is the one that concerns us most at the moment."

✳ ✳ ✳ ✳

"This is our museum, John."

McGlachlin used a key to open a heavy security door in a corridor filled with construction odds and ends, plaster dust on every surface. The area at the end of the hallway was still just undefined space, only a few wall studs in place.

The security door opened into a large viewing room, glass-faced cases along two walls displaying china in all shapes and sizes, lots of pastel-green "icing" on the edges of plates and pitchers.

"Recognize it?" said McGlachlin.

My mother had a piece she prized. "Belleek."

"Very good. The finest of Irish porcelain, kilned at the huge pottery in County Fermanagh." He waved a hand at the third wall. "And there's the loveliest collection of lace you may ever see."

I took in the white fabric spread on trays of green velvet. "You said downstairs that –"

"– this was the floor that concerns us the most right now. Yes, indeed I did." McGlachlin's voice dropped to the subdued tone of a devout man entering his church. "Over here, John."

We went through a doorway into a smaller room with soft, recessed lighting. In the center was a free-standing case about two-feet square. Its top or cover evidently had been glass, though it was hard to judge further because it was shattered into crumbly crystals lying fairly evenly on the otherwise empty green velvet.

I said, "You've had a theft."

McGlachlin looked my way as Nora Clooney began twisting her hankie again. After glancing at her, he came back to me.

"John, you recognized the Belleek. Would you also know about the Book of Kells?"

"Something the Irish monks did back in the Middle Ages?"

"Close enough. During the eighth and ninth centuries, Celtic scribes painstakingly copied each passage of the Four Gospels onto 'paper' made from the stomach lining of lambs. Every page is an artist's palette of flowing script and glorious colors, with the original Book carefully guarded at Trinity College in Dublin. However, in nineteen-seventy-four, some reproductions were permitted – they called them 'facsimiles.' Only five hundred, mind you, but they are works of art themselves, down to the worm-holes in the pages."

I looked at the smashed case. "And you had one of those."

"The Center purchased its facsimile in nineteen-ninety for twenty thousand dollars."

I thought back to my time as a claims investigator. "You've notified your insurance carrier."

McGlachlin shook his head. "On the collectors' market now, the price is ten times what we paid, but the money is largely irrelevant: Nobody who has a Book is willing to part with theirs."

"Still, the policy would pay –"

"It's not a check I want, John. It's the Book itself. There'll never be any more facsimiles produced, you see, at least not in our lifetimes. The Center needs its copy back as a matter of ..." Another sweeping gesture with the manila envelope "... heritage."

I looked at him. "Hugh, let me save you some time and possibly some fees as well. The Boston Police have an excellent –"

"Not yet, John."

"I'm sorry?"

McGlachlin seemed pained. "I'm rather hoping this can be resolved without resorting to our insurance or the police." He opened the envelope and slid a single piece of paper from it. "This was on top of the shards there."

McGlachlin tried to hand me the sheet, but instead I stepped sideways so I could read it without touching it. In simple block lettering on white photocopy stock, the words were: "TAKEN, BUT NOT STOLEN, AND WILL BE RETURNED".

"Who found this?"

"I did, sir," said Nora Clooney, the first words I'd heard her speak.

McGlachlin cleared his throat. "Nora volunteers her time to clean for us. Given all the plaster dust from the ongoing renovation, it's a tall task."

I looked at Clooney. "Where was this piece of paper when you first saw it?"

Clooney glanced to her boss. "It was just like Mr. McGlachlin told you. The note was lying atop all the broken glass."

The brogue wove through her voice much more than her boss's. "And the glass hasn't been disturbed since?"

McGlachlin said, "I've kept the room locked since Nora came to me this morning with the news."

I let my eyes roam around before returning to Clooney. "Do you clean this room the same time each day?"

"First thing in the morning, sir."

"Meaning?"

"Eight o'clock. It wouldn't do for visitors not to be able to see the Book for the plaster dust covering its blessed case."

"And nothing was wrong yesterday at eight?"

"No, sir," the lace hankie getting wrung some more.

I glanced around again. "Other than the locked door, what kind of security do you have for this room?"

"None," said McGlachlin.

I must have stared at him.

"You see, John, we've been spending every available penny on the renovations."

"No guards, no alarms?"

"As I said."

"But what about visitors wandering in here?"

"Access to these museum rooms is restricted to only those of us with a key to that door. As anyone can plainly see, there's been no attempt to jimmy it, nor the windows, even assuming the bastard – sorry, Nora – thought to bring a ladder with him to lean against the outside wall."

I thought about it. "I can see why you haven't gone to the police."

McGlachlin sighed. "Exactly so. This had to be – is it still called 'an inside job'?"

I went back to Clooney. "So the incident must have occurred sometime between eight or so yesterday –"

"– more like nine, sir, the time I was finished in here –"

"– to eight A.M. this morning."

"Yes, sir."

I looked at McGlachlin. "All right, how many people have keys to that door?"

"I do, as Executive Director. And Nora, for her cleaning and turning."

"Turning?"

She said, "Every day, sir, I go up to the Book and turn a page."

McGlachlin pointed to the outside windows. "So the sun fades the ink only the tiniest bit and more or less evenly."

I looked at the shattered glass. "How did you open it?"

Now they stared at me.

I said, "The glass cover or top here. How did you open it to turn the pages?"

"Oh," said Clooney, and moved to a wall panel that might contain circuit breakers. After unfastening the cover, she threw a switch, the remaining structure of the glass top itself clicking subtly upward.

McGlachlin went to demonstrate. "You can then lift this –"

"Don't touch it."

He looked at me.

"Fingerprints," I said.

McGlachlin looked down at the glass. "Ah, yes. Of course."

I gestured toward the paper he still held in his hand. "And please don't let anybody else touch that. As it is, the police will need elimination prints from you and –"

"Harking back to what I said earlier, John, hopefully we won't be needing the police, thanks to you."

I waited before asking, "Who else has keys to the security door?"

McGlachlin raised a finger. "The chairman of our Advisory Board, Conor Donnelly. He's a professor of Irish Studies."

"Where?"

McGlachlin named the college.

I said, "Who else?"

Another finger. "Conor's brother, Dennis, was a generous contributor to the Center, so he received a key as well."

"Dennis Donnelly, the venture capitalist?"

"The very one."

"The man kicks in enough cash, he gets his own key?"

McGlachlin cleared his throat again. "Given the amount of Dennis's contribution, John, that would be a rather awkward request to deny."

"Anybody else?"

"With a key, now?"

"Right."

"Only Sean Kilpatrick."

"And he's … ?"

"The carpenter donating his time to do our work down the hall."

I looked around me one last time. "These museum rooms look pretty well completed. Why would Kilpatrick need access to them?"

"In the event anything went 'wrong,' he said. But, John, Sean's somebody who's completely trustworthy."

"Hugh?"

"Yes?"

"At least one somebody with a key obviously isn't."

❋ ❋ ❋ ❋

"Mr. McGlachlin, will you or Mr. Cuddy be needing me any more today?"

We were back in the Executive Director's office, the door closed.

"John?" said McGlachlin.

"Not right now, thanks."

"Go home, then, Nora. And tell Bill I'll be by to visit after work."

"Thank you, that'll brighten his day for sure."

After Clooney picked up her tote bag and left us, I said, "Bill's her husband?"

"Just so. And a fine, generous man to boot, but suffering from the cancer. You know how that can be."

Though I figured McGlachlin meant his comment rhetorically, I still pictured my wife, Beth, asleep in her hillside less than a mile away. "I do."

He shook his head some more. "They met each other here at one of the Center's first socials. But then we've sparked a lot of unions from our activities."

"Hugh?"

"Yes?"

"Who else besides Nora – and you – actually knew about the way the cover over your Book of Kells opened?"

McGlachlin grew wary. "And what difference would that make, John? The case was smashed."

"That 'ransom note,' it was lying on top of the broken glass."

"As we told you."

"Being a single sheet of paper, it's pretty light."

More wary now. "Agreed, but –"

"– so the note wouldn't have disturbed the broken glass under it very much, if at all."

McGlachlin seemed to work it through.

To save time, I said, "And since the glass shards were spread almost evenly ..."

The Executive Director closed his eyes. "... the Book was probably taken out of the case before the cover was smashed."

"Hugh, somebody wanted you to think that the glass had to be broken in order to take the book. So my question still stands: Who else knew about the cover mechanism?"

McGlachlin fixed me with his blue eyes. "John, I just don't know. But I do know this. Nora wouldn't know what to do with our Book. And she's as honest as the day is long."

I filed that with his endorsement of the carpenter, Sean Kilpatrick. "You didn't mention if Grace outside there also had a key."

"She does not. But given where Grace sits, she's in a position to see who comes and goes."

"Assuming everybody comes through the main doors."

"The other outside doors *are* alarmed, John. And besides, Grace tells me she saw all three of our key-holders walk by her yesterday."

"Both in and out?"

"No, but each had either a knapsack or briefcase or tool box big enough to hold the Book."

"You have any suggestions on where I should start?"

"More a question on *how* you should start." McGlachlin paused. "So far, only Nora, Grace, and you know what's happened."

"And given the tenor of that note, you're hoping the Book will be back by the time anyone else has to?"

"On the button, John. There's an Advisory Board meeting here next week – five days hence to be exact. The members have a tradition of 'reading' a passage from the Book, as an opening benediction, you might say."

I looked at him. "Meaning, the Book is taken from the case?"

"No. No, we all troop up to the room, and thanks to Nora's turning the page each day, there're always different passages to choose from."

"Hugh?"

"Yes?"

"Anything else about this situation you haven't told me?"

"One of the reasons I'm trying to resolve things quickly." McGlachlin pursed his lips again. "You see, Conor – our Board chairman – was asked by his brother Dennis a few months ago to loan out the Book for a party."

"A party?"

"Dennis was giving a lah-de-dah affair at his home, and he wanted to have our facsimile on display for his guests."

"And what did Conor say?"

"That he'd have to put it to the Center's Board, which he did."

"And?"

"They voted *not* to allow the Book to leave its case."

"How did Dennis take that?"

"Not well. He stomped in here the next day, gave me holy hell."

"Why you?"

McGlachlin looked uncomfortable. "Dennis thought that I could perhaps permit him to borrow the Book anyway."

I thought about it. "For a small ... stipend?"

Just a nod. "I told him I couldn't do that, John." McGlachlin winced. "You could have heard him yelling all over the building."

"Dennis believed he should have been accommodated because of that contribution you mentioned earlier?"

"More specific than that, I'm afraid." Hugh McGlachlin shifted in his chair. "You see, John, 'twas Dennis's money that let our Center buy the Book in the first place."

TWO

After getting McGlachlin's home number – "Call, John, any time of the day or night" – I drove away from the Center to another repository of memories. Irish-American also, but different. And more personal.

Leaving the Prelude on the wide path, I walked through the garden of stones until I found hers.

John, you seem troubled.

I looked down. The words "ELIZABETH MARY DEVLIN CUDDY" never changed, but they'd become a little fainter, the freeze/thaw of Boston winters taking their toll even on polished granite.

"I've been asked to find a book, Beth."

A book?

I explained the problem to her.

After a pause, she said, *I remember seeing an illuminated page from it, in an art history text, I think.*

"That would make sense."

An incredible collector's item.

As I nodded at her comment, my eye caught the plodding movement of a lobster boat down in the harbor, chugging along in the light chop of a northeast wind that smelled of rain to come. Its skipper seemed intent on collecting his pots from under their buoys before the storm began to –

John?

I came back to her stone. "Sorry?"

I said, how are you going to approach these three men without tipping them to who you are and what you're doing?

"It took a while, but coming here has shown me the way."

I fooled myself into thinking I could hear the confusion in Beth's next, unspoken question.

❄ ❄ ❄ ❄

Picture the kind of campus that would bring tears of joy to a high-school guidance counselor, if that position still exists. The classroom and dormitory buildings were a Gothic design like the lower, auxiliary structures tacked onto cathedrals. Imposing, multi-paned windows, some mullioned, others of stained glass. Ivy winding like braided green hair up from the ground and nearly to the roof lines.

After stopping three students with enough earrings piercing them to fill a jewelry box, I was directed by the last to a sallow, four-story affair. Inside, red arrows with small signs beneath them directed me to the second floor, and a receptionist swamped by students picking up exams waved me toward the office on her immediate right. The stenciling arcing across the door reminded me of my own office's pebbled glass, but instead of "JOHN FRANCIS CUDDY, CONFIDENTIAL INVESTIGATIONS" in black, this one read "CONOR DONNELLY, IRISH STUDIES" in green.

I knocked, and received a "Come in" repeated three times, like an oft-intoned litany.

The door opened onto a large office with high, if slightly cracked, ceilings and two banks of fluorescent lights suspended like utilitarian chandeliers from electrical molding running to and down the book-shelved wall. The opposite wall had five of the multi-paned windows throwing as much sun as the day was given onto the head and shoulders of a standing man.

Donnelly scribbled in a loose-leaf notebook lying on one of those bread-box lecterns you can lift onto a table to make a podium. His shoulders were rounded under a vee-neck sweater that clashed with the color of his flannel shirt. The brown hair was thinned enough that the professor had resorted to one of those low-part comb-overs, the scalp showing through between the strands that were left. His bushy eyebrows made up a little for the hairline, though, twitching like mating caterpillars over filmy, gray irises. As he stepped toward me, Donnelly had to shuffle his feet around stacks of what I took to be manuscripts for articles or student term papers covering most of the floor.

His gray eyes blinked. "You're not a student."

Brooklyn instead of the brogue in his voice. "No, but I'm hoping you're Conor Donnelly."

"A fair assumption, given where you've found me." Donnelly returned to his notebook. "But these are office hours for the students, so I can't spare you much time, Mr. ... ?"

"Francis, John Francis," I said, which amounted to only one-third of a lie. "I'd like to speak with you about the Book of Kells."

That seemed to catch his interest, because Donnelly motioned me toward a captain's chair across his desk, though he stayed at the lectern. "We can speak about it, but you're a good three thousand miles from the original."

"All right, a Book of Kells, then. I represent a collector who'd very much like to own one of those limited-edition facsimiles, and I understand you have access to such."

Donnelly cocked his head. "In a functional sense, yes. However, I'm afraid ours at the Heritage Center is not for sale."

"No matter the money involved?"

Now Donnelly frowned. "Well, as chair of the Advisory Board, I'd be honor-bound to entertain any serious offer – subject, of course, to Board approval."

"Professor, I'm aware that the going rate for a reproduction is tenfold what the Center paid, and my client is prepared to substantially sweeten even that inflated price. Provided, of course, that you can open that glass cover over the book so she can inspect the item."

No reaction to my "cover-opening" comment, which told me Donnelly already knew of the mechanism. "Well, Mr. Francis, you're welcome to submit your offer in writing, but I must inform you, I doubt the Board will approve it. We take great pride in having our copy of the Book, and frankly, I don't know that any owner not desperate for money would part with one of the facsimiles."

I decided to explore what might be a gambit from Donnelly. "Would it have to be the technical 'owner' that was 'desperate for money'?"

He looked confused. "I don't follow you."

Leaning forward in the captain's chair and lowering my voice, I said, "Or, would a person even have to be 'desperate' *for* money just to be interested in having himself a little – no, a *lot* – more of it."

"Ah," said Donnelly, "the light finally dawns. A bribe, eh?"

I shrugged.

Conor Donnelly smiled and returned again to his notebook. "Mr. Francis, get the hell out of my office before I call Campus Security and have you thrown out."

❋ ❋ ❋ ❋

His brother's receptionist in a lovely office suite overlooking Faneuil Hall told me politely, if firmly, that Dennis Donnelly would not be in that day. Both of Boston's daily newspapers had run profiles on him, though, and in each story the venture capitalist's obsession with his home in Weston Hills shone through. It didn't take long to find the place – read, *estate* – and once I gave the older, hard-eyed man at the driveway's security gate two-thirds of my name and mentioned the Book of Kells, I was escorted by a younger, hard-eyed guard up the drive and into a manse on a par with the gold-domed State House on Beacon Hill.

The second guard watched me admire – without touching – a dozen paintings, sculptures, and vases in the parlor-like anteroom before a pair of gilded doors opened and a man I recognized from his profile portraits came out from a spectacular atrium to greet me.

The financier was a glossy version of his brother the professor. A hair weave of some kind made this Donnelly look like a lush bush had been planted in the middle of his head and was spreading symmetrically outward. He'd colored his eyebrows to match the new 'do, and his gray eyes had that jump in them I associate with race car drivers and serial killers. He wore a silk shirt over his own rounded shoulders. A pair of painfully casual, stone-washed jeans ended an inch above some loafers, no benefit of socks.

After we shook hands, Donnelly glanced at his security man. "I'll be fine with Mr. Francis, Rick," his brother's Brooklyn accent on his words, too. "But advise Curt 'no more visitors' until I'm done here."

Rick nodded, gave me a look that said, *Don't make me come back for you,* and left us.

Donnelly suggested the Queen Anne loveseat might hold me, while he sank into a leather, brass-studded smoking chair. "So, Mr. Francis, you mentioned to Curt a Book of Kells."

"Actually, *the* Book of Kells, but I'm sure we mean the same thing."

A look of frank appraisal. "You want to buy a facsimile or sell one?"

"Buy, as intermediary for a client of mine."

No change of expression. "I'm in and out of the art market quite a bit. I don't recall anyone with judgment I respect ever mentioning your name."

"It's an easy one to forget."

A grin that you couldn't exactly call a smile. "You, my friend, are trying to scam me. Why?"

"No scam. My client wants one of the reproductions, and I understand you have a brother with … shall we say 'sway' over one of them."

"Hah!" said Donnelly, though it came out more as a bray. "I haven't so much as spit in Conor's face for a good two months now."

I tried to look disappointed. "Why?"

Donnelly now lazed back in his chair, so relaxed as to become one with the leather. "I'm guessing you already know. I'm guessing also that you're playing me for some reason I can't figure. But I also can't see how this bit of information can hurt me. Come along."

I followed him into the atrium, even on a dark day spectacularly lit by a rotunda skylight. I couldn't describe the furnishings if I had an hour to write about them.

Except for one piece.

It rested on a pedestal in a corner, shielded from potential sunlight by a glass cover that was smoke-colored on top but crystal clear on the sides. Donnelly moved directly toward it, beckoning me.

As I looked down at the very large and open Book, Donnelly said, "You've never seen one before, have you?"

"No," I said, my voice a little clogged with something as I took in, up close and personal, the filigreed detail on the capital letter at the top of the left-hand page, the depictions of people and animals – some realistic, some fantastical – occupying the margins and trailing after the end of paragraphs. Even just the calligraphy in the text – some version of Latin, I thought.

"My brother thinks I wanted to borrow his Center's copy just to show if off for a party here. And I did." Donnelly's voice wavered. "But once I got a look at it, even in that pop-top candy case in their 'museum' room, something – a kind of tribal memory, maybe – kicked in. What Conor seemed to forget is that I could have had the Center's own copy by just buying it for myself ten years ago. And once he and his snotty Board turned me down on the party idea, I went out last month and – quietly – bought another one."

I tore my eyes away from the pages in front of me. "For how many times the twenty thousand you shelled out for the first?"

Donnelly moved over to twin columns extruding from his wall. He pushed a button, and I looked back at the Book pedestal, expecting its glass case to open the way the one at the Center had. It was maybe five seconds before the button's purpose hit me.

Almost literally.

I heard a noise behind my back, and wheeled around. The two hard-eyed security guys were standing inside the double doors of the atrium, arms folded in front of their chests. Looking a little more critically now at each, I didn't see any evident weapons.

I said to Donnelly, "That business of 'no other visitors' was code for 'hang close,' right?"

A nod with the bad grin. "And now, since you've obviously wasted my time on some sort of false pretenses, I think I'll enjoy watching Curt and Rick bounce you around a bit."

I tilted my head toward the door, my eyes still on Donnelly. "Just the two of them?"

The venture capitalist's eyes went neon. "Oh, I might jump in at the appropriate time."

I turned to Rick and Curt. "Dennis, you're one man short."

Rick, the younger one, stepped up to the plate first. He extended both his hands to push on my chest, just like a demonstration of unarmed defense back in the sawdust pit when I was an MP lieutenant. I danced to Rick's lead for two steps, then reversed my feet and sent him over with a hip-throw. When he landed on the floor, the sound of his lungs purging air was a lot easier on the ears than the gagging and dry-heaving that followed.

Curt was on me before I could turn back, clamping a choke hold across my throat with one of his forearms. I smashed my left heel down hard on his left instep, and he cried out, lifting that foot. I hammered back with my left elbow and found his ribcage, feeling some of his cartilage separating as I drove into it.

Curt slid off me and cradled his left side with both hands, eyes squinched shut like a little kid who really doesn't want to cry but doesn't see how to avoid it. When I looked at Rick, he was still trying to give himself mouth-to-mouth resuscitation.

Dennis Donnelly said, "So much as touch me, and I'll sue you and your client for every cent you've got."

I walked up to him, Donnelly apparently forgetting that those twin columns behind him significantly limited his mobility. He tried to kick me in the groin, but I caught his ankle in my right hand, then bent upward until he began to moan.

"Dennis, unless you're a ballet star, I lift six more inches, and you lose at least a hamstring, maybe an Achilles tendon as well. We communicating?"

A strangled "Yes."

"Okay. I was never here."

"Right, right."

"And I'm never going to have to worry about Rick or Curt or any of their successors trying to find me, am I?"

"No. No, of course not."

I left him then, but not before taking a last look at Dennis Donnelly's Book of Kells.

❊ ❊ ❊ ❊

I'd found one facsimile, but Dennis Donnelly's arrogance seemed more consistent with his trumping story of buying a book for himself than with stealing the copy he'd in essence donated to the Center. Which left me just one last keyholder to the museum rooms.

❊ ❊ ❊ ❊

It was nearly dark by the time Sean Kilpatrick's carpentry truck pulled into the driveway across the street from where I was getting saddle sores sitting behind the wheel of the Prelude. When the pickup approached the garage of the modest ranch, security floods came on, bathing the front yard in a yellow – and strangely warm – glow. Thanks to the lights, I could see that his truck had a primered front fender, the tailgate held in place by bungee cords.

As Kilpatrick exited his vehicle, I got out of mine and began crossing over to him. At the sound of my shoes on the pavement, he straightened up and turned to me.

Kilpatrick stood about six feet, with broad shoulders and curly black hair. He was wearing a sweatshirt with the sleeves cut off at the armpits over bluejeans and tan work boots. By the time I reached the foot of his driveway, Kilpatrick's right hand had a claw hammer in it.

Just not my day.

I stopped short of his rear bumper. "Mr. Kilpatrick?"

"And you'd be?"

A brogue heavy enough that if you didn't listen for the rhythm of his cadence, you might not catch the words themselves. "John Francis. I understand you're doing some work over at the Irish-American Heritage Center."

I'd expected him to tense even more at the mention of the place, but instead he visibly relaxed, tossing the hammer toward the passenger's seat of his pickup before wiping his right palm on his thigh and approaching me to shake. Up close, he had a pleasant face around a genuine smile with very crooked front teeth.

"Mr. Francis, pleased to make your acquaintance. What can I do for you?"

Letting go of his hand, I said, "A client of mine is a collector."

Confusion on the pleasant face. "Collector? You mean of bills, now?"

"No. Art, sculpture, rare … books."

"And what would that be to me?" Kilpatrick gestured toward the truck. "I'm just a carpenter."

"But a carpenter with access to the Center's museum."

"Yes." He actually started to pull out a key ring from his back pocket, the ring itself anchored to his belt by a clasp and coiled cord. "I've got …" Kilpatrick reined up short. "Wait a minute, now. What are you saying?"

"I'm saying there's a particularly valuable book under a glass case in one of those museum rooms, and a considerable commission to be earned by the person who obtains it for us."

Kilpatrick lost the crooked smile, the face now anything but pleasant. "You're wanting me to … steal the Book of Kells?"

"Let's not say 'steal.' Let's just say you flip open the thing's glass cover before knocking off one night, and you slip the Book itself into a –"

"Boyo, if you're not out of my sight in ten seconds, I'll kick every fooking tooth in your head down your fooking throat."

No need to listen for the rhythm there to know what he meant. "Sorry to have troubled you."

I turned, half listening for those heavy work boots to come clumping after me. But as I opened the driver's door to the Prelude, Sean Kilpatrick was still standing at the rear of his battered pickup, fists on hips and staring me down.

✳ ✳ ✳ ✳

Even after dark, you can see that dome of the Massachusetts State House from my office window on Tremont Street. It's a pretty impressive effect, the gold leaf painstakingly reapplied by artisans a few years ago for what it probably cost the Navy to buy a carrier jet. But the dome also helps me to think somehow, especially when I'm stuck.

And I was stuck fast that night.

A very valuable reproduction of the Book of Kells disappears from the locked room in which it's kept, the glass top of its case smashed. Most people with access to the museum know that top opens to allow Nora Clooney to turn a page each day, but the thief smashes it anyway, maybe to deflect suspicion onto others less informed. Hugh McGlachlin as Executive Director of the Center has a key, though he's the one calling me into the matter, and through one of the Advisory Board, Michael O'Dell. On the other hand, reacting immediately and internally like that might be a good cover story for McGlachlin himself. Of the three people he "reluctantly" suspects, none acts suspiciously – or even smugly – about my suggesting the Book could be pinched: Professor Conor Donnelly ordered me to leave his office, brother Dennis wanted me beaten up for "scamming" him, and carpenter Sean Kilpatrick stopped just short of mayhem himself when I implied he could steal the Center's copy for me.

Which, according to the note left on the broken glass, wasn't actually what had happened, anyway. "Taken, but not stolen, and will be returned." No apparent sarcasm in the words or even a double meaning.

If the one person even asking to "borrow" the Book now apparently acquired a copy for himself, who would need the facsimile only temporarily?

Then, staring at he State House dome reminded me of something else I'd seen at the Center. It was a long shot, but worth at least a call to a certain home phone.

After dialing, I got a tentative, "Hello?"

"Hugh, it's John Cuddy."

"Ah, John. You've found something, then?"

"Maybe, but I need to ask you a question first."

"Go ahead."

Looking upslope at the gold leaf through my window, I said, "Who did all that calligraphy work at the Center?"

THREE

The front door to the three-decker in Southie opened only about four inches on its chain inside. The one eye I could see through the crack seemed troubled.

"Oh, my. Mr. Cuddy, how could I be helping you at this hour?"

"I'd like to meet with your husband," I said.

Nora Clooney tried to tough it out. "He's asleep. Perhaps in the morning?"

I shook my head.

She squeezed her lips to thin lines. "Then let me just pop up there, sir, make sure my Bill hasn't –"

"Nora, we both know what I'll see. Can we just get it over with?"

Clooney's eyes closed, her head dipping in defeat. "That'd probably be best, I suppose."

❊ ❊ ❊ ❊

Terminal cancer has a certain aura to it. Not always a smell, though. More an edge in the air. That sense that something's very wrong but also irreparable.

Bill Clooney's bedroom projected that aura.

His wife led me into the ten-by-twelve space. There were matching bureaus of mahogany with brass handles, framed photos of a younger couple wearing clothes and hairstyles of the late seventies. The bed was mahogany, too, a four-poster that I could see newlyweds buying shortly after their ceremony.

A set to last a lifetime.

Bill Clooney lay under sheets and a quilt, his head nestled in a cloud of pillows. There were a few wisps of gray hair standing bizarrely at attention on top of his head, a patchy fringe around his ears. Clooney's eyes were closed, but the mouth was open, a snoring so faint you might lose it in the hum of the electric space heater near one corner of the room. His hands lay atop the quilt, bony and heavily veined, the more so against the absence of flesh on them.

Centered between Clooney's throat and waist, a breakfast-in-bed tray straddled his torso. A very large book was open on the tray, a couch cushion propping the text at an angle toward his face.

"My Bill was a graphic artist," said Nora Clooney, her voice barely louder than her husband's snoring. "He came over from Ireland five years before me, and he was ten years older to start with. The charmer told me he fell in love the moment he laid eyes on me, but I wasn't sure of him 'til I saw his wondrous calligraphy, after a social at the Center that very same night. Modest about it though, my Bill was, telling me that I'd not use the word 'wondrous' for his lettering once I saw the Book of Kells."

I kept my voice low as well. "You wanted to bring the Book home so your husband could see it again."

"See it, yes sir, but touch it and even *breathe* it as well. Only after the terrible row between Mr. McGlachlin and that Mr. Donnelly at the Center, I knew the Board would never grant my Bill what it refused a rich man."

"You took the Book out of its case before you broke the glass."

"Yes, sir." Clooney made a sign of the cross. "I'd never have forgiven myself if I'd damaged so much as a page of it."

"And you carried the Book from the Center in your tote bag."

"Brazen, I was. Walked right by Grace behind the reception counter, her wishing me a good evening and not suspecting a thing."

"Then why did you leave the note?"

Clooney blew out a breath. "I thought it might keep Mr. McGlachlin from calling in the police right away, sir. Buy me the time to let my Bill pore over the Book during his last days before I brought it back to the Center, unharmed." She turned toward her husband, and I had the sense Nora Clooney looked his way with the same expression each time. A loving one that went beyond duty and maybe even devotion as well.

"Every morning he was able, my Bill would come to the Center with me. Oh, his eyes would shine, sir, watching me turn that day's page, him feeling honored as though he was the first modern man to look upon the work of those long-ago scribes."

I waited a moment before saying, "Nora, I need to make a phone call."

Clooney closed her eyes and dipped her head again. "The one in the kitchen, please. So we don't disturb my Bill's sleep."

As I followed the woman down the stairs, I said, "You wouldn't know whether Hugh McGlachlin has caller ID on his home number, would you?"

From the look on her upturned face, I could tell that Nora Clooney thought I was crazy.

❄ ❄ ❄ ❄

The tentative hello.

"Hugh, John Cuddy again."

"John, are you calling from the Clooneys, then?"

"No, a payphone. I'm afraid Nora and Bill couldn't help me."

"Pity," spoken with genuine feeling.

"Listen, Hugh, there's something I want to pass on."

"And what's that?"

"I've traced your Book of Kells."

"Traced it, now?" His voice was thick with hope.

"Yes," I said. "The Book'll be back in the Center before your Board meets next week."

A long pause on the other end. "John, is there something you're not telling me?"

"There is."

An even longer pause. "Michael O'Dell said I could trust you."

"And you can."

No pause at all now, but a considerable sigh. "Then I will. Goodnight, John Cuddy, and thank you."

As I hung up the phone in Nora Clooney's kitchen, she blinked three times before kissing the pads of the index and middle fingers on her right hand and then touching them to my forehead.

THE LAST STANZA

"John," said attorney Steve Rothenberg to me in the corridor outside a Suffolk Superior courtroom, his tie still tugged down two inches below his collar button, "all I ask is that you just talk with the woman."

I checked my watch. "Steve, she's being arraigned on a murder charge in – what, five minutes?"

"Maybe ten. But I'm really going to need a private investigator on this one right out of the box."

"And I'm already here."

"Plus the client can pay the freight. Or so she tells me."

I took a breath. "Okay. Let's talk with her."

❄ ❄ ❄ ❄

"Just another manifestation of a male-dominated system." The woman in flannel shirt and black jeans shook her manacled hands in front of Rothenberg's face from the other side of a scarred table in the conference room. "Restraining a woman before men will deign to speak with her."

Rothenberg sighed as he gestured to me. "Kirsten Tolst, meet John Francis Cuddy. John's a private investigator I've asked to help us on –"

"There aren't any *female* investigators, or do you just not hire them?"

Thinking, This won't take long, I said, "Ms. Tolst, I'd –"

"That's *Doctor* Tolst, *Mister* Cuddy. It took me seven years to wring my doctorate out of an academic 'Old Boy's Club,' and I'm at least entitled to that much respect."

I looked into Tolst's blazing eyes, framed by heavy brows and a hairdo chop-cut into layers. "You can act out 'til your heart's content, but I'm guessing the judge won't be setting bail, so we might want to spend our time together a little more productively."

She seemed to ratchet down a notch, glancing at Rothenberg before coming back to me. "My only card against a stacked deck, huh?"

"I'd like to hear your version of what happened."

"My version." Tolst let her hands rest on the table, the chain links clunking against the gouged oak. "I'm sitting in my office two nights ago,

246

trying to come up with a list of 'lesser institutions' that might give a professor denied tenure at Claussen College another chance."

Rothenberg said, "Doctor Tolst is a post-modern feminist, Women's Studies. She was one of three professors in the faculty office building when a fourth, Mitchell Donadio, was shot to death at his desk."

I remembered the news coverage. "Donadio was a pretty senior guy, right?"

Tolst snorted. "More like 'dead wood.' A dilettante who'd gotten tenure back when the school was desperate for anybody who could get published. The last five years, Donadio never focused on anything scholarly for more than a hour."

I said, "Is your evaluation of him why the police arrested you?"

Rothenberg cleared his throat. "They had a little more to go on that that, John. Professor Donadio chaired the Tenure Committee that denied Doctor Tolst's application."

"My field is contrasting the treatment of Scandinavian women – I'm of Danish heritage – with their sisters here."

Rothenberg let her finish before adding, "And the murder weapon was found in Doctor Tolst's office, together with the dead man's dictaphone, both wiped clean of fingerprints."

Better and better. "His tape recorder?"

Tolst said, "Dead Wood had crippling arthritis that bent his fingers nearly ninety degrees the wrong way. He could barely turn a page, much less type on a computer keyboard, but he worked the dictaphone button with a knuckle."

"Doctor, do you know how the gun and recorder made their way to your office?"

"I do not," the manacles rattling, but more from rage than fear, I thought. "And how even the stupidest of police-*men* could think I'd be stupid enough myself to hide obvious evidence there is beyond me."

Toward the end of her rant, Rothenberg nodded. "Doctor Tolst was in the Ladies' Room –"

" – *Women's* Room. God haven't you ever read Marilyn –"

" – when the shots were fired."

I rolled that around a little. "Where were the other two professors still in the building?"

Tolst leaned forward. "In their offices, or so they *should* have been. That English impostor, Robert Grimes, probably was with Dead Wood's daughter, a law student named Petra."

"Meaning Grimes teaches in the English department?"

"Yes, but, despite the fact that he's originally from Cleveland, the man also affects a British accent that's like fingernails going down a chalkboard. He's up for tenure this semester."

"Who else?"

"Up for tenure?"

"In the building that night."

"Randall Hilliard, European History. Our token Southerner, and a crack shot."

Rothenberg said, "According to the autopsy report, there were three bullet wounds in Professor Donadio's chest, all within a few inches of each other, and one right through his heart. Ballistics says the shooter fired from at least ten feet away, while Donadio was sitting at his desk, reading."

Even with a stationary target, the pattern and distance both suggested a steady hand. "Then why isn't this Hilliard just as good a suspect?"

Tolst crossed her arms, the chain doing a jumping-jack. "Because 'Lock-and-Load' Randy *received* tenure from Dead Wood's committee at the same time they *denied* me, even though there were persistent rumors that Randy plagiarized student papers from his former school toward racking up publishing credentials at Claussen."

Rothenberg looked down at the table top. "Uh, there's another reason, too, John."

"Being?"

Kirsten Tolst answered for her lawyer. "I'm in the National Rifle Association myself. Best small-arms shot at our gun club. It's about time women learned how to beat men at their own modes of dominance."

I pictured a jury and thought, *That ought to help, big-time.*

❄ ❄ ❄ ❄

Outside the conference room now, Steve Rothenberg looked at me. "Well?"

"You said Tolst could pay, right?"

"I don't see she has a choice."

"All right, then. It seems to me your client's right about the evidence: She's too proud of her own superiority to be dumb enough to put the murder weapon and the victim's tape recorder in her faculty office when she'd have to know the whole building would be searched."

"Agreed."

"So I'll give it a day, see what I can find."

Rothenberg handed me the file. "Thanks, John."

"But Steve?"

"Yes?"

"Don't count your chickens on this one."

❋ ❋ ❋ ❋

Claussen College occupied a smallish cluster of hundred-year-old buildings on an odd-shaped campus shoe-horned between Fenway Park and better-known institutions like Simmons, Emanuel, and Wheelock. I'd driven past Claussen often enough, but this would be my first visit to it.

The security guard inside the faculty office building turned out to be somebody who'd grown up near my late wife and me in South Boston. He confirmed what the police report maintained: The only people in the place at the time of the killing were the four professors. Luckily, the guard also knew that the crime scene had been released by the Homicide Unit, and that the daughter was up in her father's office.

❋ ❋ ❋ ❋

I said, "Petra Donadio?"

The stout young woman standing behind a glass-cubed desk turned from the bookshelves toward me. "Yes?"

Her plain, squarish face was flushed, the eyes bloodshot. "My name's John Cuddy." I pushed the office door in a little more. "I'm sorry for your loss."

"My ... ? Do I know you?"

"I'm a private investigator."

"In-ves-tigator?" said a male voice from behind the door, an Oxford inflection on every syllable.

I moved enough to see him. He was black, at six feet a few inches shorter than I am. Medium build, bland features, cropped hair. "Mr. Grimes?"

"*Doctor* Grimes, actually."

You'd think I'd have learned. He stuck out a hand, though, and we shook manfully.

Donadio still seemed confused. "What do you want?"

"I've been asked by Doctor Tolst's lawyer to look into your father's death."

"Now, see here," from Grimes, "you must know how upset Petra is by all this."

"Not as upset as she'll be if the wrong person gets convicted."

Donadio suddenly seemed to burn through the haze of what appeared to me genuine grief, boring in on what I'd said. "You think Kirsten Tolst didn't kill my father?"

I went over the "planted-evidence" argument.

Donadio shook her head. "I'm a law student, Mr. Cuddy, so I can see your point. But my father's committee denied Dr. Tolst tenure because her writing and teaching were far too narrow for the size school Claussen is, and she complained about being 'forced' to teach what the 'male oligarchy' imposed on her. Also, as I told the police, Dad'd been troubled by something the last few days."

"Did he say what?"

"Only that it involved … 'a tenure matter.' "

"Which fits that madwoman Tolst like a glove," put in Grimes. "Talk about rather a loose cannon."

Donadio looked wearily at the man Tolst had implied was her boyfriend. "Robert? Could we, like, lose the … 'gun puns?'"

"Ah, of course. So sorry."

Addressing Donadio, I said, "Are you packing up your father's office?"

She shook her head again. "More just going through it, picking out mementos for the wake." Donadio looked up at me. "Photos, favorite books. To have on a table by the casket, so people remember him the way they should."

Searching for something to say, I pointed at the shelves behind her. "Quite a collection."

"Yes." Donadio turned that way. "Dad believed that any professor in the liberal arts should know something about all of them. But he had his pets, like 'alternative history.' " She touched the tips of her fingers to a couple of books, one face-out with the author name "Harry Turtledove" on it. "And the evolution of the Olympics," a volume with ancient Greek statuary on the cover. "Even poetry, and especially where the last words on two lines don't quite rhyme."

Suddenly Donadio frowned. "Which is kind of why I was surprised by what he was reading that night."

"I don't follow you."

She bent down, having to use the desk to steady herself. "Here's where Dad kept it."

I approached the desk. Donadio was squatting and skimming a hand over the books standing to the side of a three-inch gap on the bottom shelf, one of them having dominoed into the gap at an angle that held the rest upright. "Kept what, Ms. Donadio?"

"Dad's *Collected Works of Shakespeare*." She pointed at the gap. "The police took it as 'evidence' because they found it right by his hand on the floor here."

As Donadio raised herself back up, I walked around the desk and got down on my own haunches. The dominoed book was *Othello*, the one next to it *Hamlet*. "Your father liked Shakespeare, then?"

"Not especially, except for some of the forced rhymes. In fact, I don't recall him mentioning the Bard for quite a while now."

I straightened up and turned to Grimes, who was watching me pretty closely. "Your specialty?"

He lowered his eyes to half-mast. "My ... ?"

"As a professor of English, do you concentrate on one kind of literature?"

"Naturally."

"Which is?"

"American novelists of the early twentieth century."

I didn't want to let Grimes off the hook that easily. "Any idea why Doctor Donadio would have been reading something your department teaches?"

"None," said Robert Grimes, with a theatrical shrug, as though hoping to persuade any people sitting in the balcony, too.

❋ ❋ ❋ ❋

A man wearing a tweed sports jacket and khaki slacks was locking the door to another faculty office as two female students slung knapsack straps over their shoulders, one saying, "See you in class, Doctor Hilliard."

He waved to them, then started walking toward me. Hilliard was about five ten and around forty, with a dapper mustache over a biggish bow tie that looked as though it didn't clip on. Then he snapped his fingers and turned back toward the door.

I said, "Forget something?"

Fumbling with the key, he looked up. "I did. Money for my miserable luncheon repast."

Slow, nearly syrupy Southern veneer on the words, though if Tolst had led me to expect a redneck, Hilliard was more like an antebellum gentleman.

I stopped as he got his door unlocked again. "I wonder if I could speak with you?"

"I have class in thirty-five minutes."

"Briefly. It's about Mitchell Donadio."

A sad wagging of the head, like an old dog feeling the temperature rise. "I've already shared my best judgments with your colleagues."

"I'm not police, Professor."

As he pushed into his office, I trailed behind him, explaining my role in the drama.

"Pity about poor Mitchell," said Hilliard. "Though I had always feared Kirsten was liable to throw a hissy fit that would end in violence."

"Because she liked to shoot guns?"

A small smile as he dug a hand into the side pocket of a Mackinaw on the coat tree. "Mr. Cuddy, I prefer not to underestimate people, and it seems to me a man as polished in his approach as you are would have uncovered my own ability as a marksman."

"Did you and Doctor Tolst ever go to the range together?"

A small laugh this time as Hilliard tried another coat pocket. "Not likely, sir. No, all that Kirsten had to know about me was my drawl, and she 'knew' how I'd be as a potential companion. For whatever … endeavor."

"How about Professor Grimes?"

"Robert?" Now Hilliard pulled open a desk drawer. "No. No – ah, here we are." He lifted a long-form wallet from the drawer and slipped it into the lapel pocket of his sports jacket. "Now where were – oh, yes. Robert. No, he's made himself something of a fixture here. And will receive tenure this semester, I'm certain."

"As you did this last, I understand."

"Correct."

"Despite certain … rumors?"

Professor Randall Hilliard didn't laugh this time. Or even smile, for that matter. "I'm afraid you'll have to excuse me, sir. If I don't eat before class, my lecture won't be worth the proverbial bucket of spit."

❊ ❊ ❊ ❊

"Roses, Beth," I said, arranging the flowers so the blossoms would point toward her headstone, where I thought of her as … being.

They're beautiful, John. Special occasion?

"More a difficult case, I'm afraid."

Tell me?

I did.

Then a pause from her end. At the foot of the harborside hill in Southie, three sailboats played imaginary tag, like butterflies on a mating breeze.

John?

"Yes?"

Are you sure Professor Donadio was actually reading that book?

I looked down at her and thought about it.

❊ ❊ ❊ ❊

Back in my office overlooking the Park Street Under subway station, I wrote phrases about the players in the case on small note cards, then started arranging and re-arranging them in rows. First horizontal, then vertical, finally diagonal.

It was the last array that made me see the initial relationship. A little more shuffling, and the answer stared me in the face.

✼ ✼ ✼ ✼

"John, you have something already?"

I motioned Steve Rothenberg to sit back down in his office chair. "What if Professor Donadio *wasn't* reading Shakespeare that night?"

"The book by his hand? What else would he've been doing with it?"

I took out my little set of cards and arranged them on the desk.

Rothenberg said he didn't get it.

I pointed to the card with "eclectic reader," then the ones that had the examples Petra Donadio had given me using the books on her father's shelves as props. "Alternative history, evolution of the Olympics. Unusual poetry."

"And Shakespeare, I guess."

"No. The daughter said the plays weren't close to her dad's favorite. And in fact, the Shakespeare volumes were on the bottom shelf behind his desk, fairly out of the way."

Rothenberg canted his head to the left.

"Steve, I think this is how Mitchell Donadio tried to tell us who killed him."

"But, John, the man was shot through the heart. He would've lost consciousness in seconds."

"Even if Donadio'd had longer, his crippled fingers ruled out writing a note, and the killer took his tape recorder. So, our victim did the only thing he could."

Now Rothenberg canted his head to the right.

I said, "Once shot, Donadio's only hope would've been to yank out a book as he was falling from his chair. Or when he was already on the floor."

"And so he picks ... Shakespeare." Rothenberg pursed his lips. "To implicate the guy from the English department, Robert Grimes?"

"What I thought at first, too. But on the same shelf, and right next to the *Collected Works*, was *Othello*."

Rothenberg nodded slowly. "Grimes is African-American, and he's romantically involved with Donadio's daughter, a white woman. So, the father would have chosen *Othello* if his killer was the English professor."

"My take as well. And the other play next to the *Collected Works* was *Hamlet*."

A second slow nod. "Our client, Kirsten Tolst, studies Scandinavian society, and she's Danish-American."

"Which leaves the *Collected Works* – including some ill-rhyming poetry – which got Shakespeare the title of ... ?"

"The Bard." Rothenberg slapped a hand on his knee. "And 'Bard' almost, but doesn't quite, rhyme with 'Hilliard.' "

"The European History professor who happens to be a crack shot himself."

Rothenberg's beaming smile suddenly drooped into a frown. "But, John, what if the jury doesn't appreciate all this?"

I said, "Sounds like your bailiwick, Steve," as I stood and laid my bill on the top of his desk.

DECOYS
A Mairead O'Clare Story

"There are two reasons why people divorce," said Sheldon A. Gold, attorney-at-law. "One is that the bride expects her new husband to change, and he doesn't. The other is that the groom doesn't expect his new wife to change, and she does."

Mairead O'Clare, fresh from a discouraging experience as an associate at a large Boston law firm, stared at her new boss from the client chair across his desk. "When I signed on, Shel, you told me most of your practice was criminal defense."

Gold squirmed a little in his seat, the rumpled suit jacket scrunching at the collar against the cracked leather bustle of his chair. "And this case is no different, Mairead."

She didn't understand, but at least he'd pronounced her name correctly, "muh-*raid*," unlike that horse's ass who headed litigation at Jaynes & Ward. "Wait a minute. I thought you said –"

" – divorce. I did." Gold reached for a manila folder, one of many on his cluttered desktop. "Only here, divorce was the motive for murder. Or at least, that's the prosecution's theory."

Mairead received the file from her boss's outstretched hand, noting that their secretary – Billie Sunday – had labeled the tab, "Stanler, Harvey P.," followed by a red "H," for "Homicide."

Mairead recalled the Boston *Herald* news coverage. "The police think he strangled his wife because of a pre-nuptial agreement, right?"

"Or because of its consequences. Harvey Stanler was fifty-eight when he married Jennifer Keats, age then twenty-four."

Jennifer. There'd been one at the orphanage when Mairead was growing up. Blonde and blue-eyed, Jennifer had been adopted almost immediately, but not before making fun three times a day of Mairead's hemangioma, the purplish birthmarks covering both arms from fingernails to elbows.

Inside Mairead's head, Sister Bernadette's voice from the orphanage said, *Get over it, young lady.*

"You okay?" asked Sheldon Gold.

"Uh, sorry." Mairead refocused. "So, Harvey was smart enough to insist on a pre-nup."

"Or his lawyer was."

"And who was this lawyer?"

"Me," said Gold.

"Oh."

"It gets better." A sigh as he raked the fingers of one hand through his sandy hair. "The paragraph on lumpsum payment provided that in exchange for Jennifer's renouncing all other claims, she'd get fifty-thousand dollars if there was no divorce before two years from date of ceremony, but a hundred thousand if no divorce before year five."

"If no ... 'divorce'?"

Gold shrugged. "So, I screwed up. Should have read no 'legal separation.' Then Harvey –"

" – would have been in charge of the calendar formula."

"Right." Another sigh. "But, as I phrased the provision, he wasn't, and even though divorce proceedings had begun, the formal court hearing wasn't going to happen before the fifth anniversary."

"And her family thinks her loving husband killed her."

"No. Jennifer Keats didn't have any family, at least so far as Harvey knows."

Mairead said, "Then it's the D.A.'s Office thinks he killed her?"

"At year four, eleven months, and seventeen days."

Thirteen to spare. "Good that our client left himself some margin for error."

"I don't think he did."

Mairead paused a moment, making sure she'd gotten Gold's drift. "You're saying Harvey's innocent?"

Her boss squirmed a little more. "I've known the man almost thirty years."

"Not what a judge would call 'responsive,' Shel."

Gold looked out his eleventh-floor window, just a glance over his shoulder, really, toward the downslope of Beacon Hill. "I think he's been framed."

Mairead hadn't been working for Gold long, but she knew he had a private investigator named Pontifico "The Pope" Murizzi who'd work any case in which he – Murizzi – thought the accused wasn't the perpetrator. "So, the Pope's on board, too?"

"No." Now squirming to the point of wriggling. "He met with Harvey, but our investigator doesn't share my view of him."

"Meaning, the Pope thinks he's guilty."

"Harvey doesn't come across well, first-impression-wise."

"Shel?"

"Yes?"

"That's not exactly a positive personality characteristic, capital-jury-wise."

One last sigh, deeper than the first two. "Meet with Harvey, Mairead?"

"Where is he?"

"Should take you only one guess," said Sheldon A. Gold.

✳ ✳ ✳ ✳

"This is bullshit! The bitch is still nailing me from the grave."

Mairead O'Clare watched Harvey P. Stanler from her side of the attorney-client cubicle at the Nashua Street Jail. He had clotting hair the color of cream soda, thinning in the center of his head. Given the lines on the leathery face, Mairead voted for a dye-job, no question. The man's craggy brow gave him a brutish look, almost like those pre-humans in that flick, *Quest for Fire.*

Oh, yeah, and one other thing. There was no screen or other divider between them, so she'd extended her hand to Stanler as the guard had brought him into the eight-by-eight room. After Mairead had introduced herself, Stanler had taken a look at the color of her hand and not extended his own.

You have to give Mr. Gold credit, young lady, said Sister Bernadette's voice. *He was right about his client's knack for first impressions.*

"Mr. Stanler –"

"I mean, Mairead, what the hell can the cops be thinking? I'm gonna kill Jen to save fifty thousand against rotting in jail while my daughter runs through almost three million?"

Mairead had read the file. "Your daughter, Wendy?"

"Right, right. She's thirty-one, and if the expression was 'Wine, Men, and Song,' you'd have a pretty good idea of what she's like."

"Wendy's your daughter from a prior … ?"

"Marriage. I was born in the generation, we did the right thing. Not like you twenty-somethings."

Better and better. "Mr. Stanler –"

"Why do you think I had the vasectomy? I didn't want to knock up Jen, too. That'd be all I'd need at my age, playing father to a brat the age of my friends' grand-kids."

Mairead resisted the temptation to comment on his comfort level in marrying a woman the age of his friends' children. "Mr. Gold wants me to find out –"

"Was Shel got me into this! Five years ago, he says to me, 'Harve, you're gonna marry a young one, be sure to protect yourself. That means a pre-nuptial agreement. And, if you're not firing blanks yet, an operation, too, because once there's a brat on the scene, the pre-nup isn't worth the paper it's printed on." Stanler raked the fingers of his right hand through his hair, so like Shel that Mairead nearly jumped in her chair. "So, I listen to my lawyer's advice, and here's where it lands me."

Cut to the car chase, young lady. "If you didn't kill you wife, who did?"

"That's what ..." Stanler suddenly seemed to run down. "Look, Mairead, I don't mean to be screaming at you, all right? You're just trying to do your job, and God knows I need somebody to help me. So, okay," he straightened a little in his chair, "I admit the marriage had gone sour – hell, we filed for divorce three months before Jen died. And I admit I told half-a-dozen people I'd like to strangle the little bitch, but that was just a figure of speech, you know? I mean, I had the pre-nup, and if I didn't get divorced soon enough to keep the fifty from being a hundred to her, so be it. Dave and I gross that much and more in a good month, high season."

"Dave Poitrast, your partner."

"In the import business, right. We been together ten years, and he's like the brother I never had, you know what I mean?"

Mairead's mind ranged back to the orphanage. Boy, do I.

Stanler said, "This thing's killing him, too."

"He feels for you."

"More than that. He's got to do the work of two men!"

The prosecution would pay us for the opportunity to cross-examine this ass in front of a jury. "Mr. Stanler, is there anybody else you can think of who might have killed your wife?"

"Just that shark of a divorce lawyer she hired, try and break Shel's pre-nup."

"That's Petra Lindsay?"

"Yeah. 'Petra,' she's got the eyes of something that eats what it kills." Then Harvey P. Stanler seemed to have a brainstorm. "Hey, since when did all you female 'esquires' get such funny names, anyway?"

❊ ❊ ❊ ❊

"So, how's the new client?" said Billie Sunday.

Mairead O'Clare closed the door to their office suite behind her before replying to the middle-aged African-American woman sitting sidesaddle in the receptionist chair. "What can you do after writing 'NEANDERTHAL' in all capital letters?"

Sunday went back to her old IBM Selectric III typewriter. "Underline it, then hang the sign around the man's neck."

Mairead nodded toward the middle-office door. "Shel in?"

"Uh-unh. You need to talk with him, he'll be back around four. He said."

Which meant, *Don't count on it, honey.*

"Billie, I'll be out interviewing witnesses."

Sunday's head and shoulders rose, her trademark silent laugh. "I won't be."

✳ ✳ ✳ ✳

"You're, like, my father's *lawyer?*" said Wendy Stanler around the rim of some kind of pink fizz drink as she used a toothpick to drown a chunk of pineapple in it.

Mairead didn't have to check her watch to know it wasn't yet noontime. "Ms. Stanler —"

"As if. You can't be *that* much younger than I am, so call me 'Wendy.' "

Great, thought Mairead, a Valley Girl who speaks in italics. Stanler's streaked blonde hair was cut in a ragged shag, black tank-top over black pedal-pushers that were less sewn and more painted on. "I'm helping Sheldon Gold with your father's defense."

Wendy Stanler sat on the leather sofa in what Mairead guessed to be Harvey Stanler's den, given all the duck decoys on the fireplace mantle and the two shotguns crossed over it. Add the blood-red furniture and hunting-camp Tartan carpet, and the room reeked of testosterone.

After answering the front door, daughter Stanler had pulled down the earphones of a Walkman to her neck. Given the volume of the retro-rock music Mairead could hear from six feet away, it was a miracle Wendy had registered the bell chimes at all. And, following the potential witness through the hallways, Mairead guessed that this Stanler's butt bounced more in discos than on playing fields.

Just outside the den, though, Wendy had stopped, even shivered. "This is where it happened, you know?"

Mairead said, "I read the police report."

"Strangled, on her knees, probably. I was out at a club, but she was just, like, a couple *feet* away from a phone." Stanler had turned, her eyes not showing anything. "Bummer, huh?"

Mairead had just nodded.

Now, in the den, Wendy drew her legs up on the couch, knees nearly to her chin in the fetal position. Which didn't prevent her from taking another slug of the pink drink. "Okay, I'll bite. What *is* old Harve's defense?" She inclined her head toward the mantle. "That he would have shot the slut instead of strangling her?"

"He claims he didn't kill your step-mother, period."

A laugh, some of the liquid now fizzing out Wendy's nostrils. "More like my step-*sister*."

She moved one hand to wipe away the drink trail, but slowly, languorously. Mairead was relieved the woman didn't lick her hand after she was finished.

Then Wendy said, "The little slut was only, like, *your* age."

"Did you resent your father marrying somebody so young?"

"Why, because it made *me* feel *old?*"

Touched a nerve there, young lady. "For any reason at all."

"Look – what was your name again?"

"Mairead."

"Well, look, Muh-*raid*, here's how the old man played his cards. Even before Mom died, he was mucho macho into hunting, shooting these poor little ducks from a camouflaged box at dawn on the Ipswich River, his 'decoys' spread out on the cold water around him. But after she was ... gone, Daddy *Dear*est also liked a warm bed and a hot chick in it. He'd even take the trophy bimbette of the moment to the 'Lodge' – what him and his best buds call the place where all the hunters hang. Harve and Dave used to pass them around."

Mairead felt her head canting to the side. "Your father and his partner used to ... ?"

" ... share their chicks, like a swap shop." Wendy gestured with her glass, sloshing the drink over onto her fingers. "Those blotch thingies on your hands mean you don't have so many dates, I have to draw you a picture?"

Like father, like daughter. "Was Mr. Poitrast jealous that your father ended up with Jennifer?"

"*Jealous?* Now, that's *really* a laugher." This time Wendy did lick her fingers for the liquid she'd spilled. "To Dave, it was more like shooting the poor ducks."

Mairead put that together. "Friendly competition."

Wendy puffed out her chest and squinched up her features. "A *manly* competition," in a deep voice. Then she relented. "Aw, shit. Did I hear old Harve say he was gonna 'strangle that little slut'? Sure. But did he really kill her?" A long drag on the pink drink, and some tears actually came into Wendy Stanler's eyes. "Like I really would have cared, you know?"

❊ ❊ ❊ ❊

"I appreciate your seeing me on such short notice, Mr. Poitrast."

"Hey, for Harve? I mean, we aren't just partners, we're best friends."

Mairead O'Clare looked around the office. Orderly, with computers all over the place. The furnishings were classy and exotic, maybe the way all import companies looked. The view out the window, however, was just six feet of air well to a brick wall.

Poitrast motioned her toward an armchair while he sank into one behind his desk. Younger than Stanler by a decade, Poitrast seemed more athletic, despite a little paunch hanging over his belt. He also seemed like the personality guy, the one who'd make the rain by getting the deals that Stanler would execute.

Poitrast clasped both hands behind his head. "I am kind of under the gun, though, what with having to do Harve's stuff and my own, so I'd appreciate your getting to the point."

Anything for Harve, but ... "Mr. Poitrast, I understand from the police file that Mr. Stanler left you here after receiving a phone call?"

"Yeah. From his wife – Jennifer."

"The night that Mrs. Stanler died, she called here?"

"Right."

"Did you answer the phone?"

Poitrast shook his head. "But I knew it was her. Harve used 'Jen' – his pet name for her – and that tone of voice."

"Tone?"

" 'Pissed off' would be a good description."

"Then what happened?"

"Harve blew out of here, and when I left maybe an hour later, his car was gone."

"Did he say anything to you before he left?"

"Afraid so."

"What?"

" 'I'm gonna strangle that bitch.' "

Consistency, young lady, is not always a virtue. "The Stanlers stayed in touch, despite the divorce?"

"Well, they weren't divorced yet, and while he wasn't supposed to call her – some kind of 'personal-liberty' order, I think it was – she'd call him from their house."

Which had seemed odd to Mairead from the report. "Despite the prenuptial agreement, Mrs. Stanler was living in the house during the separation?"

"Another part of the agreement, actually. If they separated, she got to stay in one wing of the place."

Shel hadn't mentioned that, and Mairead had concentrated on the police and forensics information, not the pre-nup itself.

Poitrast said, "It's a pretty big house."

"I'm sorry?"

"Harve's place. It's plenty big enough for both of them – and Wendy, too – to live there without running into each other. While the divorce was chugging along, the arrangement saved Harve temporary alimony, and once the formal court hearing happened, Jennifer would be out of there with her lumpsum."

"You're pretty familiar with the agreement, then?"

"Harve and I are partners. Hell, Ms. O'Clare, we went over that document line-by-line with a fine-tooth comb. Missed a few things, account of we aren't lawyers. But I figured, Harve's gonna leap into the abyss, I'd help him out as much as I could."

Help him out. "You didn't exactly approve of the marriage?"

"Hey," Poitrast spreading his hands like a priest at Mass, "my view's always been, Why bother to contract for something you can pick up in a bar whenever the mood strikes?" Poitrast coughed. "Um, no offense."

"None taken," said Mairead.

Poitrast brought his hands back together on the desk. "Plus, if you are going to marry one, there sure as hell were better prospects."

"Better how?"

"Jennifer got it into her head that she was a great hostess for business meals, but the woman was a bigot, and it showed. Blacks, Hispanics, she even went off on a rant about AIDS in front of this gay client of ours, nearly cost us his business." A grim laugh. "Probably hated lesbians, too, though I can't recall she met any, you don't count Wendy."

"Harvey Stanler's daughter?"

"The one and only. Oh, Wendy always put up a good front, going to discos and dancing with guys. Even left with a few, Harve was around to see it."

"She'd leave a club with a male so her father could witness it?"

"That's right."

"Meaning, Mr. Stanler doesn't know about her orientation?"

"He thinks she's wild, but maybe not that wild."

"But you do."

Poitrast looked uncomfortable. "I tell you something, does it automatically get back to Harve?"

"Not automatically, but if it helps him ..."

"I don't think it will, but I was in your shoes, Ms. O'Clare, I'd want to know about it." Poitrast frowned. "We had a party, over at Harve's house. Just the close people, celebrate our tenth year of being in business together. Well, I go off to use the head, and as I'm coming back, Jennifer hits on me in the hallway."

"Mrs. Stanler, now?"

"Right. Makes kissy-face, even gropes me some. She says ..." Poitrast frowned a little more. "She says, 'I should have stayed with the younger stud in the stable.' "

"In other words, you?"

"I 'dated' Jen for a while before she switched over to Harve."

Jen, his *partner's* "pet" name for her. "And what did you do?"

"Pushed her off, and she goes the opposite way, none too steady, either. Well, as I turn myself, I see Wendy, standing at the other end of the hallway, this smirk on her face. As I reach her, she says, 'Dave, it's too bad I like girls, otherwise *I* could go from you to Daddy and back again, too.' "

Jesus Mary, thought Mairead. *This is grosser than the soaps.* "She ever mention any of this to your partner?"

"Wendy now, or Jen?"

"Either."

"Not that I know of." Dave Poitrast checked his watch. "I'd think Harve would have said something to me, don't you?"

✣ ✣ ✣ ✣

"Ms. O'Clare, I have a pre-trial hearing in ... twenty-seven minutes. I can give you no more than the first ten of those."

If Shel Gold had pegged Harvey Stanler just right, Harvey Stanler had done a pretty good job on Petra Lindsay. Mairead thought the woman's eyes projected that predator look Stanler had emphasized, but right now, Lindsay stood next to her desk piling papers into a tote briefcase. The divorce attorney was somewhere in her forties and not particularly attractive. However, from the quality of the furnishings, her practice was a step up the scale from even the import company Mairead had just left.

"Ms. O'Clare?"

"Yes?"

"You're down to nine minutes, forty-five seconds."

The phone bleated. Lindsay ignored it.

Mairead said, "Was your client in fear of her husband?"

"Rather a facetious question, given what he did to her."

The phone stopped in mid-ring. "Any specifics before Jennifer died?"

Lindsay seemed not to see a paper she wanted to include. Turning to a file cabinet, she said over her shoulder, "My application for the personal-liberty order is public record, so you can read it." Lindsay yanked a document from the cabinet drawer. "But, basically, Harvey Stanler threatened to strangle her."

"Why?"

"I take it he didn't care for his wife any more."

"Why?"

Lindsay looked over, showing her teeth in what Mairead couldn't really call a smile. "Like the Little Prince, who once he asks a question ..." Lindsay went back to packing her bag. "Suffice it to say that Harvey believed Jennifer was using me to stall the divorce until the anniversary date that would have doubled the pot."

"Petra, I'm sorry to interrupt, but –"

She wheeled on the male voice. "What is it?"

A slim young man held a poker hand of pink message slips between trembling fingers. "That was you car-leasing agent. And you said you'd call the bank and the –"

"Not now. I'm in conference and nearly late for an important hearing."

"But they said –"

"Not now!"

The man backed off and away.

"Temp," said Petra Lindsay, fuming.

Mairead didn't nod. A polite temp who calls his boss for the day by her first name? *I don't think so, either, young lady.*

Lindsay stuffed another sheaf of papers into her tote bag. "That going to do it, Ms. O'Clare?"

"You said my client thought yours was using you to stall until the money under the agreement doubled."

"Correct," in an impatient voice.

"And Mr. Stanler was upset about that."

"'Enraged' might better capture his mood at our settlement conference. I told him that we would resolve the entire matter sooner for the enhanced payment per the agreement, but he felt that was – what were his exact ... ? Ah, yes. Harvey felt that was 'piracy,' I suppose a bit of colorful jargon from his import business."

"So, if Mr. Stanler were just willing to pay the additional fifty thousand dollars quickly, he'd get his divorce without a trial being necessary."

"Without a contested trial, anyway."

Mairead thought Lindsay's manner had softened just a bit. "Ms. O'Clare, I didn't draft their pre-nup. I didn't even represent Jennifer before the marriage. But if I could trade that timing glitch in the payment formula for Jennifer's life, I'd gladly forget my lawsuit."

"Your lawsuit?"

"The civil case I'll file once the prosecutor has established liability in the form of a criminal conviction. The Estate of Jennifer Stanler vs. Harvey Stanler, for damages arising from his killing of her."

"You're Jennifer's –"

"Executor and sole beneficiary." Lindsay softened even more. "Jennifer really was afraid of your client, but she had no other family, so she named me in her new will, to be sure someone would have a reason to avenge her if anything ... happened."

"And the hundred-thousand-dollar lumpsum is your 'reason.' "

"Better than that, Ms. O'Clare." Now Petra Lindsay's eyes fairly glowed, as though she smelled blood in the water. "I'll be suing your client for breach of contract – the pre-nuptial agreement. By killing Jennifer, Harvey made it impossible for her to collect the lumpsum. So, I'll be seeking every goddamned dime from Harvey Stanler and his business that his daughter and partner don't spend first."

✳ ✳ ✳ ✳

"Let me guess," said Sheldon Gold, swiveling a little in his bustle chair. "Dead ends, Mairead?"

"Or a series of threads that don't tie together." She stayed standing, pacing around the office as she spoke. "Jennifer Stanler was a bigoted bimbette, according to both Harvey Stanler's daughter and business partner, yet Harvey married her. His daughter's hiding her sexual orientation from her father, if the partner's to be believed, and the partner seems not to care much about who's 'dating' whom, if he and the daughter are to be believed. Jennifer's divorce attorney tried to cut an acceleration deal for the extra pre-nup money, but Harvey supposedly bridled at that as 'piracy.' "

"He would," said Gold, clearly bemused by the word.

"Well, I hope this makes you just as happy. The one thing everybody, including our client, agrees on is that Harvey threatened to strangle his wife. Loud and often."

Gold winced. "I'm picturing a parade of his closest circle, one at a time to the witness stand."

"And that's just the criminal trial. Once the jury comes back against Harvey Stanler, Petra Lindsay is also suing him civilly."

Mairead took a small amount of satisfaction in Shel's stricken reaction. "For what?" he said. "To bring a wrongful-death suit, she'd need a surviving family member as plaintiff, and Jennifer Stanler doesn't have any."

Mairead explained Lindsay's strategy to him.

Rubbing the side of his nose with an index finger, Gold said, "Clever. And the theory just might fly. You do any research on it?"

"When?" asked Mairead. "As I was walking up the stairs, your elevator being broken again?"

"You don't mind my saying it, Mairead, you should never rely on machinery."

"Well, you don't mind *my* saying it, I got an idea from our client's decoys."

Gold blinked. "His ... ?"

"Decoys," she said. "The degenerate hunts little duckies with shotguns."

"And this gave you an idea?"

"Regarding how we might flush out the real killer."

Her boss came forward in his chair. "Tell me."

Mairead did.

Gold nodded slowly, then more emphatically. "If the Pope will go for it, I like your ploy."

"Any chance you might have the elevator fixed before I have to traipse down eleven flights to see him?"

"Mairead, feel light on your feet. I think you're about to learn that chicanery is much more reliable than machinery."

"Shel?"

"Yes?"

"The hell does 'chicanery' mean?"

✤ ✤ ✤ ✤

As Mairead O'Clare stepped onto the narrow dock running out toward Pontifico Murizzi's boat, she could see him, sitting in shorts and a tee-shirt on the back deck. The boat itself was over forty feet long, blue and white with a small top level that sported a steering wheel and two high-backed, padded bar stools that Mairead had heard the Pope call "captain's chairs."

Just one more thing about him I don't understand. Doesn't a boat have only *one* captain?

Murizzi called out to her first. "Want to go for a ride?"

Mairead got close enough to answer without feeling she was shouting. "Just a proposition."

The Pope stood up, and Mairead "appreciated" him again. A shade under six feet, his muscles were subtle and ropey, even though he was as old as his boat was long. Murizzi had black, curly hair, a lot on his head, and just the right amount on his arms and legs. His face, though, showed rugged and a little hard, what Mairead believed twenty years on the Boston Police – nine of them in Homicide – would do to you.

The Pope gave her a hand as she stepped on the ribbed, rubber strip affixed to the gunwale and then down onto the deck. Which was more like a patio, what with folding lawn chairs and a small table for drinks.

Murizzi said, "You want a beer while you proposition me."

No smile, not even a smarmy undertone to his words. "Sure."

He went downstairs – what she'd also heard him call "below." Mairead was barely seated when the Pope came back with two clear mugs of some amber ale.

"Sam Adams Summer Brew," said Murizzi, handing her one as he settled back into his chair. A couple of gulls screamed and wheeled in the air, a third in the water trying to lift off with some unimaginably ucky prize.

The Pope leaned forward toward Mairead's beer and clunked – the mugs were plastic, so they couldn't exactly "clink" – before saying, "So?"

"Harvey Stanler."

"The obnoxious asshole who strangled his wife."

"Allegedly."

"I met him, Mairead."

"And didn't believe him."

"Right."

She took a slug of the ale. Smooth, with some kind of spice flavor. "I met him, too. And some other people."

Murizzi sipped at his, then rested it on the table. "And you feel different."

"Uh-huh, and here's why."

The Pope listened, taking only one additional sip when Mairead was almost done.

As she finished her story and slugged some more of her ale, Murizzi said, "So, you want me to work the case."

"Not exactly."

Mairead was glad he waited for her to say something more, but even more glad when the Pope spoke first.

"What exactly?" he said.

She told him, and Mairead O'Clare was gladdest of all when Pontifico Murizzi began to grin.

✵ ✵ ✵ ✵

" … and you're like, *what?*" said Wendy Stanler.

The Pope, sitting in the den of the Stanler house, tried to answer her as elaborately as he could. "I'm Jennifer's brother, Bob Keats. I saw something on our local news, and I came up immediately."

"From where?"

"New York City."

"Jennifer wasn't *from* New York."

"No, but that's where I decided to settle after leaving home."

Murizzi watched the young woman try to process the news.

"Well, like, what do you want from *me*?"

"Just to introduce myself," he said.

"Why?"

"Because I think we'll be seeing a lot of each other, what with your father's murder trial and my civil suit."

"*Civil* suit?"

"Against your father, for the wrongful death of my dear sister." The Pope swung his head around the room. "Just think, all this will soon be mine."

❊ ❊ ❊ ❊

" … and you're her long lost … ?"

"Brother," said Pontifico Murizzi, watching the expression on Dave Poitrast's face as Harvey Stanler's partner half-stood from behind his desk in the nice import office. "But I haven't really been lost. It's just that Jennifer and I didn't stay in very close contact after she married."

Poitrast's expression went from surprised to skeptical. "And why was that?"

"Well, I'm afraid she was somewhat ashamed of me."

"Ashamed?"

"Of my … orientation, Mr. Poitrast. I'm gay, you see, and that gave Jennifer a lot of problems."

"Tell me about it."

"I'd rather tell you my hopes for a rational settlement."

From skeptical to shocked. "Settlement of what?"

"My wrongful death case against Mr. Stanler." The Pope looked longingly around the office. "And a good chunk of change will, I assume, have to come out of this fine business you two seem to have built."

❊ ❊ ❊ ❊

" … which may be your version, Mr. 'Keats,' but Jennifer never mentioned any 'brother.' "

"And I've already told you why that might be," said Murizzi, settling a little deeper into the chair in front of Petra Lindsay's impressive desk. "I'm sorry my sister didn't come clean with you. However, that's hardly –"

"Just what is it you want?"

"Ah, a lawyer who can get to the point. Pity I'm retaining other counsel."

"For what?"

"To represent me, of course. In the wrongful death suit I'll be bringing against Harvey Stanler. But as the executor of her estate — at least for the moment — you probably should know how to reach me, eh?"

And for the third time that morning, the Pope gave someone he'd just met the number of a room at a rundown motel just outside downtown Boston.

❋ ❋ ❋ ❋

What a dump, thought Jennifer Stanler's killer, surveying the motel that night from the driver's side window. Just two strips of rooms perpendicular to a rundown avenue, half-a-dozen vehicles parked in various slots outside the twenty-or-so doors and windows. Not exactly the Ritz, but not much chance of any "on-site security" interfering, either.

Leaving the car across the street, the killer waited for a break in traffic, then walked briskly, the trench coat flapping against shins, the baseball cap pulled firmly down around ears, the temples of the sunglasses pressing into cartilage.

But, with luck, for only a few minutes more.

In the motel's parking lot now, the killer slowed down, just another traveler unlucky enough to reserve a crummy room sight unseen. Watching the numbers on the doors, counting down to the one Bob Keats had mentioned earlier that day.

109 … 108 … 107!

A quick look around. Nobody in sight, parking lot or sidewalk.

Before trying the door, the killer peeked into the room through the window, the drapes not fully drawn. A figure lay on the bed, facing away with sheets and blanket pulled up near a chin. Black, curly hair rested on the pillow.

Jennifer's brother, asleep.

The killer's right hand went into the trench coat's front pocket, coming out with a revolver, four-inch barrel. No need to try the door or even to knock. Just six bullets through the glass and into the figure on the bed.

The killer leveled the muzzle, then squeezed off the first round, shattering the window of Room 107 and making the killer's ears ring. Five more shots followed, the figure in bed shuddering a little from each. As the person in the trench coat turned triumphantly away, however, the flat of a hand slashed down on the right wrist, causing the killer to drop the revolver while crying out and sinking down in pain.

From her knees now, Petra Lindsay looked up at Pontifico Murizzi, Mairead O'Clare coming out the door to Room 108 behind him.

Lindsay virtually barked her words. "You didn't have to break my goddamned arm!"

* * * *

"So who picked out the wig for the mannequin in the bed?" said Sheldon Gold, standing in his office suite's reception area.

Mairead raised her hand, the Pope grinning from the other reception chair as he had on his boat.

Billie Sunday stopped typing a form at her desk, swiveling her head to glance at Murizzi. "I know five reasons *I'd* kill you, but why'd the lawyer-woman want you dead?"

Mairead spoke first. "It seems Petra Lindsay had financial problems, big-time. I got a sense of that when I visited her office, her supposed 'temp' interrupting her with urgent calls from her car-leasing company and bank. But I had my doubts about Stanler's daughter and partner as well, so we kind of 'created' a brother for Jennifer."

Gold said, "A decoy who could upset everybody's apple-cart, lure the real killer into showing herself."

Sunday looked to Mairead. "Then it was this Lindsay who did the strangling?"

The Pope broke in. "At the motel, she was ticked off enough about her arm to blame Jennifer Keats for the whole thing. Seems the two of them talked about killing Harvey Stanler in his own house, make it look like a burglary gone violent. Which meant Jennifer would inherit a lot more than her pre-nup lumpsum. But then Lindsay got to thinking."

Mairead said, "Why split the money with Jennifer, when with her divorce client dead, Lindsay could bring a clever lawsuit and end up with all three million of Harvey Stanler's net worth?"

Murizzi nodded. "And eliminate an unreliable co-conspirator at the same time."

Billie Sunday shook her head. "Lindsay kills her own client instead of the husband and loses the only witness against her if anybody tumbled to the crime."

Sheldon Gold said, "Two birds with one stone."

Which again reminded Mairead O'Clare of the wooden ducks on Harvey Stanler's mantle, but she decided enough had been said about decoys.

SOURCES

"Rest Stop," *Alfred Hitchcock's Mystery Magazine*, May, 1992. Copyright © 1991 by Jeremiah Healy.

"Eyes That Never Meet," *The Usual Suspects*. Black Lizard, 1996. Copyright © 1993 by Jeremiah Healy.

"Soldier to the Queen," *Ellery Queen's Mystery Magazine*, August, 1996. Copyright © 1994 by Jeremiah Healy.

"In This House of Stone," *Ellery Queen's Mystery Magazine*, September/October, 1997. Copyright © 1995 by Jeremiah Healy.

"Turning the Witness," *Guilty As Charged*. Pocket Books, 1997. Copyright © 1996 by Jeremiah Healy.

"Body of Work," *Ellery Queen's Mystery Magazine*. January, 1999. Copyright © 1996 by Jeremiah Healy.

"Chou's Gambit," *Ellery Queen's Mystery Magazine*, November, 1999. Copyright © 1997 by Jeremiah Healy.

"Voir Dire," *Legal Briefs*. Doubleday, 1998. Copyright © 1997 by Jeremiah Healy.

"Legacy," *Irreconcilable Differences*. HarperCollins, 1999. Copyright © 1997 by Jeremiah Healy.

"What's in a Name?", *The Shamus Game*. Signet Books, 2000. Copyright © 1998 by Jeremiah Healy.

"Hodegetria," *Death Cruise*. Cumberland House, 1999. Copyright © 1999 by Jeremiah Healy.

CUDDY – PLUS ONE

Cuddy – Plus One by Jeremiah Healy is printed on 60-pound Glatfelter Supple Opaque Natural (a recycled acid-free stock) from 11-point Goudy Old Style. The cover painting is by Carol Heyer and the design by Deborah Miller. The book was printed in two forms — trade softcover and two hundred fifty copies sewn in cloth, signed and numbered by the author. Each of the clothbound copies includes a separate pamphlet, *The Safest Little Town in Texas* by Jeremiah Healy. The book was printed and bound by Thomson-Shore, Inc., Dexter, Michigan.

Problems Solved was published in June 2003 by Crippen & Landru, Publishers, Inc., Norfolk, Virginia.

CRIPPEN & LANDRU, PUBLISHERS
P. O. Box 9315
Norfolk, VA 23505
E-mail: info@crippenlandru.com; toll-free 877 622-6656
Web: www.crippenlandru.com

Crippen & Landru publishes first edition short-story collections by important detective and mystery writers. The following books are currently (June 2003) in print; see our website for full details:

The McCone Files by Marcia Muller. 1995. Trade softcover, $17.00.

Diagnosis: Impossible, The Problems of Dr. Sam Hawthorne by Edward D. Hoch. 1996. Trade softcover, $15.00.

Who Killed Father Christmas? And Other Unseasonable Demises by Patricia Moyes. 1996. Signed unnumbered cloth overrun copies, $30.00. Trade softcover, $16.00.

My Mother, The Detective: The Complete "Mom" Short Stories, by James Yaffe. 1997. Trade softcover, $15.00.

In Kensington Gardens Once . . . by H.R.F. Keating. 1997. Trade softcover, $12.00.

The Man Who Hated Banks and Other Mysteries by Michael Gilbert. 1997. Trade softcover, $16.00.

Do Not Exceed the Stated Dose by Peter Lovesey. 1998. Trade softcover, $16.00.

Renowned Be Thy Grave; Or, The Murderous Miss Mooney by P.M. Carlson. 1998. Trade softcover, $16.00.

Carpenter and Quincannon, Professional Detective Services by Bill Pronzini. 1998. Trade softcover, $16.00.

All Creatures Dark and Dangerous by Doug Allyn. 1999. Trade softcover, $16.00.

Famous Blue Raincoat: Mystery Stories by Ed Gorman. 1999. Signed unnumbered cloth overrun copies, $30.00. Trade softcover, $17.00.

The Tragedy of Errors and Others by Ellery Queen. 1999. Trade softcover, $16.00.

McCone and Friends by Marcia Muller. 2000. Trade softcover, $16.00.

Challenge the Widow Maker and Other Stories of People in Peril by Clark Howard. 2000. Trade softcover, $16.00.

The Velvet Touch: Nick Velvet Stories by Edward D. Hoch. 2000. Trade softcover, $16.00.

Fortune's World by Michael Collins. 2000. Trade softcover, $16.00.

Long Live the Dead: Tales from Black Mask by Hugh B. Cave. 2000. Trade softcover, $16.00.

Tales Out of School: Mystery Stories by Carolyn Wheat. 2000. Trade softcover, $16.00.

Stakeout on Page Street and Other DKA Files by Joe Gores. 2000. Trade softcover, $16.00.

Strangers in Town: Three Newly Discovered Mysteries by Ross Macdonald, edited by Tom Nolan. 2001. Trade softcover, $15.00.

The Celestial Buffet and Other Morsels of Murder by Susan Dunlap. 2001. Trade softcover, $16.00.

Kisses of Death: A Nathan Heller Casebook by Max Allan Collins. 2001. Trade softcover, $17.00.

The Old Spies Club and Other Intrigues of Rand by Edward D. Hoch. 2001. Signed unnumbered cloth overrun copies, $32.00. Trade softcover, $17.00.

Adam and Eve on a Raft: Mystery Stories by Ron Goulart. 2001. Signed, numbered clothbound, $42.00. Trade softcover, $17.00.

The Sedgemoor Strangler and Other Stories of Crime by Peter Lovesey. 2001. Trade softcover, $17.00.

The Reluctant Detective and Other Stories by Michael Z. Lewin. 2001. Signed, numbered clothbound, $42.00. Trade softcover, $17.00.

The Lost Cases of Ed London by Lawrence Block. 2001. Published only in signed, numbered clothbound, $42.00.

Nine Sons: Collected Mysteries by Wendy Hornsby. 2002. Trade softcover, $16.00.

The Newtonian Egg and Other Cases of Rolf le Roux by Peter Godfrey. 2002. [A "Crippen & Landru Lost Classic"]. Trade softcover, $15.00.

The Curious Conspiracy and Other Crimes by Michael Gilbert. 2002. Signed, numbered clothbound, $42.00. Trade softcover, $17.00.

Murder, Mystery and Malone by Craig Rice, edited by Jeffrey Marks. 2002. [A "Crippen & Landru Lost Classic"]. Cloth, $27.00. Trade softcover, $17.00.

The Sleuth of Baghdad by Charles B. Child. 2002. [A "Crippen & Landru Lost Classic"]. Cloth, $27.00. Trade softcover, $17.00.

The 13 Culprits by Georges Simenon, translated by Peter Schulman. 2002. Unnumbered cloth overrun copies, $32.00. Trade softcover, $16.00.

Hildegarde Withers: Uncollected Riddles by Stuart Palmer. 2002. [A "Crippen & Landru Lost Classic"]. Cloth, $29.00. Trade softcover. $19.00.

The Dark Snow and Other Stories by Brendan DuBois. 2002. Signed, numbered clothbound, $42.00. Trade softcover, $17.00.

The Spotted Cat and Other Stories from Inspector Cockrill's Casebook, by Christianna Brand, edited by Tony Medawar. 2002. [A "Crippen & Landru Lost Classic"]. Cloth, $29.00. Trade softcover. $19.00.

Jo Gar's Casebook by Raoul Whitfield, edited by Keith Alan Deutsch, [Published with Black Mask Press]. 2002. Trade softcover, $20.00.

Come Into My Parlor: Tales from Detective Fiction Weekly by Hugh B. Cave. 2002. Signed, numbered clothbound, $42.00. Trade softcover, $17.00.

The Iron Angel and Other Tales of the Gypsy Sleuth by Edward D. Hoch. 2003 Signed, numbered clothbound, $42.00. Trade softcover, $17.00.

Marksman and Other Stories by William Campbell Gault, edited by Bill Pronzini. 2003. [A "Crippen & Landru Lost Classic"]. Cloth, $29.00. Trade softcover. $19.00.

Cuddy – Plus One by Jeremiah Healy. 2003. Signed, numbered clothbound, $43.00. Trade softcover, $18.00.

Karmesin, The World's Greatest Thief – or Most Outrageous Liar by Gerald Kersh, edited by Paul Duncan. 2003. [A "Crippen & Landru Lost Classic"]. Cloth, $29.00. Trade softcover. $19.00.

Problems Solved by Bill Pronzini and Barry N. Malzberg. Signed, numbered clothbound, $42.00. Trade softcover, $16.00.

Forthcoming Short-Story Collections

A Killing Climate: Collected Mystery Stories by Eric Wright.

The Complete Curious Mr. Tarrant by C. Daly King. "Lost Classics" series.

Lucky Dip and Other Stories by Liza Cody.

Kill the Umpire: The Calls of Ed Gorgon by Jon L. Breen.

Suitable for Hanging by Margaret Maron

The Adventure of the Murdered Moths and Other Radio Mysteries by Ellery Queen.

The Avenging Chance: Roger Sheringham's Casebook by Anthony Berkeley, edited by Tony Medawar and Arthur Robinson. "Lost Classics" series.

Banner Deadlines by Joseph Commings, edited by Robert Adey. "Lost Classics Series."

14 Slayers by Paul Cain, edited by Max Allan Collins and Lynn Myers. Published with Black Mask Press.

Sleuth's Alchemy by Gladys Mitchell, edited by Nicholas Fuller. "Lost Classics" series.

The Mankiller of Poojeegai and Other Mysteries by Walter Satterthwait.

The Pleasant Assassin and Other Cases of Dr. Basil Willing by Helen McCloy. "Lost Classics" series.

Murders and Other Confusions: *The Chronicles of Susana, Lady Appleton, Sixteenth-Century Gentlewoman, Herbalist, and Sleuth* by Kathy Lynn Emerson.

More Things Impossible: *The Second Casebook of Dr. Sam Hawthorne* by Edward D. Hoch.

Murder! 'Orrible Murder! by Amy Myers.

Murder – All Kinds by William L. DeAndrea. "Lost Classics" series.

A Pocketful of Noses: Stories of One Ganelon or Another by James Powell.

Hoch's Ladies by Edward D. Hoch.

The Couple Next Door: Collected Short Mysteries by Margaret Millar, edited by Tom Nolan. "Lost Classics Series."

You'll Die Laughing by Norbert Davis, edited by Bill Pronzini. Published with Black Mask Press.

Dr. Poggioli: Criminologist by T. S. Stribling, edited by Arthur Vidro. "Lost Classics" series.

Slot-Machine Kelly, Early Private Eye Stories by Michael Collins.

The Evidence of the Sword: Mysteries by Rafael Sabatini, edited by Jesse Knight. "Lost Classics" series.

Tough As Nails by Frederick Nebel, edited by Rob Preston. Published with Black Mask Press.

The Confessions of Owen Keane by Terence Faherty.

Murder – Ancient and Modern by Edward Marston.

Who Was Guilty?: Three Dime Novels by Phillip S. Warne, edited by Marlena Bremseth. "Lost Classics" series.

[Currently untitled Grandfather Rastin stories] by Lloyd Biggle, Jr. "Lost Classics" series.

Crippen & Landru offers discounts to individuals and institutions who place Standing Order Subscriptions for its forthcoming publications, either the Regular Series or the Lost Classics or (preferably) both. Collectors can thereby guarantee receiving limited editions, and readers won't miss any favorite stories. Standing Order Subscribers receive a specially commissioned story in a deluxe edition as a gift at the end of the year. Please write or e-mail for more details.